The Reason

Also by Catherine Bennetto:

How Not to Fall In Love Actually
Make or Break

Catherine Bennetto has worked as an Assistant Director in the film and television industry, working on shows such as *The Bill, Coronation Street and Death in Paradise*. She can generally be found travelling the world and spends her time reading healthy cookbooks (not necessarily cooking from them) or at the beach.

To families affected by bullying

First published in Great Britain by Simon & Schuster UK Ltd, 2022

1 3 5 7 9 10 8 6 4 2

Simon & Schuster UK Ltd
1st Floor
222 Gray's Inn Road
London WC1X 8HB

Simon & Schuster Australia,
Sydney
Simon & Schuster India,
New Delhi

www.simonandschuster.co.uk
www.simonandschuster.com.au
www.simonandschuster.co.in

A CIP catalogue record for this book
is available from the British Library

Paperback ISBN: 978-1-4711-6579-5
eBook ISBN: 978-1-4711-6581-8
Audio ISBN: 978-1-4711-8069-9

Typeset in Bembo by
Palimpsest Book Production Ltd, Falkirk, Stirlingshire

Printed and bound in Great Britain by CPI Group (UK) Ltd, Croydon, CR0 4YY

MIX
Paper from
responsible sources
FSC® C171272

CATHERINE BENNETTO

The Reason

**SIMON &
SCHUSTER**

London · New York · Sydney · Toronto · New Delhi

Chapter 1

It was the stuff of dreams.

Caused by a nightmare.

Still scanning the offending email on my open laptop I lowered a plate smeared in congealed fish curry towards the dishwasher, gagging at the smell. And the mild hangover.

'ARGH!' Pain shot up my arm. I yanked it out of the dishwasher to see a deep slash across my wrist.

Blood the colour of last night's Merlot leached out and I watched as it swelled into a single, glistening globule then fell to the floorboards.

'Gross,' I said, stifling a retch while tugging a ratty tea towel from the oven door with my uninjured hand. I gave it a sniff – a bit fishy, a lot musty, likely to give me a disease – then tossed it aside and opened the drawer that held the paper towels. As I did, a bubble of blood seeped from the now gaping wound and coursed, warm and nauseating, down my arm. I paused, mesmerized by the maroon stripes against my pale skin. *I look like a candy cane*, I thought, but was jolted out of my daze as another glossy bubble glooped out. Followed rapidly by another, then another.

'Oh shit . . .' Instantly woozy, I slid to the floor next to the fishy dishwasher. 'HANNAH!' I yelled while holding my dripping arm aloft. 'HANNAH, I NEED HELP!' Fighting panic,

I snatched the paper towels from the open drawer. 'AND WHAT DID I TELL YOU ABOUT STACKING KNIVES BLADE UP!?'

Cookie, our mixed-breed, knapsack-sized dog with scraggly straw-like fur and a toothy underbite, appeared at my feet.

'Hey, girl,' I said while struggling to tear off some towels with one hand. 'Go, get Hannah!'

Cookie wagged her scrubby tail.

'Where's Hannah? Where is she?' Nothing. 'You're no use in a crisis,' I growled. The paper towels fell from my grasp and rolled across the floor. Blood dripped onto the men's boxers I used as pyjama bottoms as I lunged at the roll. 'Lassie would know what to do. Lassie would get Hannah, call the ambulance, alert the neighbours, finish my sudoku, then help me get these fucking paper towels off the fucking roll! You need to up your game, Cookie. I am not impressed. Not impressed *at all.*' I wedged the roll between my knees and tore.

As I positioned the wad of paper over my wrist, I caught a glimpse of muscle or tissue or, I don't know, but it was wet and red and *disgusting*. I averted my gaze, only for it to land on Cookie lapping at my blood on the floor.

I vomited.

Seconds later, Hannah walked into the room in her school uniform; rummaging through her school bag, headphones on, nodding to a beat. She looked up, dropped her school bag, and let out the kind of piercing scream only a 10-year-old girl can make.

'MUM!' She flicked her headphones back so they hung around her neck as she fell to her knees. 'What happened!? Are you all right!? Should I call an ambulance?'

'No, I'm okay . . . I just—' We both watched, horror-stricken, as the paper towels reached their absorbency threshold and turned from dimpled white to lipstick red. 'Actually, sweetie . . .' I said, my voice sounding like it were underwater. 'Perhaps . . . we ought to . . .'

★

I came to and heard Cookie yapping and footsteps in the hall. Hannah had arranged me in the recovery position, cleaned up the vomit, and there was a fresh tea towel around my wrist, secured with masking tape. I fought another wave of nausea as I pushed myself to sitting and with my one good arm, reached up to the countertop and snapped my laptop shut. Had Hannah seen the email . . . ?

'She lost consciousness,' Hannah said, arriving with two paramedics and emulating Ted Danson in *CSI*. 'And threw up,' she added, wrinkling her button nose at the lingering smell.

The paramedics, one male and handsome and one female and sturdy, glanced at the two empty wine bottles on the kitchen bench. Embarrassment heated my cheeks. *One had only been a quarter full!* I wanted to protest.

'I'm Dan,' the male paramedic said, stepping around a cupboard door hanging open on dodgy hinges and coming to kneel beside me. 'This is Shelley. Can you tell me your name?'

'Brooke,' I said, as Shelley navigated masses of washing spilling from a tatty clothing basket and crouched on my other side.

Dan unwound the red-soaked tea towel while Shelley attached a blood pressure sleeve to my other arm. I smiled at Hannah to let her know everything was just fine but as the final swathe of tea towel was tugged open, the wound gaped and Shelley placed a pot from the kitchen bench in my lap as I retched.

'Can you tell us how this happened?' Dan asked while making a quick assessment of the wound before dousing it in saline.

I told them about the knife in the dishwasher; the blade

pointing up instead of down. They asked to see the knife. Hannah produced it in a plastic Ziploc bag with a sombre, 'I've bagged it', and I made a silent vow to branch out from our *CSI* marathons.

'You haven't hit any arteries,' Dan said. 'But you'll need to go to hospital to have the wound sutured.'

'Stitches,' Shelley clarified, then offered me a glucose lozenge.

The word 'hospital' conjured images of machines and scalpels, anaesthetic and MRSA. A shiver travelled down my spine. 'Can't you just do it here?' I said, talking around the lozenge.

Dan shook his head as he removed sterile wads of gauze and other bits of medical padding from single-use packets that were opened by Shelley.

She turned to Hannah with a kindly smile. 'Why don't you go and put some things in a bag for your mum? A change of clothes, toiletries. Something to read. And bring something for you to do as well. There can be quite a wait sometimes.'

Hannah nodded like she'd been tasked with something the level of National Security and raced out of the room.

'And a bra too, please, Hannah?' I called after her, remembering that my threadbare, only partially ironic Taylor Swift T-shirt offered little modesty.

'Ma'am,' Dan said as he wound a crepe bandage around my wrist.

'Brooke,' I corrected with a smile. I know I hadn't moisturized yet but I refused to accept that forty-three was old enough to be a 'ma'am'.

He smiled briefly. 'Was this an accident?' His probing eyes were on mine; trying to ascertain if I had attempted suicide while my 10-year-old daughter was getting ready for school and my dog was watching.

I glanced towards Shelley who was in the process of what *CSI* would probably call a 'situational assessment'. When looking at your home through someone else's eyes certain things can become alarmingly misconstrued. A note stuck on the fridge from the school about their 'No Bullying' policy, certain passages underlined in angry red lines; a pile of unread self-help books my mother sent at regular intervals arranged haphazardly on the sideboard with titles like *Do You Have Depression?* and *Sad To Glad In 12 Weeks*. Cookie humping a raggedy lion toy then biting its face and hurling it across the room.

'She has . . . issues . . .' I said.

Shelley raised her brows and continued her appraisal of my home life. Dirty dishes, unopened mail, broken cupboards, last night's congealed curry in takeaway containers. The two empty wine bottles (it had probably been more a sixth!)

The one glass.

Her gaze made its way back to me. Me, on the floor in my oversized men's boxers with a slit wrist, an unwashed topknot, panda eyes, and an aroma of vomit.

'I know what you're thinking,' I said, smiling perhaps a tad too wide. 'But this was an accident. I'm not depressed or anything.'

'Mum, you only have two clean bras left!' Hannah hollered from my bedroom down the hall. 'Do you want the one with the rip or your depressed one?'

Dan and Shelley gave me a look.

'I did *not* try to kill myself,' I said firmly, then turned towards the hall. 'The depressed one please, sweetie!'

I turned back to Dan and Shelley. 'It's not called my "depressed bra" because I wear it when *I'm* depressed,' I explained with an air of everything being very extremely normal. 'It's because my friend, Trish, pointed out that it made my boobs point away from each other and downwards,' I mimicked this action with my fingertips, Dan and Shelley watching with blank expressions, 'and made it look like *they* were depressed.' I paused for understanding. None was forthcoming. 'The boobs . . . You know, downwards and sad?' I said and mimed being a sad boob. 'But I wear it anyway because it's the most comfortable thing I've ever had on my boobs and that includes Blair Ferguson's strong, competent hands when I was—' I stopped as I realized I'd said the word 'boob' (and pretended to *be* one) to paramedics more times than was considered normal for someone who did not have a boob-related injury. ' . . . nineteen,' I finished and offered a grin that was not returned.

*

The ambulance pulled up at the back of St George's Hospital and Hannah helped me out at the same time as a man lying on a stretcher was being pulled from the back of another emergency vehicle. Bloodied bandages covered his nose, he had a split eyebrow and blood-caked hair. He flashed Hannah a cheerful smile, revealing blood-stained teeth, and she smiled warily back.

A clicking of low heels sounded down the side of the building then my mother came into view, my father lolloping behind her with his stiffened leg and his cane.

'There she is!' Mum said, squinting in the early morning sunshine. 'That's my daughter!'

I shot Hannah a look. 'What are they doing here?' My parents lived in Sussex, an hour and a half's train ride away.

'I called them while you were unconscious,' Hannah said, looking guilty.

'We were on our way to the accountant's,' Mum said, navigating the man on the stretcher and his paramedics with complete disregard. 'Very happy to miss *that* meeting.' She arrived by my side and gasped at the bulky bandage round my wrist. 'What have you done!?'

'*I* haven't *done* anything.'

Dad reached us with a look of concern on his usually quietly amused face. He was wearing his customary belted shorts with knee-high ribbed socks, a blue patterned waistcoat buttoned over a crisp white shirt, and a brightly coloured neckerchief. With his snowy white beard he looked like an eclectic Santa about to give a lecture on ancient botanicals. Across his body was the khaki strap of his side-satchel. And it was moving. 'Dad,' I said leaning towards him. 'Is there a chicken in your bag?'

Dad's beard twitched with a hidden smile as he poked a baby chick's fluffy head back inside his bag with a thickened finger. 'A gift for the accountant.'

Mum shook her head then turned her attention to Hannah and commenced an inquest that would have made Sherlock need a lie-down.

*

In the bustling reception area the man on the stretcher and I were greeted by two different nurses. Mine looked to be about fourteen.

'Lacerated left wrist,' Dan said with emotionless efficiency. 'Patient had lost consciousness but was coming around by the time we arrived on the scene. Applied direct pressure. She's no longer actively bleeding.'

'Self-inflicted?' the fresh-faced nurse asked.

Mum drew in a theatrical gasp and the man on the stretcher shot me a sideways glance as he was wheeled away.

'Patient claims no—' Dan said.

'Patient can *hear* you,' I said and Dad's beard twitched again.

Dan and Shelley passed on more medical titbits before departing and our nurse walked us to what appeared to be a wide corridor full of other waiting patients.

'We're very busy so you'll have to wait here,' she said, guiding us to a parked stretcher and one tatty plastic chair before leaving to find a working pen.

The man in the stretcher with the bloodied face was parked next to us. 'Hello again,' he chirruped cheerfully, flashing his horror-movie smile as I climbed up on my stretcher and Mum wiped the plastic seat with a tissue.

Everyone except my mother smiled politely back.

'I'm going to find a bathroom,' Hannah said, tearing her gaze away from the collection of damaged and bored patients parked up on the other side of the corridor.

'It's just down here,' a passing orderly said. 'Follow me.'

Hannah trotted off as my nurse arrived back, scanning the paramedic's form.

'So, Mrs . . . '

'Paige,' Mum answered for me. 'With an "I". And we'd like a psych assessment, please.'

'What?' I frowned. 'No, we wouldn't.'

The nurse glanced between us then scribbled on a form. I noticed she held the pen like a preschooler, with all her fingers gathered around the tip.

'You don't know your mental state because you're in it,' Mum said. 'It's up to your loved ones to tell you when you've gone too far. And this . . .' she said, giving my bandaged wrist an accusatory look, '. . . is too far.'

'This,' I waved my injured arm, 'was an accident.'

Mother pursed her lips and turned to the nurse. 'Is it protocol to have a psych assessment with an injury like this?'

'Mum, don't be ridiculous!'

The nurse's inexperienced glaze flicked between us again. 'Ahh . . . the doctor will be able to . . . make that call.' She looked back at her form. 'Do you know your NHS number?'

I looked it up on my phone, rattled it off then turned to my mother.

'All I did was reach into the——'

Mum spun to face Dad. 'I told you I should have come up yesterday.'

'I'm *fine*,' I growled.

'*This* is fine?' She turned to the nurse. 'You see, a very big thing happened yesterday, and I just knew it had the potential to push her over the edge. And look where we are. Over. The. Edge.'

'Oh my *God*. All I did was—' I stopped and leaned towards Dad. 'Is there a duckling in your bag?' I whispered.

Dad poked the duckling's fluffy head back in. 'So the chick didn't get travel anxiety,' he whispered back.

I glanced towards the man on the stretcher, who seemed unapologetically fascinated by us, then turned back to my mother. 'This isn't even the correct direction to slice your wrist. We've all watched *Grey's Anatomy* and know how to do it properly if we wanted.'

She narrowed her eyes. 'Peter-from-Pétanque's daughter's husband is a psychiatrist, isn't he, love?' she said, turning to Dad again.

I rolled my eyes. 'Good for Peter-from-Pétanque's daughter's husband.'

Mum pursed her lips. 'I'm sure we can get you an appointment.'

'I don't want an appointment.'

'Wants and needs are two very different things. What you need—'

'Stop telling me what I need.'

'I wouldn't have to if you'd at least look at the self-help books I've given you.'

'They're *self*-help books, Mum. You defeat their entire purpose by thrusting them upon people.'

The man in the gurney chortled and Mum stopped him with a glower.

'I do not *thrust*,' she said, indignant, 'I—'

'And the injury is on your . . . ?' my nurse said.

I glanced towards Dad whose beard was twitching again, then looked pointedly at my arm, with its bulky bandage. 'Wrist,' I said clearly.

'Yes.' The nurse blinked, her pen poised over her form. 'Which one?'

I avoided eye contact with my father. 'The left one.' I lifted it and gave it a 'here it is' waggle.

The nurse scanned the wrist, blinked, nodded, then did some more scribbling while Mum observed her with blatant displeasure.

'And the injury was sustained with . . . ?' the nurse said.

'A knife.'

Mum inhaled another sharp breath.

'Mother,' I said in a level tone. 'I did not *try* to hurt myself. So can you please stop with all the dramatic gasping.'

'My gasps are perfectly in line with the current situation.'

I answered the nurse's questions about date of birth, address, was I a smoker etc, then the nurse left – either to enter all the info into a computer or reattend nursing school.

Mum turned to me, her brow creased. 'Brooke, love, your father and I *are* concerned. And we think—'

'Hannah's coming back,' I said as I spotted my daughter walking up the hall chatting to the orderly. Her knobbly knees stuck out the bottom of her uniform skirt and her blondish hair, forever straggly, was tucked behind her ears.

Mum pressed her lips together, thwarted.

For now.

*

'Margo's daughter is no longer in a cult,' Mum said, as I watched yet another patient who wasn't me get taken away by a nurse. 'Now she sells sparkling water. But she's a little cult-ish about that, if you ask me.'

It had been six long hours since we'd arrived at A&E. Urgent patients had come and gone, scant updates on time frames were delivered from harried staff, and Dad had fed mealworm to his satchel. I managed to get through to Mum that my injury was a genuine accident and instead of sympathy got outrage. She'd given a lecture on dishwasher stacking (I'd had to stop her Googling a tutorial) then taken off her 'business' earrings and spent an hour going through her receipts and the rest of the time reporting to an unengaged audience on the gossip from her Pétanque club. After a few hours Hannah had declared herself '*so freakin bored*' and the bloodied man on the stretcher had extended an arm, introduced himself as Dennis, pulled a deck of cards from his rucksack, and asked if anyone wanted to play Last Card.

'How'd you hurt your face?' Hannah had asked as she settled cross-legged at the foot of his stretcher while Dad moved alongside, his peeping satchel keeping the other waiting patients entertained.

'Rugby training,' Dennis had said with a broad smile, which had disappeared as he'd added, 'I tripped on the ball and hit the goalpost.' He'd pulled his collar to the right and shown Hannah a silvery line near his shoulder. 'I got this one skydiving.'

'Skydiving!' Hannah had exclaimed.

'Yes,' he'd grinned. 'I tripped on the parachute cord on the way to the plane.'

Hannah had shown him her best scar, which he'd enthused about, then he'd rattled off a list of incidents and injuries that made it sound like he walked through life looking for hazards where there were none.

As Mum moved on to listing things other than sparkling water that made Dad gassy, an orderly arrived at the foot of my stretcher.

'You're up.' He kicked a lever at the bottom of my bed and turned to Hannah. 'Hitch a ride?'

Hannah looked at her cards then back to me. 'But I'm winning.'

'Ha!' Dennis said, mock-affronted. 'Ha!' He glanced at his large handful of cards and dropped his brow. 'She is, actually.'

'I'll bring her along in a minute,' Dad said, placing a card down. 'Pick up,' he said, his beard quivering, and Dennis struggled to add more cards to his already messy hoard while Hannah giggled, her nose wrinkling in her customary scrunch that melted my heart every single time.

With Mum at my side, I was settled in a cubicle and moments later a woman with red lipstick and hair like liquid chocolate walked in and introduced herself as Doctor Singh. Despite me convincing her earlier that my slit wrist was not a suicidal act, Mum immediately started asking about the effects of sustained strain on a person's mental health. Off my look, perceptive Dr Singh asked Mum to wait outside and with a scowl of betrayal, mother clip-clopped out.

'I'm sorry about the long wait,' the doctor said as she sat on a wheeled stool at my bedside and scanned my clipboard. 'It's been one of those days.' She took a few moments to check my details and confirm how I'd sustained the injury then met my gaze.

'It was an accident,' I said.

Doctor Singh smiled then began to undress the wound. 'A nasty one it seems.'

After injecting a local anaesthetic, the doctor got to work with her needle. 'You've been under some strain recently?' Her voice was smooth and comforting, like listening to one of those meditation apps.

I thought about the email that had warranted the one and an eighth (it was probably more an eighth) bottles of wine.

'A bit,' I said, averting my eyes. 'Nothing that requires any kind of "intervention". Just regular busy life kind of stuff.'

'What kind of work do you do?'

'Event management, but I stopped a little while ago. I work from home now, for the same company. Just a few hours a week. Sending invoices and chasing payments.'

'Anyone else live at home with you?' she asked in her velvety voice.

'Just my daughter.'

Her gaze flicked to my wedding band, its golden shine muted with age, then back to the wound. She 'hmm-hmm-ed', then we exchanged stories about our pre-teen daughters for the twenty minutes it took to complete the suturing.

Half an hour later, with my wrist neatly bandaged, Mum, Dad, Hannah and I schlepped towards the exit, drained from our full day in A&E. As we passed the busy nurses' station we saw Dennis being wheeled towards a cubicle. He raised his arm in a wave and whacked his orderly in the face, making Hannah giggle.

Outside the sun was already starting to set. Dad and Hannah went ahead to find our Uber and I turned to Mum. 'Thank you for staying with me today.'

Mum nodded. 'Well, as long and as dull as it was, it was still preferable than meeting the accountants.'

I smiled and scratched a spot at the edge of my bandage while Mum watched me for a moment. 'Brooke, love, I know today was an accident, but we have been worried about you for a while. And with yesterday's outcome . . .' She shook her head in disbelief. 'You probably ought to talk to a professional. A counsellor-y type who can help you move forward with this. And a financial advisor or something. As I said before, Leslie's son does something in finance, we should ask him, don't you think? You really do need to think about what to do.' She gave me a grave look. 'It's an awful lot of money.'

My heart sank.

It was.

It was an awful lot of awful money.

Chapter 2

'I do wish they'd hurry up. We've got to get home to put the chickens away.' Mum leaned obtrusively across the Uber driver and glared towards the open front door of my ground-floor flat. Seeing no movement from inside, she huffed her irritation then glanced at her watch, Dad's baby chick in her hand going upside down with the motion. 'Would you look at the time! I've new guests arriving tomorrow and I haven't aired out the yurt from the last lot! Now *they* were a smelly bunch.'

And while Mum recounted the smelliness levels of their last few rounds of yurt guests I called out to Hannah and Dad to hurry up.

My parents lived in Sussex in an inherited country pile that consisted of a rickety barn, an overflowing cart shed, a pool area well past its heyday, a scrubby field (home to a smattering of rescue farm animals), an ancient orchard, and the brick manor house surrounded by a vast lawn. It required constant maintenance but Mum was damned if she was going to let Dad's childhood home go to ruin. Since they'd both retired, Mum from being a receptionist at the local vets and Dad a philosophy professor, they'd had to batten down the financial hatches. In a bid to keep up with the endless repairs, Mum had erected three glamping yurts and a basic bathroom block in the old orchard. The yurts were immediately popular and year-round Mum was checking guests in and out, washing bedding, and delivering eggs. When we stayed, it was Hannah's job to collect the eggs and drop them outside each yurt in a little wicker basket. She'd often end up playing with any kids that were staying; a blessing for an only child.

Hannah ran out of the house and Mum terminated her smell inventory to scan what she'd changed into: tie-dyed shorts, an oversized Nirvana T-shirt, mismatched manga socks and battered purple Converse with the rainbow laces undone. Dad hobbled behind carrying Hannah's duffle in one hand and the duckling (who'd apparently needed a quick splash in the kitchen sink) in his other.

Hannah looked at my neat bandage. 'Sorry, Mum.' She threw her arms around my waist.

I hugged her back, marvelling that her head came up to my chin now. I still remembered, as vivid as if I'd been doing it that morning, pacing the kitchen while waiting for her bottles to sterilize, her tiny body warm and heavy over one shoulder. There's nothing quite like nuzzling the head of a baby with the underneath of your chin. Now, I was nuzzling a collection of knots that, I sniffed, needed a shampoo.

'That's okay, honey. You've learnt now, haven't you? Blade down.'

Under my chin, Hannah nodded. She gave me an extra squeeze then leapt in the back of the Uber, yanked the door shut, and reached through the front for the baby chick.

'Are you sure you don't want to get the train with us?' Mum said, stretching through the driver's open window, her fluffy grey bob tickling the Uber driver's face. 'We've still got . . .' She looked at her watch again. 'Oh, my gizzards! Not much time!'

I shook my head, giggling at the driver's attempts to curtail a sneeze. 'I'll come down tomorrow. The kitchen is a mess and I have to get Cookie from Penny.'

'Righto, love.' Mum turned and gave the driver some

exasperated 'hurry up' directives as though she'd asked him to get a hustle on a thousand times before and couldn't understand why the car was still stationary, then waved as they drove off.

I locked the front door, swapping from my right hand to my left when the act of turning the key in the lock sent a spasm of pain across my injury, then walked around the corner to Penny's.

'AGH!' Penny flew to one side as she opened her front door making me 'AGH!' right back.

She wore a transparent shower cap over her jet-black hair and had a strong waft of chemicals about her. I looked where she was looking; a section of wall near the floor. Nothing. I looked back at her.

'Oh great,' she said, her tiny shoulders relaxing. 'I'm seeing tarantulas again. I think it's the fumes.' She pointed to her head.

'Okay,' I said, stepping inside and giving the spot where the fictitious tarantula was a wide berth. 'You smell terrible, by the way.'

'I know,' Penny slammed the front door. 'Elise came home with a note saying there are nits in her class so we checked and we all fucking have them.'

'Yuck,' I said, immediately itching as I followed Penny down their immaculate hall. In direct contrast to my typical 'at-home' ensemble (PJ bottoms and an old T-shirt) Penny wore her standard home-wear; a grey cashmere jumper/leggings combo that displayed yoga-toned thighs and a bubble butt.

We arrived in their cavernous kitchen with its high ceilings, warm lighting, and neutral hues. Cookie trotted over, licked my shin by way of a greeting, then immediately started humping my handbag.

'She did that here all day too,' Penny said. 'I just thought she liked the new green sofa as much as I do.'

I laughed and nudged Cookie off my bag with my foot. 'Thank you for picking her up.'

'No problem.' Penny slid a hotel box containing a shower cap across the marble-topped kitchen island. 'Put this on. I know they don't jump but they are probably *every*-goddamned-where,' she said, scanning the room with irritation.

I looked through the closed glass doors to the family room where her three kids, Elise (ten), Rosa (eight) and Lorenzo (four), were doing some colouring in, watching cartoons, doing homework. All of them wearing cheap hotel shower caps and grim expressions. Her husband, Rog, travelled a lot for work and they had a never-ending supply of tiny shampoos, soaps, sewing kits and tampons. Yes, he collected the tampons. And no, he wasn't embarrassed by it. He's a good guy, is Rog.

'Put it on!' Penny squawked when she turned back and saw me sneaking prosciutto from a platter laid out for their regular Friday 'make your own pizza' night. 'I don't want you to have to go through this. My God, it took us eight weeks to get rid of them last time! We kept re-infecting each other. The newspapers called it a super nit. Do you remember that? *Super fucking nit! Dios mio*, I still have nightmares. Didn't you find one on Cookie? Didn't your Mum get them? What a nightmare to have nits in your seventies, can you imagine the horror? Do you want a wine?'

Penny didn't give me a chance to reply to any of the questions and got out two glasses while I positioned the clear shower cap over my topknot.

'Before we get into all this . . .' she glanced at my bandaged wrist while pouring us Rioja from her home town in Southern Spain, '. . . I need to tell you that Elise heard Livie telling some of the girls the nits must have come from Hannah. That's why she wasn't at school.'

I sighed as I pulled out a cream leather-topped bar stool and sat down. Livie again.

'Elise told them Hannah was with you at the hospital but you know how kids are, once the rumour is out there . . .' Penny shrugged as she picked up her glass.

'That's very kind of Elise,' I said looking at Penny's eldest daughter doing her homework at the coffee table.

She'd been standing up for Hannah, in her own gentle way, for a while now. But she was a quiet girl who just wanted to get on with her studies and navigate her school life with as minimal fuss as possible. I understood. It wasn't fair to expect Elise to keep stepping out of her comfort zone to defend Hannah.

I turned back to Penny. 'Livie has made her point. She doesn't like Hannah any more, why can't she just leave her alone now?'

Penny, who understood schoolgirl dynamics like she'd done a thesis on it, launched into an impassioned theory about Livie's mum doing a new vlogger hairstyle on Livie every morning, letting her wear lip-plumping gloss to school, buying her tiny but real diamond studs for her tenth birthday, and dressing her in labels while Hannah tied her hair off her face so she could get on with things, and dressed like she ought to be attending an ecstatic dance festival in Hove, or giving a talk on bathing your crystals in the light of a new moon. 'Hannah is so uniquely herself it confuses kids who are still trying to figure themselves out,' Penny said, flouring her countertop. 'Also Hannah is friends with boys. Livie wants to talk about them and Hannah actually hangs out with them.'

'They're different. Big deal. She doesn't need to be a little bitch about it.'

'That's the world over these days, no?' Penny said slamming home-made pizza dough on the countertop a few times and sending puffs of flour into the air. 'I think Melody's had another boob job,' she said, referring to Livie's mother. 'She was wearing that compression bra thing under her vest again today. And talking about some kind of GOOP-approved post-surgery energy field recalibration treatment.'

'God,' I said shaking my head. I went to steal an olive, then snatched my hand back as Penny swiped at me.

'You staying for dinner?'

I nodded and Penny smiled then looked away as her phone dinged.

'Oh, not again . . .' she groaned as she looked at the screen. She fell quiet for a second while she read, then began shaking her head. 'No. No, no, *no*, I do not accept!'

'What is it?'

'My mother-in-law. Look!' She held up the phone.

I'm in fashion! the text read, above a link to an article titled 'The Full Bush is Back.'

I sniggered. Rog's mother was a chronic oversharer and I very much enjoyed Penny's outrage on the matter.

'That woman!' Penny said, firing off a fierce reply. 'Last month I sat her down and I told her *no more* and that she is making me very uncomfortable but she continues! She spent the weekend with a Turkish sailor — he's so young he doesn't even *shave*! I could be his mother! Then she calls me and tells me all about it!' She shook her head, finished the furious text then dialled Rog and verbally downloaded about how she did not want to hear another thing about his mother's pubic hair, her weekend with a smooth-skinned man-boy, or her urinary tract infection, and that he needed to tell her to stop, with Rog's audible awkward response seeming to be a general reluctance at broaching any of those topics with his mother.

I sipped my wine and giggled at my friend's robust indignation. As Penny moved on to regaling him with their childrens' achievements from the day my smile faded and my thoughts went to the Hannah and Livie situation. It was concerning me more than I was letting on.

Livie and her parents, the Smith-Warringtons, had arrived in the area two years previously. Livie was shy and Hannah had made an effort to include her. She'd been a sweet girl to start with but in the past year it had become obvious that she was maturing quicker than some of the other girls. She got an Instagram account, encouraged the others to get them, then set up chat groups and speculated on which girl liked which boy, or started kissing rumours. Hannah and a couple of the other girls, who still very much had young minds and bodies, had felt uncomfortable with the boy talk and Livie had teased them.

I'd spoken to Livie's mother about it and her response had been, 'Livie has been spending some time with my sister's children, they live in France and are very sophisticated. I'll talk to her and let her know that kids aren't like that here.' Soon after though Livie began posting pictures of herself in bikinis, adding filters to make herself look older and prettier and pressuring her friends to do the same. If they didn't she'd Photoshop their photos herself and send them from their accounts to boys in their class (they played it a little fast and loose with passwords), asking which girl the boys liked the best. Other parents were upset but, after speaking to Melody again with no change to Livie's behaviour, only I had gone to the head teacher. The Smith-Warringtons were called in to the school, the office sent out a generalized note on what constituted bullying and appropriate online conduct, and called the matter dealt with. The next day Livie had blanked Hannah and whispered to the other girls that Hannah couldn't take a joke. A few days after that Hannah had sat in melted chocolate and later found a note saying 'poo smear' on her desk. And more inside her pencil case and schoolbag. Hannah was positive Livie had put the melted chocolate on her seat because that day she'd brought a giant duty-free Toblerone to school.

As the weeks went on, Livie began saving seats for everyone except Hannah. Or saying something cutting then following it with a smile and a 'just joking'. She'd laugh a little too loud when Hannah missed a shot during basketball or answered a question incorrectly in class. Sleepovers and playdates began to happen without Hannah. And because it had all started after I'd gone to the head, Hannah refused to let me intervene. She kept her head down and hoped it would blow over.

'So,' Penny said, getting off the phone and throwing it on the counter. I quickly plastered on a smile as she turned in my direction. She grabbed a blob of pizza dough and began stretching it on a tray. 'Tell me.' She indicated my wrist with a head tilt.

Two hours later, we'd eaten, cleaned up, combed the kids' hair for nits and were lounging on the new green sofa with the last of our wine. Elise could be heard doing her piano practice, Rosa was practising ballet with a friend on Zoom in her bedroom, and Lorenzo would fly through the living room at regular intervals wearing a different superhero mask. We were debating the merits vs pitfalls of a full bush when Penny received a text from Rog. He'd finished his late meeting and was looking forward to coming home to heat up his pizza and watch *Line Of Duty*.

'Oh shit,' Penny said, tapping out a super-fast text. 'I watched an episode without him and now I have to fake shock and outrage and all of that while we watch it again.'

'Only one?' I said, taking our empty wine glasses to the kitchen with Penny following behind, texting furiously.

'Okay, two. Three. Ah fuck it, I watched the whole goddamned season. But I can't tell him. He'll divorce me and we'd never agree on who got to keep the new sofa.'

'I'd better get home,' I said, walking over to where Cookie was asleep upside down on the floor, legs splayed like she was awaiting a gynaecological exam. I clicked the lead on her collar and Cookie sprang to attention, the abrupt movement on the end of the lead letting me know the anaesthetic was wearing off.

Penny threw her phone on the countertop and followed me down the hall. The promise of a warm summer floated in on the temperate April evening as I opened the door.

'Are you sure you don't want to come to Hammertime?' Penny said, referring to a school fundraising 'charity auction' event where parents of the school donated prizes. The last couple of years it had been sponsored by one of Livie's father's companies; an online wine subscription. He'd spend the evening looking smug while being fawned over by the spinster head-mistress and we'd all be heavily encouraged to sign up for a case as an extra fundraising push. 'I hear the De Klerks have donated a vasectomy and the Knowles have donated a weekend in Cornwall. Rog donated a financial planning session. Nobody in their right mind is going to bid. He's going to be devastated. So, you want to come?'

I said I'd think about it and Penny's expression said she knew what that meant.

I stayed in the doorway not making any move to leave.

'What?' Penny said, sensing, as good friends do, that something was up.

Behind her, Lorenzo, in a Hulk mask and *SpongeBob* pyjama bottoms, zoomed out of one room and disappeared into another.

'The money's coming through,' I said, a lump forming in my throat.

'*What?*' Penny's eyes searched mine.

'I got an email yesterday.'

'The whole amount they went for?'

I nodded.

Penny's eyes grew wide. 'Does Hannah know?'

'No.'

'Okay.' Penny gave a slow nod. 'Okay, we can deal with this.' Her liquid brown eyes assessed me. 'Do you want me to ask Rog his advice? I'd be discreet, of course, I wouldn't say it was you.'

'I don't know, I—'

'Mama, I need a kingfisher costume for ballet tomorrow,' Rosa said from the top of the stairs.

'Ay,' Penny said to me with a roll of her eyes before turning around. 'You're telling me this now, *cariño*? At 8:45pm on a Friday night? What do you want me to do about it? Call Cinderella's mice and birds?'

'Ma*ma*, I have to!' Rosa said with a fierce foot stamp.

Penny stamped her foot right back and they launched into rapid Spanish.

With a giggle at Penny's match in feistiness being her 8-year-old in a tutu, I waved goodbye and two minutes later closed the door behind me at home. After the vibrancy of Penny's my place seemed tomblike. I flicked the kettle on and the rumble of the water echoed in the unsettling stillness. I grabbed my phone and dialled Mum.

'Hello love, everything okay?' she answered.

'Yes, I just wanted to say goodnight to Hannah.'

'Oh, you missed her. She's asleep already. What time are you getting her to bed these days?'

I endured a five-minute speech about sleep deprivation in minors, agreed to trial a fifteen-minute-earlier bedtime, said goodbye, and I was in a silent house again.

I collected my tea and laptop, sat down at my weathered pine dining table that, if you looked close enough, had an etching of a penis my brother Martin had done when he was nine and I was loath to remove because it still made me giggle remembering Mum's week-long reaction, and reopened the email from my lawyer. I clicked on the attached document and stared.

I never imagined I'd ever see that many zeros on a document with my name on it.

Chapter 3

The next morning I walked out of the station to find Mum sitting in her silver estate on the phone.

'Yes, two nights,' she said as I wedged my overnight bag in the boot between her industrial supermarket shop. I let Cookie into the back seat then hopped in the front. 'It's rustic, remember . . . Oh no, we have lavatories but they aren't in your yurt of course. Ha! . . . Lavatories? Well, what do you call them? Toilets.' Mum's expression soured. 'Yes, we sometimes use that term here, too.'

She started the car, her phone flicked to Bluetooth, and as we drove through country lanes I listened to a man from Argentina book a two-night stay in one of the glamping yurts. She finished the call as we swung through open lichen-covered gates and the old brick manor house I'd grown up in came into view. Wisteria tangled over the front entrance was beginning to blossom and Dad's sweet peas in concrete planters either side were already a flurry of peachy colours.

'Hannah's over at the school,' Mum said unnecessarily as we passed the cart-shed crammed with broken ladders, ancient bicycles with cracked leather seats, outdated gardening tools like hoes and scythes, and a rusty Triumph Spitfire with deflated tyres Martin and I used to pretend was KITT from *Knight Rider.* 'We checked her for nits first thing this morning. I didn't want your father getting them in his beard again, I couldn't sleep after he'd shaved it. Very unsettling seeing his chin.'

'Did you find any?'

'Course not,' Mum said, yanking the handbrake on in her usual spot under an old oak tree next to the house. 'I wouldn't have let her go over to the school if she had.'

Mum and Dad's orchard backed on to the sports field of the local private school. When Hannah was seven the rugby coach had taken pity on the girl in red wellies who'd spent a full season perched on the fence following the ball with the intensity of a sheepdog and, after official training, he'd allowed her to join in. It was where she met Tom, her best friend, and she'd been playing with the team ever since.

As we headed inside, laden with bags, Mum answered another call and immediately began apologising.

'That bloody pony!' she said, dumping her phone on the hall table. 'He's been holding the Americans hostage in their yurt while he eats their croissants. They managed to distract him with jam so they could reach their phone and now he's pulling clothes out of their suitcase!' Her eyes fell to the bandage on my wrist. 'How is it? Sore?'

'Not too bad,' I said and Mum gave a nod then strode through to the laundry, the words 'asshole pony' echoing off the tiles.

Mum and Dad's neighbour, Noel, was a former senior editor for Reuters News Agency, and now a (hopeless) animal husbandry hobbyist. His front paddock contained a smattering of old cows, a female alpaca, two very nice horses, and one 'asshole pony', Crumpet. A Houdini-level escape artist who was frequently found eating the fruit in the orchard and intimidating the yurt guests. He kicked and bit and would charge at you if you tried to get him away from whatever contraband he was eating. Mum was the only one who could control him. She'd march him back to his field, scolding him like a belligerent child and when she got there she'd scold Noel as well.

★

Despite Mum's industrious shop there wasn't anything I, or anyone not laying down blubber for an arctic winter, liked to eat. So after checking on Hannah at the school field, and reminding her to be back in time for her drum lesson, I jumped in Mum's car and popped into the local village. When I stepped through the front door an hour later Hannah's lesson was in full swing. I smiled as I heard her nail a complicated fill.

As a toddler, she had showed a devout fascination with percussion and beat. Anything stick-like was a drumstick and *anything* was a drum. Including Cookie. By the time she was four she was having lessons. It wasn't very neighbourly to play the drums in a flat in Earlsfield, so she had an electric drum pad in her bedroom that plugged into headphones. But a few weeks ago, Hannah's teacher in London had said that to progress at the rate she currently was, she needed to know the feeling of performing on a full kit.

Before I knew it, Dad had popped over the back field to the college and enlisted Gus, the Head of Music, and the two of them had scoured eBay for a second-hand kit. Hannah's face when Mum led her down the cellar to show her her first full drum kit in a specially-appointed music room was one of those moments I'll keep going back to in darker days. Her face when she saw Mum's choice of posters was another I'll go back to but for different reasons. Justin Bieber still hangs on the wall because Hannah doesn't want to hurt her grand-mother's feelings, but she's angled her kit so that she doesn't have to look at him. Or his crotch.

'Are you sure it won't get on your nerves?' I'd asked after the first lesson the previous weekend had reverberated through the house, making the glass in the cellar door rattle. Hannah favoured drum heavy rock anthems and Gus seemed keen to comply.

'Of course not,' Mum had huffed. 'I find the beat quite invigorating as I do my chores.' And she'd stalked off to secure the trembling glass with electrical tape. The fact that Gus looked like a 'scruffier Paul Newman' might have had something to do with her delight at the new arrangement.

'This is a jaunty little number, isn't it?' Mum said arriving at my side in the kitchen moments later and searching though my bags-for-life for a receipt, her hips moving absolutely not in time. 'Who is it?'

'Rage Against The Machine.'

'Lovely . . .' she said, wincing at the thunderous beat. 'I think I should like to get their CD.' Then she found the receipt and analysed how much money I'd wasted on extravagances such as avocado, sourdough and mixed leaf lettuce.

'What's this?'

'Mushroom pesto,' I said taking it out of my mother's hands and spreading some on a slice of sourdough. 'Want some?'

'No, thank you.' Mum pulled an expression as though I'd offered her fermented goat tonsils. 'I've invited Gus to stay for lunch. If he's going to be here every weekend we should show him some hospitality. I've put a pie in the oven.'

Poor Gus didn't know what he was in for.

Lunch was called, Hannah raced over to the school to grab Tom from the boarding house and, on account of Gus joining us, Mum directed us to the formal dining room despite there being a perfectly good outdoor table in the spring sunshine.

'A word for the uninitiated,' I said to Gus as we walked through to the dining room. 'Next time, arrive full.'

Gus gave me a quizzical look but as Mum dumped a sunken pie that was leaking a strange orange fluid on the dining table realisation/alarm spread across his features.

'Hello Gus,' Dad said, hobbling in with his cane, his lager, and trailing two Japanese girls who looked about seventeen.

'This is Yumi and Noriko,' Mum said gesturing vaguely so we didn't know which one was which before leaving the room.

Renting a room to students before or after they attended a full-immersion English language school near the coast was another way my parents had of bringing in money. Usually, though, there was only one. Depending if the students stayed before or after their time at the school their level of English made for interesting conversation at the dinner table. Mum made all their meals and believed that we should just talk to each other as normal and they would pick things up. Or not. By the way the girls stood silently smiling, they were yet to attend the school.

The girls shuffled their seats together at one end of the table, Hannah and Tom tumbled in with grass-stained shorts and flushed cheeks, plonked themselves in their regular seats, and lunged for their waters.

'Hi, Tom,' I said.

Tom raised his eyebrows in a hello over his water glass. His dark hair was in all directions.

I took my seat opposite Gus, pushing up the sleeves of my denim shirt. Both Yumi and Noriko's eyes went straight to my bandaged wrist.

'Could you cover that up, love?' Mum said, coming in the room carrying a mountain of peas. 'It looks a little call-for-help-ish. It's not appropriate at the dining table.'

Dad's eyes flicked to me as he reached for his lunchtime lager.

'Well, I don't think it's appropriate to imply that this was anything other than an accident in front of my daughter—'

'I'm okay,' Hannah said eyeing the pie in the middle of the table then sharing a giggled grimace with Tom.

'And Tom.'

'I'm okay,' he said.

'And Gus.'

'I'm . . . fine,' Gus said, tearing his apprehensive gaze away from the pie to smile at me.

'And students,' I flicked my eyes to Noriko and Yumi.

'Well,' Mum said glancing at the girls. 'Perhaps not. We haven't exactly started with the best of impressions.' She sat at the head of the table, flapped her linen napkin onto her lap and tugged the pie towards her, trailing orangey goo across the table like a gruesome crime scene. 'I gave them a tour of the garden,' she said as she slashed into the bunched up pastry, 'you know how I like to do; showing them the herbs and veg they can help themselves to and came across yet another,' she leant away from Hannah and Tom, '*marijuana* plant,' she said in a whisper, while spooning wadded pastry and fluid with bits of mangled meat onto Gus's plate while he made unnoticed motions that that was enough.

'We know what marijuana is, Nan,' Hannah said with a conspiratorial look to Tom who grinned his double-dimpled smile back. 'It's weed. Uncle Martin smokes it.'

Mum – mid spooning – glanced at Gus then back at Hannah, horrified.

'I'm ten,' Hannah said as if that explained her worldliness.

'Well, *that's* inappropriate,' Mum said dropping the spoon into the pie and leaving the rest of us to serve ourselves. She turned to Dad. 'Did you get those plants behind the barn?'

Dad nodded. 'On the manure pile, love.'

'He thought we wouldn't notice. I really wish he'd stop,' Mum said, meaning my digital nomad brother, Martin, currently believed to be in shared living accommodation in Bali, who'd been growing weed around the house in various hiding spots since he was sixteen and often planted a couple of small shrubs when he was back home. 'Don't burn them again, will you, love,' Mum continued. 'You know what happened last time.'

Dad's eyes twinkled. 'Yes.'

'You stoned that dear young couple from Perth.'

Dad's beard twitched.

'My goodness, I'm surprised they didn't give us a bad review on TripAdvisor!' Mum said.

'I'm surprised they didn't give you a five-star review,' I said.

Mum looked up, confused. 'They did.'

Gus caught my eye, and I realized Mum was right. He *was* gorgeous in a Paul-Newman-in-his-forties kind of way; it was the aqua eyes and cheekbones perhaps. A graze of grey-tinted stubble covered his jawline, and his white T-shirt highlighted his tan. He had a blue-ish faded tattoo of what looked like a swallow on his forearm and a few knotted cords round his wrist. His resting face made him appear like he had something he was really looking forward to and his thick blondish hair looked like he'd run his hands through it that morning then let the wind take care of the rest.

'And what did the students think of you vacuuming Clint?' I said looking away from Gus before it got weird.

Mum pursed her lips.

'Who's Clint?' Gus asked.

'Nan's alpaca,' said Hannah.

'He's a rescue,' said Tom.

'Mum vacuums him,' I added.

'He likes it!' said Mum.

'*You* like it,' said I.

Mum shot an embarrassed look at Gus. 'Let's change the subject,' she huffed and turned to Tom. 'So Tom, love, what movie are your parents on?'

'The same one,' Tom said, politely putting his cutlery down

while an adult spoke to him. 'They had to fit a nose on George Clooney last week.'

'Did they?' Mum said leaning forward, eyes alight. Tom's parents both worked in the Prosthetic Make-Up Department for big budget films and Mum loved to hear gossip from set. Especially if it were handsome male lead-orientated. They owned a cottage at the end of the lane but because they spent a lot of time on overseas jobs Tom was in the boarding house most of the year. And often spent his weekends with us.

'You've got leave to stay tonight?' I asked after he'd answered all of Mum's questions as best he could about how one 'fits' a fake nose, what George ate at lunchtimes, and if he were still with his wife.

'He's not allowed,' Hannah answered for him.

'What did you do this time?' Mum said.

'Yes,' said Gus with a knowing look. 'What did you do?'

Tom and Hannah grinned at each other. They reminded me of Martin and me as kids; racing around the garden until we were called in for dinner, giggling and muddy-kneed at the table, hiding food in our pockets/socks/pencil cases during the course of every meal. Hannah adored him like a brother. We all adored Tom.

'Can he tell them?' Hannah asked Gus.

Gus smiled. 'Go on.'

Tom's eyes shone with mischief. 'You know how we had camp last week?' he said to the rest of us.

Everyone nodded as we assessed from which angle to approach the 'pie' on our plates.

'Well, on the last night I snuck into Mr Marshall's—'

'You can call me Gus when we're here,' Gus said, smiling.

Tom nodded. 'I snuck into Gus's cabin in the middle of the night and—'

'Tied a goat to the end of his bed!' Hannah blurted.

'A *goat*?' I said.

Hannah and Tom nodded with enthusiastic glee.

'Have you ever woken in the middle of the night to *a goat* licking your toes?' Gus said.

'Yes,' said Mum, hacking at her pie.

We stared at her.

She looked up. 'Well, ex*cuse* me for having a life before you lot!'

Dad looked at his wife as if she were just the most delightful of creatures.

Laughing at Gus's expression I turned back to Tom. 'And they took your leave away because of that?'

'No.' Tom grinned.

'When they got back to school he got the whole class to call him Mr *Maaaa*shall,' Hannah said making the 'maaaa' sound like the bleat of a goat.

'By the end of the day the entire school was calling me that,' Gus said. 'Even the receptionist. The kids kept asking if we could learn Bob *Maaaa*rley or *Maaaa*donna. We couldn't get any work done.'

'But then you told us to get ready to learn the *maaaa*ndolin!' said Tom.

'Which was when Mr Franklin from next door came in and said we were disturbing his Geography test.' Gus made an 'oops' face.

'And Tom asked if they were using *maaaa*ps!' Hannah squealed.

'And *that's* why I'm not allowed leave this weekend.' Tom turned to Gus with a placating expression. 'We would never tie a goat to Mr Franklin's bed. You should feel flattered.'

'Oh, I should, should I?' Gus said, grinning.

'How did you happen across a goat in the middle of the night?' asked Dad, forever concerned with details.

'They stole it from a farmer's field next door,' said Gus with a reproachful look at Tom.

'We didn't steal it,' Tom protested then his expression turned crafty. 'We *kid*napped it.'

In the middle of our laughter the front door slammed.

'Oh lordy, Sasha's home,' Mum said. 'The date mustn't have gone well.'

Sasha was my much younger sister who'd moved home from London two years previously so she could save for a flat. She lived in her old bedroom, helped around the house (ish), and had taken Mum's old job as receptionist at the local vet despite barely knowing the difference between a poodle and a parrot. At twenty-nine Sasha hadn't yet found 'the right man' but was vigorous in looking. Tinder was undertaken as part of a daily routine. Like brushing your teeth.

'MUM!' Sasha bellowed from somewhere in the house. '*MUM!*' She appeared in the dining room doorway, her tiny frame quivering with rage.

'Hello, love. Date not go well?' said Mum.

'What do you think?!' Sasha replied, her green eyes flashing beneath her blonde fringe.

'I think perhaps not, dear,' said Dad, supping his frothy lager and leaving a white moustache across his white moustache.

'And why do you think *that* is?' Sasha said thrusting her hands on her slim hips, her numerous bangles clinking.

Mum blinked. 'We don't know, love.'

'Okay, let me paint you a picture,' Sasha barked. And without any acknowledgement of Gus and the students she commenced pacing. 'We're sitting outside at the café having a coffee and he seems nice and I think, *Finally!* Not a complete psycho like the last one, who got drunk and stole the naan off the plate of a lady at the next table then had to borrow money for the bus home, and not in assisted living with his carer waiting outside like the one before.'

Gus glanced at me and I strained to keep a straight face.

'And we start discussing maybe we make it lunch not just

coffee. I thought I'd have the halloumi salad and he said he liked the look of that too and was also trying to eat less meat and we were just about to order when he gets a Facebook notification, which he says he needs to check because it might be his ex-girlfriend who is dropping off his keys, and who he broke up with because her mother was always interfering and his girlfriend seemed to be unable to make any decision without consulting her. So, of course, I said – *Yes, check it!* – because it makes me look chilled and so I sat there and . . . *he checked it.*' Sasha stopped pacing and glared at Mum, her chest rising and falling.

Noriko and Yumi looked at their laps.

Gus adjusted his cutlery.

Tom and Hannah gaped.

Dad appeared to be elsewhere. The finer details of nocturnal goat-napping perhaps.

Mum blinked. 'Go on, love.'

'He got all weird and I thought, *Oh great – another guy with an ex he hasn't quite finished with.* Then he showed me his phone and said . . . *"Is this your mother?".*'

Mum flushed a deep crimson.

'YOU SENT A FRIEND REQUEST TO A GUY I WAS ON A DATE WITH! WHILE I WAS *ON* THE DATE!'

'I did not!' Mum gasped. 'I think . . . I think *he* requested *me*!'

Sasha's eyebrows shot up. 'WE BOTH KNOW THAT'S NOT *AT ALL* TRUE!' She yanked out a chair next to Hannah and sat down violently. 'I'm going to end up forty and single and will have to spend every weekend hanging out here with you like a complete loser!' She flicked her eyes toward me. 'Sorry.'

I blushed and glanced towards Gus who offered a kind smile.

'By the way,' Sasha said, dragging the bowl of peas towards

her. 'I saw Jeffrey in the village and he asked if you could look after an old dwarf horse till he finds him a home. His name is Pedro. Or Pepe or something.'

'That man!' Mum said. 'Tell him no. We've enough waifs and strays around here.'

'I already said yes. It's in the hall.'

Hannah and Tom turned to me with pleading faces, both to see the old dwarf horse and be released from the pie.

'Off you go,' I said and they clattered out.

Gus leaned towards me. 'The hall?'

'Yes. Where do you keep your old dwarf horses called Pedro or Pepe?' I said and Gus chuckled.

'*God,*' Sasha said throwing the spoon in the bowl of peas, sending them in all directions. 'I am never telling you the name of a guy I'm going on a date with again. You're a complete stalking psycho.'

'I was merely trying to find out a little bit about the fellow,' Mum said, happy to be back to speaking in level tones with her youngest, most volatile child. 'Like any normal mother would when her daughter is off with a total stranger who could have a shovel and some chloroform in his boot.'

Gus choked on a pea.

'*NORMAL?*' Sasha boomed again, startling Noriko and Yumi. 'YOU TAGGED YOURSELF IN A PHOTO OF HIM ON A STAG DO IN MALTA!'

Mum coloured and shot a sideways glance towards Gus. 'Well, I always say the measure of a man is to see how he reacts to adversity.' She gave an indignant tilt of her chin. 'How did he react? Favourably or . . . ?'

'WE DIDN'T GET THE HALLOUMI!'

★

'They seem sweet,' I said, referring to Yumi and Noriko who, after moving Mum's pie around their plates without taking a mouthful, had politely excused themselves from the table and come back with exquisite squares of thick paper. They were now teaching Dad, Tom and Hannah origami at the outdoor table with the old dwarf horse called Pepe or Pedro (which turned out to be a miniature donkey named Pablo) munching grass at their side. Gus had left with a sweaty Tupperware box full of leftover pie and a weak smile of gratitude and Mum and I were on dishes. 'But why two?'

'They are very tidy, very quiet, and they take up very little room,' Mum said, handing me a suds-covered pan to dry which I handed back for rinsing. 'They paid in advance so I was able to get the bricks round the pool sorted. Which reminds me. I've put them in your room because it's bigger. I moved your stuff into the student room. I hope that's okay.'

'Of course,' I said handing back another pan for rinsing which Mum wordlessly undertook and then handed back to me.

'When the money comes in I can help fix up the house,' I said.

'You'll do nothing of the sort. That money is for your future.'

'But—'

'I won't hear of it.'

'I—'

'Absolutely *not*, young lady. You can stop even entertaining the idea. We do fine here on our own with the yurts and the students. We do fine.'

Knowing when to back down I dried my dish.

'I think you need to look at investing,' she said, handing me another sudsy platter that I handed back. 'Bonds and property and the like. You've got to be sensible. That's the thing. It's easy to think you have plenty when you have such a large sum but a bit here and a bit there and all of a sudden you don't know where it all went. What about school?' Mum said, referring to Tom's high school over the back field where Hannah was enrolled to start in September. 'Ms Potts said you haven't confirmed Hannah's place?'

'No.'

'But it's only five months away?'

'I know.'

'Best to get a hustle on, love. With the money on its way you can pay the deposit and look for a place down here now. Shall I get Joan's son round with his property portfolio?'

I grabbed the sudsy dish from Mum's sudsy hands, rinsed it, dried it, and placed it on the bench with Mum waiting for my response. 'I'm going to see if Hannah and Tom want to get ice creams in the village,' I said and headed out the back door to the garden, Mum watching after me.

★

On Sunday I helped Mum with the glamping laundry, watched Hannah and Tom do flips on the trampoline, listened to their movie script idea, argued with Mum while she vacuumed an alpaca about it being a bit mental to vacuum an alpaca, and around 4pm Mum drove Hannah, Cookie and me to the train station. And so another weekend in Sussex had passed. Hannah sat in the back with her headphones on, tapping her drumsticks on her lap, Cookie panting next to her.

'Your father and I have been talking to the accountants,' Mum said abruptly at the end of a protracted story about Brenda-from-Pétanque's daughter who Brenda said was a legal secretary in the city but who everyone knew was a society 'companion'. 'And they said that although the yurts and students are keeping it all ticking over, we need to come up with ways to create more income streams, to make the property profitable.' She hesitated. 'Well, not so much *profitable*, but less of a financial drain, and . . .' She glanced at worriedly me as we bumped into the train station.

I frowned. 'And . . . ?'

She pulled into a car parking space with a jerk and wrenched the handbrake, giving those of us with a compromised pelvic floor a challenge. 'We're going to need the barn cleared out.'

Her words knocked my spine out of me. 'Oh.'

'We're hoping to turn it into more accommodation. No rush though, love, I know it will be hard . . .' She gave a nervous titter. 'Well, I say no rush but there does need to be a bit of haste because we've booked in the draftsman.' She gripped the steering wheel. 'Just something to think about.'

Chapter 4

'Hannah Paige,' I said to the lady in her late sixties peeping out from behind a sleekly curved silver monitor atop a white marble reception desk.

'Of course! Lovely to meet you.' She handed me an iPad with an online form then popped out from behind the desk in a cloud of powdery perfume, and guided us across plush cream carpet to two chrome and leather chairs. 'Dr Anning won't be long. Would you like a magazine?' She smiled at Hannah. 'Let me guess . . .' She tapped a glossy red nail to her chin. 'Something with animals . . . ?' She grinned and trotted off on ruby pumps.

Once seated Hannah turned to me. 'Is it going to hurt? Will he use a needle?'

'He's just going to look at your teeth today and tell us our options,' I said, checking boxes on the iPad.

Hannah's baby canine had never fallen out and the adult tooth had grown over the top causing it to twist and protrude. She'd become self-conscious about it, more so after Livie said her teeth looked like the llamas Hannah had all over her exercise books. I'd barely finished telling Mum the wait list for braces was over a year on the NHS and she was on the phone. Half an hour later we had an appointment with a Harley Street dentist who, I imagined, had been manhandled by his mother, Frances-from-Pétanque, into allowing us to skip what was probably a six-month wait list.

Hannah fiddled with the hem of her uniform skirt while I agreed to the terms and conditions I hadn't read and made a spaghetti-like disaster of my digital signature.

'How'd you go in the trials this morning?' I asked, resting the iPad on my lap.

Hannah shrugged.

'Do you think you qualified?'

There hadn't yet been a year when Hannah hadn't qualified for the class relay team for their annual Sports Day. She shrugged again.

'Who was in your heats?' I was trying to ascertain how Livie, who used to be her main adversary in any races, had behaved but Hannah knew what I was angling at.

When I'd collected her from school at lunch she'd been quiet. And after pressing her I'd found out that nobody had wanted to partner with her during science class because of the nit rumour. One girl wouldn't even touch the microscope after Hannah had used it, and at lunch Livie had made a show of running away from the basketball if Hannah passed it. She'd let everyone know that we'd checked over the weekend and she didn't have them, but that didn't matter. The rumour was out, the damage had been done.

The receptionist came back with a copy each of *Pony* and *Popstar*, both in pristine condition, and handed me an *Interior* magazine. 'For Mum,' she said, smiling before returning to her desk. She slipped on some ruby-framed glasses, stared long and hard at the iPad then tapped with a single hooked finger at her keyboard.

'Will I have to have an X-ray?' Hannah said, flicking the edges of a magazine.

'Maybe.'

'Will you stay in the room with me if I do?'

'If I'm allowed, of course.'

Hannah fidgeted some more.

'Sweetie, you have nothing to worry about. Grandma said Doctor Anning is the best dentist in the whole of London, remember?'

'He is,' said the receptionist, peeking around her computer screen with her glasses lowered. 'We get all sorts of celebrities coming in here, expecting the best.' She smiled reassuringly. 'And they can go anywhere.'

Hannah relaxed a fraction.

'See?' I smiled. 'You're in good hands.'

The consulting room door opened and there, in a white coat, shaking hands with a patient, stood the rugby ball-tripping, parachute cord-tangled, orderly-face-smashing, pack-of-cards-dropping Dennis from the hospital the week before. I tried very hard to not say 'fuck'.

Hannah started typing furiously into her phone and held it up.

Fuck

'Put that away,' I hissed.

'I'll watch it tonight,' we heard Dennis say, nodding and opening the door wider for his exiting patient.

'Make sure you do,' the striking young woman said in a sing-song voice through the one half of her mouth that still moved. She looked like I'd find her in the social pages of a newspaper supplement, if I cared to look. She held Dennis's gaze through thick false lashes as she sashayed into reception, her efforts at coquettishness making the rest of us recoil. Nobody finds drool attractive. Except maybe bloodhounds.

I could see why she was flirting, though. Without his face covered in bloody bandages and his horror-film smile, Dennis turned out to be a good-looking man.

'Bev will sort you out for next time,' Dennis said, walking the glamazon to the reception desk, his hand hovering at the small of her back but not actually connecting. 'Six weeks follow-up please, Bev, and . . . ah . . .' he leaned closer and lowered his voice, 'the bill from last time was a bit wrong so . . .'

Bev frowned at the computer.

'Never mind,' he said with a smile as he turned back to the woman. 'We'll email it to you later. And, ah, good luck with your movie.'

'Thank you. Bye, Dr Anning,' the patient trilled as she sashayed through the door, oblivious to the river of saliva making its way down her chin.

'Yes, bye,' Dennis nodded. He gave the iPad Bev held out a quick scan then spun on a heel to face us and said 'Hannah Paige?' For a brief moment, his brow creased as he tried to place us then his expression brightened with recognition. 'Well, hello there! It's you!' He moved energetically towards the open door to his surgery. 'Come in, come in!'

I encouraged Hannah off her seat with an elbow nudge and followed her reluctant form into the room with all the sharp things and a man who apparently once twisted his ankle while colouring in with a niece.

'So,' Dennis said, settling himself onto a low stool on wheels. He beamed at Hannah and me. 'Fancy seeing you here!'

'Yes,' I said forcing a smile while looking at the dental assistant who was lining up a tray of pointy implements.

'Are you . . .' He glanced at my wrist, now sporting a simple adhesive bandage over the stitches. 'Better?'

'Yes, thanks. You?'

Up close I could see that he was, in fact, *very* handsome. He was probably in his early thirties, had floppy brown hair, hazel eyes and a fresh, youthful appearance, like he hadn't suffered a day's stress in his entire life. He was quick to smile and probably only needed to shave once every two weeks. 'Yes, thank you.' He touched the strip bandage on his forehead. Stitches crossed through his right eyebrow, making him look a little rakish, and only slight bruising was evident under his eye. 'But I snore now, apparently.'

I gave a polite little laugh and wondered briefly who'd told him that; a girlfriend? Boyfriend? Wife? He didn't wear a ring.

The three of us were quiet for a moment. Only the noise of the dental assistant clinking items on a metallic tray and the hum of various machines could be heard.

'Well,' he said eventually, still grinning like he had all the time in the world. 'Why don't you take a seat there, Hannah.' He gestured to the chair then wheeled across the room and snapped on some blue rubber gloves from a box on the wall.

Hannah's nervous gaze darted between Dennis's stitched eyebrow and the tools surrounding the dental chair. I was equally apprehensive. He was going to be in my daughter's mouth with sharp things and he'd managed to sustain a concussion while perusing the dessert buffet at a golden wedding anniversary.

His assistant held out another iPad which Dennis scanned while pulling a paper mask from another box. He looked up with a smile then frowned when he saw us standing motionless. 'Oh, I see,' he said, his grin returning. 'You're worried about these.' He indicated to his injuries with a rubber-gloved hand. 'But you needn't be.' He wheeled across the room, took Hannah by the hand and guided her into the chair. 'I can assure you that in here I'm as calm and controlled as . . . as . . .' He searched for a word as he adjusted the overhanging light. 'As . . .'

'As the Dalai Lama?' Hannah offered, lying back and blinking as the light beamed in her eyes.

'Precisely.' He grinned and adjusted the light again while the assistant fastened a paper bib behind Hannah's neck. 'Nice fellow, the Dalai Lama,' Dennis said. 'Met him at a conference once.' Both him and his assistant donned their surgical masks. 'This is my domain,' he said, his voice slightly muffled.

'Everything in here is exactly . . . exactly . . .' He looked at the little tray table to his left while his assistant held out something at his right. 'Everything is . . .' He turned to his right as his assistant moved the item to his left. 'Just exactly . . .' His assistant put her hand on his shoulder and handed him some tiny tongs. ' . . . exactly where I need it!' He held up the tongs and clicked them together, his eyes crinkling above the mask.

Hannah's eyes bored into mine at me as Dennis used the little tongs to place cotton rolls in her cheeks. I smiled my reassurance.

'In here I'm in complete control,' Dennis continued peering into Hannah's mouth with a little angled mirror on a stick. 'I think I must use up all my "clumsy" in my personal life.'

The dental assistant's eyebrow raise told us that was definitely the case.

In between rattling off tooth name and numbers to his assistant who typed things into a computer, Dennis kept up a comfortable chatty stream about the Dalai Lama, and how after meeting him he immediately booked a trip to climb Kilimanjaro.

'I got my friends and colleagues to sponsor me via a JustGiving page. I was going to donate the money to a school in Rwanda. I got as far as the airport in Nairobi and was getting my bag off the carousel, I was wearing those trousers, you know the ones with the zip-off legs at the knees?' He made a motion with his hand of zipping trousers at the knees.

Hannah and I nodded.

'Well, the zip got caught in the carousel and I sort of hopped alongside before tripping over someone's trolley and breaking my wrist.' Dennis called out another tooth number to his assistant. 'I got stuck in the trolley and unfortunately the carousel continued on and took my trousers with it.' He stated another tooth number. 'I wasn't wearing underwear as the heat had been too much. It was quite a drama after that.'

'I can imagine.' I said, trying not to laugh out loud at the thought of Dennis lying naked from the waist down on an African baggage claim floor and silently cursing my mind for going directly to where it shouldn't have: the size of my daughter's dentist's penis. His assistant caught my eye; her eyes twinkling as if she'd seen my penile thoughts, and I felt a heat creep up my neck.

'So,' Dennis said, putting his gloved fingertip into Hannah's mouth and attempting to wiggle her offending snaggle-tooth. 'The tooth seems to be very strong.' He moved his gaze between Hannah and me. 'And there's considerable crowding causing this protrusion. We'll do an X-ray but I'm pretty sure the root hasn't dissolved. In that case we'd need to do an extraction and—'

'Ochs ang ich-schak-hyun?' Hannah interrupted.

'It's when we take the tooth out,' Dennis said, understanding, unfathomably, what Hannah had gurgled. 'We need to do that so we can—'

'Ill I nyeeg a nyeegle?' I could see Hannah's fists balling her pleated school uniform skirt.

'A needle? Yes, but not to worry. It'll—'

'Eare?' Hannah said, looking increasingly panicked.

Dennis sat back and glanced at me then leaned forward and gently placed a gloved fingertip to her top gum. 'We put some gel here first then the anaesthetic—'

Hannah made a strangled kind of yelp and clawed at the paper apron while her legs kicked out. One foot knocked a hydraulic cantilevered arm that was attached to the chair and a series of tools attached to hoses fell to the floor with a loud clatter, startling both Dennis and his assistant into a momentary static shock.

Hannah spat out the cotton rolls. 'MUM!' she cried, terror

in her wail. Her hands flailed, trying to extract herself from the chair while Dennis and the assistant ducked out the way of all the flying instruments.

★

'She seems better now,' Dennis said, sucking strawberry milkshake through a striped paper straw. He touched a finger to a new red mark on his cheek.

While Hannah had been trying to get off the reclined chair and out from behind all the angular arms holding mini sinks, tools, lights, screens and trays – and making as much progress as a ferret trying to get out of a buttered bucket – Dennis had taken an elbow to the cheek. Once we'd disentangled her and she was in my arms, her breath coming in anxious pants, Dennis had asked Bev to give his remaining patients of the day to a colleague. He'd taken us to nearby Regent's Park for milkshakes. We'd kicked off our shoes, Hannah had immediately gone to watch a busker, and Dennis and I had stood against a low rock wall in the spring sunshine.

'I'm sorry. She's a bit anxious about anaesthetic.' I looked over at Hannah. 'You were really good about calming her down, though.'

Dennis looked humbled. 'My sister suffers from anxiety so I've learnt a few calming tricks over the years.' He smiled and I smiled back. 'Sometimes you just need to get outside, take off your shoes and ground yourself.' He wriggled his toes in the grass to emphasize his point then held up his takeaway cup. 'And milkshakes always help!'

'You're a dentist. Aren't you supposed to frown on sugar?'

He grinned and shuffled back to sit on the wall, his feet dangling in mid-air. 'Milkshakes make you happy! And we should all do more things that make us happy.'

'I concur.'

'And anyway, I'm an orthodontist,' he said with meaning.

I raised my eyebrows.

'We're cooler.'

We laughed and Dennis nearly fell backwards off the wall.

'Can I ask you something?' Dennis said once he'd righted himself.

'Sure,' I said, steeling myself for the question about why Hannah would have such a visceral reaction to the thought of anaesthetic.

'Why did your father have baby farm birds at a hospital?'

'Oh,' I laughed, surprised. The steel in my stomach dissolved and I shuffled up on to the wall next to Dennis. 'Dad has show chickens and had promised his accountant a baby chick from his award-winning hen.'

'I see,' said Dennis, not seeing. 'And . . . and the duckling?'

'Company for the chick. But because of the day in A&E they both went back to Sussex and now Dad doesn't want to split them up because he says they bonded on their excursion to London.'

'I see,' Dennis said again, *really* not seeing and I laughed again. 'Why were they in a satchel?'

'Dad likes to do things a bit unconventional to see people's reactions and analyse why they respond the way they do. He doesn't do anything with the information, he's not writing a paper on it or anything. He just likes to have it in his head so he can mull it over whenever he likes. He's a retired philosophy professor and I think he sees the world as one big university.'

Dennis appeared to be delighted. 'That's a fine way to look at life.'

I smiled. 'I guess it is.'

'I didn't know people showed chickens.' He paused to take a deep contemplative suck on his milkshake straw. 'My grandfather had show dogs.'

'Oh.'

'Boxers. Did you know that male show dogs are neutered to keep them from becoming aggressive but many then get silicone implants in their . . . ah . . . region . . . in order to preserve the illusion of intactness?'

I paused. 'I did not know that.'

'Yes. And the same silicone implants used for dogs are used in humans to replace the intactness of ah . . . the . . . area after testicular cancer. It's also very popular in the commercial sex industry because you can go up a size. Well, not just one size, many sizes, if that's what you wish.' Dennis stopped and looked at me, his cheeks colouring. 'I'm so sorry. I seem to have taken our conversation to a strange place. If I'm not stopped I often end up somewhere unusual.'

I smiled at this peculiar, friendly man. 'I like unusual,' I said and Dennis's blush deepened.

Hannah trotted over. 'I left my phone at the dentist's.'

'Orthodontist's,' I said which made Hannah frown. 'They're cooler,' I added and Dennis grinned.

★

'Let's not do anything else today,' Dennis said as we arrived back in his reception area. Bev jumped up, wrapped an arm around Hannah and walked with her into the surgery. 'Shall we try again next week?'

'But you're booked up?' I said. Mum had made sure I knew she'd pulled in a big favour from Frances-from-Pétanque with her extremely busy and important son.

Dennis shook his head. 'No, I have space. Life can get away from you if you're not vigilant so I'm a big believer in scheduling down. You never know what opportunity might arise and you want to have the time to take one if you fancy.'

'That's a fine way to look at life,' I said.

Dennis smiled and blushed. His humble nature was endearing. 'I guess it is.' He glanced at Bev exiting the surgery with Hannah looking at something on her phone. 'Here, I'll book it for you now.' Dennis said in a lowered voice. 'Bev doesn't quite know how to do it yet.'

'Is she new?' I followed him to the reception desk.

'No, been here for ages. She's just terrible with computers,' he said while he clicked a few buttons. 'But she puts the clients at ease and I think that's more important. Strangely though, she's a whizz on social media and has a huge TikTok following. She does cooking demonstrations to Joe Cocker songs. There's a fan base for everything these days I gather.'

We checked schedules and booked an appointment for the next week then waited for Bev to stop cooing over pictures of Cookie as a puppy.

'Why is Hannah anxious about anaesthetic?' Dennis said as we waited. 'Did she have a bad experience?'

His face was open, his smile genuine. My stomach clenched and I swallowed. 'Her father died on the operating table.'

Dennis stared at me in that horrific way people do when they've asked where Hannah's dad is, or what my husband does for work, and I've told them he's dead. It was a combination of embarrassment, guilt, and fear that I might burst into tears.

'How long ago?' he asked, his smooth Adam's apple bobbing as he swallowed.

'Twenty months.' I watched Hannah while twisting my wedding ring round and round. 'Twenty months and twenty-seven days.'

Chapter 5

'I'm *starving!*' Chris had moaned twenty months, twenty-seven days previously.

The nurse walking alongside my husband's moving hospital bed had smiled. 'I'm sure your wife has a marvellous meal planned for you tonight?'

'Percy Pigs and a samosa party pack?' I'd said and Chris had rolled his eyes and grinned as he was wheeled through the double doors. He'd been the natural cook in the family whereas my skills lay in following a recipe to the letter and nailing our regular Sunday night takeaway.

That morning had been a scramble. Cookie had humped then taken off with one of Hannah's basketball shoes and we couldn't find it anywhere. Hannah had try-outs that afternoon so was uber pissed. I'd been preoccupied with making sure I took everything for a final briefing at my office about a huge event we had that evening, and Chris couldn't find his earbuds, phone charger or James Patterson book he'd read ten thousand times already. We'd dropped a sullen Hannah round to Penny's early, sans basketball shoes, and carrying the scolded Cookie under her arm. Hannah had given Chris a disheartened hug goodbye and he'd told her that Michael Jordan still played like Michael Jordan even in his slippers. He promised he'd get her the new basketball boots she'd been coveting if she made the team.

'Really?' she'd said and Chris had made a 'cross my heart' motion from the front passenger seat. Hannah had given a lopsided smile then headed inside.

After mouthing 'I love you' at Chris through the double doors and waving until he was out of sight, I'd left the hospital, picked up a joke bag of Percy Pigs, then raced to my briefing. But halfway through my briefing I'd gotten a phone call.

Complications. Unexpected reaction to anaesthetic. Get back to the hospital.

Hannah never went to try-outs. She didn't get her new basketball boots. My huge event went on without me.

And we never saw Chris alive again.

★

If I tried to recall what happened in the weeks immediately after he died, time warped and made no sense at all. Like trying to follow *Pulp Fiction* while drunk. I know Mum was there. She'd moved in to Hannah's room and Hannah had slept with me. My brother Martin had flown in from Seattle (I think that's where he'd been – he'd had a lot of waterproof clothing with him) and slept on a camp stretcher on the floor of the office, working from the kitchen table at the odd hours he liked to keep. Penny liaised with the school about Hannah and took Cookie for all her walks. My friend Trish called banks and insurance companies and dealt with the admin side of death. No one ever tells you how *much* admin there is and how catastrophically heartbreaking it is to have to deregister your loved one from the administrative world. Sasha would pop up to London on weekends and play with Hannah or watch movies with her, and Dad was my shoulder to cry on. But I know nothing else. What did Hannah and I talk about? What did she ask me?

After six weeks Mum went back to Sussex and friends took over. There was a constant stream of people. Some dropped off casseroles, some cooked that casserole in front of me. Some did my shopping and some (Trish) turned up at my house, put my feet in sneakers, a hat on my greasy hair, dragged me to the market, and held eggplants up in front of my face. People vacuumed my living room, stacked my dishwasher, took bins out, and demanded I hand over my pyjamas so they could do a load of washing. I'd have moments where I was desperate for my own space. Then about four months down the track they went back to their own lives and it felt like Hannah and I were old news. Not in an uncaring way, in a practical way. People can't keep coming around every Wednesday to make mushroom risotto you barely have an appetite to eat. They need to make their own mushroom risotto for their own family not to eat.

And during that whole time-bending period, where busy bodies passed to and fro in front of me, I'd sat on the sofa with one thing running through my head. The last words I'd ever said to my husband were *samosa party pack*.

Hannah eventually went back to school and I went back to work. But daily I found myself either hovering outside my boss's office toying with the words 'I can't do this' or fighting a panic attack at my desk about not being home if Hannah needed me. I found I no longer cared about putting on Christmas parties for indie record labels or launching a celebrity's first novel with book-themed cupcakes at a members only club. It felt frivolous and pointless and overnight it seemed I'd developed a zero tolerance for pedantics.

'I think you may have come back to work too soon,' my boss, Abdul, had said one day after calling me in to his office.

'What? Why?'

'We've had a complaint. A couple actually.'

Abdul's PA, Tiff, held up two hands, all fingers splayed. Abdul glanced at her then turned back to me.

'Ten. We've had—'

Tiff held up another full hand and two fingers.

'*Seventeen?!*' He turned back to me, his brow lowered. 'We've had seventeen complaints.'

I thought back to my last client meeting.

Oh.

'Nobody gives a crap about your gift bags,' I recalled to Abdul in a monotone voice that admitted fault. 'They're full of flyers for 10% off stuff no one ever wants, your branded candies taste like Tide Pods, and no one is ever going to wear your company-branded wristband because it's not the 1980s. And you're a nasal spray manufacturer. So for goodness' sake pick a colour and move on because they'll all be left behind for me to clean up the next morning anyway.'

Abdul looked over the top of his on-trend glasses. 'Yes. But instead of "gives a crap" you said,' he glanced at a sheet of paper Tiff held, '"gives the tiniest of fucks" and instead of "for goodness sake" you said—'

'For fuck's sake.'

Tiff jabbed at the paper and Abdul read with a frown. 'For Jesus mutha-fucking Christ's sake pick a mutha-fucking colour and move the fuck on because they'll all be left behind for me to clean up the next fucking morning any-fucking-way.' He looked up.

'I think I may have come back to work too soon.'

★

Abdul had kindly found work I could do from home rather than let me go. From then on it had been tight money-wise. Life insurance had paid off the mortgage and it was just those ten to fifteen hours a week that scraped us through the day-to-day bills. The house was falling apart around us. The toilet plumbing rumbled all night despite a plumber coming out twice, floorboards were lifting and cupboard doors were hanging off their hinges. But I hadn't been ready to go back to work and leave Hannah with a nanny.

★

I looked down at Cookie sitting at my feet. I was in Battersea Park at 11.45am on a Thursday, sitting on a park bench watching ducks. Or people. Or nothing. I'd started walking a few weeks after Abdul had sent me home and, with little work, I couldn't see how I was going to get to the end of the long and lonely week. The emptiness of my home had felt both cavernous and claustrophobic. I'd grabbed Cookie and headed out intending to walk round Wandsworth Common. But before I knew it I'd walked all the way to Battersea Park and had found a bench and watched people walking by. After some time I'd headed home in time for Hannah's return from school. The next day I headed for the river, turned left and found myself walking the Putney Sculpture Trail. The day after that I picked up my pace and made it to Westminster Bridge and had sat watching tourists taking photos of Big Ben.

After a while it became what Cookie and I did while Hannah was at school. Walk, sit, watch a world I didn't feel part of. I'd wonder at all the people who passed me by. Who did they go home to? Were they sad or angry about anything? Were they lonely? Did they have worries they couldn't see a way out of? A depressed family member? Crumbling marriages? Sick children? Why did we go everywhere with our headphones on and our eyes cast downwards, feeling alone? I'd wonder if the passing people wondered about me; why I was sitting with my dog in the middle of a weekday, not at work. Could they see my grief in the way I sat, the way I held my mouth? After a while I'd get off my bench, having realized no one had noticed me at all, and Cookie and I would walk home. I'd spend an hour or so generating invoices, maybe make the odd call to chase a payment, and that would be another day done. Even though the walks were purposeless I felt like I had a purpose; put one foot in front of the other until you get somewhere then turn around and put one foot in front of the other until I got home. I was Forrest Gump.

Just without influencing any significant moments in history. *So far.*

About eight months after Chris died I'd thrown a dinner party. I don't know why, I was still so fragile. I think I'd wanted to feel normal for a moment. Chris and I had put on great dinner parties so I'd just done what we always did. But I'd done it on my own and had spent most of the evening racing from the drinks area to the kitchen to the dining table never having a full conversation with anyone. Previously, when guests had left one of our dinners, Chris and I would have one last glass of wine, turn the music up and deconstruct the evening while stacking the dishwasher; debating who told the funniest story, which wife had been mad at which partner for drinking too much, scoffing leftover pavlova as we worked. I'd get to the end of the clean-up having had almost as much fun with my husband as I'd had during the party. But after that first evening without Chris, when the guests had left amid laughs and declarations of having had a great time, the abrupt silence had been jarring. And it had been up to only me to load the dishwasher, empty crumbs from the chip bowls, scoop olive stones into the bin, and put the leftover pavlova in a Tupperware box. It was silent and laborious and I'd cried the whole way through. The next morning snippets of conversation ran through my head; '*our* heating bill is ridiculous', '*we* are going to Wales for Christmas', '*our* kids love the new babysitter'. We, Our, We, Our. I'd realized those words were no longer mine to use. Now it was just *my* heating bill. *My* child. I'd felt raw and exposed. And no longer safe in the world. So from then on I'd just declined to join it.

*

Just over a year and a half later and I was now at that part where everyone assumes you're better. Not over it, obviously, but functioning. Yet if anything, I was finding this part harder. The all-consuming agony has passed, which is like a full-time occupation where no one even expects you to be able to feed or wash yourself, but I still felt weighed down, like I was carrying an invisible boulder everywhere I went. Grief was still like a gaping nothingness inside of me but nobody could see it anymore so their expectations rose. I must be a good mother again, a good friend again, a good PTA member again, and a good supermarket shopper who definitely does not put a cantankerous old hag of a woman who terrorizes the staff in her place.

'We all dislike Mrs Canvill,' said the junior assistant manager of my local Tesco's Express as he'd escorted me out of the store. He'd been Hannah's babysitter and I'd written a reference for him so he could get the job. 'She's an old cow but we can't have people feeling threatened in our store.' He'd looked at me apologetically as I stood on the footpath with my empty bag-for-life and my shopping list.

'Jonathan, she was being racist.'

'Yeah, but it was kind of like you implied you wanted her dead, Mrs Paige.'

'Implied?' I'd mused. 'I should have been more clear.'

I shop at the big Sainsbury's now and Hannah doesn't get to chat to her old babysitter about Harry Potter.

★

My phone vibrated in my hand with a WhatsApp message from Martin. It was a link to a *HuffPost* article which I opened and began reading. A few minutes later a call came through from Trish.

'Hey,' I said, my voice croaky from not having used it since wishing Hannah a good day at school a couple of hours previously.

'What are you doing?'

'Sitting on a park bench reading an article about people who taxidermy their pets and wondering if I should get Cookie stuffed when she dies.'

'Cookie looks stuffed now.'

'She does.' I appraised my aesthetically unpleasant dog sitting at my feet, her protruding, unevenly sized eyes following the ducks. She'd been such a cute puppy when Chris had brought her home but had done the whole ugly duckling journey in reverse. Now she frightened small children.

'What are you doing?' I asked.

'Having a smear.'

'Wha— like, *right now*?'

'Uh-huh.'

'You're actually on the bed . . . ? Or are you just in the waiting room?'

'I'm on the bed. I'm on the bed and . . . Sorry, what was your name?'

I heard a muffled reply.

'Nurse Caitlin is down the other end with her duck bill-shaped gadget; which is extremely *cold*.'

I heard Nurse Caitlin request that Trish stay still and relax.

'I must say,' Trish said. 'I think she's got the better view. I'm looking at a faded poster of The Wirral.'

I heard a muffled giggle from Nurse Caitlin then another request for my friend to relax.

'Okay, I think you should go and "relax" for Nurse Caitlin and I should do a full body shudder. I feel kind of icky bearing auditory witness to this.'

'Fair enough. I was just seeing what's for dinner tonight?'

'Schnitzel—' Another call beeped in my ear. I looked at the screen and my stomach cramped. 'I've another call coming through, I'll see you later.' I flicked over to the other call and stood. 'Hello?' I said, tugging on Cookie's lead. I needed to be in motion for this call.

'Good afternoon Mrs Paige, it's Will. From Bingley and Frankton. How are you?'

'I'm okay, thanks,' I said, my hands starting to shake. 'Is this the call?'

'It is. I'm pleased to inform you that the agreed amount arrived in our holding account yesterday. As requested, a trust has been set up for Hannah's future, the instructed amount has been sent to Mr Paige's parents in New Zealand, and the remaining funds have been transferred to your account.' Will's voice was respectful and businesslike but also the voice of someone delivering what they thought was welcome news.

I was silent.

'I do need to remind you of the confidentiality agreement you've signed and the ramifications if it's broken.'

'I remember,' I said, vivid images of a boardroom and a document and a weighty Mont Blanc pen popping into my head.

'Very good. Nevertheless, my secretary will email you copies of the documents. Breach of contract in this situation is serious so I suggest you read over the terms of payment again just to be very clear.'

'I will.'

'Congratulations on the outcome, Mrs Paige. I trust you and your daughter will be able to create a good future with it.'

'Thank you,' I said, my voice barely a whisper.

'Is . . .' Will's voice, formally lawyerly, took on a more human tone. '. . . is there anything else I can do for you, Brooke?'

I swallowed. 'No,' I said, clearing my throat. 'I mean, no *thank you.* This is . . .' I forced the words out of my mouth, '. . . good news. Thank you.'

After a brief pause, he spoke again. 'You and Hannah take care. And please do contact me if you want to be put in touch with a financial advisor. I know you were initially reluctant but with a sum this large, it's advisable to make wise decisions early.'

'I'll think about it. Thank you.'

'You're welcome. Goodbye, Brooke.'

★

Two hours later I sat on the sofa in my coat staring at the blank TV screen.

Mum was the reason I'd received that call. Unable to heal her daughter's pain, she'd got on the phone to Lesley-from-Pétanque about her son, a highly regarded solicitor (Will). All of a sudden, I was in the shiny offices of Bingley & Frankton, submitting my financials, sitting across from emotionless lawyers and pharmaceutical representatives, hearing the painful details of how an unexpected reaction to anaesthetic, a piece of malfunctioning new machinery they hadn't disclosed they were trialling, then a lack of critical action that constituted as 'gross medical negligence' had caused my husband to go in for relatively routine elective surgery and come out dead. Months went by where it was all boardrooms and litigation, accusations and defences, and heart-shattering debates over what my husband's life was worth. Will and his besuited team of slick underlings had hit the medical people with everything while I'd wrapped my cardigan tighter, picked my nails, and prayed to be out of there.

Then last week the email.

They'd ruled in my favour. Hannah and I were to be awarded a truly enormous sum. According to Will it was the largest individual payout for a wrongful death claim in the UK. His firm would probably receive some accolade at the British Legal Awards. How weird that my and Hannah's devastation could result in an engraved glass award, a night of drinking, and people cheating on their partners behind velvet drapery in the conference room of a posh hotel. But the payout had come with a non-disclosure clause; essentially a gag order. And *that* was the bitter pill. The new piece of medical machinery had been advance-sold all over the world.

The company behind it was a subsidiary of a billion-dollar pharmaceutical behemoth and if it got out that in its infancy stages of use a patient, my husband, had died, it would be catastrophic for their shareholders. I didn't see how the loss of money, no matter the sum, was 'catastrophic' when compared to a loss of life but I'd been incapacitated with grief and hadn't had the fortitude to go all Erin Brockovich on them. The company was pulling the machine from use to undertake more rigorous testing and I was to never mention the details of my husband's death. To anyone. And I couldn't shake the feeling that I'd betrayed him.

Hannah knew about the court case, of course; it had taken up many months of our lives. I'd told her it was to find out how her father had died so that it wouldn't happen to anyone else. But she didn't know about the money. How could I tell her I'd chosen silence and cash over honesty about his death? But my other option had been to tell everyone how he died and walk away with nothing. Or worse, likely being sued by *them* for libel. It wasn't fair but Will said they were a giant corporation with endless funds and zero integrity. Much better to take what to them was a small hit but to Hannah and me was life-changing than risk financial ruin and years of litigation.

But the contract had been signed; the money was in my account. My lips were sealed and my heart was broken. I felt like I walked around with a scream I couldn't let go of.

*

I looked down and realized Cookie was at my feet, still on her lead. I let her off and made a cup of tea. Then, still in my coat, I sat at the dining table, flipped open my laptop, tapped in my passcodes and stared at my bank account.

Zero after zero after zero.

What one pharmaceutical company and a bunch of lawyers with luxury pens thought a man's life was worth.

More money than Hannah or I, or Hannah's children, would ever need. It was obscene.

Tears trickled down my face and fell on the table. My nose ran into my tea. I picked up the cup and hurled it at the wall.

Chapter 6

'Come listen!' I heard Hannah say by way of greeting to Trish at the front door.

The door slammed. Hannah clattered down the hall to her bedroom and Trish popped her head in to the kitchen.

'Hey,' she said then clocked me stacking washed lettuce leaves in the dish rack and shook her head.

★

'If I buy a salad spinner I'll be one of those people who owns a salad spinner,' I'd said the first time Chris had witnessed my drying rack method and he'd turned to Trish with alarm.

Trish, over for what would become our regular Friday night dinner and drinks that would end up in a 1am fight for control of the stereo (Chris: 90s grunge, Trish: the latest club tunes, me: Salt 'N' Pepa's 'Push It' Every. Single. Time.) had rolled her eyes and continued making margaritas.

'You know what I mean?' I'd said.

'If you buy a salad spinner you'll own a salad spinner, yes,' Chris had replied flatly.

'You don't know what I mean,' I'd sighed and slid another lettuce leaf in the rack.

'Not in a logical sense, no.'

Trish had snorted as she'd tested the margarita directly from the blender.

'What I'm saying is, with kitchen gadgets it's a slippery

slope. If I'm the kind of person who needs a device to get water off my lettuce, soon I'll be the kind of person who needs an apple corer, not just a knife. Or a yolk separator not just the shell. Next thing you know I'll have a battery-operated twirling spaghetti fork, a heated butter knife, and a mono-grammed steak branding iron.'

Chris's eyes had lit up.

'I'll get one for you for Christmas,' I'd said and gotten back to stacking lettuce leaves.

It had even been in our wedding vows. . . . *in sickness and in health, and even though you dry your lettuce in a dish rack . . .*

★

Trish and I locked eyes over the expanse of kitchen. I could tell we were sharing the same memory.

'Go hear the latest,' I said.

After listening to Hannah play Green Day's 'Holiday' three times over Trish strode in to the kitchen and, as familiar in mine as she was in her own, reached her long limbs effortlessly over my head to retrieve glasses and a bottle of red.

'Let's see,' she said, leaning her bony hip against the counter and nodding towards my wrist. As usual she'd encased her lean frame in form-fitting black. She had a smattering of tattoos (a blurry-edged Byzantine cross at the base of her thumb, a Sanskrit symbol behind her ear, three dots that meant some-thing personal to her on her left shoulder, her mother's death date on the other, and a black heart on the inside of her wrist), an inscrutable I-could-be-regal/I-could-be-about-to-fuck-you-up resting face, and an undercut to her blonde, slicked-back hairstyle.

Chris had once called her Trinity from *The Matrix* and she'd floored him with a jiu-jitsu move before deciding she actually quite liked it.

'It's nothing,' I said, holding out my arm to show a flesh-coloured bandage with ratty edges.

She raised a single, impeccably sculptured eyebrow, an act she'd spent an entire summer perfecting when we were thirteen. 'If you say so,' she said then crossed the room and settled herself at the kitchen table. Her intelligent blue eyes, the exact colour of the waves on a beach we'd stayed at on the west coast of Chile, registered the tea stain on the wall and I watched her mentally file that information away for a later inquiry. 'So, I went out with a man on Tuesday who tried to "romantically" force me aboard the Eurostar to Amsterdam.'

'*What?*' I said, glugging olive oil in a pan while reading the recipe on my laptop.

'Yup,' she said, kicking off heavy boots and putting her feet up on a chair. 'We'd been chatting online for a few weeks and at some point I'd mentioned I carry my passport with me because you've got to be up for an adventure and who knows where the day was going to take you.'

I nodded. It was a theory we'd come up with aged eighteen and it had served us well through our early twenties when Ryanair had 50p trips to places that required a Google search.

'We were having a drink at a bar near St Pancras when he said he'd forgotten to meet his cousin at the train station. We rushed over, but no cousin. Instead he produced two train tickets and started frogmarching me towards International Departures while talking about this room he'd booked us at a hotel in the red light district.'

'What a creep!' I said, dropping schnitzel in the sizzling pan.

Trish shrugged. 'He owns a couple of twenty-four-hour gyms in Croydon and was massive. Very protein powdery. No neck.'

'What did you do?'

'Elbow strike, back hammer lock,' Trish said with the casual air of someone reciting the route they took on their recent trip to Margate. 'Then I went to Amsterdam and bought this jacket. Do you like it?'

'You still went to Amsterdam?' I said, incredulous but also eyeing up the buttery soft leather jacket.

'The tickets were already bought, so why not? I hadn't seen Hans and Hestia since they had their new baby, and I didn't have anything on the next day that I couldn't do over Zoom. Hans and Hestia say hi by the way. They had another friend staying and *he* was lovely,' she said with a grin.

'Of course he was,' I grinned back.

Trish then detailed how she'd sent No Neck Man links to courses he could take on Developing Healthy Relationships With Women and how he'd messaged her back an apology and said he'd misread her 'up for an adventure' as 'up for anything (wink wink)' and Trish has reflected on how nuance was lost on dating apps and how she ought to remember that and anyhow, now they were text pen pals. Trish was like that. She didn't write people off for one wrong step. Even if that step was attempted kidnapping across international borders.

★

'Mum got asked back to work yesterday,' Hannah said as we took our places around the dinner table a little later. We all had our usual spots. And no one ever sat in Chris's chair.

'Really?' said Trish, serving herself salad.

I nodded as I handed out home-brand paper towels as napkins.

Trish arched those flawless eyebrows in my direction. 'And?'

'She said no, of course,' Hannah said. 'She says no to everything.'

'No, I don't,' I said feeling a pang of guilt. Was that how my daughter had come to see me?

Hannah turned to me, eyebrows raised. 'Are you going to Hammertime?'

'No.'

'See,' she said, getting back to her schnitzel. 'Mackenzie's mum is donating one of her paintings. We could donate one of Dad's sculptures?'

'No,' I said again which caused Hannah to roll her eyes. I looked at the nearest sculpture on the messy sideboard; a bronze cast of Hannah's head and shoulders, about the size of the cookbook it sat alongside. The idea of a piece of Chris leaving the house . . . I turned back to Hannah. 'I'll think of something else.'

'What*ever*,' she said, showing hints of a new pre-teen attitude that made Trish and me share a suppressed giggle.

'What did the email from your boss say?' Trish asked.

I opened it on my phone, slid it across the table and waited while she read.

'Doesn't it sound cool?' Hannah said as Trish handed me back my phone. 'They want *camels* in the city. Camels! Could I come watch, Mum?'

'It sounds like fun,' Trish said, looking at me.

'It does,' I admitted.

A few years before Chris died I'd put on a treasure-hunt-style wedding proposal for a wealthy man from Saudi Arabia. It had woven through Belgravia and Hyde Park, with performers in the street doing dances, singing songs or drawing caricatures for the recipient and handing out clues. It had ended at a jewellers in Mayfair where a ring had been picked out. I'd then done something similar for an elaborate pregnancy reveal. After that, requests came in for similar events and I sort of got a name in the industry. I'd loved creating the secretive yet public events and Hannah had loved seeing the photos and comments from the public on social media. The email from my boss was about another elaborate marriage proposal, an associate of the first Saudi man, and they'd asked for me personally.

'So?' Hannah said, grinning with anticipation.

I smiled at her. 'It's not the right time for me to go back to work.'

Hannah dropped her grin. 'See,' she huffed. 'No to everything.'

Trish watched me from across the table. Was there disappointment in her expression? She was often unreadable, even to me, her oldest friend.

We'd been friends since we were eight. With neither of us sure what we wanted to do as a career, we left school and worked in food trucks during the summer festival season then went travelling as soon as we'd saved enough. We picked up odd jobs in order to keep ourselves out of England until the next festival season. We worked at nail salons in Brazil, hired out wetsuits and paddle boards in the Caribbean, worked in a bookstore in the Northern Territory, and were extras for a Bollywood movie in India.

When we were on our flight home, tanned, broke and tired, Trish would skooch down with her eye mask on, lean towards me and say, 'It's been a fun ride, babe.'

I'd lean my head against hers and say, 'I can't think of anyone I'd rather have done it with.'

For five years we lived that carefree life, until one year while sitting in a sweaty open-walled bar in Vietnam, the rain falling in sheets off the tin roofs and our tickets home booked and paid for, we decided to 'get serious' and when we got back to London we volunteered at Childline. Trish immediately showed a strength I didn't have. She could handle hearing about the abuse and the violence but I couldn't even make it past the first round of call shadowing. That was where we parted ways. In a work sense. Trish went on to attend university, taking an array of subjects which enabled her to work with at-risk youths and I put my skills of quick decision-making, the ability to go without sleep, and spout the odd white lie in order to keep people happy to monetary use and got a job in event management.

Trish picked up her wine and turned to Hannah. 'So Chickpea, how is school? Did you have music today?'

I grinned and shook my head. Trish had a thing for Hannah's music teacher, Ms Beadle, after meeting her at Hannah's end of year concert.

'Yes,' Hannah said, and a sudden cloud crossed her face.

Trish and I exchanged looks.

'What happened?' I asked.

'I got chosen for the end of year concert again.'

'That's great!' I said, confused at her manner. 'Are you happy?'

'Yes,' she said, emanating anything but happiness. 'Well I *was*, until Livie said that drums were a boys' instrument and the whole class laughed.'

'There's no such thing as a boys' or girls' instrument,' I said, annoyed.

'I *know* that. But everyone laughed.'

'Even Zara?' Zara was a sweet girl but a weak girl. She hadn't aligned herself with anyone and didn't seem to have her own opinions about anything. She'd be dominated by Livie in due course.

Hannah shrugged and looked at her plate. 'And . . .'

Trish and I met each other's gaze again. 'And what?' I said.

'When I put my hand up to be on the costume committee Livie said "you can't be on the costume committee because you dress like a rainbow vomited".'

I bit my lip and Trish's eyes crinkled at the edges as we held back a smile. It was cruel but bang-on.

'The whole class laughed again.'

I put my hand on her shoulder but she sunk away from it. 'Maybe we should have a word with your teacher again?'

'No,' Hannah said, scowling at her dinner. 'I just want her to shut up and leave me alone. I can't wait till I go to school with Tom and never have to see her *ever again*.' She put her cutlery together on the plate. 'I'm not hungry. Can I be excused?'

'But, Hannah—'

'Please?'

'Okay, honey. Jump in the shower.'

Hannah scraped her chair back, tipped her leftover dinner in Cookie's bowl and put her plate in the dishwasher. Eventually we heard the bathroom door shut and the shower turn on.

'So the Livie situation isn't getting any better?' Trish said.

'Nope.' I told her about the recent nit rumour that was still causing kids to shuffle away from her in class, the dwindling playdate invites, and the increasing jibes that Livie innocently explained away as jokes. 'It seems like her goal is to isolate Hannah completely. I think she's still pissed she got in trouble for the Instagram Photoshopping.'

'That was, what, over a month ago?'

'Two.'

'The need to be mean comes from a place of fear,' Trish said, settling back in her chair, comfortable dissecting a topic she had dedicated her life to. After years of working in the charity sector she'd founded an initiative that helped vulnerable teens and youths who'd been excluded from mainstream education. It had been going for the past six years and was proving so successful at reintegrating troubled kids back into society that it had been recognized by The Prince's Trust. Trish was due to have dinner with Charles and Camilla at the end of the year. Hannah and I were beside ourselves with excitement. 'Maybe there's something else going on that's making Livie act out. How's her home life?'

'Perfect,' I said, noting a hint of bitterness in my voice. 'They have plenty of money, they're good-looking, they throw lots of parties, and are friends with minor celebrities; baking show types and low-grade footballers.'

Trish nodded. 'Kids don't just "decide" to bully.'

'Unless they're a sociopath.'

'Is she?'

'It helps to think of her that way.'

Trish laughed.

'Is it bullying, though?' I asked.

'Sustained torment. Intentional exclusion.' Trish nodded sadly. 'It sounds like it is.'

'What can I do if Hannah won't let me go to the teachers?'

'Bullies often stop or move on to someone else quite abruptly. But that's not in your control. What *is*, is making sure Hannah's self-esteem isn't damaged in the meantime,' Trish said. 'She will probably be doubting herself and searching for reasons why Livie has chosen her. You have to continually remind her that there is no reason, and that bullying is more to do with how the bully feels about themselves rather than anything about Hannah that is 'wrong' or unlikable.'

I nodded grimly. I hated the idea that Hannah might be wondering which aspects of herself were 'unlikable'.

Trish gave a me a supportive smile. 'And if she's struggling to have meaningful connections or joy at school then you have to find her joy and connection in another area. Make sure she spends time doing things she is good at, like her drumming, and organize extra playdates, sleepovers. Things that strengthen her self-esteem.'

I had a sudden pang of guilt. I couldn't remember the last time Hannah had a sleepover or playdate at our home. 'Connection has been missing for Hannah lately,' I admitted.

'And for you.'

I avoided Trish's pointed gaze.

'I see you avoiding my pointed gaze,' she chided.

I smiled at my friend. She would have been an awesome parent but had decided biological children were not part of her future, instead choosing to put her love, diplomacy and fierce intellect into helping her troubled youths. They'd never know how lucky they were she'd made that choice.

★

While Trish cleaned up in the kitchen I tucked Hannah in to bed.

'Are you ever going to go back to work?' she said, pulling her tie-dyed duvet up to her chin.

'Do you want me to?'

Hannah shrugged.

'If I went back to work there'd be lots of days I wouldn't be here when you got home after school. And I'd have to work some weekends.'

'I could stay with Zara? Or Penny?'

I smiled. 'I'd miss you though. Wouldn't you miss me?'

Hannah nodded. 'I miss seeing the videos of all the crazy stuff in the streets.'

'You just miss the *free* stuff!' I said grabbing the to-scale feathered cockatoo from her headboard and pretending to nibble her ear with it while she giggled and squirmed.

The cockatoo was from a tropical-themed thirtieth. Somewhere in Hannah's bric-a-brac of a bedroom there was also a toucan and a sequinned python. At the end of an event any decorations left over were either put into the company's stock or allowed to be taken home. My work in events had instigated Hannah's obsession with colour and street parties, and her room was a cacophony of glittery bowler hats, neon feather boas, disco balls, and crystal-encrusted bunting.

I replaced the cockatoo, who Hannah called Reginald, and flicked off her side lamp. 'Night, honey. I love you.'

'I love you too,' Hannah said.

I gave her an extra squeezy cuddle then rejoined Trish in the kitchen.

'I have to show you something,' I said, grabbing my laptop off the sideboard and taking my seat at the table. I opened internet banking, typed in my security info then spun it to face my friend, biting my nails while her eyes darting across the particulars before widening.

She lifted her wine without taking her eyes off the computer and took seven gulps before plonking the empty glass on the

table. 'Holy freeze-dried nutsacks.' She flicked her attention to
me. 'They paid it.'

I nodded.

She stared at the screen again before shuddering and looking
abruptly away. 'You know, I can't look directly at it. It's making
me nauseous. Where do you start with a sum like that?'

I shrugged.

Trish turned back to the laptop, cocking her head to the
side. 'You could buy Australia?'

I snorted.

'But what to do with the other half . . . ?'

I didn't reply and looked away, focusing on the red sediment
at the bottom of the glass. I was feeling weirdly detached from
the gigantic figure on the screen. How could it be mine?

'It's definitely enough for you to bankroll your ultimate
fantasy,' Trish said.

I looked up, the corner of my lips lifting in a smile. 'The
entire male cast of Marvel's *Infinity War* performing Colour
Me Badd's "All 4 Love" in their spandex suits?'

Trish shook her head, disappointed in my choice of fantasy.
Hers was unrepeatable.

★

After Trish left I brushed my teeth and climbed in to bed in
the quiet, dark house. I navigated to the banking app on my
phone and stared at the unfathomable amount in my account.
I felt . . . nothing. I shut down the page, opened the photo
app, found the video, propped my phone against the pillow
on the empty side of the bed, and pressed play.

'I'm just saying, it could help.' Chris grinned down the lens as
he lay on his pillow in the glow of his bedside light. *'It's science.
Here, I'll look it up.'*

'You do that,' came my yawning voice as Chris leaned to retrieve
his phone from his bedside table, his naked back filling the screen.

He rested back on his pillow and I could be heard giggling while he tapped at his phone. 'Just as I suspected,' he said, channelling Angela Lansbury. 'It says that having sex, although you may not feel like it at the time, releases a rush of endorphins that are a natural pain relief.' He looked towards the camera again. 'See? Science. And I'm only offering to do it to help you because I won't enjoy it.'

'Oh really?' my chuckling voice said.

'Nope. I'm not in the mood.' He turned away from the camera with a haughty look, then shot some side-eye and cracked into a grin. 'Who could be with those saggy pyjama bottoms you're wearing? Would you like me to remove them in the interest of science?' Still grinning he lunged towards the phone and it moved around displaying quick flashes of the ceiling, the duvet, his shoulder, while I could be heard laughing in the background. 'It might be your disgusting pyjamas causing the headache,' Chris's disembodied voice said.

'Get them off then!' my squealing, giggling voice said.

More laughter, more duvet/ceiling/shoulder/grinning face images.

The video stopped on a wonky out-of-focus angle of Chris's bare shoulder.

I was in my bed in a quiet, dark house again.

My eyelids blinked heavily. I yawned as I pressed play.

'I'm just saying it could help . . .'

Chapter 7

Hannah and I walked through the back door into Mum and Dad's kitchen that Saturday morning each carrying a basket of freshly picked spoils; radishes, asparagus, rhubarb, spinach etc, that Mum would cook until their cell walls gave up and they turned into a greyish mush. Trailing behind us, who'd been making not at all furtive snatches at our haul as we'd meandered around the sunny garden, was Clint the rescue alpaca. Trish appeared, sweaty from her two-hour morning run. When she'd heard I was having to clear out the barn she insisted on being at my side when I did it. 'I just met Gus,' she said, filling a water glass at the sink.

'My lesson!' Hannah dropped her basket on the counter and raced towards the cellar throwing a scowl my way. 'You didn't tell me the time!'

'He's early!'

Trish grabbed a couple of cherry tomatoes from Hannah's abandoned basket and bit down on their sun-warmed skin. She noticed Clint standing at the kitchen back door, said, 'Hello, buddy,' and turned back to me like having an alpaca watching you from the kitchen back door was perfectly normal, which in this house it was. 'Gus arrived on a *horse*.' She grinned. 'You never told me Gus was hot. Or that he drives a horse.'

I held up my index finger, a silent 'do not sleep with my

daughter's drum teacher' and Trish pulled a 'we'll see' face then chugged back her water. I'd felt these rules (teachers off limits, parents of school friends off limits, Prince Charles off limits) needed to be laid out ever since we were 20 and I found out she'd slept with my 17-year-old brother, Martin. Then his friend. Then *his* brother.

★

'It's the inconsistency I can't cope with,' I said an hour later, as Trish and I followed Mum into the laundry where the washing machines had rumbled to a halt; the end of Hannah's drum lesson, a continuous attempt at the transition to the 'break' from Tone-Loc's 'Wild Thing', reverberating up from the cellar. 'She's sweet then sarcastic then sullen then shirty. I'm sure I wasn't like this till I was at least fourteen.'

'Oh no, love,' Mum said, pulling wet sheets from her industrial washing machine and dumping them into a huge basket on wheels. 'You were vile from about nine.'

Trish, leaning against the tiled laundry bench gulping back a sewerage-coloured smoothie, nodded her agreement. I made a face. She grinned, put her smoothie down and helped me untwist heavy wet towels from a wad of heavy wet sheets. It was a changeover day for two of the glamping yurts which meant a day of washing and cleaning. Mum had two industrial washing machines installed in her large utility room when they'd moved in, plus two dryers which, because of thriftiness, were only to be used in emergencies. Like Noah's Ark level rain.

'Well, I wasn't as bad as Martin,' I said, my voice echoing because I was up to my waist inside the washing machine reaching for a towel suctioned to the bottom.

'Oh, Brooke,' Mum puffed as she wrestled with a wet king duvet cover. 'You were a *nightmare* as a teenager. Right into your twenties really. Martin just did pot, but you? Pills, pills, RTDs, STDs . . .'

'I didn't do pills and I never had an STD!' I said indignantly, hoisting myself out of the bottom of the washing machine in a sweat to see Gus at the laundry room door.

'Ah, sorry to interrupt,' he said.

I felt my face flame while Trish hid her mirth behind a wet towel.

'We've finished so I was just coming to say goodbye.' He was wearing a plain grey T-shirt and, without needing to check, I knew Trish was scrutinising his bicep area.

Hannah was still practising and I could hear one of her favourite drum breaks; the Phil Collins one that the gorilla did in that Cadbury ad.

'Would you like to stay for lunch?' Mum said, smoothing down her hair and flinching at the increased volume of Hannah unbridled on her kit. 'We have meatloaf. It's Bill Cosby's recipe.' She beamed then dropped her smile and looked serious. 'From before he did all those horrible things.'

'Not before he did them. Just before we knew about them,' Trish corrected.

'I won't, thank you, Iris,' Gus said while Mum gave Trish a look of incomprehension. 'I'm taking some of the boarders cycling around Hesworth Common. My friend has started an e-bike hire business and needs the branded bikes cycled around at weekends to advertise.' He turned to me. 'Hannah has been asking to give one a go. If it's okay with you I could take her after our lesson next week? Tom as well.'

'She'd love that,' I said.

Gus broke into a smile that was all white teeth and appled cheekbones. 'Great! Will you come too?'

'Oh . . . maybe . . .' I said.

'Love to,' said Trish.

'I think I might be a bit past that kind of thing,' said Mum, 'but you never know.'

We all smiled and Gus smiled awkwardly back.

'Great,' he said again, his gaze flicking between the three of us. 'Next week?'

'I'll be there,' Trish grinned while I said 'perhaps' and Mum said she'd have to look at her calendar.

'Okay.' He nodded then left the room.

Trish spun round. 'Is that a date, do you think?'

'Who for?' I said, recoiling at the notion.

'Not me,' Mum said, but her blush said something else.

'Maybe me?' Trish said. 'I'm sure he was directing the conversation mostly to me.' She winked.

I snorted and shook my head and we all got back to the laundry.

'It's STI now,' Trish said after a few moments.

'What?' said Mum.

'What you were saying before. The terminology got updated a while ago, it's just a bit more enlightened. Not every infection turns into disease, especially if treated straight away.'

Mum frowned and looked at Trish like she'd just outlined the Mongolian government's sanitary plan for Ulan Bator. In haiku.

'Brooke had pills, pills, RTDs and STIs not STDs,' Trish explained.

'Brooke had *no* STDs *or* Is, or *anything, okay*?' I said, punching some dirty towels in to the washing machine. 'None! And except for the odd bout of thrush, I've always had perfect vaginal health!'

Gus appeared in the doorway holding a pair of Hannah's favourite drumsticks. The tips of his ears were the colour of Mum's rhubarb (pre her boiling it to oblivion).

'Christ,' I muttered, feeling my own cheeks begin to flame.

'Sorry,' he said, waggling the drumsticks and avoiding eye contact. 'I nearly left with these.'

Trish shot Gus a winning smile whereas Mum shot me a glower of disgust.

'I'll just leave them . . .' he placed the sticks on the counter. '. . . here.' He gave a short wave and was off again.

'Well,' I said turning back to Mum who had pursed her lips and Trish who had dissolved into laughter. 'That was indisputably mortifying.'

*

After helping us hang out the washing, Hannah was excused to go and find Tom, and Trish and I headed to the barn where Mum had left some empty storage boxes.

'Gus is gorgeous,' Trish stated.

'Is he?'

'You know he is. Does he have a girlfriend? Boyfriend? Wife? Husband?'

'I don't know,' I said realising that at lunch that previous week I hadn't asked him about himself at all. The realisation unsettled me. When had I become *that* kind of person?

'Hmmm,' Trish said, her eyebrows activated.

'Not happening.'

'We'll see.'

Together, we tugged at the shabby oak doors of the old barn. They swung back on perilous hinges and banged against the wooden walls wafting out a fug of dust and stale air. Coughing, we stepped forward. As our eyes got accustomed to the gloom inside, a bulk in the centre came into focus. I gazed up at it while Trish strode past and disappeared into the dark, musty depths.

'Fuck!' she yelled and a clattering of metal sounded from the shadowy void.

'Are you okay?'

'Yes,' she said, as something wooden collapsed. '*Ow*! No! Owwww.'

'What are you doing?!'

'Where are the—?' Three hanging bulbs that hung down the centre of the barn flickered on. 'Ah, that's better.'

Trish hobbled out from behind some cluttered shelving, rubbing her shin with one hand and her bony hip with the other. She arrived next to me and looked up. 'What was this one going to be?'

I stared at the last sculpture my husband had been working on before he died. 'Me.'

Trish jerked her head to assess my reaction. Once I'd assured her, with a weak, one-sided smile, that I was okay, she turned back to the 8-foot structure, cocked her head to the side, and took in the crude form. Hardened yellow expanding foam clung in porridge-like clumps to a vaguely human-esque wooden armature. Eventually my husband's skill would have shaped the giant mound of solidified gloop into a sculpture that, once cast in bronze, would appear as fluid as floating silk. But at this stage it looked like a zombie carcass emerging from the decomposing flesh of some kind of porridge/mud monster.

She wrinkled her nose. 'Didn't like you much, did he?' She flung a toned arm over my shoulders. 'Where shall we start?'

*

When Hannah was a toddler Chris had come home from his work as a (mostly ignored) geography teacher at a South London comprehensive, plonked on a chair at the kitchen table, and said he didn't know how much longer he could do it. I'd made him a vodka lime and soda and sat on a chair opposite him, watching him drag a palm over his brow.

'Those kids are sucking the life out of you,' I said. 'They're pre-teen Dementors.'

Chris slunk down in his chair, leant the crook of his arm on the back rest and gave a smirk. Despite his weary limbs and flat gaze, he was still sexy. He'd trained to be a teacher knowing it could take him anywhere. And he'd loved it while he was in Dubai or Argentina, Cape Town, Australia or Korea, but now that we'd bought a flat and had a baby, and travelling was something we had to plan and save for rather than a lifestyle, he'd realized the travel was what he loved, not the job.

'I've been doing some figures,' I said, getting up and retrieving an A4 envelope from a kitchen drawer. I slid the envelope across the table then headed to the kitchen to start dinner. 'If I went back to work, I can cover us.'

Chris looked at me for a moment. He placed his glass carefully on the table and opened the envelope.

'They have space because I called,' I said as Chris pulled out a prospectus for a sculpture course he'd been talking about for years.

Chris glanced towards Hannah, on the sofa watching *Dora*, and opened his mouth to speak, but I held up my hand. I told him that my old boss had recently sent an email asking if I'd like to go back to work earlier than we'd discussed. He'd been so keen to have me back he'd said he was sure he could make the hours work for Hannah. Chris was wary. Events was not an industry that made life with young children easy. But after another vodka, a thorough read of the prospectus, and an in-depth explanation of the childcare logistics I'd been quietly organising in my head, he started to come around.

With his elbow on the table and his chin resting in his upturned hand, Chris watched me stir mince in the kitchen with smiling eyes. 'We're really doing this?'

I grinned. 'If it's what you want, then we are.'

He pushed his chair back, crossed the kitchen and arrived behind me at the stove, wrapping his arms around my waist. 'I love you,' he murmured into my neck.

'I love you too.' I twisted my head to meet his kiss which deepened quickly into something more passionate.

'Dora finish!' Hannah called from the living room.

Chris groaned as I pulled away from him. With my arms resting on his shoulders I glanced down. 'I'm getting lucky tonight, aren't I?'

'Very,' he said, touching his forehead to mine. He looked at me, his eyes glinting. '*Very.*'

★

By the end of that year he was coming home from his course covered in dust and clay, enthusing over moulds and mediums, and gushing about guest tutors. We managed to bumble along with me working full time and Chris doing his course, completing various other modules and honing his artistic abilities. But when he finished his course and decided his preferred medium was bronze and his preferred scale was giant, we needed more money.

'We'll get a second mortgage,' I said as we walked through Wimbledon Common one chilly Sunday.

'What?!' Chris said, stopping to watch Hannah approach a man with three Yorkies.

'I've been doing the figures,' I said.

'You and your figures. When did you learn to do figures?'

'When I met you, my love, because you're terrible at them.'

'I do the family spelling.'

'You do. And I do the figures. And I'm telling you, the figures work.'

We continued to walk, again working through logistics (Mum had offered the barn as his workspace in exchange for help around the manor), and pausing to let Hannah pat every passing dog.

'But I'll be away from you and Hannah?' he said.

'Two nights. You leave Wednesday after Hannah goes to school, we come down on Friday evening and we all go back on Sunday together. Mum will love having Hannah every weekend, and I get to binge watch the shows you hate on Wednesdays and Thursdays.'

Chris smiled then pondered in silence for a few moments. 'What if no one buys my work?' he said as we turned towards the pub for a post walk pint.

I didn't have an answer to that question. But he wouldn't know if he didn't try. And I told him so. And he hugged me and told me he loved me and I got very lucky that night.

★

For the next three years every weekend was spent in Sussex. Chris would work in the barn with the doors open and I'd sit on the grass just outside in summer or wrapped up in blankets inside in winter. We'd sip wine and chat while Chris's old 90s CDs played on his plaster-splattered stereo. Chris managed to sell a few pieces, mostly to friends of Mum's who she'd harangued, but gallery owners suggested he scale down his sculptures in order to make more sales. Then one day Hannah scored her first try against the older kids. She flung her arms out, threw her head back, and ran across the field, hair splaying behind her. Chris sketched Hannah's pose and went super giant with that piece, despite his gallery contacts expressing their concerns that it was a risky (and expensive) move. He'd barely put the finished 14-foot, 700-pound bronze statue on his artist's Facebook page when a Singaporean collector contacted him and bought it, requesting its immediate shipment. Almost instantly an esteemed dealer got in touch; he had a list of clients wanting commissions. Apparently, the art world is vastly competitive, and no collector wants to be the one who misses out on 'the next big thing'. The commission deposits rolled in and we made plans for me to quit my job and move to Sussex. We put Hannah's name down to attend the private school with Tom and even looked at a tiny office space I could lease for me to potentially start my own event business in the village.

But then Chris died.

Before even finishing his first commission. Which was looming before me now.

'Oh my God!' Trish said from somewhere down the back. 'I'd forgotten about this trip.'

I ducked under the outstretched 'arm' of the sculpture and joined Trish, who was leaning over a messy work bench looking at a collection of photos pinned to the wall next to pencil sketches and exhibition cards.

She unpinned a photo, spun around and rested her slim hips against the worktop. 'I thought he was looooovely,' she said tapping a fingertip on the smiling face of a friend of Chris's. He had goggle marks around his eyes and his teeth shone white against his skier's tan.

'I know you thought he was lovely,' I said, taking the photo out of her hands and looking at the rest of the people in the picture; Chris, me, Chris's 'lovely' friend, two other guys and two other girls, all of us red-cheeked from mulled wine and a roaring fire. 'The whole chalet knew you thought he was lovely. We all *heard* you think he was lovely about twelve times a night.'

She grinned. 'Shame he went back to New Zealand.'

'Probably good for his hydration levels that he did.'

We went back to looking at the photo, both smiling but for different reasons. Trish, because she was just remembering a holiday where the majority of riding was done in the thin-walled bedroom instead of on the new snowboard she'd carted all the way to Chamonix, and me because I was pretty sure Hannah had been conceived on that trip. I looked at my face; big grin, eyes sparkling. Cheeks flushed from wine and happiness. I felt like I was looking at a totally different person.

Trish gave my shoulder a squeeze then scanned the room full of tools and materials, pencils and plaster. Even an empty coffee mug, all left pretty much where my husband had last used them.

'Gunge.' She picked up a box, handed it to me, then unpinned another photo and placed it in the box. 'That's a cool word that's underutilized, don't you think?'

I smiled at my best friend; as nuts as a Snickers and as loyal as a rescue pup. I loved her as much as I loved my parents. I swallowed down a lump and took down another photo, briefly noting the dimples in my husband's face before putting it in the bottom of the box.

Trish kept up a distracting and amusing stream of chatter while we worked on the walls, then taped up and labelled the boxes. Once the workbench was clear, Trish opened a set of drawers that looked like a Pandora's box of shit and I opened a cupboard and stopped.

'What?' Trish was at my side, holding a fistful of metal Allen key type tools gummed together with plaster.

I pulled out an A3 sheet of newsprint. It was a study of me he'd done for the sculpture, with closer studies around the edges. I remembered him catching me while I cooked dinner, or played Lego with Hannah, or once, for which I was outraged, while I was plucking my chin hairs. It was strange to see myself through the eyes of my husband. He'd made me look way prettier than I actually was. I pulled out the rest of the sheets; all of them complimentary close-ups of my face. You could tell the subject was drawn by someone in love.

The emotion I'd been holding back broke free.

'You're doing really well,' Trish said, placing an arm around my shaking shoulders, the Allen keys clunking on my upper arm. 'But I think you need a break.'

*

The day was blue-skied and warm and, inspired by Gus and his talk of e-bikes, I decided to take Martin's old bike and cycle to the local bottle store to take the edge off the rest of the pack-up.

'Oh hello, Brooke love, how are you? How is Hannah holding up?'

'Holding up' was an expression I heard often now that my husband had died. It was a strange term. What were we expected to be holding? I imagined it to be my body. And yes, there were times when I couldn't construct any emotional scaffolding and the idea of holding it upright for a day was inconceivable.

'We're both doing well, thanks,' I said as I put a bottle of rosé on the counter. 'What vodkas do you have?' I looked beyond Kirsty, a lady in her sixties who'd been running the little bottle shop in the village with her husband since I could remember.

'Oh, we just got this one in,' she said, suddenly animated. She turned and pulled a bottle from the wooden shelf behind her where other bottles glistened under the overhead lights. 'It's made entirely from milk by a man in Dorset! And it's gluten-free, like you young things like.' Her face dropped. 'Hasn't been selling well, mind. I think people find it unusual.'

'It's weird. I'll take it,' I said and Kirsty beamed. I pulled my wallet from my bag and saw a little plastic collection box on the top of the till. A picture of a boy not much older than Hannah was sellotaped to the side. 'Who's that?'

Kirsty's face was suddenly downcast. 'Ah, that's a wee lad from the next village over. He's got leukaemia, the poor mite. His parents can't afford to take time off to be in hospital with him.'

Chapter 8

The next couple of hours of barn clearing was less painful with the addition of rosé, and Chris's old CDs on the stereo. Cookie scurried in and out, nose to the ground, and I got the feeling she was looking for Chris. With the doors flung open to the warm afternoon, and my best friend and me reminding each other of some teen debacle we'd got ourselves into each time another 90s song came on, there were moments when I'd forget that I was dismantling another tangible mark of my husband's existence.

'Mum,' Hannah's voice sounded from the front of the barn. 'Tom got a pass. Can he stay for dinner?' She arrived behind the sculpture where I was sorting through a box of plaster-caked carving implements.

I looked up at her; muddy knees, bare feet, rugby ball under her arm, scraggly hair, wonky teeth, Iron Maiden T-shirt, and green and yellow dip-dyed shorts. She was perfection. She kept her eyes resolutely on me, avoiding the undoing of her father's studio. Tom, in a neat polo shirt and tidy shorts, stood next to her taking in the formerly busily adorned walls and bench-tops, struck silent by their sudden bareness.

'Sure, sweetie. Just check with Grandma if there'll be enough, okay?'

'How's school, Tom?' Trish asked as she hefted another full box towards the pile of taped-up boxes.

'Good, thanks,' he said with a comfortable grin, having known her for years. 'We've got a new rugby coach – Mr Taylor. He's also the deputy housemaster.'

'What's he like?' she asked and I flashed her a look that said 'don't sleep with Tom's rugby coach'.

'He's cool,' Tom said. 'He likes Post Malone.'

'A rapper,' Trish informed me before taking a swig from her sporty water bottle and flashing a look that said 'If he's even remotely interesting I'll be trying my darndest'.

Mum burst into the barn. 'I just had a call from Kirsty saying you'd put a rather large sum in a charity box!?'

I glanced meaningfully at Hannah who was half hidden behind the sculpture. 'It's a collection for a local boy who has leukaemia so his parents can be in the hospital with him. And it wasn't *that* large.'

'I know that boy,' Tom said. 'We play against his school in cricket.'

'Oh hello Tom, love,' Mum said, her face softening upon seeing the two children. 'How's Mr Taylor getting on?'

'He's good.'

'He likes Post Malone,' Trish said.

I rolled my eyes and returned her grin.

'Lovely,' Mum said with a flutter of confusion then she turned to me and her expression hardened.

'Did you really give the boy some money?' Hannah asked, frowning. She was used to us buying everything on sale, getting a bus not an Uber, and putting her school jumper on the radiator instead of in the dryer. 'How much?'

'Just a few pennies,' I said and Mum made a scoffing noise.

'Dinner will be ready in an hour.' Mum turned away from my hard stare. 'Tom, love, do you have a pass to stay?'

Tom nodded.

'Lovely,' Mum said with a smile which dropped when she

noticed the children's bare feet. 'Run inside and put shoes on, will you?'

Hannah grabbed Tom by his sleeve and made her way towards the house with her grandmother watching after her. When Mum turned back to me the kids made a cartoon-like direction change and bolted across the gardens towards the back field.

'We'll come inside and help with dinner,' I said, pushing myself up off the dusty barn floor. 'It's mosquito time now anyway.'

'Yes, thank you,' Mum said, then she looked around the barn, taking in the boxes in the corner, taped-up and labelled in black sharpie, the bare walls where previously there'd been photos and sketches, and the workbenches that were now clear except for splashes of paint and plaster. She turned back to me with a mollified expression. 'You're all right, love. I can manage.'

*

'Charity is all well and good,' Mum said, ferrying in a heavy dish of worryingly wobbly lasagne and placing it on the table in front of Sasha who openly sneered at the sight of it, 'if you're okay yourself. But a bit here and a bit there and it can all go without you even realising it.'

'Most of us at this table are in a position to help others out now and again, Mum.' I placed the salt and pepper on the table and pulled out my chair.

'*No one ever becomes poor by giving,*' Dad quoted, taking his seat and placing his lager down with the reverence he believed it deserved. 'Anne Frank.'

'Well, that's clearly incorrect,' Mum said, annoyed. She gestured impatiently to Yumi and Noriko, who were politely waiting for her to sit, to take their seats. 'If you have a finite amount and you keep giving, it will eventually all go. It's just basic maths.'

'*We make a living by what we get. We make a life by what we give*,' Trish said putting the salad on the table and sitting down. 'Winston Churchill.'

Dad gave a nod of respect.

'Of course, the act of giving is admirable,' Mum said, accustomed to being the only one fighting her side of an argument as she took her own seat. 'But money is so easy to fritter. Especially if you have a lot,' she said, attempting a covert pointed look in my direction as she took her seat. 'And then the frittering can become the whole thing and you end up like Nicolas Cage.'

I wrinkled my nose. 'Swapping faces with John Travolta?'

Mum scowled.

'On a doomed plane full of convicts with Steve Buscemi?' Trish queried.

'Stuck on Alcatraz with Sean Connery?' I offered.

Mum pursed her lips and dragged a knife through the soupy-looking lasagne.

'I would've gotten stuck *anywhere* with Sean Connery,' Trish said, making Hannah and Tom giggle.

'Yes, well anyway,' Mum said, getting back to her agenda. She always had one. 'I think that if *I* were to come into a lot of money the thing to do would be to invest in property. Joan-from-Pétanque's husband, he's the one who gets a bit flirty at the tournament after-gala, he invests in property and says it's the way to go. Financially speaking. That's where that saying comes from – "as sure as houses".'

'Did you win the lotto or something, Mum?' Sasha said. 'Why are you obsessed with money all of a sudden?'

'I did not win lotto. And I'm not obsessed,' Mum said. 'It's just good to be mindful of what comes in and out of our accounts, that's all. I'm having a practical conversation. Something not done often enough around this table.'

'If I won lotto, I'd buy one of Dave Grohl's old drum sets,' Hannah said.

'I'd get a motorbike,' said Tom. 'And a football team.'

'Tattoo parlour,' said Trish. 'And I'd fund a series of climate change symposiums in low-income boroughs.'

'If I won the lotto I'd probably only just be able to afford a basic place to live,' Sasha lamented. And while she segued into her regular complaint about how hard it was to get ahead in this day and age – especially in property etc – after the baby boomers had ruined everything and how her entire generation had to live at home until their late thirties, like back in Victorian times, just without shingles, Mum passed plates of sloppy lasagne down the table and the rest of us semi-tuned out. Sasha always seemed to be striving towards something. And always so vocally. We all knew about her efforts to secure a boyfriend/promotion/goal weight, or a particular pair of shoes that would help her get the boyfriend/promotion/goal weight.

'Delicious,' Noriko said unconvincingly, as Mum handed her a plate.

Each pasta layer had slipped in a different direction, leaving a watery, meat-coloured sploosh in the middle.

'I'm not eating that,' Sasha said as a plate was offered to her, and when we all stared at her she added 'I have a date picking me up in ten minutes.' She passed the plate to Tom then went back to her phone.

'I didn't think you were supposed to give out your address to a Tinder date?' I said. 'In case they're a murderer or whatever. Didn't you see *Dirty John?*'

Mum glanced at Hannah and Tom, who were enthralled. 'Well, he seems very nice, doesn't he, love?' she said loading Dad's pasta massacre with parmesan.

Sasha made a vague noise of affirmation from behind her phone.

'He's an administrator or something at the architectural firm in the next village,' Mum continued. 'And he does a lot of different sports and seems a very clean-cut, respectable young man. I think he has a sister too, doesn't he, Sasha love? Seems very family orientated.'

Sasha glared across the table. 'I have no idea if he's got a sister! WHY DO *YOU?*'

The table winced at Sasha's burgeoning rage.

'HAVE YOU BEEN FACEBOOK STALKING AGAIN?"

'Stalking?' Mum got busy with the pepper while Yumi and Noriko watched with nervous eyes and Tom and Hannah were gleefully gripped. 'Hardly, love. I was merely checking the suitability of the young man seeing as you'd got him to pick you up here, which is not one of the Tinder-izer rules, is it, Brooke, love?' Mum looked delighted to have made a connection that she thought would get her out of trouble with my industrial-dating sister.

I shook my head, wanting no part in another tiff.

Sasha opened her mouth to reply but her phone dinged. 'He's here,' she said getting up from the table.

Mum also made to stand. 'Lovely, shall we—'

'SIT!' Sasha commanded.

Mum sat.

Sasha glared at Mum. 'Do *not* follow me and do *not* stare out the window,' she said heading towards the door while keeping her hand out at Mum in a 'stop' motion.

'Have a lovely evening, dear,' Dad said, flapping out his napkin and laying it beneath his belly. He grinned at Hannah and Tom for no apparent reason.

Mum tracked Sasha's departure with desperate eyes and twitching limbs, like a collie told to stay when there was an open field of sheep calling, while Trish and I sniggered.

★

After dinner Trish went with Hannah to sign Tom back into the boarding house, Mum pottered in the kitchen while Dad, the students and I settled in the den with a plate piled high with home-made (best avoided) biscuits. Dad was in his armchair with a thick hardcover face down on his lap, Noriko and Yumi were on the floor watching K-pop videos on an iPad, and I was on the sofa flicking the pages of the *Investing for Dummies* book Mum had thrust at me; my mind on the barn and Chris's things sitting in taped-up boxes in the dark.

Trish entered the room, sat cross-legged on the floor next to the girls, inexplicably sang a few lines of the K-pop song, making the girls giggle, then reached for a biscuit.

'You speak Korean now?' I said.

'Just enough to get in to clubs and ask for a condom,' she grinned.

Dad's fluffy eyebrows shot up as he hid behind his book.

Trish's grin dropped as the biscuit hit her taste buds. She twisted her mouth in disgust, and searched for somewhere to offload it while I snorted at her mistake.

'Hannah told me about what happened with Niko,' she said after spitting her mouthful in my half-empty mug.

I stopped giggling. 'What happened with Niko?'

'Livie started a rumour that Hannah asked Niko to be her boyfriend and he'd said no.'

Dad lowered his book.

'Niko is her friend,' I said with a frown. 'They play rugby together at lunchtimes.'

'He doesn't play with her anymore, apparently,' Trish said with an empathetic expression.

'That little bitch.' I threw the investing book to the side and stood.

'She's in the shower,' Trish said.

'Something the matter?' Mum said, coming in to the room with a pile of mending and settling herself in her own armchair.

I growled and fell back on the sofa. 'Hannah is having a bit of trouble with a girl at school.'

'What?!' said Mum, sitting erect, instantly at maximum fret

level. 'We can't have that! Who is she?! What's she doing?! Have you gone to the head teacher? There's no excuse for bullying – it must be stamped out *immediately*.'

'It's okay, Mum,' I said, backtracking before she got on the phone to her Pétanque friends and incited a hostile takeover of the school. 'I'm sure it'll blow over. The girl is probably having a hormone surge or something.'

I could feel Dad watching me. He'd always been able to tell when I was bending the truth.

'Well,' Mum said, sitting back with a wary expression. 'It's best to keep a close eye on it. I was bullied by a girl once. For a whole year when I was twelve. We didn't do anything about it back then, it was part of life. But I'm not sure I ever got over it. I heard she died about six years ago and I must tell you, I felt relief. Even though I hadn't seen her in over fifty years. Isn't that horrible? I felt terribly guilty afterwards. But it just goes to show how long lasting a stint of bullying can be.'

Dismayed, I looked to Trish. I couldn't bear it if the effects of Livie's torment today were still being felt by Hannah in her seventies.

'*The antidote to fifty enemies is one friend*,' Trish said with a smile.

'Aristotle.' Dad nodded, impressed.

'Thank goodness for Tom then,' said Mum, putting her mending to the side. 'You know, Belinda's daughter was bullied. I think I'll just give her a call. It was thirty years ago but she might have some insight.' She got up again and marched out the room.

I turned to Dad, anticipating his input.

He blinked a few times, evidence of his whirring brain. '*A healthy mind does not speak ill of others*,' he said eventually. 'John Selden, I think. I have a book . . .' And he got up and hobbled towards his library.

'He has a book,' I said to Trish with a sigh then fiddled with the TV remote.

Mum would come back with a list of outdated things Hannah must do and Dad's advice was usually ambiguous and cerebral and required one to read a tome on philosophy, or take a short course in anthropological sciences.

Trish watched me for a moment. 'Iris said you haven't confirmed Hannah's place at the school,' she said. 'Any reason why?'

'Did she ask you to speak to me about it?' I said, thinking myself clever for avoiding the question.

'Ask?' Trish said, one eyebrow raised. 'No. Demand? Also no. Threatened . . . ? Yes.' Trish grinned then fixed her shrewd gaze on me. 'And you didn't answer my question.'

'I haven't had time yet,' I said getting off the sofa and heading towards the door while Trish gave me a knowing look. 'I'm going to get Hannah into bed.'

★

'Trish told you,' Hannah said, her expression clouded, as I tucked her in.

'She just cares,' I said, smoothing out her duvet. 'And so do I. Why didn't you tell me?'

Hannah shrugged.

'Because you thought I'd go to the teachers?'

Hannah nodded.

'You don't think they'd be able to help?'

'They made it worse last time.'

'Okay.' I said pulling the duvet up to her chin. 'We'll think of something else.'

'I can handle it,' Hannah said, her efforts at maturity making my heart clench.

I looked down at my 10-year-old daughter with her snaggle-tooth and her zany-coloured pyjamas, desperate to be able to be herself without persecution. My chest burned with injustice. I stroked the hair out of her eyes.

'Mum,' she said, her voice quieter. 'Why do the other kids believe everything Livie says about me?'

Because she's a manipulative, entitled little fuckwit, I thought. 'Because she has a very strong personality,' I said instead. 'And it takes a while for people to realize when they're being lied to.'

Hannah nodded then yawned. I gave her another hug, flicked off her light, then watched from the door as she turned over. I just hoped they'd realize sooner rather than later.

'How is she?' Trish asked as I took my seat in the den a few minutes later.

'Okay, I guess. Still won't let me go to the teachers.'

Trish shuffled closer and leaned against my legs. 'We'll figure this out.'

For a few silent moments we watched Noriko and Yumi demolish the rest of the hideous biscuits and giggle at the iPad.

'You know,' Trish said, 'I do believe they have the munchies.'

★

On the Sunday, before we left for London, I took a moment to visit the barn alone. With the afternoon sun warming my shoulders I stepped through the open doors and stood before the zombie porridge sculpture. I ran my hands across the rough surface and imagined Chris's plaster-covered hands touching the exact spots I was. I saw him bending and crouching in that unique way he moved his body; his well-worn T-shirt straining across his deltoids and triceps as he carved and sculpted. The way he'd turn at the sound of me arriving in the barn doorway, brushing hair out of his eyes with the back of his hand and grinning.

I had always been attracted to the way he moved. Can you fall in love with someone because of the way they cross the road? Yes, you can. Because I did.

★

Aged twenty-six, Trish and I were travelling in-between event jobs for me and her final year at Uni. We were thinking it might be our last big trip together because once she graduated she'd was due to start a grown-up job in the charity sector. We'd been in a rental car in Cuba waiting at a pedestrian crossing and dancing in our seats to Wham's 'Wake Me Up Before You Go, Go' on the radio when a guy walked across, his movements conveying such casual confidence that I was captivated. He wore a plain white T-shirt, brightly coloured board shorts, and carried absolutely nothing. Like life was just there to be sauntered cheerfully through. When he passed in front of us he turned and grinned and I couldn't believe the flurry under my ribcage. His skin was tanned, his teeth were white and his blond hair was cut short in a functional manner, like he'd got it done on a whim by some lady with a 1960s pair of clippers in a side street a few days before.

'Oh. My. God,' I'd gasped and Trish had chuckled.

The lights turned green and Trish pulled over at the footpath where he was waiting. Like in that split moment we'd silently agreed we needed to meet.

'Hey,' he said, leaning his arms on the shiny powder blue edge of the 1950s convertible, giving us a wide and curious grin.

'Hey,' we'd both replied.

And while Trish asked him where he was from (New Zealand), where he was going (a food truck near the beach where a lady served barbequed seafood caught that day), what his name was (Chris), and if he minded us joining him (not at all), I listened to his kiwi accent with its shortened vowels and, behind the safety of my mirrored neon-green sunglasses I'd picked up at a street stall, ran my eyes over his tanned, muscled arms, and his I'm-on-holiday stubble.

'Jump in,' Trish had said and shot me a look that said *What the hell has got your tongue!?*

I cleared our gear off the back seat and Chris leapt in, the smell of his suntan lotion and aftershave causing a prickle up my neck. On the way to the food truck he leant between the seats and over Wham's Greatest Hits asked us where we were from, where we were going, and where I'd got my sunglasses. We sat at a plastic-covered table surrounded by scrappy-looking dogs and ate barbequed seafood with our hands then went into town and drank beers with condensation weeping down their thick glass bottles at a wall-less shack bar till the wee hours. That night he went back to his accommodation and we to ours, organising to meet the next morning where we would take him to a waterfall you could jump off. The day after that he took us to another food truck at another beach and the day after that we went on a guided hike in the national park. We snorkelled, paddle-boarded and bar-hopped the next day, and the day after that we lay under sun umbrellas around a hotel pool nursing hangovers, playing endless rounds of five hundred. Before long we no longer asked if he wanted to meet up the next day, it was just assumed we would do things together. The three of us left Cuba and headed to Belize via Cancun then on to Honduras, Chris hunting down food trucks at every turn; if it was served from a hatch out the side of a vehicle he was eating it. By the time we got to Costa Rica it was obvious that two of our trio were wanting to get closer. Trish met some people who were heading off on a diving/philanthropic trip to Dominica so she boarded their yacht and Chris and I stood on the jetty waving her off, shoulder to suntanned shoulder, every nerve ending in my body alert. The boat drifted off in the distance and we dropped our arms. Chris turned to me and flipped his sunglasses up on his head.

'Please tell me it's not just me who wants to go back to either your or my room right now.'

The intensity of his look was heady. I thought my chest might explode.

'It's not just you,' I replied and we jumped on our scooters, raced back to our jungle guest house and, with the doors to my room open to a sudden tropical downpour and the mosquito nets wafting in the strong breeze, had the kind of frantic sex you have when you've been kept from having it for months.

Hours later we sipped beers on the balcony, watching the rain bounce off the tropical foliage.

'I've been wanting to do that since I saw you staring at me at that crossing in Cuba.'

I laughed. 'I *was* staring.'

Chris and I became a couple immediately, as though the months of travelling, holding ourselves back so as not to make a third wheel out of Trish, had intensified everything. Neither of us had a job to go back to so we travelled together through India and Sri Lanka, and down through Cambodia, Thailand and Malaysia. We stopped in at Sydney, then Auckland where I met his family and we both worked at an Irish pub for a couple of months. With our bank accounts replenished we travelled through Indonesia then the Philippines, and six months later I arrived back in West Sussex with a boyish New Zealander who hardly ever wore shoes, and told my parents I was getting married.

*

The mental image faded and I was left looking at the looming human-ish figure.

Dad had said he'd get Gus in one afternoon after school to help move it to the cart shed. For what purpose, I'm not sure. It was essentially junk but throwing it away wasn't an option. Yet. I plonked down on an upturned plastic bucket Chris had used to mix plaster in, opened the photo app on my phone and scrolled back to the last photo I'd taken of him. He'd been asleep on his back on the sofa and had his hands clasped beneath his chin like a little baby. I flicked through a few more – Hannah and Chris; Cookie, Hannah and Chris; Cookie and Chris – and settled on a group shot of him and his friends in various stages of hilarity around a vigorously smoking BBQ they'd forgotten about while watching rugby on TV. Chris was flapping at the billowing smoke with a tea towel and laughing at me taking the photo. I felt my stomach flutter. I got the surge of wanting to be in his arms, wanting to drag him to the bedroom. It was weird to still have those sexual urges for someone who was dead. I wanted to sleep with my husband. My love for him was still real and my attraction to him still made the hairs on my arms prickle. But he didn't exist anymore. I was attracted to a memory.

'Time to go,' Trish said, arriving behind me, her overnight bag slung over her shoulder. She crouched next to me, looked at my phone then checked my expression, gauging, as best friends do, the best course of action. She slipped the phone from my fingertips and gazed at it for a moment before tapping at a hunky guy with green eyes she'd met at Chris's funeral. 'I'd still like it noted that I turned this guy down out of respect.'

★

'I could just transfer it to you, you know,' I said as Mum drove us to the station and Hannah and Trish listened to music via a split cable in the back.

She had asked, again, if I'd had any thoughts about the money and I'd offered to pay for the barn renovations.

'You absolutely will not,' Mum declared. 'And no more of that over-generous donating nonsense either. I know it's for a good cause and you do rather have a lot of it but until you've made your own plans it's best to be frugal. It's very easy to fritter when you feel like you have a lot to fritter with.'

'Yes, Mum, you said that already.'

She flicked me a stern look, then went back to driving aggressively. 'And anyway, I could just transfer it right back.'

And she would. We'd end up in a lengthy game of money ping-pong, probably inciting lots of transfer fees along the way.

I couldn't just enlist the labourers and pay them direct either. Mum would stand at the gate with Crumpet at her side and refuse entry to the nice workers with ladders and saws. I could appeal to Dad but he would defer to Mum. She ran the house and the finances and he grew great peonies and kept the hens laying. No, I'd have to find another way to help my parents with the house. Perhaps put the money in a trust, apply pressure, and wear her down over the years. I had more chance of carving my initials in Stonehenge by blinking on it.

'Noriko and Yumi are off on Wednesday and I only have a single fellow from Finland or somewhere coming next. Would you like me to get Gus to move your things back in your room?'

'No, it's fine. Thanks though,' I said, looking out the window. 'The new room has a good view of the yurt field and I like watching the guests trip over the guide wires on their way to the bathroom.'

Mum shot me a series of troubled looks. 'You're a wicked child, you are,' she huffed. While she was throwing me another dismayed look she caught sight of her watch and pressed her foot on the accelerator. 'Oh my goodness I'm going to be late for that silly lady Flo's silly rescue greyhound fundraiser. I've got to drop off a fruit cake!' she said, lurching the car into the train station. She jerked us into a car park, wrenched the handbrake on and spun around to the back seat. 'Time to go, loves!'

Chapter 9

'There she is,' I said at the school gates on Monday morning, pointing towards Zara and her mother getting out of their 4×4.

Hannah hesitated at my side. That morning she had come out of her bedroom with her hologram pencil case and asked if there was a plain one she could use. I'd found her an old navy one of Chris's and watched, holding in my wretchedness, as she swapped her pens and pencils from the vivid, cheerful case to the dull, unremarkable one. And when I went to check she'd turned her bedroom light off I found her llama-covered science folder and all the band, animal, and neon rainbow key chains that usually adorned her school bag on her bed. We'd walked to school side by side, and with Trish's 'make connections' advice in my head I'd suggested she invite Zara down to Sussex the following weekend. Hannah had been reluctant, stating that Zara probably wouldn't want to but I'd reminded her that Zara had visited before, when her father was alive, and had loved playing with the animals and having a picnic in the tree hut.

'Come on,' I said, encouraging Hannah along the busy footpath with a hand on her unembellished backpack. 'I'll come with you.'

'Oh, hi,' Rachel, Zara's mother, said in her declarative voice when she saw me approaching through the kid/parent swarm.

Her eyes took on the 'empathetic' look people give when your partner has died. 'How *are* you?'

'I'm good, thanks,' I said in a much quieter voice than Rachel. I glanced at Hannah at my side looking shyly towards Zara, a girl she'd been friends with for years, who she should have no reason to be shy in front of. 'Hannah and I were wondering if Zara would like to come and stay in Sussex this weekend?'

'Oh right,' Rachel barked, beeping her giant SUV locked while holding her handbag and Zara's school bag while Zara stood there with empty hands that were, in my opinion, perfectly capable of holding her own pink glittery bag. We walked together towards the throng of kids and parents streaming through the school gates. 'Zara is going to Livie's sleepover party this weekend? Is Hannah not going to that?'

Zara, with her pale blonde hair and her limp limbs, looked blankly at Hannah from her mother's side while other children and parents glanced in our direction. Hannah glared up at me, cheeks burning and eyes that screamed *I told you!*

I wanted to shake Rachel and say 'Think about it, woman! Would I have asked Zara over if Hannah were invited?! Can't you see my daughter's embarrassment?! Did you need to be so loud?! And why did you take your husband's last name – it's Cockram?! *Cockram!*' But of course I politely said 'another time' and waved my humiliated daughter off to school.

*

I couldn't get Hannah's look of betrayal out of my head all morning. Even during the uncomfortable process of having my stitches removed at the GP. And when I picked her up at lunchtime to take her to the orthodontist she was still mad. Zara had ignored her for the rest of the day. Why, I'm not sure. I guessed at that level of emotional maturity it was easier to ignore an awkward social situation than discuss it. Like an ostrich who puts its head in the sand. Or a child who has a mother with the emotional delicacy of a salami. Hannah had overheard Livie telling one of their mutual friends that she was annoyed with Hannah for 'trying to stop Zara coming to her party'. Jesus, that little cow!

But by the time we exited Oxford Circus Tube Hannah had marginally thawed and as we navigated the crowds along Regent street she told me about being paired with Mackenzie for a science project. Mackenzie was another girl who was friends with Livie as well but Hannah seemed happy enough to be paired with her and from my as-subtle-as-possible probing it seemed Mackenzie was fine being with Hannah. As we turned on to Harley Street and the noise of central London became muffled by the tall buildings my phone rang with a Facetime call from Mum. I answered and she appeared.

'Hi Mu—'

'Somebody made a rather large anonymous donation to Flo's rescue greyhound foundation. You wouldn't know anything about that, would you . . . ?'

'No, Mum.'

She peered closer to the phone, eyes narrow and suspicious, nostrils flared and (unfortunately) very much in the foreground.

I stifled a giggle. 'We're nearly at the orthodontist's, so was that all?'

'That's all,' Mum clipped and hung up.

I slipped my phone into my pocket with a smile. A unexpected feeling had transpired when I'd put money in the box at Kirsty's bottle store. And again when I'd Googled Flo's greyhound rescue foundation, discovered that the racing industry created a surplus of dogs each year and those that aren't rescued are killed, and immediately donated. The money going to someone who needed it. It felt like a weight had been lifted. It was . . . invigorating.

Hannah and I arrived in reception to see Dennis in the

middle of the room with a striking blonde woman. A fawn Panama hat was balanced on her silken hair and she'd tucked a crisp, white shirt into on-trend jeans.

'I've been asked to do a fake paparazzi shoot,' the girl was saying in a cut-glass accent as Hannah and I took our seats. 'To raise the profile of a married star.'

Bev gave us a wave then went back to openly observing the exchange.

Dennis nodded.

'I can't say who,' the young woman said.

Dennis blinked and nodded.

'He's very famous.'

Dennis blinked.

'It's a cheat speculation. For magazine sales.'

Dennis nodded.

'I can't say which one.' She waited for Dennis to react. He looked like he was waiting to be told how to react. 'Anyway,' she continued, with a swish of her golden hair and complete disregard for Dennis's next patients. 'I just wanted to run it by you first because we're going to have to look intimate, you know? It'll raise both our profiles. I'll get called a "mystery blonde" but there'll probably be a follow-up piece – maybe even a sidebar in the DM outing who I am.'

Dennis seemed unsure as to the best course of action.

'And that's when we say it was just a meeting about a role coming up. It'll raise both our profiles,' she said again and waited for Dennis to say something. The room was deathly quiet. 'So are we okay? It's just how the industry works. You understand I'm not going behind your back?'

Dennis glanced to Bev who smiled back and carried on watching. 'Ah . . . yes?' he ventured.

The woman stretched enhanced lips to reveal a whitened smile. 'Amazing! Okay, call me later!' She kissed the air next to Dennis's left cheek and strutted out of the reception.

Dennis watched the glass door easing shut behind her, seemingly confused.

'I didn't know you two were dating . . . ?' said Bev, peering over her red framed glasses with a 'what's this I see?' expression.

Dennis blinked out of his reverie. 'Neither did I.'

★

In the surgery room Dennis chatted to Hannah about music and her drumming while his assistant prepared machines and trays of tools. He told Hannah what bands he liked and I could tell she thought his choices were supremely uncool but she liked him so didn't say anything. And finally, after I was sure we'd gone well over our appointment time and must be holding another patient up outside, Dennis casually suggested we crack on with the X-rays and Hannah, almost but not quite at ease, slid into the chair and allowed his assistant to put an X-ray protector apron type thing on her. Dennis snapped into work mode but still did everything with an unhurried chatty air, letting Hannah know what each item he put in her mouth was and what it did. He used three different apparatus to take X-rays, photos and a 3D digital scan, which he then studied on his computer before wheeling across the room on his stool and examining more closely the baby tooth that was refusing to come out. All the while, I couldn't get the image of Dennis and the blonde girl out of my head. They seemed so unsuited. He was gentle, kind and genuine. Not a fake-paparazzi-shoot kind of guy. For some unexplainable reason I felt protective over him.

'Do you have a favourite drummer?' Dennis's voice was muffled behind his paper mask.

'Huah–huah huah,' Hannah articulated as best she could with her mouth wide open and full of cotton rolls.

'Sheila E. did you say?' Dennis said.

'She played with Prince's band,' I explained.

'Oh yes, she's ah . . . *very* good,' Dennis said and I got the impression he didn't know Prince had had a woman drummer. Or who Prince was. 'I had a client in yesterday who is a music promoter or . . . something along those lines. He was telling us the band he's working with now has a drummer who only has one arm. How he manages—'

'Ik A-ung?!' Hannah gurgled, her feet at the end of the chair flexed to attention.

Dennis leant out of Hannah's mouth, looking surprised. 'Rick . . . *Allen* was it?'

'Another one of her favourites,' I said.

'Ee oh eh eh-arh!' Hannah glugged.

'He's from Def Leppard.'

'Yes,' Dennis said, bemused. 'Yes, I think that's who he said.'

'They have a concert coming up,' I said. 'We tried to get tickets but it was sold out.'

Dennis pulled down his mask and looked between Hannah and I. 'He offered me tickets but I wasn't sure if it was my kind of thing . . .' He glanced at Hannah then back to me. 'If they're still on offer would you like them?'

Hannah made a strangled kind of noise, her feet eagerly activated, her fingers gripping the sides of the chair and her eyes in a desperate plea. Like if I didn't say yes right then and there the tickets might somehow evaporate.

Five minutes later Hannah and I were sat on two swivel chairs in front of the surgery computer, looking at an X-ray of Hannah's teeth.

'So,' Dennis said, choosing his words carefully. 'There really is only one effective option.'

Hannah slumped. 'It's braces, isn't it.'

Dennis gave an understanding smile. 'It is.'

He waited while Hannah looked up at me with pitiful eyes and I gave her shoulder a squeeze.

'They won't stop you playing rugby. You'll just wear a mouth guard like usual but it will be specially fitted to go over your braces.' He paused a moment for the information to sink in. 'Do you want to have a look at your options?'

Hannah, still slumped, nodded.

'There is every colour of rubber band these days,' he said moving closer to the computer and navigating to a webpage. 'Not like when I was young. There's even neon. You can have all sorts of fun. I have a patient who wears hers in a rainbow.'

'Really?' Hannah said, straightening, a hint of a smile beginning to grow.

I grinned at my daughter. Any chance to wear every colour the universe had to offer.

'Oh yes,' Dennis said, giving me a wink before wheeling Hannah's chair closer to the computer. 'She's just been signed for a record deal. I do believe you'll be seeing her on your TV very soon.'

When we walked out of the surgery into the waiting room no one else was waiting. Dennis booked us in for our next appointment while Bev asked Hannah about her hobbies and I paid the bill. As I waved my card over the payment terminal I had a brief moment where I realized that affording braces was not a concern anymore. Chris and I had noticed Hannah's wonky teeth and were hoping as more adult teeth came through they'd sort themselves out so we didn't have to go on a potentially interminable NHS waitlist or squeeze the money out of our already tight budget to go private. If Chris were here he'd be relieved we didn't have to worry. If Chris were here we wouldn't have the money. I pushed aside my conflicting emotions and slipped my wallet in my handbag as Dennis handed over his personal number, in case Hannah had any questions and told us that in the meantime, we needed to go to a regular dentist to have the baby tooth extracted. He made the appointment with a friend on his mobile, even offering to come along to put Hannah's mind at ease as it was only a few doors down.

'The anaesthetic will be a local,' he said to Hannah. 'You won't have to go under, it will just numb the area around the tooth.'

Hannah nodded. 'Mum told me.'

Dennis smiled. 'What are you doing for the rest of the day then?' he asked as he walked us to the door, grinning for no reason from ear to ear. 'Not going back to school, are you?'

'We thought we'd go to the new Marvel movie,' I said, giving him a 'you've-caught-me' look.

'Wonderful idea! I'm going to tidy up here then head off to a parkour class.'

'Parkour?' Hannah said, trying to contain a giggle.

Bev appeared to find such folly exasperating.

'That's the leaping from building to building, running up walls and along railings thing, right?' I asked, trying not to let my doubt at his ability come through in my voice.

'Exactly!' Dennis grinned.

I did a brief scan of his handsome face and wondered which part would be dented next time we saw him. 'Well, have fun!'

As we walked to the Tube, Hannah was a different child. She skipped alongside me chittering non-stop about the foot pedals Rick Allen used to be able to continue drumming after losing his arm in a car accident and double/triple/quadruple checking that Dennis had meant it when he said he'd call and let us know if he was still able to get the tickets.

But by the next afternoon, the slump in her shoulders was back.

'What happened?' I asked as she unloaded her school bag and thumped her homework on the kitchen table.

She shoved a notice at me. It was about the school Sports Day. It had a schedule of events and at the bottom Hannah's name was one of two girls' in the mixed relay team. 'That's great, sweetie,' I said. 'What's wrong?'

'After the teams were read out Livie said they picked girls

with no boobs because they could run faster,' Hannah muttered. 'She said it loud enough for the whole class to hear. I know she was meaning me. Everyone laughed.' The effort Hannah was putting in to not cry was immense.

With her still not allowing me to go to the head teacher I felt helpless and wretched. I ordered her favourite pizza and as we ate it on the sofa in front of *Harry Potter* I noticed she didn't laugh at Ron's antics like she usually did. And there was a furrow between her brows that didn't melt away, like she were harbouring a constant concern. I looked away, swallowing down a lump in my throat.

Chapter 10

'She didn't think the boob comment was specifically aimed at Hannah, she hasn't noticed anything going on between the girls, and when I asked her if she wouldn't mind keeping an eye on Hannah she acted like I'd asked her to cut my toenails,' I said, watching Penny shovel in toast at my kitchen table after school drop-off the next morning. I picked up my mug. 'That woman possesses the emotional intelligence of a monitor lizard. I don't know why she chose a career with children. She seems more suited to laying tarmac or euthanising kittens.'

Penny laughed through her mouthful.

Hannah's teacher, Miss Shuker, was a 27-year old, fluffy-haired, maths-obsessed weirdo (Penny thought she masturbated to Pythagoras and acute angles), who seemed overwhelmed by the notion that in order to teach her beloved maths, children had to be involved. I'd popped in to her class early that morning but it had been a waste of time asking for her discreet help on the Livie matter.

'Rog had a sex dream about her,' Penny said, dusting crumbs off her lips then fingertips

I choked on my coffee.

'He was so disturbed he nearly went to confession. So,' Penny said exchanging her toast plate for her coffee mug and barrelling the conversation on as she usually did. 'Let's talk about this money.'

My body stiffened.

'Obviously you're buying a house and moving to Sussex, which I'm still dark about, you understand, but I know that's always been the plan so of course I'll get over it. Eventually. God, maybe *I* should move to Sussex. But, I mean, it's just *so much money*. What will you do with the rest?'

I squirmed in my chair and shrugged.

Penny's mouth gaped. 'You have no ideas?'

'No.'

'But . . .' Penny said, eyes wide. 'But you could do *anything*!?'

'I know. I think that's the problem.'

Penny glared at me like I were truly unhinged.

'There are too many options. It's like having five streaming services but you can't pick anything to watch so you just watch *Bake Off* even though you hate it.'

'*Bake Off* is amazing,' Penny countered sternly.

'I guess it would be easier if I were one of those people with strong convictions; tunnel vision on saving the narwhal, or campaigning for cycle lanes across the whole of the UK, or eradicating a fungus that decimates heritage tomatoes.'

Penny looked at me strangely.

'I don't have a burning passion,' I said, leaning back in my chair. 'I'm one of those people who can say "yes, I see your point" and if someone comes up with a counter opinion I say "yes! I see your point too!". I see all the points. Does that make me pointless?'

'Yes,' Penny deadpanned. 'What about getting a boat? Or a villa in Sardinia? Or a boat *and* a villa in Sardinia? And staff! Oh, can you imagine having *staff*?!'

The idea of splashing out on all of the typical things one dreams of if you struck it rich triggered a visceral response of revolt. I looked at Penny, her eyes already on her own ergonomic sunlounger next to the pool at my Sardinian villa. How could I explain the feelings I had towards the money in my bank account, and the idea of getting on with 'the plan', when I didn't fully understand them myself?

'I was buying steak the other day,' I said, causing Penny to drop her dreamy expression.

'Right,' she said, frowning as if she'd missed an integral part of the conversation.

'And I picked up a pack on special. Next to it was a stack of the expensive organic eye fillets Chris and I bought on special occasions. And I realized I could afford that steak now, so I put the one on special back and picked up the organic one. Then realized the only reason I had the money to buy the posh steak was because my husband had died. Would I really enjoy eating posh steak knowing that my husband losing his life was why I could afford it?'

Penny's dark eyebrows drew together and she reached across the table and squeezed my arm.

'So I put it down again. Then I realized that Chris would want me to have the steak. So I picked it up again. Then felt awful, so put it down again. And up. Then down. Then up and down. And so on and so on until twenty minutes later I left with nothing and we had jam on toast for dinner.' I sat back in my chair with a 'see?' expression.

Penny, admirably, nodded her understanding. Then frowned. 'I don't get it.'

'Why should I get to have nice things when my husband had to die in order for me to have them?'

'Oh,' Penny said. 'Of course. It's too huge. Sorry, *cariño*, I get *so* carried away. I blame my mother. One hint of a suggestion from my father and she was off packing the bags to Uzbekistan or signing up to adopt a family of rare pigs. Ay, that woman. I did love those pigs, though. Okay. One step at a time. Like that psychologist philosopher man your father is always quoting; *the next and most necessary thing.*'

'Carl Jung,' I said with a smile.

'Yes, him. That's the move to be near Hannah's school, right?' My stomach dropped.

'Shall we look online?' Penny snatched up her phone and started jabbing with a glossy red nail. 'How close do you want to be to your parents? Close enough for babysitting, not so close for daily pop-ins?'

I looked out my back doors to the tiny garden Hannah had learned to walk in and tuned out Penny's description of just how very far she'd need to live from her mother-in-law for optimal happiness.

Everyone had assumed that when the money came in I would follow 'the plan' that Chris and I had had to move to Sussex and put Hannah in school with Tom. And so had I. Or I'd been too preoccupied with grief to think about it. But the money was here now and I felt . . . confused.

I glanced around my kitchen. My flat was where I felt closest to Chris. It was where he had his last meal and his last glass of wine. Where he'd lost his keys for the final time because I'd driven him to hospital the morning that he never came back. Earlsfield was where I still felt like myself – Chris's wife, Hannah's mum. We were supposed to move together to Sussex as a family. Who would I be if I moved to Sussex and bought a new place with no ghosts of Chris in the cracked panel of glass in the French doors from when he tried to teach Hannah to skateboard inside? Or the dent in the floorboard from when he'd tried to flip pancakes and had flipped the pan as well making Hannah do her nose wrinkle and collapse on the floor cackling? My eyes rested on the wall behind the kitchen table where there were four stripes of paint in different shades of cream. We'd painted them two weeks before Chris died when the commission deposits had come in and we'd planned on doing the place up a bit before selling and moving. I swallowed and looked away from the wall.

'I . . . I don't think I want to go to Sussex,' I said.

Penny looked up from her phone. 'But that was the—?'

'"The Plan". I know. But now the money is in my account and it's all a reality, I . . .' It finally dawned on me. The nausea that had been churning my stomach ever since the money had arrived in my account. 'I don't want to leave here.'

Penny knitted her eyebrows.

'This was the last place Chris was alive.'

Penny's expression changed from confusion to under-standing. 'Of course.' She waited a few beats before adding. 'But what about school? If you don't move to Sussex you'll send Hannah where? The local girls school? With Livie?'

'No,' I shook my head. 'I couldn't.' Not only because Livie would be attending, and probably be quite intolerable as a teenager. But also, I didn't think I could send Hannah to a girls-only school. So many of her friends were boys.

'So . . .' Penny said. 'The school in Sussex, then . . . ?'

I twisted my coffee mug around, watching the dark liquid swirl.

'You've got less than five months before the new year starts,' Penny said gently. 'I know "the plan" was to go to Sussex *with* Chris and of course everything is different now but . . .' she glanced around my tiny kitchen/dining space. 'Don't you think Chris would want you to live in the area you both agreed on? To let Hannah go to the school you both picked for her? And buy a nice big house with a pool that your friend Penny can visit to escape her mother-in-law for the weekends and all the holidays and maybe even have her own room with a big-screen TV?' Penny smiled. 'Sussex is a good plan, *cariño.*'

I looked across the room at Cookie humping a raggedy lion soft toy. It had been Hannah's and when she'd found Cookie defiling it, in the most vigorous of manners, I'd been worried she'd be upset. Instead she'd erupted into giggles but said emphatically that it didn't matter how many times I washed it, it was Cookie's 'sex friend' now. I pictured her doing her

nose-scrunch cackle. Like a cheeky little witch. I turned back
to Penny. 'Hannah barely ever laughs anymore,' I said. 'You
know that adorable one she does with the nose wrinkle?'

Penny nodded fondly.

'She hasn't done that in ages. The only thing I really want
is for Livie to leave Hannah alone,' I said. 'And money can't
stop that.' I sat back in my dining chair. 'I don't know what
I want anymore. For the future, for Hannah's school, for where
I want to live. Not even what bloody steak I want.' I swallowed.
'I know it sounds outrageously ungrateful but . . . I think I'm
starting to resent the money.'

Penny nodded. 'Maybe it is time I get Rog's advice, *cariño*?
Like I said, I wouldn't say it was for you.'

'Sure,' I said, feeling adrift.

A little while later Penny left to get Lorenzo from nursery
and around 1pm I received an email from Miss Shuker.

Hello Mrs Paige,
I'm just checking in with you after our chat this morning.
The girls seem to be getting on fine in science class with
Mr Harris. They were in the same group for their
experiment. And Hannah lent Livie her P.E. clothes for
netball because Livie had forgotten hers. Perhaps it has
all blown over. It can so quickly at this age.
   Regards,
   Miss Shuker

Could that be true? Could it all be over just like that? With
the simple act of lending something? I sent a thank you reply
to Miss Shuker then, with a lighter, hopeful heart, sat down
to do a couple hours of work. Around 3:30pm Hannah came
in from school and instead of heading straight to the kitchen,
like she normally did on the days Penny walked her home, I
heard her moving around in the laundry.

'Hey!' I said, popping my head around the doorway. 'How was your day?'

Hannah had her back to me. She stayed silent while rummaging in her bag.

'What are you doing in here?' I took a step closer. Hannah was pulling sodden P.E. gear from her gym-bag and stuffing it in the washing machine. 'What's this?'

My daughter remained silent. I began to feel panicky.

'Hannah, talk to me!'

Hannah turned around, soggy P.E. shorts hanging from limp fingers. 'I lent Livie my P.E. gear,' she mumbled.

That I knew. But what the fuck had Livie done? 'And?' I coaxed.

'When I asked for it back, she said she must have left it in the changing rooms.' She paused. 'I found it on the floor all wet.' Her voice faltered and I could see how desperate she was to not cry. 'There was . . .' her voice became a mere whisper. '. . . a trail of water from one of the toilets . . . to my gear.'

I was stunned. 'Let me get this right. You think she dunked it in the toilet?'

Hannah gave an minute nod. 'I had to miss P.E.'

I looked at my daughter. Skinny and wiry, with only me to help her steer her through this crap. And I was deathly afraid I wouldn't be enough.

'I just wish she'd leave me alone,' Hannah said to the floor.

'Then don't lend her your things, honey.'

'She'd tell everyone I was stingy or a bitch.'

'*She's* a bitch!' I cried and Hannah looked like she was going to burst into tears. I reined in my fury. 'Sweetie, I really do think we need to speak to the head teacher about this.'

Hannah crumpled. But she didn't rage against me like she had before. Her silence was her conceding she needed help. I stepped forward and pulled her into a hug that she didn't reciprocate. Her arms hung lifelessly at her sides.

'Remember that this is something that is going on with her, not you. Okay? There's no reason for this. It's nothing to do with who you are as a person. Do you understand that?'

Hannah waited a beat before nodding, her head moving against my shoulder. We stayed there for a moment then she extracted herself. 'I'm going to my room,' she said.

'Do you want to bake cookies or watch a movie?'

'No. I just want to be on my own. Is that okay?'

'Sure, sweetie. If that's what you want?'

She nodded.

'How about I bake cookies anyway and we can eat as many as we want while they're still warm?' It wasn't the best offer, I was a shocking cookie-maker – they'd probably taste like cat dander – but it was all I could offer her right now.

She nodded again then walked away with her head down. As she turned to close her bedroom door, she caught my eye and what I saw devastated me. She was sorry. Sorry for coming to me with a problem. Furious and feeling shackled by helplessness I picked up her discarded school bag and took it to the kitchen to empty. As I tugged out her drink bottle a tightly crumpled sheet of A4 fell on the floor. For some reason dread engulfed my body. I snatched it up, flattened it out on the bench and read the three lines of Comic Sans.

My diary by hannah paige
    I miss my daddy. I want to kill myself to be with him.
    I think I mite be a lesbein thats why I love rugby so much.

The cruelty took my breath away. The thought of Hannah reading the note at school alone caused a rush of nausea. I raced to the bathroom, locked the door, and dry retched over the sink, tears streaming down my face.

After a few minutes I splashed cold water on my face, dried it with a towel that definitely needed washing and waited for my breathing to return to normal. Rage surged inside me as I read the note again. How dare Livie torment my child. A child who'd lost her father. How *dare* she. And she couldn't even spell! I grabbed the printout and headed down the hall.

I knocked on Hannah's door before opening it. 'Honey?'

Hannah was sitting on her bed with her legs crossed. She looked up, saw the printout in my hand, then dropped her face towards her lap. I moved across the room and sat next to her on the anime duvet cover Martin had sent from Tokyo.

'Where did this come from?' I asked in a gentle voice, hiding the fury that was causing a fire at the back of my throat.

Hannah said nothing.

'Sweetheart?'

She looked up. Dark bags under her eyes showed she wasn't sleeping. Her cheeks, usually pink with how much energy she exerted, were white. Anxiety is physical. Blood rushes to your organs because your body believes it's in danger. I fought the urge to race out the front door all the way to Livie's house and shake her till her diamond studs fell out.

'Honey, this is serious now, where did you find this? Did Livie do it?'

'I found it in my bag after lunch,' she croaked. Her lip trembled and tears trickled down her pallid cheeks. 'I don't know who did it.'

I shuffled up the bed and pulled her into a hug as she allowed herself to finally cry.

Chapter 11

Don't get angry, don't accuse, don't swear, don't cry; don't get angry, don't accuse, don't swear, don't cry. I silently repeated the advice Trish and Penny had given me over a group Facetime that morning as I followed Louise, the school receptionist, towards the head teacher's office.

'They've been waiting for you,' she said as she tapped on the door with a knuckle.

They?

Louise opened the door to the office strewn with positive mottos and a faint smell of synthetic gardenia that always made me gag, and conducted me in with an outstretched arm.

'Mrs Paige. Good afternoon,' Ms Galloway, the head teacher, said standing up from a small brown sofa adjacent to her desk. She wore a loud red and pink top with an asymmetrical hem and a below-the-knee black skirt; both with a polyester sheen. She was knocking fifty and I imagined she collected things with owls on them and thought herself kooky. 'I'm pleased we could all make it for this meeting.'

We? All?

I turned to where she was looking behind the half-opened door. In two upholstered chairs, with half-drunk cups of tea on the table in front of them, sat Livie's parents.

What were they doing here? Everything I had prepared to say to Ms Galloway – could I say it in front of them? Was it appropriate to invite the other parents to *my* requested meeting? Was it fair? I instantly felt on the back foot.

'Mrs Paige, this is Mr and Mrs Smith-Warrington,' Ms Galloway said, her obsequious smile mostly directed at Livie's father, Justin.

'We already know each other,' Melody said, smiling up at me. Her blush-coloured silk top displayed tanned, fake boobs, and a chunky gold watch hung loosely on her thin bronzed wrist. Her ever-present Louis Vuitton sat boxy and big at her loafered feet. Justin, with his salon haircut, tailored trousers and white shirt that skimmed his gym-honed physique, gave me a nod.

Self-conscious in my white tee and black jeans alongside this shiny Hugo Boss advert, I managed a smile back.

'Oh good,' Ms Galloway said as though we were already on the right track and halfway through solving everything. 'Please take a seat there, Mrs Paige.'

I took the seat opposite the Smith-Warringtons and rested my handbag on my lap. Ms Galloway sat while Louise made a show of offering us tea and biscuits. I declined, not trusting my shaking hands to hold a cup of tea, Melody declined on account of the fact she was on a cleanse, and Justin shook his head.

Louise left the room, closing the door behind her, and in the resulting silence Ms Galloway smiled in my direction. 'Mrs Paige—'

'Brooke, please,' I said, my voice catching. I coughed to clear it.

'Brooke,' Ms Galloway said with another smile as Melody passed me a glass of water from the coffee table. 'You wanted to discuss Hannah and Livie and some potential hiccups they may be experiencing with their friendship?'

I took a sip of water.

Don't accuse.

Justin turned his attention fully towards me. His impassive scrutiny put me on edge. Melody waited with giant blue eyes. I keenly felt the airy gap next to me where Chris would have been, disarming everyone with his easy-going nature.

'Yes.' I said putting the glass on the coffee table, noting the wobble in my hand. 'Some of Livie's behaviour over the past couple of months has made my daughter extremely unhappy. Hannah has tried to ignore it and hope it stops, but it hasn't. And now I'm worried about her wellbeing.'

'Livie talks fondly of Hannah,' Melody said, glancing from me to Ms Galloway. 'They're friends. She wouldn't do anything to upset her.'

'Hannah *is* upset,' I said. 'And they *aren't* friends.'

Melody glanced to her husband who kept his emotionless eyes on me.

'It's not been obvious bullying,' I continued, noticing a tiny flinch from both Justin and Melody at the claim. My hands were sweating where I gripped my handbag tightly. 'It's exclusion. Or blanking. It's digs at things Hannah says or does, laughing at her not with her, and spreading rumours.'

Melody blinked as if to say, *is that all.*

'Can you give specific examples?' said Ms Galloway. She was sitting with a pen poised over a pad as if waiting for something worthy of noting down.

I nodded. 'Yesterday Hannah lent Livie her P.E. gear for netball. Hannah found it soaking wet on the floor and it looked like it had been dunked in the toilets.'

Melody put a hand to her chest. 'Livie would never do anything like that.' She turned to her husband. 'Would she?'

Without removing his eyes from me, Justin gave a curt shake of his head. Was he trying to intimidate me? It riled me that it was working. I looked away from him to Melody.

'Livie was the one who borrowed her kit,' I said.

Melody blinked again. 'If Livie left it in the changing rooms other children could have gone in after her. It could have been anyone.' She turned to Ms Galloway. 'How much time was there between netball and Hannah's P.E. class?'

'I can check that.' Ms Galloway got up and moved behind her desk to look it up.

With Melody watching me with her fluttery blue eyes and Justin essentially ignoring me, the seconds ticked by painfully. God, how I wished for Chris to be at my side. I blinked back tears.

'Netball was from 11–12 and Hannah's P.E. class was in the afternoon from 2pm,' Ms Galloway read from her screen. She looked up.

Melody and Mr Smith Warrington turned to face me with expressions that said, *There you go.*

Who the fuck else would do that? I wanted to scream.

Don't get angry.

'Why would somebody randomly put someone's P.E. kit in the toilet?' I said, working hard to keep my voice level.

'Children do some strange things,' Melody said with a smile as if this were all just so silly and not the damaging situation it was. 'It sounds like something a boy would do,' she said, looking to Ms Galloway for endorsement.

I wanted to slap her. Trish and Penny never said I couldn't hit.

'I'll ask the P.E. teacher to look into it,' Ms Galloway said, taking her seat again and making a note. 'You said there were other incidents?'

Stunned that the toilet-dunked P.E. kit didn't seem to be taken seriously I was momentarily speechless. 'Yes,' I said, after a few quiet seconds where the room waited for me to continue. 'Hannah gets picked for the rugby team, Livie says rugby is a boys' sports; Hannah gets the drum position in the school play, Livie says drums are a boys' instrument.' I listed the nits rumour, the laughing at mistakes in class, the increasing exclusions, the melted chocolate and 'poo smear' notes, the comments about how she dressed, and the rumour about Niko that caused him to no longer play with her. I avoided the 'no boobs' remark. I didn't want to bring that up in front of Justin. 'A few weekends ago someone hacked into Hannah's Instagram account and posted a picture of her face and a famous rugby player's superimposed on a pair of mating llamas,' I said, feeling my cheeks flame. I hadn't told anybody else about that one and had deleted it immediately. I was mortified on behalf of my daughter.

'Are you aware that Instagram has a recommended age restriction of thirteen?' Ms Galloway's tone implied I'd made a poor parenting choice, and perhaps I had. Chris and I had told Hannah she could have a phone at thirteen. But a few months after he'd died Hannah had been dropped home from rugby practice early. I'd popped out to the supermarket and had forgotten my phone. When Hannah had run around to Penny's and they'd called me but still got no answer, she'd become so panicked she'd gotten light-headed. So, I bought her a phone and she was less anxious.

'Nearly every child her age has a phone and an Instagram account,' I said, keeping my tone level when I wanted to cry *fuck Instagram, this is about my daughter being bullied!'*. 'And I agree, they are young and the potential to misbehave on there is limitless. But shouldn't we be teaching our children *how* to behave on the internet rather than totally banning them?' I looked to Livie's parents. Melody seemed mildly interested in my theory. Justin watched me coldly. It was unnerving and I looked away to Ms Galloway. 'If we don't let them have accounts, they'll just go and set up secret ones. And anyway, the fact they have accounts is not the issue here. It's the hacking into each other's pages, the anonymous nasty comments from fake accounts, and the sexualized Photoshopped images. She's only ten, for God's sake!'

Ms Galloway flinched at my emotion and I chastised myself for displaying it.

'It is very hard for us to take a role in events that happen outside of school hours, Mrs Paige,' she said. I was back to being Mrs Paige.

'Are you implying the photos and comments were posted by our daughter?' Justin spoke for the first time, and by the steely tone of his voice I realized he was furious. 'Because, as you said yourself, they were anonymous. They could have been from anyone.' He turned to Ms Galloway. 'We've heard this all before from this family. It feels a lot like victimisation here, Mrs Galloway, and I won't have members of my family accused without proof.'

Ms Galloway nodded and turned to me. 'I'm sorry, Mrs Paige, but we do need some kind of proof. Before we're able to take any sort of official action. If Hannah were to come and see me—'

'No.' I said. 'Hannah just wants this all to stop. She doesn't want to come in.'

Ms Galloway nodded again. 'You said in your email you found an upsetting entry in Hannah's diary . . . ?'

'Not *Hannah's* diary,' I said, reaching into my handbag. 'It was a fake one. Written by someone else.' A curdling sensation twisted in my stomach as I pulled out the diary printout. I felt I was betraying Hannah by showing people. Exposing her humiliation. 'This was put in her school bag.'

As I handed over the note Melody's gaze flicked to the red scar on my wrist then quickly away. While the three of them leaned together and read the printout I picked at my cuticles and tried to will away the hotness developing behind my eyes.

'Oh.' Melody's eyes welled. 'That's horrible.' She looked at me with, I must admit, sincere sympathy.

Justin said nothing but the muscles in his jaw flexed.

Ms Galloway shook her head sadly. 'This is awful, Mrs Paige, and very concerning.'

'It is,' I said quietly. 'Which is why I want, *need*, something to be done to stop this whole thing.'

'Livie would never write anything like this,' Melody said, and I was touched to hear her voice crack. 'I'm so sorry Hannah had to read that.'

'Thank you,' I said, then, keeping my tone as neutral yet firm as possible, I continued. 'I know I don't have any proof but based on Livie's recent actions towards Hannah I'd like her questioned about the diary page.'

Ms Galloway opened her mouth to speak, as did Melody, but Justin got in first.

'Enough,' he said, his eyes flashing. 'Livie took the heat last time for what everyone was doing. It caused her a lot of distress. We didn't make an official complaint against you and your accusations because of what you'd recently been through.'

I felt like I'd been punched in the guts. Melody had the decorum to look mortified.

'But this is where it stops,' Justin turned to Ms Galloway. 'We do not give you permission to speak to our daughter.' He turned back to me. 'Maybe you should be asking *your* daughter why she wants to blame everything on Livie.'

I was shocked, but managed to find my voice. 'Why would Hannah make this up? What has she got to gain from this?'

'Attention?' he spat.

'She doesn't want this!' I spat back. 'She's *miserable!*'

'Okay,' Ms Galloway said, making a pacifying palm-down gesture. 'Putting aside, just for the moment, the note—'

I jerked my head towards Ms Galloway. 'Putting it aside?!'

'Because, right now, we don't know who wrote it,' Ms Galloway placated. 'We will investigate that separately, I assure you we will, Mrs Paige. But let's deal with what we can, here and now. The friendship challenges the girls seem to be having in class.' I felt my breathing become quicker as Ms Galloway began a speech about misunderstandings and the prepubescent way of seeing things from an emotionally heightened point of view. Especially when the children involved were so different from one another. When she said the word 'different' she looked at me. I know Hannah was still considered an oddity for liking rugby and rock music and shorts, and not wearing shoes or putting her hair up in elaborate styles with glittery accoutrements. The subtle insinuation that if Hannah were the same as everyone else this wouldn't be happening enraged me.

This was not a 'joint friendship challenge' as Ms Galloway was now saying, or 'misinterpretations of attempts at cementing bonds through humour'. I gripped my handbag straps so tightly my hands ached. This was bullying. Why couldn't they see that? What else could I say to *make* them see?

'Yes,' Melody said, nodding at Ms Galloway and turning to me with appeal. 'Maybe Hannah is misunderstanding Livie's comments in class. She does like to joke around and has a rather mature sense of humour that some children don't get. Considering what Hannah has been through nobody would blame her for getting it a bit wrong.'

I felt a boiling tide of injustice rise up.

Don't swear, don't swear, don't swear!

'SHE'S *NOT* GETTING IT WRONG! LIVIE IS BEING A LITTLE BITCH!'

Melody gasped and clutched her husband's arm. Justin's jaw tensed.

Shit.

'Please refrain from remarks like that, Mrs Paige,' Ms Galloway said, her lips tight.

'I'm sorry.' I turned to Melody and Justin, who were regarding me with distaste. I was desperate to make them see that the Hannah I knew and loved was fading away. 'I'm really sorry. But if this were happening to your child—'

'We're not staying here and listening to this.' Justin, his face and neck flushed with wrath, got to his feet. He was at least 6 foot 3 and cast an imposing figure. 'Unless there is something concrete, I do not want my time wasted, or my daughter being accused and called names, again. Hers isn't the only child in this school dealing with something. But she's the only one causing trouble.'

Melody shot me an embarrassed glance.

'Of course,' Ms Galloway said, standing. 'I'm very sorry.'

I felt winded.

Ms Galloway accompanied Justin to the door, but Melody stayed in her chair. She seemed like she wanted to say something to me, but Justin turned back into the room.

'Melody.' He sounded like an owner calling their dog to heel.

Her gaze flickered away from me as she hastily gathered her Louis Vuitton and followed him out. The door closed behind them.

Fuck it. Fuck it, fuck it, fuck it all over the damn place.

I could hear the murmurs of their voices and cringed when I heard Melody mention Chris again and the scar on my wrist. Why was Chris's death clouding their ability to hear what I was saying? After a minute or so Ms Galloway came back in and, instead of sitting on the sofa, sat behind her desk in her chair.

'I'm sorry about losing my temper,' I said, swivelling in my seat to face her. 'But I am very worried about Hannah. It's been a hard year and a half for her and now this with Livie . . .' My eyes grew hot.

Don't cry, don't cry. Oh come on, please don't cry!

A tear trickled down my cheek.

'It has been a hard time for you and Hannah,' Ms Galloway said, handing me a box of tissues. 'And the school is keen to support you in any way we can. But we must consider the damage it could do to another child if we take official action when it is possible, considering the stressful time Hannah has had recently, that she is misinterpreting the comments.'

'She isn't! What can I do to make you see that she isn't misinterpreting *anything*?' Tears of frustration were coursing down my cheeks.

Ms Galloway waited while I dried my eyes. 'I understand you're worried, Mrs Paige. The note is disturbing and I'm very sorry that someone has chosen to write this about Hannah. But if you don't want Hannah to come and speak with me, and if the Smith-Warringtons won't allow me to speak to Livie about it, then I'm afraid, in regard to the note at least, my hands are tied.'

'But what about her P.E. kit? And the comments Livie makes in class?'

'I will ask the P.E. teacher to investigate further and will get back to you with what he finds. And in regard to the comments we do have some options that I was hoping to outline to both sets of parents,' her cheeks coloured at her words 'both *sets*' and she gave an apologetic smile before continuing, 'so it's a shame the Smith-Warringtons aren't here to hear them, but I will email them what we discuss.'

'Okay,' I said, balling the soggy tissues in my hand, eager to hear what steps could be taken to stop this horrible situation.

'We operate with a Restorative Justice method,' she said, settling in to her role of 'educator'. 'The victim of the purported bullying is asked to draw a picture or write a poem, without using names, about the effect the mistreatment has on them. We hold a meeting with a group of students – we call that Circle Time – which includes the alleged aggressor and other neutral members of the student body. The group reads the poem or assesses the picture then talks about how the victim feels and workshops solutions.'

I was momentarily aghast. *A picture or poem? Circle Time?*

Hannah sitting in front of a group of her peers talking about how she feels? Was this woman on mushrooms? 'Hannah will absolutely not be comfortable with that situation.'

'It's a valuable tool which helps children realize the consequences of unkind words and behaviours. It is often the only reform needed for the alleged bully, achieved namelessly without proportioning blame, which can cause resentment and negative self-worth in the accused.'

'No,' I said firmly, incensed that the focus seemed to be on how the bully felt.

'Okay,' Ms Galloway continued. 'If the group situation feels too confronting for Hannah it has been proven effective to get two children together, without parents present but with a mediator, and allow them to tell each other how they feel about each other. It's a less daunting method still in the Restorative Justice framework. Again it helps children to understand how words and behaviours can hurt without anyone feeling blamed. Would you like me to see if the Smith-Warringtons would agree to that?'

'That's a terrible idea! Do you honestly think Hannah is going to have the confidence to tell the person tormenting her how she is making her feel?'

Ms Galloway bristled. 'Or if Hannah isn't ready for a face-to-face she could write a note. It's important Hannah convey to Livie how she is feeling. Livie may not know some of her comments are hurtful.'

'Of course she knows! That's why she's doing it! She is bullying my daughter *on purpose*.'

'We are careful to avoid the word "bully" in these situations, Mrs Paige.' Ms Galloway said, flinching as though I'd called Livie a whore. 'A label like that can stick with a child throughout their school years and affect emotional development and future friendships. Now, if Hannah is reluctant to share her experiences, we do have other options. She could keep a notebook and note down the times, what occurs, and who else was present so they can be looked in to.'

'You want her to keep a bullying diary? Can you imagine how bad that would be if Livie or another child found it?'

'In order for us to be officially permitted to take any enquiries further,' Ms Galloway said, her voice taking on a tinge of impatience, 'as outlined in our policy, which is available to view online, we will need to have some kind of proof. Date and time-logged, and with witnesses.'

'Hannah and I want this to stop,' I said, reaching the end of my own patience. 'Without Hannah having to come in and relive it all. *I'm* telling you. I am her mother and *I'm* telling you. Why is this not good enough?'

'Mrs Paige,' Ms Galloway clasped her hands together on her desk. 'I am outlining all the government-endorsed options and you are not happy with any of them. You are leaving me no other options.'

'Because they're ludicrous!' I said. 'Your whole system is geared to protect the bully, not the victim. What about *my* daughter's emotional development?! *My* daughter's self-worth? Livie is being horrible and Hannah is extremely distressed. She's lost confidence, self-esteem, her laugh.' My voice cracked. 'If you have a zero tolerance for bullying then you need to damn well show that!' I swiped angrily at another tear.

Ms Galloway took a breath and as she spoke any hope I had at receiving real support faded. 'I understand you're upset, Mrs Paige. And we want to help. I'm very sorry Hannah is feeling unhappy at school. But as you can see it can be a tricky situation to solve if she is reluctant to talk about it. If you can bring me proof, in the form of times and dates and with witnesses, as I said before, then we can move forward. Just because an accusation exists does not mean the accused is automatically guilty. We have to consider the emotional needs of both children in a situation like this. Right now we have one child saying another is being mean and parents unwilling to get the children together to share their sides of the story.'

'Why does there have to be two sides?' I spat. 'Nobody ever said about the Holocaust, "Well, there are two sides to everything, let's just hear Hitler out"!' I stood and tugged my handbag over my shoulder as Ms Galloway's mouth fell open at my Hitler reference. 'You might have all your up-to-date policies and take Teacher Only days to attend the relevant courses that allow you to put a certificate on the wall but *YOU. AREN'T. LISTENING.* My daughter is *very* upset. And your PC bullshit is getting in the way of helping her. You can be sure that if anything happens, anything at all, to my daughter – I will be the first to say that I came to you for help and got nothing!' I yanked open the door and stormed out of the room and down the hall past Louise on the phone.

Shaking with anger I stepped out of the office building as the children were being let out of class. I rushed towards the gate hoping Hannah wouldn't catch me coming from the direction of the head teacher's office and bumped into someone, sending a cascade of folders and papers to the ground.

Today was a freaking disaster.

'Oh, Mrs Paige, hello,' said Mr Moody.

He'd been Hannah's teacher when she was in Year 3. Now he took her for English. He'd always been complimentary of Hannah's writing, saying she had a distinctive 'voice' and often wrote from a thoroughly unique point of view. He regularly read her short stories out in front of the class.

'Gosh, I'm sorry, I wasn't looking at all!'

'Not a problem,' Mr Moody said as we bent to retrieve the dropped folders. 'I was actually going to contact you.'

'Oh yes?' I straightened, clutching a mess of papers.

'Yes.' Mr Moody said, his kindly old face a furrow of smile wrinkles. 'I've noticed Hannah's interest in writing has changed.'

'Oh?'

'She used to be happy to offer up ideas and have her pieces read out to the class, she's so highly imaginative, but recently she's . . . well, not to speak out of turn for the other students, but now she's merely one of the pack.' He watched me absorb the information. 'She's had a tough time recently, I know.' He paused. 'But it seems to me like she's trying not to get noticed.'

I didn't trust myself to speak without my voice breaking. My little girl was losing pieces of herself.

'Here, give me those. I'll sort it.' He smiled and held out his hand for his folders. 'There's Hannah now,' he said nodding towards the gate where Hannah was scanning the street looking for me. She stood alone to one side while other children bustled around each other in boisterous knots, or walked out in pairs; off to have afternoon playdates. Livie was climbing in the back of Melody's white Range Rover with two other girls; Zara and Mackenzie. I was sure Melody would be treating the trio to a delightful afternoon that involved cupcakes and manicures.

I handed over the paperwork. 'Thank you, Mr Moody. I appreciate you noticing.' It was more than I could say for Ms Galloway. I said goodbye and wove through the busy playground to Hannah.

'What were you doing in there?' she asked suspiciously.

'Sports day stuff.'

We walked the short distance home at a subdued pace, both occupied with our thoughts.

At the front door she turned to me. 'Mum, I've decided I don't want you to talk to the teachers. If Livie found out it'd just make everything worse.'

Shit.

Chapter 12

'You cried.'

'Yes.'

'And swore.'

'Yes.'

'Accused their child?'

'Yes.'

'And got angry.'

'Very. And brought up Hitler.'

'*Dios mio*,' Penny exclaimed the next morning as she stirred three sugars into her coffee at my kitchen table. 'It went well, then.'

'You should have seen the way Justin looked at me. It was like he hated me.'

Penny's expression darkened. 'Do you think that if they knew you were richer than them they'd make sure their daughter treated Hannah better?'

'That's an ugly thought.'

'They're ugly people.'

'On the inside. That woman has the cheekbones of a goddess.'

'And the skin of a 12-year-old mermaid who washes her face in cherub tears.' Penny grinned, then switched to concern. 'So what now?'

I reached for my coffee. 'Mrs Galloway sent an email this morning listing the options she'd mentioned in the meeting and some links to resources on "maintaining the wellbeing of your child". I think she's just creating an email trail so she can prove protocol is being followed rather than having any true desire to solve anything.'

'That woman is all talk and no balls on the grindstone.'

'That is *not* how that saying goes.'

Penny shrugged. 'Does she still have that awful fucking *Kindness is Coolness* cross-stitch on her desk?'

'She's added one that says *You're Important. Treat Yourself The Same Way You Treat Others.*'

'I hate others,' Penny said, appalled. 'On a daily basis I want to tell everyone to eat a bag of ferret entrails. I treat myself *way* better than that.'

I gave a short snort of laughter. 'She suggested Hannah see a counsellor or child psychologist and emailed some names and numbers. I called every number. None have any availability until next month,' I said fighting a growing sense of defeat. 'Some weren't even taking on new clients because their lists were full.'

Penny shook her head. 'That's terrible. How's Hannah?'

I sucked in a breath and eased it out. 'She's pale, quiet. Sad. Can't sleep. Doesn't eat much. She won't wear her colourful clothes or take her neon basketball to school anymore.'

Penny's dark eyes rounded in empathy.

'I can't believe this is happening to my little girl.' I shook my head. 'It's like she's had all the joy sapped out of her.'

Penny squeezed my arm, her glossy red talons gripping me. 'Then it is up to us to give it back to her.'

After Penny left I flicked open my laptop to do a couple of hours' work. I was wading through an email chain from Abdul about an urgent invoice abnormality that was causing one of his regular clients conniptions when my phone rang. Hannah. Calling during her lunchbreak.

I swiped at the screen. 'Hello darling, is everything—?'

'I can't believe you told Ms Galloway!' Hannah's distraught voice was loud and gasping in my ear. It echoed, like she were calling from a toilet cubicle. 'I told you not to!'

'But sweetheart—'

'Livie came to school and told everyone I made up lies about her!' she cried. 'She said she's in trouble with the head and her parents are super embarrassed because of how much they do for the school and Livie told Zara and Mackenzie I've probably made up lies about them too and now they aren't talking to me either! *Nobody* is speaking to me!'

'Honey, listen I—'

'Everybody moved away from me in class! Now I have no friends! None! Everyone hates me! You've made *EVERYTHING* worse!' And she hung up but not before I heard her break down into wet, tragic sobs.

I jabbed at the screen trying to call her back but she sent me to voice message. My heart thudded in my chest. What had I done? My baby was at school, isolated and hated, without anyone she could turn to for comfort. I felt sick. I typed out a text to Hannah, my vision swimming with pooling tears.

Honey, I'm so sorry. Please call me. I can come and pick you up if you want? I love you so much.

I clutched my phone, waiting for a reply, but none came.

The next few hours passed at an agonising pace. When school finished, Hannah marched across the playground to where I was waiting with Penny.

'Hi, honey,' I said but she trudged past me in the direction of home and Penny threw me a sympathetic look.

I caught up with her and tried to apologize. She didn't respond. I asked how the rest of the day had gone but she kept her furious gaze on the footpath and ignored me. When we got home, she went straight to her room. Penny called and said Elise had told her Livie had cried all day and played the victim and Hannah had been completely ostracized. Again, I tried to talk to her but she sat on her bed not responding and after I'd explained why it was important to stand up to bullying and that I loved her so terribly much, she asked me to leave. She barely ate any dinner, showered and went to bed early. I called Trish but her phone was off. I'd forgotten she was speaking at a charity gala. I spent the rest of the evening pacing the living room, trying to figure out what I could do, and when I checked on Hannah at 10pm she was wide awake.

'I don't matter,' she said in a tiny voice.

'What do you mean?'

'If I lived or died no one would care.'

'I would, honey,' I said, supressing a howl of anguish. 'I would care very, *very* much.'

I listed the people who loved her because of everything that she was, and tried to remind her, as Trish had advised, that Livie's nastiness was because of something going on with Livie, not her. That she mustn't doubt herself because there was no reason for Livie's persecution.

'There must be a reason. Otherwise the other kids would still be my friend and not believe her. There's something wrong with me.'

'There isn't anything wrong with you at all,' I said, but my protestations fell on deaf ears.

After stroking her hair till she fell asleep I sat on the sofa with Cookie, tears trickling off my chin. There were less than three more months of the school year. I just wanted to get Hannah to the end of it without losing herself completely in the process. But how?

I remembered Abdul's urgent invoice and, wiping my cheeks, pulled my laptop on to my knees and spent a couple of distracting hours finding the source of the problem from a stack of purchase orders. At midnight I sent Abdul an email with the correct invoice attached and the numbers of the incorrect purchase orders and an apology for it taking so long. A moment later – Abdul was a night owl – his reply pinged back.

My friend, thank you. Ingrid was struggling to find where it had all gone wrong.

And in regards to not returning for the proposal event, I understand you are not yet ready. It is a great shame for us but you must put your family first.

I will let the client know you are not available to us at this time. He was adamant he wanted you. You really do have a particular knack for creating somebody their own personalized day of joy. I hope we see you back here again one day, working your magic. It is always available for you.

Perhaps you'd be more comfortable on a contract by contract basis? Have a think about it, but of course, no pressure.

Go well, my friend.

A

I was about to shut down my computer, I'd reply to Abdul tomorrow, reiterating that even on a contract by contract basis I would not leave Hannah, especially at the moment, when my phone dinged with a text. I was surprised to see it was from my mother. What was she doing awake at seventeen past midnight? I opened it and began to read and scroll through one of her stream of consciousness texts.

Sorry to message so late. I suppose you're asleep but I'm at the Pétanque annual fundraiser and George has had a bit to drink and has let on that his son is putting his cottage on the market tomorrow, he's having a terrible divorce, his wife won't let him see their Schnoodle, but anyway, it's not far from the village and I thought if you called tomorrow before it officially goes on the market you might nab yourself a deal. Not that you need a deal, but there's no sense in throwing money away unnecessarily. Even with that ridiculous amount in your account. Gosh you know, sometimes I do forget quite how much it is. Anyway, I'll forward you George's son's number if I can figure out how to do it. Just a thought, time is a-marching onwards and upwards or what's that saying. Oh I don't remember but best be getting on with the plan now love, don't you agree? Must go and get your father away from the karaoke machine. Nobody wants to hear Part Time Lover from a septuagenarian with a cane.

Ugh. The plan, the plan, the goddamned plan! Well, Hannah was losing herself so I needed a new fucking plan.

I stopped.

I looked at Abdul's email. '. . .*personalized day of joy* . . .'

I looked at Mum's text. '. . .*ridiculous amount* . . .'

I tossed my phone on the sofa, clicked on my Excel icon and opened up a new template.

Chapter 13

Penny and I stood at the school gates in reflector vests waiting for the children to come out of their classrooms with the other Sports Day parent helpers, which included Melody and her gaggle of fawning mothers. Since Chris had died I'd felt like an outsider at the school gates as everyone around me made normal playdate/quick-coffee-before-Pilates plans while I was too disassociated to remember if I'd put on pants. But today I was grateful for my 'outsider' status. I didn't trust myself to be near that gaggle and not give Melody an unedited piece of my mind. Or fist, or foot or . . . I looked away from her, breathing out my violent inclinations.

In the two weeks since the head teacher fiasco Hannah had been excluded and ignored at school. Elise had asked her to join her at lunchbreaks and Hannah sat at the edge of their group, silently watching the other kids play basketball as Elise and her friends did their homework on the benches.

I blinked away the image of my daughter alone and miserable and took a moment to appreciate the blue sky and brilliant sunshine. I couldn't have hoped for a better day.

I was distracted by a text and while I read it Penny grumbled at my side about her mother-in-law.

'If she shows me any more photos of her microdosing, magic mushroom, healing weekend I will insert a magic mushroom in the area she keeps showing me!'

'Ew.'

'Apparently nudity was optional. *Optional*. But am I given the "option" of not seeing my naked 73-year-old mother-in-law's crazy bush? No, I am not.'

I sniggered while texting the words 'white alpaca'. Penny glanced at the screen then gave me a weird look. But before she could quiz me the kids tumbled out of the classrooms slicked in sunscreen and with their backpacks low on their pre-teen backs.

My phone dinged again and I smiled at the text.

'What?' Penny said, stepping closer to look over my shoulder.

'Hannah's orthodontist. It's the Def Leppard concert tonight.'

Penny made a face. 'It's great that you're actually going out, but *so* weird you're going with him.'

'It's the first time Hannah has smiled in weeks.' I finished my text, slipped my phone in my pocket and scanned the crowd.

Hannah had had her baby tooth extracted the week before and Dennis had unexpectedly popped down to his friend's dental surgery to check it was going well. He'd noticed the change in Hannah and I had a feeling it was after that he'd made an extra effort to obtain the concert tickets.

Hannah emerged from the pack of children on her own and stood at my side, her shoulders hunched. She'd been unhappy about wearing the sports uniform because the shirt was white and she was worried everyone would see that she didn't wear a bra. I couldn't believe this had become a concern. At her age I'd still liked cuddly toys.

'Two lines please!' said an officious teacher in a reflector vest.

Hannah's old friendship group orbited Livie, who basked in the devotion. Zara glanced over then looked away when she caught my eye. It was a strange phenomenon in the school yard, how a nasty child could become kingpin and other children flocked to them, more out of fear of being cast aside than actually liking the child. And the fear was real. I could see how nobody wanted to be near Hannah in case her social rejection could somehow be 'caught'. It was like she didn't exist. It broke me.

'Dramatic little *princesa*, no?' Penny said, her eyes on Livie. We watched as she made a performance of who got to be paired with her for the walk to the high-school field down the road. Hannah surveyed through heavy eyes. When she saw me watching she quickly looked away.

'Perhaps you could help her in front of a passing truck on the way, no?' Penny said with a wicked grin. 'Probably not the kind of parent "help" the school has in mind.' When she saw me looking at my phone again, she frowned. 'You're distracted today, *cariño*. Are you okay?'

'Yes,' I said, replying to another text then slipping my phone in my pocket. 'Just got a lot on.'

Penny raised her eyebrows above her sunglasses as if to say *You? A lot on?* and I laughed.

After watching teachers tick things off clipboards and repri-mand children for not standing in line, or forgetting their sun hat/drink bottle/manners, the gates were opened and the restless double line began to move out of the grounds and down the straight footpath. Penny and Elise were six sets of children in front of Hannah and me. Behind us meandered the rest of the senior school, a parent every sixth pair of jabbering children. Two boys in front of us shoved each other to and fro like a couple of tumbling Labrador pups. Hannah's stillness was like a dark cloud among the excitement.

I kept an eye on the front of the line and as it neared a certain point I pressed send on a text:

Now

Then, anticipation fluttering in my chest, I waited.

Seconds later a lady pushing a retro stroller emerged from a front garden on the other side of the road a few paces ahead of us. She wore a baby-blue T-shirt tucked in to high-waisted white denim shorts, mid-calf retro sports socks, and a pair of vintage Reebok high-tops. Her dark brown legs were smooth and firm, like she hiked every Sunday or did hot yoga five times a week, and she wore her hair in a natural afro.

'Look,' I said to Hannah.

Hannah looked at the lady, who we could only see from behind, then frowned at me. 'What?'

'It's nice to see a lady out in the sunshine walking her baby. That's all.'

Hannah gave me a strange stare but before she had a chance to say anything the song 'Iko Iko' burst forth from the lady's direction and she pranced behind her stroller, her hips sashaying to the beat.

Our snaking line of parents, teachers and kids giggled at the lady strutting to the music but as the song kicked in to the second verse and two ladies and a man, with matching strollers and retro outfits, appeared from a side street and fell into formation behind the first lady, there was a stunned silence. In unison the dancers spun to face us, pushing their strollers with one hand. Across the front of their sherbet-coloured T-shirts in big white letters it said 'NO REASON'. Giving our group wide grins, they whirled their strollers to reveal speakers in the place of babies and a cheer erupted from the school kids. Excitable chatter rippled down the line as everyone realized something exciting was happening.

Penny, up ahead, turned around, walking backwards, and mouthed 'WTF'.

Hannah shot me a baffled look but jerked her head back to the dancers as 'Iko Iko' scratched to a halt and was replaced by the chorus of Twisted Sister's 'We're Not Going To Take

It'. Two men in overalls who were on the back of a removal truck back-flipped onto the footpath and fell in to a co-ordinated dance step to a cacophony of whoops and laughter. For the next minute and 37 seconds (timed to fit in with the length of the street) seemingly ordinary passers-by joined in with each new chorus. A woman who'd been putting some-thing in the boot of her car and two men clipping a hedge fell in behind to Pharrell Williams's 'Happy'. A jogger, coming the opposite way, then a woman with a briefcase joined to Chaka Demus and Pliers' 'Twist and Shout'. Five dancers in glitter wigs, neon leggings, leotards and leg warmers, all with No Reason T-shirts in a rainbow of sherbet colours, burst out from a side street to The Monkees' 'I'm A Believer' followed by a person (who I knew to be a guy called Brian) in a chicken suit, the lilac No Reason T-shirt stretched over his fluffy yellow belly.

The school group clapped along as we snaked down the suburban street – the thirty-strong troupe of multicoloured dancers matching our pace on the opposite side twirling and leaping. Residents stepped out of their front doors to watch the jubilant performance. Hannah was confused and captivated. A few yards from the end of the street the music paused and the dancers froze. The school group waited. Hannah's favourite drum break from Phil Collins' 'In the Air Tonight' echoed, followed by her second, the bongo break in Cindy Lauper's 'Goonies R Good Enough'; the dancers mimed drumming then fell into a synchronized dance move, prompting an enor-mous cheer from the kids. To the last bars of the Cindy Lauper song the dancers did a final pirouette, back flip, or twerk (the chicken), then one by one fell away down side streets or back to 'work vans' until we were left with just the original lady and her stroller and the fading out song. We reached the end of the street and the lady made a sharp turn in the opposite direction we were heading. The music stopped and she and resumed her normal stride, like she'd never known all that was happening behind her. The school group pooled at the corner, staring after her in edgy anticipation. Just when it seemed it was all over the lady looked over her shoulder, threw us a wicked grin, then disappeared down a side street and the children exploded into excited hollers and shrieked theories.

'Who were they?!'

'That was *EPIC*!'

'What the fu–?!'

'*Liam!*'

Parents drew together and speculated.

'What was *that?*'

'Did anyone know that was going to happen?'

'Why here?'

'It must have been for us!'

I looked down at Hannah watching her classmates shriek and squeal and compare videos on their phone. 'Did you like that?' I asked.

She nodded emphatically.

'That's good,' I said casually, then bent down and whispered in her ear. 'Because I did it for you.'

I straightened and Hannah jerked her head up, eyes wide.

'Cross now please, children!' commanded a teacher before Hannah could quiz me and we jostled to the other side of the road, Hannah's open-mouthed stare sending prickles of happiness down my neck.

Teachers grappled to regain order as we swarmed through the high school gates and onto the field.

'Mum!' Hannah breathed once we were through. 'Did you–'

'LOOK!' A boy pointed at the sky.

Everybody looked up while I looked down at my phone. Right on time. I grinned and waited as Hannah squinted at a circling plane trailing a pink, peach, yellow and purple banner that popped against the clear blue sky. Once she clocked the giant swirly white letters saying 'No Reason', she jerked her head to me again. I winked and her jaw dropped comically.

Penny sidled up to me and I curtailed my giggle. 'This is fucking weird.' She looked up, shielding her eyes even though she was wearing the most giant, glossiest sunglasses known to Instagram. 'What do you think's going on?'

'Banksy?' said a mum.

'Like he gives a fuck about our school,' Penny scoffed, and got a sharp look from a teacher in a reflector vest and a responsible amount of visible sunscreen.

After a series of loops over the field, the plane zoomed off and Hannah tugged at my arm. 'Mum?!'

'Not here,' I whispered, putting my finger to my lips. 'At home.'

Hannah stared at me, a tiny spark of confused delight dancing behind her eyes. If that was all I got from the day I'd be happy.

The teachers rounded up the kids to start the races and Hannah reluctantly left my side. Parents settled in the shade of some trees and Melody curled her legs on her designer picnic blanket and took a sip from her designer drink bottle. Her eyes landed on me, sitting at a distance.

'It's nice to see you again, Brooke.' She followed my gaze to Hannah, standing alone at the back of a group of bustling children waiting to start their race, then turned back to me. 'I hope the girls are getting along better?'

'No, I don't think they are.'

Melody smiled. 'Well, you know how girls are.'

'I know how *some* girls are.'

Melody looked taken aback but the arrival of Penny stopped any chance of false platitudes.

'Don't be alarmed, ladies – I'm eating cake.' She plonked herself down next to me, pulled a crumpled paper bag from her tote, wrestled free a gigantic piece of carrot cake and took an enormous bite.

'Whangk shomg?' Penny said, proffering the wedge to me.

I leaned forward and took a huge bite, getting icing on my cheek and a look of disgust from Melody.

'So,' Penny said, swallowing down her mouthful and chugging back water from the eco-friendly stainless-steel bottle all us conscientious parents also owned. 'What do we think all that was about? Any ideas?'

'I think the school should have been warned,' Melody said. 'It could have been dangerous. Especially around children.'

'It was dancers!' said Penny, her mouth full again. 'On the other side of the road. How can that be dangerous?'

Melody raised her eyebrows. 'Unknown people.'

'You're mad,' Penny said, but it was without malice and Melody stood, brushed down her spotless Lulu Lemons, and headed towards the gathering teachers with a smile.

'Dangerous?' Penny hissed. 'People like her are the reason we have to have police checks in order to walk our own kids to their fucking Sports Day.'

*

Distracted from her misery by the morning events, Hannah was able to focus on her relay and her team won. She competed in hurdles, sprints and the 800 metres, and at the end of the day the kids, parents and teachers gathered on the field in much the same knot as the beginning of the day, just less chatty, and more sunburnt. Parents had been encouraged to turn up to watch the finals and most children were being signed out at the high school and heading home with a parent or guardian.

'Now what?' Penny said as we walked out of the gates to see kids and parents merging on the sun-drenched footpath round an ice cream van, Otis Redding's '(Sittin' On) The Dock Of The Bay' drifting out of its serving hatch. A second van surrounded by a logjam of kids and parents was parked a few yards away.

'Free ice creams!' said a boy to the kids arriving behind him in the line. 'For *no reason!*'

Hannah turned to me again, gobsmacked, and I chuckled. Knots that had been in my stomach for weeks began to unfurl as Hannah stared at the ice cream vans in wonder.

Melody trotted down the side of the eager swarm. 'What's going on?' she called over their heads to the young man in the van closest to us.

'We got booked to be here and told to give out ice creams till we run out. And someone dropped off this.' The man pointed to his sherbet-yellow T-shirt with 'No Reason' across the chest, grinned, then took the next desperate child's order.

'Outstanding,' Penny said and hustled to join the queue, not at all making allowances for any child. She turned and made an urgent motion for me to get in behind her.

'Who booked you?' Melody said.

The man grinned as he shrugged. 'I was just told to say "someone who wanted to spread a little joy for no reason".'

Melody frowned.

'Can I have an ice cream?' Livie asked as Hannah and I joined the queue.

'Dairy lines the gut with mucus and lowers the immune system,' Melody said and guided her away.

Penny threw her eyes to the heavens and I grinned.

On the sunny footpath, with beachy music wafting from the vans, parents took photos while kids waited in line, scouring the menu board, declaring their choices, then changing them to match their peers. Cheery energy crackled across the crowd. Hannah watched with awe and I could feel her desperate itch to ask me what was going on. I loved it. Once she'd been passed her swirly strawberry cone covered in sprinkles with a flake sticking out the side, and I'd received my vanilla one, we joined Penny and Elise, both with colossal spirals of ice cream loaded with every accompaniment on offer, and started the walk back home. A boy ran past us to catch up with his friend, hooting about how his ice cream was so much bigger than his friend's, then dropped it and the friend creased up with hilarity. The boy did an abrupt U-turn and joined the back of the queue, a pained expression on his face, leaving his friend doubled over in hysterics.

Hannah uttered the tiniest giggle with her mouth full. Affection moved liked a soothing balm across my chest at the sound.

As we walked Penny, through mouthfuls of ice cream and flake and marshmallow, rattled off their plans for the weekend, bemoaned how she was already late for picking up Lorenzo from her mother-in-law and that she had to collect Rosa from her friend's house and scoot her across town to ballet, but that there was no way she was missing out on a free ice cream, and spewed forth speculations about the strange events of the day, barely noticing that I wasn't offering my opinions. When we arrived at the spot where we'd turn right towards home or left towards the school I stopped.

'Aren't you going home?' Penny said, already angled towards the direction of both our houses.

'I need to drop these back,' I said holding up some coloured sports bibs. 'Come with me?'

'Ms Shuker will do it,' Penny said, indicating to Ms Shuker crossing the road behind us with a mob of kids she had absolutely no control over.

'It's fine. I'm enjoying the sunshine.'

Penny frowned heavily at me for a moment then glanced at her watch. 'Ugh, I'm *so* late already, I may as well walk with you,' she said, a suspicious note in her voice.

We turned on to the road back to school, Elise and Hannah trailing behind totally absorbed by their sugary good fortune, and stopped.

'What *the hell* is going on today?!' Penny said.

The road back to school was teeming. Kids were gathered around a popcorn cart or were squealing and clambering to have their effigy sketched by a caricaturist. Others stood in clumps laughing and taking photos of brightly coloured chalk drawings that ran the length of the street. A girl in a rainbow-painted cart handed out whimsical tufts of candy floss, and giant pearlescent bubbles floated across the sky. Music emanated from somewhere further down the road and every single cart owner and performer wore a sherbet-coloured No Reason t-shirt. I smiled. It was quite astounding what could be quickly permitted if money was thrown in the right direction.

'Is that a llama?!' Penny squawked.

'It's an alpaca,' Hannah said, grinning at a man holding a pink rope with a fluffy white alpaca at the end of it. His pink T-shirt with white lettering clashed with his farmer-style shorts and dirty work-boots.

'Is that a *pig?!*'

'Yes,' Hannah giggled.

Penny turned to me to see why I wasn't commenting on the extraordinary events and caught Hannah and me grinning at each other.

'Wh . . . ?' With her ice cream melting down her slim fingers she took in the popcorn cart, the bubble machine, the animal handlers letting kids pat their owl or goat or donkey, the magician pulling giant chocolate buttons out of a child's backpack, all the No Reason t-shirts, and the white alpaca then spun back to me. '*Is this you?*' she hissed.

Saying nothing, I held her gaze while Hannah and Elise joined a cluster of kids and parents chuckling at the magician as he clapped his hands, sending a cascade of confetti over the everyone. Parents and kids bumped past us on the footpath, keen to get among the fun. Penny flipped her sunglasses up on her head and her eyes bored into me. When I smiled a torrent of Spanish fell from her lips and when she switched to English she was still no more decipherable.

'What in the . . . !? How . . . !? Where did . . . !? *Why!?*'

I looked at my daughter patting the alpaca and dissolving into giggles as it slurped her ice cream. 'For Hannah.'

Penny's eyes widened. 'I don't even know what—!' she growled as her phone rang and she pressed ignore. 'Are you *completely* mad!? How did you—?' Her phone rang again and she glared at the screen. 'Ugh! I'm *so* late picking Lorenzo up and I have to get Rosa and . . .' Still holding her ringing phone she scanned the throng of kids. 'Elise!' she called, beckoning her daughter over. She turned back to me with a fierce glare. 'I'm calling you later.'

'Okay.' I grinned.

'Ay,' she said shaking her head. 'You crazy woman!' She turned back to her daughter who'd been distracted by a baby goat. 'Elise! I'm going!' She answered her phone with a terse 'I'm on my way!' and strode off.

'Mum!' Hannah came rushing up, her entire face lit up with delight. 'Come and look at this!' She grabbed my arm and tugged me into the fray.

We zigzagged down Tranmere Road, laughing at the magician, nibbling on popcorn, getting our caricatures drawn, petting the pig, the giant lop-eared rabbits, and the owl on a man's shoulder. After visiting every animal twice, Hannah dragged me from chalk drawing to chalk drawing. Some were on the road, some on the footpath. Some even went up garden walls. We saw a zebra with a top hat, meerkats spinning decks, orangutans taking selfies, a troop of tigers doing the floss, elephants in wireless headphones, puppies working on the engine of a VW camper, horses making tacos, donkeys at a coronation, and llamas running a hair salon. The words 'no reason' in swirly white lettering were interspersed throughout. Kids raced around with fists full of candy floss, snapping photos and selfies. Parents too. After an hour, the snack carts handed over their last snack, the caricaturist did his last sketch, the magician pulled his last hamster out of a child's backpack, and we walked home, Hannah with a giant fluff of candy floss, reeling in the joyful chatter from the other families. A warm glowing sensation settled down my spine. I'd done it. Two frenetic weeks of secret emails, bookings, payments and rehearsals and I had done it. Well, Trish and I had done it. And Hannah had smiled.

'Mum?' Hannah said when we reached our gate, but stopped when she spotted Mrs Webb, our upstairs neighbour, hefting a folding shopping trolley up her garden steps.

'Oh, hello pet,' Mrs Webb said. Her usually dour face lit up when she saw how animated Hannah was. 'What's that lovely grin for?'

Hannah beamed at me as she helped Mrs Webb up the steps with her shopping. 'No reason.'

Chapter 14

Hannah rounded on me as soon as we were inside. 'Did you really do that? Like *really* really?'

Cookie raced down the hall to greet us, evidence of her afternoon unsupervised all over the floor.

'Really, really,' I said, grinning as I picked up a chewed sock and a wellington boot on my way to the kitchen.

I opened the French doors to the garden and Cookie raced outside and weed on my parsley.

'All by yourself?' Hannah said, plonking her bag on a dining chair and standing next to the table with her candy floss, her sun-pinked nose and a smattering of heart-shaped paper confetti flakes in her hair.

I smiled. 'I had help.'

'Who?'

'Trish,' I said and Hannah's eyes widened.

With neither Trish or I being particularly materialistic, the idea of spending a large chunk of money trying to distract Hannah from her misery at school and bring her some much-needed joy for a day had been immediately embraced by my friend.

'Most of the dancers were students or tutors from her organisation. They were co-ordinated by a musical theatre director who is one of their mentors. Did you see the guy up the ladder fixing the street lamp?'

Hannah nodded.

'That was him. Anton. He was cueing everything from up there.'

Hannah listened, her eyes moving back and forth, as I told her how Trish and I had organized everything in two weeks; our combined attributes of event management and being extremely well connected making the entire operation relatively easy. Residents had been told it was to spread a little bit of joy in the community for 'no reason' at all and had been happily on board. Even more happily when they'd received a healthy 'donation' for the inconvenience. I told her the ideas had been mine and Trish had executed them; speaking to the pilot, the magician, the animal handlers, the chalk artists and the food carts, and getting her students and staff involved. When I finished, Hannah was quiet. She chewed her bottom lip.

'And you did all that . . . for me?'

I smiled as I grabbed the water jug from the fridge. 'Yes.'

'Why?'

'Because you've been having a tough time recently,' I said, pouring the water into two glasses. 'And I wanted to remind you that there is 'no reason' for anyone to be mean to you. And that life can be fun.' I looked up from the drinks. 'I've missed your laugh.'

Hannah's cheeks flushed as she lifted a corner of her mouth in a tiny smile then she frowned. 'Did it cost much money?'

'Yes, some.'

'Where did you get the money from?'

This was the moment I had known would come after the day's events. Hannah had been aware of our tight money situation, our humble home with its multitude of things that could do with a fix-up, our home-brand food items, and our low-key Christmas presents. Of course she was going to ask how I'd managed to pay for it.

'Come and sit in here,' I said, picking up our glasses and heading into the living room. 'I want to tell you something.'

I placed the glasses on the coffee table and we took our favoured positions at either end of the sofa. Hannah's was Chris's old spot. Hannah used to snuggle in the middle when we'd watched family movies. Now the middle was Cookie's spot. And she just sat there licking her bits and pieces.

'Do you remember that man who came around in a suit a couple of times last year? After Dad died? His name was Will?'

Hannah nodded.

'And you remember after that I had to go into the city a few times to meet with the hospital people and a judge so we could find out what happened to make sure it never happens to someone else's dad? And Penny looked after you?'

Again, Hannah nodded.

A silent stillness settled over her as she listened to me explain the malfunctioning bit of new machinery they hadn't told us they were trialling, the succession of negligence, and the tennis game of blame the hospital, surgeon and machine manufacturer had played. Injustice flickered in her eyes as she heard for the first time that her father's death was not an accident. But she fell back in to sad resignation as I explained the details of the mediation and she realized that it didn't matter who was at fault – her father was still gone.

'And the judge made them pay us some money,' I finished quietly.

'How much?' Hannah asked while running her fingers through the scrabbly fur on Cookie's neck.

'A lot. Too much.'

Hannah looked up, her mood still tempered. 'Are we rich?'

I waited a beat. 'Yes.'

She frowned. 'How rich? As rich as Penny and Rog?'

Penny and Rog were Hannah's benchmark because not only did they have Netflix *and* Disney+ subscriptions, they also had

Amazon Prime and an Xbox (that only Penny used). 'Enough that we don't need to worry about money. Ever.'

Hannah's eyes widened a fraction but she didn't react like any other nearly 11-year-old who'd been told in the past that they couldn't have the latest pair of 'must have' shoes or a light-up scooter because they couldn't afford it, and was now finding out they were wealthy. She didn't leap up and start requesting this and that. She simply nodded and continued running her fingers through Cookie's fur.

'But you mustn't tell anyone about it, okay? Not ever.'

'Why?'

'Because that was part of the agreement. No one must ever know about the money or they will take it all away. You know what being sued means?'

'Duh,' Hannah said, rolling her eyes.

I smiled, loving seeing a hint of her former sassiness. 'Ok, well they might sue us. And we'd have to pay them.'

Hannah's eyes flashed. 'But it's *their* fault!'

'I know, honey, it's not fair. But it's what we must do. It's very, *very* important. I'm trusting you to keep this secret.'

'Even from Tom?'

'Even from Tom.'

'Tom and I never keep secrets from each other.'

'But this one is one we *have* to keep. You think you can do that?'

Hannah chewed her lip, grappling with the notion of keeping something from her best friend, before nodding.

I watched my daughter, her expression unreadable; her buoyant mood from earlier tempered by the talk of her father's death. Had I burdened her too much? 'Are you all right, honey?'

Hannah eventually looked up and nodded, her expression unreadable.

'I love you,' I said, bopping her on the nose with a fingertip.

She forced a lopsided smile. 'I love you too,' she said in a quiet voice.

My phone, lighting up with messages from Penny and Trish, caught my attention and I noticed the time. 'We've got to get ready for the concert. Are you sure you're okay?'

'I'm sure.' She pushed herself off the sofa and took a step towards the hall but then turned back and a tiny smile lifted the edges of her lips. 'I loved the alpaca the most.' She wrapped her arms around me. 'Thank you.'

One good day wouldn't bring Hannah's self-confidence back to head-to-toe-neon-tie-dye/breaking-into-an-unexpected-Queen-drumbeat-in-the middle-of-the-nativity-musical levels. And it wouldn't change Livie's behaviour. But one day of joy meant one less day of misery and I allowed myself to enjoy that small victory as I hugged her back. 'You're welcome, honey.'

While Hannah got ready I called Trish and told her everything had gone *exactly* to plan.

'Anton said it was brilliant.' Trish's voice came in huffs as she walked briskly somewhere important, the sounds of a busy London street in the background. 'The dancers want to know if anything else is planned.'

'No, nothing else. It was a one-off.'

'Thought so.'

'I wish you could have seen her face.'

'That girl's sweet face is etched on my soul.'

My chest swelled at how much my daughter was loved by my best friend. She held Hannah's heart in her hands as reverently as I did. We hung up and I dialled Penny.

'*What the fuck, woman?!*' Penny said instead of the traditional 'hello' and I laughed.

'I'm only ringing to tell you I can't talk. Hannah and I have to get into Greenwich in . . .' I swivelled to see the kitchen clock on the wall behind me. 'Oh shit! Soon!'

'*Mierda*. Okay, come for dinner tomorrow? How did you even — I can't believe it! I mean . . .'

'Can't do dinner tomorrow. I'm in Sussex.'

'Sunday when you're back? Oh, double fucking bugger that won't work, we've got Rog's sister coming and she's a vegan and I won't inflict that sort of shit on anyone. Monday?'

'Monday sounds great,' I said while throwing the rest of the morning dishes in the sink and heading down the hall.

'I still think it's weird, you going with the dentist,' Penny grumbled. 'You don't see me going to the cinema with Rosa's podiatrist. I mean, I *would*. He's sexy, my God he is. I'd sit in the back and—'

'I have to go!' I said, giggling.

Penny made frustrated noises, muttered a goodbye and we hung up.

'Hannah, we have to leave in seven minutes!' I said, passing her bedroom and heading to mine. I threw my phone on the bed, and tugged clothes indiscriminately from both the clean and dirty washing piles. Then the doorbell went. 'God dammit,' I said hopping down the hall, shoving one leg into a pair of questionably clean jeans. I shoved the other leg in, zipped up my fly and swung open the door to a man with a stubbly chin, skew-whiff hair, a faded Harry Styles T-shirt stretched across his plump little tummy, and a belt bag slung diagonally across his chest. He looked like Jack Black. If Jack Black been up all night with a teething child. And got dressed in the dark. From his niece's wardrobe.

'Hello,' he said merrily. 'I'm—'

Cookie hurtled out the door and made bouncy leaps up the man's creased trousers.

'Oh God, sorry. Cookie!' I said, trying to grab her. 'She never does this. Cookie!' I said, not managing to capture her.

'That's okay,' he said cheerily, catching Cookie mid-boing. 'Dogs love me.'

'Clearly,' I said, flinching as he let her lick his face all over. 'How can I help you?'

'I'm a journalist,' he said then stopped to chuckle as Cookie licked in his mouth.

I recoiled and noticed his hair sticking out the left side of his head like one of those feathery owl tufts. 'You don't look like a journalist.' I held out my hands to take Cookie back but she 'ruffed' at me. 'Gosh, she's never done that before,' I said, glowering at my traitorous dog.

The man smoothed down the tuft while holding Cookie with one arm and it popped back up. 'I'm off duty because I was on a night shift last night. This is my morning. My *early* morning. You see my flatmate has a *Hello Kitty* problem and couriers turn up all hours of the day or night and they have to be signed for because they've come from Japan and . . .' he trailed off as he noticed my frown. 'Anyway, I live around the corner and a courier woke me and when I answered the door I saw the street party thing and well, here I am!' He smiled then smoothed his tuft again.

My heart instantly leapt into my throat. A journalist sniffing around? *That* I hadn't anticipated. The man put Cookie down, who immediately leaped at his legs to get back up, and pulled a tatty wallet from his pocket.

'Here you are,' he said, holding out a credit card-sized press I.D.

I scanned the particulars while trying unsuccessfully to coax Cookie away from his legs. 'Julian P *Tickle*?'

'That's me,' he beamed, sliding the I.D. back in his wallet and the wallet back in his scruffy . . . were they pyjama bottoms. . .? I looked back at his cheerful expectant face while Cookie still boing-ed at his feet. He was not at all the fox-faced, shifty journalist of my 90s-TV show-inspired imagination.

'Have you been knocking on all the doors round here?'

'Yes!' he said cheerily and my heart rate slowed. He hadn't knocked on *my* door specifically.

'Did anyone . . . say who was behind it?'

'You were there?!' he said, looking in awe of his good fortune.

'Oh . . . just for a little while . . .'

'Great!' he said lifting his belt-bag over his head, getting it caught on his left ear, stumbling on Cookie and eventually wrestling free of it. 'Would you mind if I asked you some questions?' He dug around in his bag and pulled out a ratty-looking notepad and a pen.

'I actually have to—'

He placed his belt bag on the ground

'Oh don't put that—!'

Too late. Cookie pounced on it and began humping.

'*Cookie!*' I tried to grab her but she picked up the bag in her jaws, did a manic loop of Julian's legs then ran through my legs into the house, bits falling from the open bag zipper all down the hall. 'Shit,' I said, racing after her.

'I only saw the mini carnival . . . thing . . . ' Julian said, unfazed about his belongings being humped then strewn through a stranger's home as I headed down the hall and bent to collect his phone then a half packet of gum. 'And just the end of it really, when they were packing up.'

'Right,' I said, picking up his chapstick, noting that it was a *Hello Kitty* one.

'But I've been told there was a sort of street theatre in the morning,' he said, raising his voice as I moved further away to retrieve a dice. 'I must have slept right through that, and also a sky banner. Did you witness the other two events as well?'

'Yes,' I said from further down the hall where his keys were.

Cookie could be heard growling as she attacked her new beltbag lover in the living room.

'Awesome,' he breathed, just like Jack Black in *Kung Fu Panda*. 'What do you think it was for?'

'I don't know,' I said, picking up what looked to be an old life jacket whistle.

'Do you have any idea who might have organized it?' he called out as I went into the living room.

'No, sorry!' I called back, wrestling with Cookie over the belt bag. 'Give it here, you little psycho,' I muttered.

'The words "no reason" were written in chalk on the road,' his disembodied voice echoed. 'And the sky banner and T-shirts! Do you know what "no reason" might mean?'

'No idea!' I hollered, finally getting the bag out of Cookie's jaw with a 'ha!' and walking back to the front door with a sweaty sheen and my hair falling out of its bun while Cookie ran down the hall, probably off to hump my slippers in revenge.

'Do you think they were trying to make a political or environmental statement?' Julian P Tickle said calmly, like nothing sexual had just happened between my dog and his belt bag, which I handed to him while puffing slightly. 'Or were perhaps part of an advertising campaign?'

I curtailed a laugh. A political statement? With ice cream? 'I don't know.'

'One woman said it felt like it was meant for the local school because it seemed to follow the timing of the sporting event.'

'I . . . guess it did seem like that.'

'And the magician said he'd been booked by someone called Patricia. Do you know who Patricia might be?'

'Not a clue,' I said, believing myself to not be lying because I had only called Trish 'Patricia' once and the resulting wrestle to the ground meant I'd never uttered it again. 'Why is . . . sorry, what publication do you work for?'

'Well, technically I'm a freelancer. But I mainly do shift work for the *Daily Dispatch*.'

'Oh,' I said and felt bad when he blushed at my involuntary sneer. 'Why does the *Daily Dispatch* care about a little thing like this?'

'Well, it probably won't,' he said with an expression of defeat. 'But you never know what might turn into a story.' He shrugged as he slid the bag back over his shoulder then perked up as though he'd just thought of something. 'Did you get any photos?' He looked at me with naive hopefulness.

'Sorry, no,' I lied.

'Really?' he said, genuinely surprised.

'I was . . . too busy enjoying it all.'

Julian nodded as if that were an admirable, if not slightly annoying for him, action.

'I'm sorry but I have to—'

His attention was suddenly diverted and he glanced behind me.

I turned to see Hannah walking up the hall, still in her school uniform, Cookie under her arm.

Julian's gaze flicked to the school logo on Hannah's shirt and his eyes lit up. 'Hello!' he said chirpily. 'I'm a journalist and was just asking about the exciting events that happened near your school today.'

Hannah's eyes grew wide and she shot me a worried look. 'Did you have fun?'

Instinctively I held my arm out in front of Hannah, half pushing her back. 'Look I'm sorry but we're due out in a minute. Hannah, go and get ready please.'

'Right,' Julian P Tickle said, watching as Hannah stared at me then walked down the hall looking at us over her shoulder. He turned his attention back my way and, after a brief search of my expression, smiled. 'Would I be able to take your name? Just for quotes.'

'I'm . . . shy,' I said, shaking my head.

Julian bobbed his head as if he fully understood. 'Well, if

you do hear anything about who might be behind it please get in contact.' He handed over a creased business card.

'Do you think this will be in the paper?'

Julian's smile faltered. 'Probably not. Community events like this are not really on the *Daily Dispatch*'s radar, but,' he shrugged, 'you never know what it may end up being.' He paused and smiled. 'It sounds like it was a fun day.'

I nodded.

'Have a good evening,' Julian said, and he turned and left.

I shut the door and stood in the hall running over my actions to see if Julian would be able to trace anything back to me. I'd transferred the money to Trish and all the payments to the performers, food trucks and animal handlers had been untraceable cash deposits. Trish had been the one to speak to everyone. She'd told the pilot where to fly, the chalk artists what to draw, and the food carts where to set up. And she'd done it all with her phone number blocked and from a purposely set up Gmail account. Oh yes, I watched my crime shows. The only people who had face-to-face contact with her were her own students and staff, and the theatre director. And according to Trish they were as reliable as the law of gravity. None of them knew I existed. Julian only had the name Patricia and that wouldn't get him anywhere. My apprehension dissipated. I tossed his card in the bin then hustled to my room to continue getting ready.

Chapter 15

Dennis stood outside the Tube station scanning the crowd spilling out and swarming towards the O2 Arena. He wore a dorky floral, short-sleeved shirt, and beige shorts that displayed beige, sinewy legs.

The entire journey Hannah had quizzed me. What was the pilot's name? What was the banner made out of? Who had it now? How long would the chalk drawings on the road last? Did the alpaca need adopting? The closer we got to our stop the more excited she became. When she saw Dennis, she squealed and ran towards him. He spotted us and waved back, revealing a bandage wrapped around his palm.

I reached him moments after Hannah. 'Parkour?' I said, looking at his hand.

He beamed. 'I underestimated the permanency of a fence.'

It took half an hour to get through the ticketing gates, have our pockets and bags checked, find the toilets, the food stalls, and the merchandise stall (for which Dennis insisted he buy us all T-shirts even though they only had XLs left, then insisted on putting his on over his floral shirt). The rigmarole had not been conducive to conversation so Dennis and I had those awkward half-sentence exchanges you have with someone you don't know very well when you're busy trying to order hot chips and popcorn, handing over tickets while holding hot chips and popcorn, or making sure your daughter doesn't get lost in a crowd.

Finally we sat in our seats, Hannah (her giant T-shirt covering her knees), then me (T-shirt in my bag), then Dennis (floral collar poking out of his neckline and the arms all bunched up like a weird rock n roll-Popeye), and we took in our surroundings. The stage was the same level as our seats and perhaps only ten yards away. We were the front row of our section, and below the metal railing in front of us was the standing area. Beside Hannah were five middle-aged ladies probably three large Chardonnays into celebrating their proximity to their former teen crushes. I looked away from their sequinned excitement. It felt strange being out at night. Evenings were for dinners with friends, drinks with colleagues, going to a show or movie. Evenings were for happy people. I felt out of place among the lipstick and the cologne and the excitement.

'Are we in the VIP section?' Hannah asked, leaning across me to Dennis.

'Yes,' he replied, looking somewhat self-conscious. 'My client said the section is usually full of competition winners, friends of management and such like.'

'Wow . . .' Hannah breathed and turned to take in the 'VIPs' around her.

I twisted in my seat and clocked the rows stretching steeply up behind us till they faded into the dark area near the roof.

'Brooke is a nice name,' Dennis said.

I turned back around, wondering if he was scratching at the bottom of the barrel of how to make conversation. 'Thanks.'

'It's not often you meet Brookes.'

'No. My dad chose it,' I said, holding out the bag of crisps for Hannah to dig her hands into. 'Mum thought he'd suggested naming me Brooke after a country brook they'd had a particularly "romantic" picnic beside.' I pulled a gagging face which Dennis chuckled at. 'It wasn't until my twenty-first that she found out Dad suggested it because he liked Brooke Shields. And he couldn't even remember the picnic.'

Dennis laughed. Then there was an awkward pause when we realized that we were client and professional and didn't really know each other and had a long evening ahead of us. Well, I realized it. Dennis appeared to be unusually content to just sit and smile.

'Hannah has been so excited about tonight,' I said, finding amenable silence extremely unamenable. 'Thank you for inviting us. We don't really go out much these days. This means a lot to her.'

Dennis looked both chuffed and embarrassed by the acknowledgment. 'Oh. It's my absolute pleasure.'

We lapsed into silence again. I couldn't bear it.

'What do you like about teeth?' I blurted then cringed. 'I mean, what made you choose orthodontics as a career?'

'It's a family business. My grandfather went into it for the status, my father went into it because my grandfather made him. But I wanted to do it.'

Who wants to stare into gross mouths each day? My thoughts must have been evident in my expression because Dennis smiled.

'I liked the idea of helping someone become more confident about their smile. It's the first thing we hope to see from a newborn; the first sign of connection between baby and world. If correcting someone's teeth makes them smile more, then that benefits not only them but all the recipients of that smile,' he said with an endearing shrug. 'I guess going into orthodontics was my way of adding a little bit of positivity to the planet.'

I smiled and Dennis made a 'see' gesture then beamed and asked what I did for work. I told him about my former job in events and how I now only did a few hours a week from home.

'I think everyone assumed I'd be back at the office by now. Even I did. But . . .' I shrugged. 'The idea of putting on parties for strangers and being away from Hannah . . .'

'I understand,' Dennis said, nodding.

'How did you meet your girlfriend?' I asked then blushed, realizing he might think I was fishing.

Dennis squinted for a moment as if he were trying to understand the question, then his eyebrows shot up. 'Oh,' he shifted in his seat. 'Sienna. Well, I did her teeth and my friend did her, ah...' He checked that Hannah wasn't watching but she was absorbed by some tech guys on the stage, then indicated bosoms with his hands.

'Boobs?'

'Er, yes. And, well, then she invited my friend and me to an opening of a new restaurant, which ended up being a loose interpretation of the word because it was in a garden shed. Pop-up, she said it was called.' He shook his head. 'And then I met her again at a launch of a new cosmetic surgery down the road, and after that she just kept turning up.' He looked hunted. 'Everywhere.'

While we waited for the stadium to fill up Hannah asked Dennis lots of questions about his celebrity clients. She showed him videos of her drumming and he showed her another collection of cuts and scrapes he'd obtained while on a weekend hike in Snowdonia. He'd stretched while yawning and had fallen backwards off a reasonable sized cliff. Moments later the stadium lights lowered and the stage lit up with criss-crossing laser beams as the music boomed. Hannah spun towards the stage and Dennis began clapping furiously, forgetting about the large paper cup of lemonade in his hand, and splashing it all over his knees. I grinned at my daughter captivated by Rick Allen's foot pedals as the opening beat to 'Rocket' boomed so loud I felt it in my chest.

*

'And "Pour Some Sugar on Me" made the album go to number one in the charts because strippers in Florida kept requesting it,' Hannah said, skipping breathlessly along between Dennis and me through the crowds of concert-goers swarming towards the Tube station.

'Strippers?' Dennis said. 'How fascinating.'

'Yes. And in an interview they said when they play the song in America for some reason it seems to make women take their shirts off. And they actually love—'

'Okay,' I said, laughing. 'That's enough Def Leppard/stripping trivia for tonight.'

Accustomed to getting carried away with the details of her favourite bands, Hannah looked up at Dennis to see if she'd bored him.

'I very much appreciated the trivia,' Dennis said, smiling genuinely. 'It enriched my concert experience immeasurably.'

Hannah turned to me and grinned, triumphant.

'Thank you again for getting us the tickets,' I said to Dennis as we reached the spot where we needed to part ways.

'My absolute pleasure,' he beamed again then quite suddenly his face loomed towards mine. For a horrifying second I thought he was going to try and kiss me but he tumbled past my shoulder. 'Watch out for . . . er . . . that,' he said, righting himself and pointing at a smooth and faultless area of pavement. Then he told us he'd see us at the surgery in two weeks for Hannah's braces to be fitted, trotted towards his platform, and was absorbed by the crowd.

'He's an unusual man, isn't he,' I said, putting my hand out for Hannah to hold. My heart soared when she took it.

'I like him,' she said, as we negotiated the underground tunnels. 'He's weird and funny.'

'I like him too,' I said.

At home Hannah and I headed down the hall towards our bedrooms.

'Mum?'

I turned to see Hannah in her doorway. 'Yes, sweetie.'

She smiled. 'Today was awesome.'

She disappeared into her room and, basking in the glow of her contentedness, I stepped into my own reflecting that being out hadn't been so bad. I hadn't been entirely comfortable, but I'd survived. And my daughter had had one very good day among her horrible ones.

Seconds later Hannah rushed in clutching her phone in her oversized Def Leppard T-shirt, one sock half off, and no trousers. 'Mum, look!'

'Hannah, put that away, it's very late,' I yawned while pulling my shirt over my head. 'We have to get the train to Sussex in the morning.'

'*Look!*' she said, stepping in front of me holding her phone up. With one finger she scrolled through Instagram.

I stopped, my arms entangled in my top. Photos rolled up of the chalk art, the sky banner, the magician, the man in the chicken suit, the pigs, the alpaca. Ice creams with flakes, ice creams with raspberry swirls. 'What . . . ?'

Hannah clicked on a photo of the man in the ice cream truck grinning while pointing to his No Reason T-shirt. 'They've made a hashtag!' she gasped. 'Look how many people have commented!'

There were 1,431 comments. More were popping up as we looked. Hannah scrolled further and stopped on a close-up of the sky banner.

'That's Liam from my class!' Hannah said, pointing at a comment by someone with a handle that seemed to be more XXs and dashes than any real name. 'And that's Brianna!' She scrolled some more, gasping and pointing at the comments.

'Mum,' Hannah said turning to me, her eyes wide. 'It's *trending*.'

Trending?

I dropped my shirt and snatched my own phone from the nightstand, opened the Twitter app and searched #NoReason. The first thing to pop up was a video of the dancers with the strollers. And it had already been shared hundreds of times!

Breathing quickly, I scrolled through videos and photos and stopped at a clip of the man in the chicken suit; the caption said *'I ♥♥♥ that big yellow butt!'*. I clicked on the play symbol. The chicken began crumping to 'Twist And Shout' and from my shoulder I heard a sound I hadn't heard in a long time. Almost but not quite the whole thing. Hannah's cackle. Just the initial tinkle of it.

She looked at me, eyes shining. 'Can we do more?'

Hearing that almost-cackle was like taking your first sip of champagne at a wedding where an extremely hot, extremely single groomsman had been making eyes at you during the ceremony. I felt giddy with potential.

I wanted more of that almost-cackle.

She stood with one half-off sock and no trousers, waiting for the 'no' she was accustomed to getting from me.

'Yes,' I said.

Chapter 16

'Hannah wants to do more,' I said once Trish, Hannah and I had nabbed a coveted table on the train to Sussex early the next morning. Trish was coming to join us on the bike ride with Gus, but mostly, I suspected, to make sure I didn't back out.

'More . . . ?' Trish said, placing her studded leather bag on the spare seat next to her.

Hannah, in a window seat next to me, leaned forward and cupped her hands around her mouth. 'Secret No Reason stuff,' she whispered.

'Oh,' Trish said, raising her eyebrows in my direction. 'What kind of stuff?'

Hannah wriggled. 'Mum said she did it to make me smile. And I did. Like, *all day*.' Hannah threw me a grin, then turned back to Trish. 'And my smile made Mrs Webb smile and she *never* smiles. And that secret fun stuff made me feel really special. And all day I had this good feeling in here,' she put both her hands on her stomach. 'And I was thinking there might be lots of other people who are feeling sad, like, people we don't even know! And maybe they might feel better if someone did stuff to make them smile. And then maybe they'd have the good feeling all day. And maybe if that person smiles they might makes someone else smile. And *they* might get the good feeling too! And then it was on Instagram! And people who *weren't even there* liked it! And I bet they smiled. And that smile might have made another person who wasn't even there smile!'

My heart swelled at hearing my daughter describe the ripple effect without any awareness of its existence.

Hannah fixed her eyes on Trish, eagerly awaiting a reaction. Trish turned to me.

'I know what you're going to say,' I said.

'The journalist.'

'He'll have found a cheating girlfriend from a reality show I've never heard of by now.'

'The social media interest?'

'Not an issue. It could be anyone, anywhere. As long as I don't ever post my face.'

'Yeah,' said Hannah, appealing to Trish. 'There's a boy at my school who makes videos of his mum's really horrible dinners. It's really funny! He puts like, vomiting sound effects and that scary music from *Jaws* and does like, mash-up videos from old movies where everyone runs out of a building, and he's got this big TikTok following and *no one* knows it's him. An American rapper even follows him.'

'*Really?*' I said, recalling a similar-sounding video I'd seen shared by Chrissy Teigen. 'Which boy?'

Hannah shook her head as if my inquiry were naïve, making Trish and me giggle.

Then Trish turned to me, her expression becoming serious. 'What about the cost?'

'Duh,' Hannah blurted.

I giggled. 'Yeah, duh.'

Trish held my gaze for a moment then fished in her bag, pulled out a sleek notebook and an even sleeker pen, then turned to Hannah and said, 'Well then. What makes people smile?'

Hannah and I grinned. 'Ice cream!' we said in unison.

For the rest of the journey Trish recorded whatever was thrown at her and added a few of her own.

'Llamas.'

'Being thanked.'

'Tacos.'

'*Free* tacos!'

'Colour.'

'Being complimented.'

'Pizza.'

'*Free* pizza!'

'Music.'

'Love.'

'Yuck,' said Hannah.

'Coffee.'

'Babies.'

'Yuck,' said Trish.

'Cupcakes!' Hannah said, getting overexcited. '*Free* cupcakes! Glitter! Glitter *on* free cupcakes! That are shaped like llamas!'

'Shhh,' I said, giggling and looking around the train carriage at the other commuters with their earphones in.

When we got off the train in Sussex, Hannah skipped alongside Trish's long strides, rattling off things that could make strangers smile. I followed behind, thinking how special and kind my little girl was and how unfair it was that Livie had chosen not to see it.

At Mum and Dad's, Hannah went into her lesson with Gus and, after Mum offered to pack us up some leftover mussel and salami pie for the bike ride, I popped to the village for some picnic food.

An hour later Trish walked in to the kitchen where I was unloading my normal person food purchases, Hannah's lesson echoing up from the cellar. 'I met Inga,' she said.

'Inga?' I directed this to Mum who walked through from the laundry and slammed a flyer for a selection of local cottages with open homes on the counter in front of me. 'I thought you had that Finnish kid with the eyeliner?'

'He got homesick,' Mum said, rummaging through my shopping and examining a pottle of stuffed peppers with a disproving eye. 'I've got Inga from Germany now. She's just come from the school. Her English is good and she won't shut up. You know, I really prefer them when they haven't been yet. Much quieter.'

'She seems nice,' Trish said, walking over to Clint who'd arrived in the doorway and scratching him under the chin.

'Hmmm,' Mum said, scanning my receipt. 'She eats like Martin did when he was on the pot. I can't fill her up. And she's always running everywhere – even into the village! And wearing that Apple wrist tracker thing. It's like she's on house arrest from prison – always beeping at her telling her things she has to do. Your father can't stand it.'

'*Who* can't stand it?' Dad said, coming into the kitchen.

'Who's this?' Mum said ignoring Dad and attempting to move her hips in time to the crashing cymbals.

'Metallica,' I said.

'Lovely,' Mum said, wincing as she left the room.

*

'Oh my,' Trish purred as we arrived outside to see Gus unloading bikes, his arm muscles popping with the effort.

He'd tanned up over the past week of early summer and I elbowed Trish to stop her indecent mutterings.

'Tom can't come!' Hannah puffed as she ran around the side of the house. 'He put fake spiders in his housemaster's breakfast and the housemaster threw his plate across the room and it hit this really old important painting and he's not allowed leave again.'

'I will come,' Inga declared, appearing out of nowhere. She was blonde, tanned, 5 feet nothing and all muscle.

Gus glanced at me and I shrugged.

★

The day was sunny, the lanes we wove through were lush with spring growth, and the wafting scent of sun-warmed grassy fields gave a sense of optimism. Trish spent most of the trip biking alongside Gus, discussing the best places in the world to surf, education reform, and their various views on what struggles today's youths were facing while Hannah and I biked side by side behind them discussing more ripple effect ideas, the movie she and Tom were writing, and our various views on taco fillings. Inga would cycle around us assessing our form and enlightening us on how we could all pedal more efficiently.

At Hesworth Common we picnicked under an old oak; Hannah confidently chatting with Gus, a different girl to the one she was at school. On the way back Inga took a 'long cut' and pedalled off in a different direction saying she required the extra cardio but that she'd be back well before us on account of her superior speed and skill, and on the final stretch down Mum and Dad's lane Hannah fell behind to discuss a beat with Gus. Trish sidled up next to me.

'Gus has a pub quiz team,' she said. 'He started a quiz cup challenge down at the Gentle Goose.'

'Cool,' I said, struggling to adjust my gears.

She grinned the kind of grin that preceded mischief then angled her head behind to Gus. 'You should get Brooke to join your team!' she hollered. 'Brooke is a fount of that useless trivia that gets asked in a pub quiz!'

I gave her an appalled look. 'What the fuck?' I hissed as my gears clunked into high gear and my legs rotated furiously.

'You *should* join his team,' Trish said unapologetically, changing her gears like a pro. 'You're here every weekend.'

'So? I don't *want* to join his team.' I flicked the gears again. 'Orff,' I gasped as the gears became so heavy it felt like I were peddling through treacle. 'And useless trivia?' I narrowed my eyes at my duplicitous friend who glided ahead with a breezy smile. 'One day I may save your life with what I know about Wham!'

'Maybe,' she said and called for Hannah to race her home.

'We did actually lose a point on a Wham! question last month,' Gus said, arriving in Hannah's vacated spot at my side, not at all breathless from the acceleration. 'How old was George—'

'—Michael when he wrote "Careless Whisper"?' I finished, while finally attaining the correct gear for the gradient; completely flat. 'Seventeen.'

Gus grinned. 'We could use someone with that kind of Wham! intelligence on the team. I started the cup challenge a year ago, won the first month, and haven't touched it since. It's embarrassing because I called it the Marshall Cup.'

'You named it after yourself?' I puffed, watching Trish and Hannah up ahead, giggling as they raced each other through Mum and Dad's gates.

'Yes. And it's a regret of mine.'

I laughed as we glided through the gates and stopped beside the trailer where Trish was helping Hannah off her bike.

'The quiz is every Saturday at 6. Would you like to join us tonight?' Gus said dismounting with ease.

Trish looked over expectantly.

'Oh I . . . can't,' I said, concentrating on flicking out the kickstand. 'I have to make a miniature donkey a birthday cake.' It sounded like a lie but it was not.

Trish shook her head.

'Right.' Gus smiled. 'Maybe next time.'

'Yes, maybe,' I said peeling off my backpack and ignoring Trish's disappointed stare.

Gus looked around the empty courtyard. 'Where's Inga?'

We moved to the gate and looked up and down the empty country lane. Nothing.

Mum arrived behind us leading Crumpet, who had mud around his muzzle, and the fronds of a pilfered carrot sticking out of his white pillowy lips.

'Mum, I think we lost Inga,' I said.

'Thank God for that,' she said and carried on out the gates telling Crumpet he was a naughty, naughty boy and mustn't follow the yurt guests into the showers.

With tired limbs and sun-warmed skin, we helped Gus load the bikes on the trailer. Hannah thanked Gus then raced off to see if Tom was allowed to play rugby, and Trish, Gus and I walked back to the gates and peered up and down the lane again. It was deserted except for Mum coming back from the neighbours' field cursing.

'That bloody Noel,' she said. 'He's trying to get me to swap Clint for Crumpet again. I'll *never*. Clint is a gentleman. Crumpet is an asshole. He only wants Clint to breed with his alpaca Rosy. Well, I will not be coerced into pimping. Not again. Far too much co-ordinating, I haven't the time. And all that shunting!' She stopped her rant and joined us watching the empty lane.

'Shunting?' Trish mouthed and we giggled at Gus's bemused expression.

Sasha roared her retro Mini Cooper through the gates sending gravel everywhere and Gus relocated his attention from Mum to her.

'How was the date? Where did you go? I didn't see you in the village?' Mum said through Sasha's open window.

Sasha gave Mum a hard state as she slid out of her car. 'He's an obstetrician and he's travelled to Rwanda and Greenland and he's just signed up to volunteer with Doctors Without Borders,' she grumbled. 'He said his purpose in life was to help others then asked what I did and what my purpose in life was. When I said I was a receptionist and didn't really know what my purpose was he shut down and ten minutes later he,' she paused to do the finger quote thing, '"got an emergency call" and had to leave. So, I went shopping to cheer myself up.' She tugged glossy shopping bags from the back seat. 'I need to find a purpose in life.'

'*You are a function of what the whole Universe is doing in the same that a wave is a function of what the whole ocean is doing,*' Dad said, arriving round the side of the house with a chicken under his arm. 'Alan Watts.'

Gus looked from Sasha to Dad. Trish and I giggled as we clocked that the chicken was wearing a bow tie.

Sasha frowned. 'What?'

'You have no purpose, and you have all the purpose,' Dad said, and nodded as if he'd explained everything perfectly clearly before sauntering out the front gate with his chicken.

'Whatever. I'm widening my Bumble radius,' Sasha said and stormed inside.

'Expanding your horizons!' Mum called after her with a delighted smile. 'Lovely!'

'It means she's run out of men in West Sussex,' I said and Mum's jaw dropped.

Gus watched Trish and me giggling at my scowling mother then went back to looking down the empty lane. 'Inga will bring the bike back, won't she?'

'She's probably circumnavigating Sussex,' huffed Mum and she took off round the side of the house.

At Gus's concerned look I added, 'Of course she will.'

Trish and I watched Gus secure the bikes with a firm pull on some bungee cords that made his biceps pop (and Trish make more purring noises), then waved him off.

'He probably thinks this is a mad house,' I said, picking

up my backpack and schlepping towards the house, hot and weary.

'This is a mad house,' Trish said, striding alongside like she'd undertaken nothing more taxing than sneezing.

'Why'd you bring up the pub quiz?' I grumbled.

'Hannah and Tom are together every weekend, I thought it might be nice for you to have a friend down here too. You guys have a lot in common.'

'I can make my own friends, thank you.'

'You don't, though.'

I gave her a look.

'He's your age, he's divorced—'

'So because we're both the same age and single we should fall in love?'

'Love?' Trish sneered. 'No. You should have sex.'

'What?!'

'It's probably time you got back in the saddle. The sex saddle, if you will.'

'Ew,' I said and stalked ahead of her through the front door. We arrived in the kitchen and poured ourselves cool glasses of water from a jug in the fridge. 'I wonder if there is a sex saddle,' I mused.

'There is.'

I screwed up my nose. 'How do you know?'

Trish shrugged. 'You're waiting to give a TED talk, you Google . . .'

I shuddered, gulped back my drink, then wriggled uncomfortably in my lycra leggings.

'What?' Trish said, watching me squirm.

'The bike seat was hard. I think I bruised my vagina.'

I turned to see Gus in the doorway, red to his collar, as was his customary hue when he caught me talking about my vagina, which had become a regrettably frequent occurrence.

Trish didn't even try to hide her glee.

'I, ah . . .' Gus cleared his throat. 'I just wanted to let you know that when Inga comes back with the bike she can leave it in the cart shed and I'll swing by and pick it up later, if that's okay?'

'Of course,' I said, my throat also in need of a clear.

Gus said thanks, gave a nod, left, and I rounded on Trish. 'Why am I always talking about my vagina when that guy walks in the room?'

'Why you talk about your vagina at all is beyond me,' Mum said, coming into the kitchen and dumping a basket of dirt-encrusted carrots, some partially munched, on the countertop. 'What could possibly need to be said about it that you haven't already in your forty-three years.'

'I talk *to* mine,' Trish said.

Mum shot her an exasperated look and left the kitchen again.

'Just little words of encouragement,' Trish said as she leaned against the counter. '*Doing all right there, little love cave? . . . I appreciate all your hard work . . . sorry about the synthetic fabrics . . .* that kind of thing.'

'Hard work!' I snorted then looked at my crotch. 'Sorry little friend, but I'm afraid you've had all the action you're going to see. I hope I gave you a good time.'

Gus walked back in the back door, placed a bike lock on the counter and silently left, trying to hide a grin.

Trish and I looked at each other and burst into the kind of helpless laughter that requires crossed legs.

Around 5pm, I dropped Trish at the station so she could get back to London in time for another important charitable event she had to attend.

'What do we have in common?' I asked, pulling into a car park.

'Huh?' Trish said, I grabbing her bag from the back seat.

I gave her a 'you know what I mean' look. 'Gus. What do Gus and I have in common?'

'Oh,' Trish said, smiling at the flush rising in my cheeks. 'He likes horses and . . . you liked that TV show with the horses.'

'Eh?'

'*Taboo.*' Trish said opening the car door. 'It had horses in it.'

'It had *Tom Hardy* in it. With his shirt off.'

Trish smiled. 'You're both lonely.'

Chapter 17

'What *The Hell* was Friday all about?' Penny said on Monday morning as she slid a pod into her coffee machine.

I sat on a stool and filled her in, apologising for keeping it a secret.

'And you did all that to make Hannah—'

'Smile. Yes.'

Penny stared. 'That's excessive. You know that's excessive, right?'

'I tried everything else,' I said, accepting the coffee she slid across her marble counter top.

'Everything else?' Penny said pausing half way through loading the next coffee pod. '*Everything* else? No, *cariño*. You went from asking the head for help to hiring a *pilot*, buying ice creams for an entire senior school, and llamas in suburbia. There were a lot of trips to Hamley's, sleepovers in the Natural History museum, order-pizza-and-let-her-buy-a-movie-on-iTunes you skipped over.' She dropped the pod and slammed the lid.

'Trish said I needed to find Hannah joy and connection. But I couldn't. How can you find it if it's not there? It needs to be *created*. So I did. And she smiled.' I shrugged. 'And it was an alpaca.'

Penny scowled. 'Did it cost much?'

'Some.'

'Fine,' she said, stirring mounds of sugar into her coffee. 'I get your theory of creating your own joy and all that, very admirable and proactive you should probably become a life-hacking influencer blah-de-blah, but maybe you create the next "joy and connection" without, you know, shutting down an entire street for an afternoon and learning the flight zones of a school field?!' She gave me a pointed glare as she moved to my side of the kitchen counter and settled on a stool. 'So, moving on to something *not* crazy, I asked Rog what he would recommend to someone who'd had a windfall. He was a bit suspicious, but I said I'd read an article and he seemed okay, although weirded out I was interested in his work after all these years. Ay, once he starts talking about investing he can go on for hours! I can't understand what he finds so fascinating about base rates and whatever but anyway, each to their own.' She reached for a packet of biscuits even though it was only 9:15am. 'Anyway, Rog said you need to . . . hang on, I had to make notes on my phone, so I didn't forget this crap. You know, you really do owe me for this, it was *so* boring.' She navigated her phone with one hand and grabbed a biscuit with the other. 'Okay, so you need to . . .' And while Penny said words like 'equity', 'investment', 'returns' and 'hedge funds' my mind wandered.

After I'd dropped Trish to the station the rest of the weekend had progressed as it usually did. By which I mean, chaotically and full of animals.

We'd baked a cake and sung happy birthday to a miniature donkey named Pablo, Mum then realised we'd forgotten Clint's so we'd put a party hat on him too and sung it all again, and Sasha had brought an African Grey Parrot with an injured wing home from work. Mum had called her old boss and given him an earful, then backtracked immediately when he said he'd find Leo another foster home. Tom had quickly discovered that Leo had a wide and colourful vocabulary and took every opportunity to incite it. Martin had Facetimed us from an island in the Philippines, a realtor turned up (apparently off the cuff) with a little portfolio of cottages in the area that could be good for a parent and child and close to the college. Crumpet had gotten loose in the early hours of Sunday morning and was found in the orchard having chewed a yurt rope making the canvas collapse on a sleeping couple from York. Penny kept calling at inconvenient times wanting to ask about the Sports Day #NoReason stuff and I'd call her back when she was unable to talk because she was at Rosa's ballet recital garnering slitty-eyed evils from the thrice-decade starved ballet teacher, or at Lorenzo's jiu-jitsu tournament, or Elise's lacrosse. And over Sunday lunch Sasha had found out she was named after a Serbian gymnast Dad had been particularly enamoured with in the 80s and Mum had got in a huff.

'Oh love, we all know you named Martin after Martin Sheen,' Dad had soothed and Mum had blushed deeply then served us a radish, egg and curried lamb pie.

And all the while Hannah and I struggled to discuss more ripple effect ideas without Mum appearing from every direction like an overly suspicious meerkat.

'Maybe we could . . .' Hannah would whisper and Mum would pop up from behind a tomato plant.

She'd narrow her eyes. 'What are you whispering about?'

'Nothing,' we'd chorus, plastering on wide grins.

'I think we should . . .' I'd begin and Mum's head would nip through the yurt flaps.

'What if we . . .' Hannah would attempt and Mum would stalk past with Clint, the vacuum cleaner, and a mistrustful frown.

On the train on the way home Hannah had fallen asleep with her head in my lap and I'd watched Sussex fly past the window thinking about the simple act of making strangers smile with a flutter of excitement beneath my ribcage.

Penny reached the end of her notes, and the biscuits, and looked up, waiting for my response.

'Hmm,' I said, nodding. 'Lots of options.'

Penny lowered both her phone and her brow. 'You're not going to do any of it, are you?'

I made an apologetic face.

Penny's mouth dropped open. 'But I endured two hours of finance talk! He got out spreadsheets! He's put a pile of equity management publications next to my side of the bed! *And* folded down pages he thinks I'd like. He's booked me in to watch a webinar. On *Friday night*! It's three hours long. Not including intermission! What are you going to do? More crazy person llama stuff?!'

'Mum won't let me help her with the house, Trish won't let me donate to her organisation, something to do with being eligible for funding, and you refuse all my gifts. What else am I supposed to do?' I shrugged. 'And it was an alpaca.'

*

'Here,' I said, dumping a cap on Hannah's head after school that afternoon then pulling my own down low.

We were on sunny Clapham High street happily unnoticed by the passing public.

'What are these for?' Hannah said, adjusting hers.

'Security cameras,' I said, jerking my head in an upwards motion, and because Hannah loved a good crime show she nodded knowingly, pulled her cap even lower, and followed me into the bookstore.

'Put one in any book you like,' I whispered while walking down a quiet row.

'Not ones on how to make a bomb or kill anyone,' Hannah whispered, trailing behind me and scanning the titles.

'No, Miss Macabre, not ones on weapons and murder. But I very much doubt they stock books on how to kill people.'

'Oh yeah?' Hannah held up a book titled *How To Kill Friends and Implicate People*.

I laughed as I wove through the book stands.

It was one of Hannah's ideas. People love books. People would like a free book even more. We'd bought some colourful envelopes in the village over the weekend and while Hannah was at school I'd stuffed each envelope with a £20 note and a printed message that said:

Hello Wonderful Person We Don't Know,
    We'd like to treat you to a book today. Have a great day!
    #NoReason

We spent fifteen giggly minutes slipping envelopes inside any book that took our fancy then met in an aisle, did a clandestine high-five and made for the exit. As we neared the doors a woman in her fifties picked up a book from a table and Hannah tugged me behind a bookstand.

'I put an envelope in that one!' she whispered.

We peeked around the stand watching the woman read the blurb then turn it over and open it. Hannah let out a tiny gasp as a coloured envelope dropped to the ground.

'Shhh,' I said, grinning at my overexcited daughter with her cute ears poking out each side of her oversized cap.

The woman picked it up, frowned, scanned the store, then opened it. Hannah and I clutched hands as she read the note. When she pulled out the £20 note her hand went to her chest and she scanned the shop again with a furrow in her brow.

We waited, still clutching each other.

The woman looked back at the note, at the £20, around the store again, then broke into a smile and trotted to the counter. Hannah and I hustled out of the store in fits of supressed giggles.

The next afternoon I picked her up from school and we sat on a sunny bench near London Bridge and watched passers-by enjoying free ice creams. The same bearded man in a #NoReason T-shirt from the Sports Day proudly handed his ice-cream creations out of his truck's serving hatch to thrilled customers. The day after that we watched strangers lining up for free tacos from a taco truck in Southbank, and the next we loitered on the street and watched cupcakes decorated as puppies and kittens get delivered to the volunteers at Battersea Dogs and Cats Home.

We'd set up a #NoReason nerve centre at the kitchen table with a white board and multicoloured post-its, and dinnertime became lively brainstorming sessions. At school Hannah was still being excluded and ignored. Livie had achieved her goal; Hannah had no friends and Livie was queen bee, not that she'd ever needed to knock Hannah off that status to achieve it. Each afternoon Hannah would exit the school gates with her gaze on the footpath, acutely aware of the playdates being organized and the knots of children jumping into other kids cars. But as soon as she was watching strangers enjoying our secret acts with her cap down low, she was smiling.

★

The day her braces were to be fitted, Hannah was obstructive in getting out of the house. She didn't feel like the eggs I'd made for breakfast so remade herself some toast. She sloped off to the shower but fifteen minutes later I found her thrashing 'Offspring' on her electric drums. She couldn't find her favourite T-shirt then when it was located in the dirty washing pile decided for the first time in her life that she wanted to learn how to hand-wash.

'Hannah, sweetheart, I know what you're doing,' I said, while she sprawled miserably on the floor of the hall complaining that none of her shoes fitted.

'Why are we rushing?' Hannah puffed beside me as we hurried towards the Victoria Line after I'd eventually got her out the front door.

'Because we're late,' I said.

'Why'd you let *that* one go?' Hannah said, watching the third Tube that had come screeching into the station barrel out without us on it.

'Because we're early.'

Hannah fixed me with a peeved glower which I tried not to giggle at.

A blast of dusty air let us know the next train was approaching. As it rattled in I clocked a yellow teddy bear in the window of the driver's compartment. The train came to a stop with a set of double doors directly in front of us. Through the oblong windows I spotted a man and a woman holding on to a pole, him with a yellow cord wound through his dreads and her in a yellow vest. Both had ukuleles strapped across their backs.

'*This* one okay for you?' Hannah said through heavy eyelids.

'Yes, this one seems great,' I said, offsetting her caustic tone with an overly chipper one.

Hannah shook her head and stomped into the half-filled carriage, muttering about me 'losing it in my old age'.

I removed my denim jacket, exposing my yellow T-shirt, and a thrill rushed through me as the man with the dreads noticed, gave a tiny nod, then winked at two people in seats opposite him. They got up as we approached and I guided Hannah towards their vacated seats. Hannah slumped in hers, tugged her phone from her satchel and set about locating her headphones.

The doors clattered shut, the train lurched forward, and, unnoticed by Hannah who was scowling at her playlist, the guy with the dreads and the woman in the yellow vest swung their ukuleles from their backs to their fronts and strummed the first chords to The Travelling Wilburys 'End of The Line'. Hannah looked up as did a handful of other passengers in that way Londoners on the Tube do; boredom tinged with vague wariness. Movement opposite us caught Hannah's eye and her mouth dropped as every person on the seats opposite us produced bongos or ukuleles, castanets or tambourines from their bags and joined in.

'*Well, it's all right, riding around in the breeze,*' a voice sang and everyone spun in the direction it was coming from. A young man walked the length of the carriage towards us, peeling off his jacket to reveal a sherbet green #NoReason T-shirt as he sang.

Hannah gasped and clapped a hand over her mouth.

As the singer reached the end of the first verse people who looked like regular commuters scattered through the carriage removed jackets, or turned away from facing doors to reveal #NoReason T-shirts and sang the second verse.

'Oh my God!' Hannah squealed, turning to me, and I grinned.

The energy in the carriage crackled. People tugged earphones from their ears or filmed with their phones. A father jiggled his daughter on his knee in time to the beat and she watched the musicians, her youthful cheeks bouncing in her unconvinced face. Faces from the adjoining carriages appeared in the end windows as the singers moved through the carriage handing out multicoloured envelopes. Hannah and I received ours from a guy with multiple earrings in one ear, a tiny star tattoo under his left eye, and a mischievous grin. A student of Trish's.

'Thank you!' Hannah said, her eyes alight. She flashed me a grin then tore open her hot pink envelope.

With a bubbling sense of accomplishment, I watched passengers receive their envelopes and glance at people sitting next to them before tearing them open. I opened mine and pulled out a gift card to a café called 'Ozone' and a bright orange notecard:

> *Hello, stranger!*
> *This voucher is for you and a friend to enjoy a drink or snack on us. It's a café we love. Try the cinnamon buns – they're amazing! Also, a donation to the National Animal Welfare Trust has been made in your honour. We hope you have a great day.*
> *Love #NoReason.*

Beaming, Hannah showed me hers. It was exactly the same, except her donation was to the Gingerbread Solo Parent Charity and her gift card was for free drumsticks from an independent drum store in Lavender Hill.

'What a surprise!' I said and Hannah dissolved into giggles.

As we pulled into Pimlico, passengers waiting on the platform hesitated, but the singers beckoned them in. Curious smiles spread across faces as new passengers received envelopes and Hannah and I delighted in watching them leave their detached state and connect with their fellow passengers.

I was buzzing.

When the doors opened to the busy platform at Victoria the expressions were, again, hesitant and wary. But one guy leapt into the carriage and launched into an animated dance and a cheer erupted. Two young women with rucksacks on their back joined him. Hannah laughed and clapped along and I joined her, my cheeks aching from smiling so wide. When the train pulled into Oxford Street station the singers and musicians moved towards the doors. They took a bow and the last note of the song was drowned out by applause. The doors opened, the performers alighted the train and dispersed throughout the crowded station and, apart from passengers clutching coloured envelopes and smiling, the Tube was quiet again and it was like it had never happened.

Unable to ask me anything among the crowd Hannah raced up the escalators, through turnstiles and we emerged on to sunny Oxford Circus.

'Mum, that was . . .' she said then stopped as a man in rainbow shorts held up by glitter braces held out a yellow daffodil. 'Thank you,' she said guardedly.

'You're welcome!' The man curtsied and Hannah clocked his #NoReason shirt and giggles overtook her again.

I waited, itching for her to notice that Oxford Circus was littered with people in vibrant outfits and #NoReason T-shirts handing out flowers and more coloured envelopes. When she did her mouth formed a perfect 'O' and I laughed out loud.

'Come on,' I said pointing down Upper Regent's Street, which had had the chalk drawing treatment.

'Oh my God!' Hannah raced from one chalk drawing to the next, taking photos and beaming at other passers-by appreciating the bright and wacky illustrations of unicorns and witches, planets and animals. More people (Trish's students and their friends) in #NoReason shirts and vivacious clothing handed out envelopes to members of the public whose expressions would switch from wariness to delight once they'd ripped them open.

'Let's go this way,' I said, guiding Hannah away from a drawing of a llama as a barista. 'I have a feeling it could be interesting . . .'

'*Mum!*' Hannah laughed. 'You're crazy!'

As we turned the corner classical music became faintly audible. Hannah raced along the footpath until Cavendish Square Gardens came into view, then wove through foot traffic, around the circular walled garden and stopped among an amassed crowd.

Twelve ballet dancers – the men in dove-grey tights and tight vests, the women in white tutus and sparkling tiaras – faced a twelve-strong motley crew of Trish's students in multicoloured tights and rainbow tutus, Wu-Tang Clan and

NWA T-shirts, and beat-up Timberlands or sneakers. Tchaikovsky's *Trepak (Russian Dance)* from *The Nutcracker* played from large speakers and the ballet dancers performed quick-as-a-wink pirouettes, arabesques and grand jetés around the gardens. They landed in 1st position and gracefully gestured that it was the motley crew's turn.

The inelegant bounds, off-centre whirls and cumbersome leg hoists had the gathered crowd in hysterics. Laughing, Hannah filmed it on her phone. The classical music scratched to a halt and Young MC's 'Bust A Move' blared across the green. The crew instantly fell into a slick hip-hop routine while the ballet dancers watched; their feet in vees and their postures impeccable. The crew landed in a co-ordinated knot, their arms outstretched in a challenge and the crowd cracked up at the petite ballerinas crumping, twerking and nae nae-ing in their tutus. Hannah beamed at me.

After a few minutes we shuffled back, making room for new bystanders to watch, and headed in the direction of Dennis's surgery.

We turned on to Harley Street, the music became a distant hum, and Hannah spun to face me. *'Mum!'*

I grinned then dropped it and affected innocence. 'What?'

She erupted into giggles.

*

Hannah bounded up the stairs, her phone in her hand, ready to show Bev everything, but when we arrived Bev was trapped behind her desk with a skinny man in an IT branded polo shirt, both of them frowning at his laptop. Beneath them were the burly legs of another man and a mass of electrical cords.

Dennis stood nearby, awkwardly countering Bev's answers as to what systems were used for what. It all seemed a bit fraught, so Hannah pocketed her phone.

'Oh, hello,' Dennis said with a smile, stepping away from the reception desk and tripping on the legs of the burly IT man.

Bev waved from where she was hemmed in.

'I'm sorry about this,' Dennis said, righting himself. 'Our entire online system has, well . . . disappeared, it seems. But I'm sure these wonderful gentlemen will be able to locate it. Shall we go in?' he said, doing an exaggerated step over the IT man to retrieve a file from behind the desk and another one back again.

Dennis closed the door of his surgery behind us. 'I have something for you,' he said, crossing the room and opening a cupboard. He placed a single, well-used stick in Hannah's hand. 'Rick Allen's drumstick. Just the one because, well, that's all he uses being one-armed. My client dropped it off for you last week.'

Hannah stared wordlessly at the drumstick in her hand and Dennis glanced apprehensively in my direction.

'Hannah is short circuiting right now,' I explained, grinning at my daughter. 'But I can tell you that she is very, *very*—'

Hannah launched herself at Dennis and wrapped her arms around his waist.

'Happy,' I finished, swallowing down a lump of emotion. 'Thank you,' I said and Dennis blushed deeply.

★

Fitting the braces took just over an hour. Dennis was focused and methodical, yet still friendly and chatty. He played Hannah's recently curated playlist through a speaker on his desk, asking who each and every band was. Even Queen. At the painful parts he distracted her with Rick Allen trivia he had garnered from his client especially for her and his assistant and I exchanged looks of appreciation for his kindness. Hannah had chosen metal braces over clear ones and once they were fitted Dennis gave Hannah detailed instructions on how to clean her teeth while she listened, the knitting of her brows revealing she was in a bit of pain. Her fingers fidgeted with the hem of her shorts as Dennis listed the foods she'd best to avoid if she didn't want a brace to fall off, while his assistant put together a package of special toothbrushes and toothpaste.

'How does it feel?' he asked.

'Bit sore.'

Dennis nodded. 'Eat soft foods for a couple of days. Yoghurt. Boiled vegetables.'

Hannah nodded grimly.

'Custard?' Dennis said.

Hannah gave a weak smile. She didn't speak as we made to leave the room. She appeared to not know how to hold her lips. Dennis opened his surgery door and ushered us out to reception where Bev was still surrounded by wires, men and frowns, looking mighty unimpressed at Dennis's 'girlfriend' standing in the middle of the room on the phone.

The next patient, a man in his late fifties, was in a chair, with a fishing magazine.

'The shoot I did is out,' the girlfriend said, getting off the phone as soon as she saw Dennis.

She didn't acknowledge either Hannah or me. Her jeans were so tight she looked like she'd used that vacuum sucker thing you use to suck the air out of bags you store your off-season clothing in and she held a weekly magazine to her pert chest.

Dennis blinked. 'Oh, good,' he said as Hannah and I tried to reach the reception desk amid IT legs and wires.

'Not really,' she said.

'Oh,' Dennis paused. 'That's a shame.' He acknowledged the waiting patient with a head bob then tried to guide Sienna towards the exit.

'Look,' she said, not moving. 'We explicitly told the photographer to shoot me from the right. That's my best side. And all these shots are from the left.' She huffed, then commenced a thorough analysis about her best angles, her laugh face, her listening face and the way her hair fell. 'The photographer definitely favoured me on the day but the editor obviously chose pictures that have more of the male star. *So* misogynistic. Haven't they heard of #metoo?'

'Wonderful!' Dennis said.

'*What?*'

Dennis looked up from the magazine. 'Er, what?'

'*What's* wonderful?' Sienna said, her eyes narrowed.

'Oh!' He broke into a smile. 'This.' He pointed at the opposite page. 'No Reason. It's brilliant!'

Hannah and I looked at each other, stunned.

'Look!' Dennis said, sliding the magazine from the young woman's talons and striding towards Hannah and me.

Bev navigated the IT bungle and trotted around the desk to join us.

Dennis held the magazine out for us all to see and opposite the quarter-page piece on his 'girlfriend' and her male 'star', who I definitely didn't recognize, was a full page piece on the phenomena popping up around London that was #NoReason.

Hannah shot me a wide-eyed stare then we both inched closer. The first photo was of a woman in the process of giving blood holding up a brightly decorated cupcake and a pink notecard.

'Cupcakes and vouchers turned up for people volunteering at Citizen's Advice as well,' Dennis said pointing to the next photo.

'Isn't that just precious!' Bev said, tapping a glossy ruby nail to a photo of a young woman holding a woeful-eyed puppy.

The caption beneath read *Jess, a volunteer from an animal shelter, said the cupcake and voucher for a movie for two had made her feel like people cared about volunteers.*

Photos of food trucks and grinning customers holding up their free culinary treats, a post taken from Instagram of someone with the book they bought with their found £20, and people cashing in their vouchers for a 'free coffees for you and a friend' covered the glossy page. All the things Hannah and I had been doing in the afternoons, there *in a magazine*! I couldn't believe it. It was surreal!

'Nobody knows who it is,' Dennis said, his voice full of awe. 'Or *what* it is, but it's wonderful!'

Hannah and I exchanged tiny grins.

'I got an envelope on the way here,' said the male patient who I hadn't noticed joining us.

'Really?' Dennis said, fascinated.

'There was one on the Tube today!' Hannah said, digging out her phone. 'And on the streets on the way here!'

'Why didn't you say?' Dennis said, passing the magazine back to Sienna without looking at her and bending to look at Hannah's phone.

The two IT men joined us and the six of us huddled together and watched over Hannah's shoulder as she pressed play on a video of the singalong on the Tube.

'Oh my!' Bev said when the video ended. 'That looks like such fun! My grandson sent me a link to one in Earlsfield. I think I still have it.' And while she went to her desk I was suddenly struck that this was an actual thing. That Hannah, Trish and I, at home in our pyjamas, were making people we didn't know smile. And an article had been written about it. It was frightening and thrilling in equal measures.

'We saw that one, too!' Hannah said excitedly.

'You were at both?' Dennis said, looking from Hannah to me.

'Ye-es,' I said, sharing a worried look with Hannah while scrabbling for a believable reason why that unlikely coincidence could have happened. 'We ah . . . we—'

'You're so lucky!' he said and I exhaled.

'Here we go,' Bev said, passing Dennis's girlfriend by the main door looking outraged that no one was paying her article any attention. She tapped at the screen, far more proficient with it than she was with the booking system, then angled it so we could all see a video of the street carnival. 'Isn't it wonderful?' she said when it finished.

'It's amazing,' Dennis said, looking towards Sienna and giving a little start when he saw she'd left.

'It makes me feel all warm and fuzzy, like,' said the burly IT guy.

Hannah looked up at me from the centre of the cluster of entranced adults and grinned a completely metal-filled mouth.

★

The next afternoon she came home from school and dumped her school bag on a chair at the kitchen table where I was on my laptop. I looked up questioningly.

'Yep, Livie had something to say about the braces,' she said as she clocked my expectant expression. She dug out her laptop, drink bottle and other bits and pieces that needed putting away and were part of her afterschool routine.

'And?' I prompted.

'She called me metal mouth and said my favourite music must now be heavy metal.'

'What did you do?' I said, shards of unease twisting their way into my stomach.

'Ignored her. She's a dick. And heavy metal is great.'

The unease disbanded and was replaced by a fizz of happiness so real it buzzed all the way to my fingertips.

Chapter 18

The next day I stood on the footpath opposite the school gates with Penny, watching a handful of journalists approaching parents, Julian P Tickle among them.

'Do you know anyone at the school with the means to orchestrate something of this magnitude?' said a woman with her phone held out like a recording device towards Melody.

Penny spun her head my way. Behind her polished Versaces I knew she'd be giving me a reprimanding stare.

'What?' I said casually as I turned towards home. 'It's fine. She doesn't know the meaning of the word "orchestrate" anyway.'

★

Hannah and I arrived in Sussex on the Friday evening and the family gathered round, commenting on the new braces.

'Nice colour choices,' said Sasha, flying out the door.

'You look marvellous,' said Dad, giving her a cuddle.

'Tom Cruise had braces,' said Mum with a flush creeping up her neck.

And Hannah's bubbly mood was noticed by all. Mum thought it was the orthodontist sorting out her teeth. Tom thought it was because the All Blacks had recently won against the Irish. Sasha put it down to Hannah not yet experiencing the traum of striving in a world that wanted you to fail at every turn. An Dad thought perhaps his convoluted oration on bullying across various species explained via the hierarchical system of social dominance in female lemurs was the cause. Only I had the private thrill of knowing the real reason.

'Would you like to come to the pub quiz tonight?' Gus asked when he arrived for Hannah's lesson on Saturday morning, his guitar case over his shoulder and his freshly showered hair wafting a sea-spray-ish type scent around the front entrance.

'Oh I can't. I have to teach an African parrot to say *Hello* instead of *Hello shithead.*'

'Right,' he said with a smile. 'Next time, maybe.'

The Smashing Pumpkins' 'Bullet With Butterfly Wings' reverberated around the house while Inga taught Dad how to make her 'better German bread', and Crumpet decided that if Clint were allowed inside he should be too. Sasha emerged from the wrong side of the bed and, upon seeing an alpaca and a pony in the kitchen where her father was proving dough with an African parrot on his shoulder, declared her lack of boyfriend to be the fault of living in a madhouse and the whole village called us a zoo, and Mum got on the phone to her Pétanque friends to see if that were in fact the case. And seemed chuffed to discover it was.

And Dad made me talk about my vagina in front of Gus again.

'A university student has made vagina yoghurt,' Dad said from his iPad, Leo the parrot still on his shoulder, while his baking bread filled the kitchen with a comforting aroma.

'Ew,' scowled Sasha.

'Spike!' scolded Mum.

'How?' queried Inga.

'*Why?*' said I.

'It says here in this article,' said Dad, 'that she made it using the bacteria from her own vagina.'

'*There's* a great business idea for you,' I said to Sasha, who'd transitioned from lamenting her lack of boyfriend to the lack of career prospects for her generation.

'It's disgusting,' she sneered.

'It's *indecent*,' spat Mum.

'It's entrepreneurial,' said Dad.

'It is organic,' Inga offered.

'And,' I said, 'you've already got all the start-up costs.' I pointed to my vagina just as Gus arrived in the doorway to say goodbye. Which he did hastily and left.

I turned back to the family. 'He's going to quit soon, isn't he?'

'Well,' Mum had huffed, looking alarmed that Gus's handsomeness may cease darkening her hallway, 'Perhaps you should stop talking about your . . . zone.'

'Dad brought it up.'

'Not your vagina specifically,' said Dad, rocking on his plimsoles. 'Just vaginas in general.'

At dinner that evening Inga told us about her life. Non-stop. She ate more than one side of the table put together. Mum looked on aghast, while Dad, Hannah, Tom and I were anthropologically enthralled.

'How does that girl put away so much food?!' Mum whispered. 'She must be at least thirty per cent potato.'

After dinner, we dropped Tom back to the boarding house and everyone convened in the living room, Inga with a giant mug of soup and a wedge of her bread. Mum walked in with a tray of delicate biscuits.

Inga leaned across and took four. 'The news programme,' she stated, through her biscuity mouthful. 'We watch the news programme.'

Dad obligingly turned up the volume and we listened to political updates, royal updates, and climate updates, while Mum gave Leo, who sat on her lap like the cat he wasn't, looks of adoration, and Cookie watched from the floor, her eyes in resentful slits, and Hannah and I played Uno. The news reached the part where light-hearted stories come on and I stretched for the remote but as a reporter came on the screen something behind her looked familiar and I stopped.

'In a world where royal scandals and dirty politics, celebrities behaving badly and the climate crisis dominate our news feeds it can be all too easy to forget that life can, and should, be joyful. Perhaps Britain is tired of being in a bad mood but a series of seemingly random acts have captured the public's attention. It's called No Reason and it seems to have originated in the form of a mini street party here in Earlsfield.'

Hannah was instantly alert. Mum squinted at the TV. Riveted, I kept my expression neutral as the reporter walked the length of Tranmere Road and listed the events of Hannah's Sports Day while videos of the dancers and the street party played in the corner of the screen.

'Envelopes in bookshops, singalongs on the Tube, cupcakes and notes that simply say "Thank you" at blood donation centres.'

The shot of the reporter on the street was replaced with images from social media of #NoReason envelopes, swirly ice creams, the students in colourful #NoReason T-shirts handing out flowers, the ballet dancers, the alpaca and the owl from the street party, and the singers on the Tube.

I could hardly believe what I was watching. A magazine was one thing but this was *the news*! I glanced at Hannah but she was glued to the TV.

While the reporter's voice continued to list events and their locations, Inga dug her phone out of her cleavage making Mum do a revolted double-take.

'I have been following the hashtags,' she said. 'It is nice. The world needs positivity. Not the negativity of now.'

'Shhh,' said Hannah and we all looked at her.

'On Oxford Street people in extravagant outfits gave out

envelopes containing vouchers for independent businesses and donations to various charities. We contacted some of these charitable organisations but the donations have all been anonymous. This owner of a popular café in Camberwell loves the movement."

A man came on the screen standing on the footpath outside his café.

'I got a phone call from someone saying they represented the #NoReason team. Yeah, I'd heard of them. They explained what they were doing and an hour later the money was in our account and the next day someone came in to pick up the gift cards. The people who received them haven't been in yet but when they do they'll be greeted with excitement by our staff. We can't wait to see you!'

The image then flicked to a guy from one of the ice-cream trucks.

'We got told it was to spread a little joy. Well, that's what ice cream is all about, innit? So of course we said yes! We could all do with a bit more of that. That's why I'm in the ice-cream business!'

Off camera the journalist asked, 'How does it feel to be a part of it?'

The guy grinned. 'Wicked.'

The news reporter came back on with the Tranmere Road sign behind her.

'Tranmere Road . . .' mused Mum as she stroked Leo's feathers. 'Isn't that near you?'

Dad's astute eyes flicked my way over the leather-bound tome in his lap.

'It's a few streets away,' I mumbled.

'Maybe these acts of joy and acknowledgement for the little things ordinary people do is just what the public needs. Perhaps these seemingly random deeds are something to give us hope in an unpredictable world. Who is behind it? We don't know.

Why is this happening? We don't know that either. But maybe the answer is right here in front of us.'

The screen filled with a close-up of a pink T-shirt, the white #NoReason lettering filling the screen, then flicked back to the smiling reporter.

'What we do know is that it seems to be giving people a much-needed sense of fun.'

The reporter stopped at the gates to Hannah's school. She smiled at the screen then the anchors came back on thanking her and I turned the volume down. In the resulting silence I glanced around the room. Hannah was wide-eyed, Dad's gaze twinkled at me over the top of his book, Inga was finishing off the last seven biscuits and scrolling on her phone, and Mum was scratching Leo's feathery neck and frowning to herself, seemingly on the edge of figuring something out. She glanced up at me, her mouth open and her brow furrowed.

'Tea?' I said, standing, and quickly left the room.

Chapter 19

'I know how to follow your twitters!' Mum shrilled down the phone first thing Monday morning. 'It's you, isn't it?!'

'I don't have "twitters", Mum, what are you talking about?'

I flicked my phone to speaker and put it on the kitchen bench so I could continue filling the dishwasher. Hannah listened as she packed her school bag at the dining table.

'Inga showed me! On the Twitters! It's you! I know it's you! At the school! And the bookstores! And *on the Tube*! I know what you've been up to! WHAT ON *EARTH* HAVE YOU DONE, YOUNG LADY? It's a mania! You've caught a mania! And you don't even have a working car! I don't know why you insist on . . . I mean *really*! It's you, isn't it? Admit it!'

Hannah and I shared a glance.

'It's me, Mum.'

'*WHAT*? Oh my God! I can't believe it! I can NOT believe it! This is ridiculous. You've always had to be so grand with everything – all those dramatics as a teen! Why can't you behave like a normal person? It's madness! What *on earth* were you . . . You just wait till I tell you father! It's utter madness and I forbid it. I forbid it! I can't understand why you would . . . I absolutely for*bid* it!' She hung up and Hannah and I looked at each other for another moment before bursting out laughing.

Half an hour later, when Hannah had been dropped to school and I was walking Cookie, Mum rang again.

'Hello, Mother,' I answered.

Her unnervingly casual voice came down the line. 'I'm coming to London tomorrow to see the accountants. Will you meet me for lunch?'

'It depends.'

'On what?'

'If you're going to yell.'

Mum huffed and puffed and said she'd never yelled a day in her life.

*

The next day I trotted down Great Portland Street, navigating city workers on their lunchbreak, while Mum kept checking the time and rushing ahead. I was in a good mood despite being called into the head teacher's office the afternoon before to be told, in a severe voice I'd taken instant offence to, that Hannah had used an 'inappropriate conflict resolution' that day.

'What did she do?' I'd said from a chair lower than Ms Galloway's, a Freudian tactic if ever I saw one.

'She used a certain curse word towards another student.'

'Right. Do you know why?'

'The reason why is not the issue. We encourage our children to resolve conflict with constructive words and actions.'

'What was the conflict?'

'I believe it was a misreading of another student's words.'

A mis-fucking-reading. Yeah *right*. 'She told Livie to fuck off, didn't she?'

Ms Galloway had stiffened in her seat, then nodded.

'About time.' I'd gathered my bag and stood. 'Is that all?'

Ms Galloway had also stood. 'We won't allow that kind of language in our school, Mrs Paige. If it happens again—'

'Do you have proof, Ms Galloway? Date and time logged and with witnesses?'

Ms Galloway had kept her gaze level but said nothing.

'I'll let myself out.'

*

'What's the rush?' I said now, jogging to catch up with Mum. I'd been momentarily distracted by a busker, and she'd sped a few yards ahead. It dawned on me that I was noticing all sorts of lovely, London life details – things I hadn't noticed in a long time. Ooh! Like that shop over there with the pretty flower display in the window and that—

I crashed into the back of my mother, who'd come to an abrupt stop outside a très trendy restaurant. 'Oof, sorry!' I looked up and down the street. 'This is nowhere near your accountant's?'

'I've been recommended this place,' Mum said tugging open an oak and decorative-iron door.

What was she talking about?! Mum knew no one in London who would recommend such a place. We stepped inside, and the noise of the street was replaced by the tinkle of ice against glass, delicate fork against oversized plate as it scooped partridge and artichoke confit, and the kind of carefree chatter that comes from people who have a lifestyle where they attend unhurried lunches on a Tuesday in an oak-floored, leather-chaired restaurant in Marylebone. While wearing fedoras.

'Wow, this place is *nice*.' I stood next to a brass-framed 'Wait here to be seated' sign and scanned the restaurant, noting an ornately tiled pillar holding up the double-height ceiling, a beaten copper bar, and waiters in full-length black aprons tending to the clientele; a mixture of business people and fashionable (see fedoras) others.

A maître d' approached us. 'Good afternoon,' he said in an Eton accent. 'Table for two?'

I pointed to a table in the sun. 'Yes please, could we have—'

Mum strode across the room in the opposite direction.

'Where's she going?' I said.

The maître d' shrugged.

We watched as Mum approached a man sitting alone at a table with his coffee and a couscous salad, and pulled out a seat.

'She's gone mad,' I said. I left the maître d' and when I reached the table the man and Mum were chatting. 'Oh, you know each other.'

'Yes,' Mum said. 'This is Brooke.'

'James.' He smiled warmly and put his hand out then gestured to a spare chair, which I pulled out and sat in. Once I was settled James smiled. 'So, how can I help you?' he said. It appeared he was saying it to me.

'Eh?' I said.

'Well,' Mum wriggled in her seat. 'It's just . . .' She glanced at me, then back to James. 'Brooke has been acting strangely and—'

'Eh?' I said.

'Love,' she said, facing me, 'this is Peter-from-Pétanque's son-in-law. He's agreed to chat to you.'

Peter from Pétanque. . . I rifled through the mountains of gossip Mum regurgitated at nearly all her waking moments. Oh. I turned to James. 'You're a psychiatrist?'

James nodded.

I spun back to Mum, my cheery mood from earlier instantly absconded. 'You tricked me into a psychiatry appointment?!'

'Now, don't say "trick", it's not entirely—'

I stopped her with my most furious glare then turned back to James. 'I'm so sorry, I didn't know anything about this. It appears you've been brought here under false pretences. As have I. It was very nice to meet you but I don't need to see a psychiatrist and I'm sorry that *my mother*,' I glared at her and she recoiled, 'has wasted your time . . .' I stood, 'but I'm leaving.'

I heard Mum's chair scrape back as I stalked away from the table. 'Just one moment,' I heard her say. 'We'll be right back.'

'No, we won't!' I said over my shoulder as I wove through tables towards the door. Mum caught up with me at the 'wait to be seated' sign. 'Brooke, please!'

'I cannot *believe* you,' I said as I waited for a slow-as-tectonic-plate-movement couple to enter the restaurant and clear the doorway.

'Please talk to him!' Mum said, stepping in front of me as I made to leave. 'You have to! Peter said his son-in-law was very busy and he's really pulled in some favours to get him to meet us and it would be *so embarrassing . . .*'

'It already *IS* so embarrassing!' I hissed. 'I can't believe you did this!' I sidestepped Mum but she sidestepped me right back.

'You have to talk to him! Peter is picking teams for the upcoming championship and we're hoping he'll pick us. If he finds out we've wasted his son-in-law's time we'll be off the list for sure!'

'What *are* you talking about?'

'Pétanque,' Mum said as if it were plainly obvious. 'James's father-in-law picks the teams and if he finds out we requested an appointment with his daughter's husband then abandoned him in a restaurant, your father and I might not get picked!'

'You know,' I said narrowing my eyes, '*you* could do with talking to a psychiatrist.'

'Oh love, please say you'll talk to him? Please? I just want to make sure you know what you're doing.'

'I *do* know what I'm doing!'

'But I don't think you do!' Mum implored. She stepped closer and lowered her voice. 'Throwing away all that money on street parties and free ice creams for the whole of London?! When you have a future to plan for? It's madness! And what for? To cheer Hannah up? Why can't you cheer her up like normal person with a nice day out and a new dress? It's crazy. Utterly crazy! And crazy people don't *know* they're crazy – that's why it's called crazy!'

'Mum stop saying crazy – people are looking.'

'LET THEM LOOK!' Mum shrieked.

'Christ, Mum, calm yourself!' I said through gritted teeth. I watched as she dabbed at the corners of her mouth with her kerchief.

'You seem intent on wasting it and being reckless, but this money can give you a new life!'

'I don't want a new life,' I said, my voice catching in my throat. 'I want my old one.'

Mum eyed me. 'Stubborn as your father. I don't know why I'm surrounded by Saggitariuses. Nettie *said* I should be with more Pisceans. Oh love, please talk to him? Please? Just to hear another opinion?' Mum's expression was desperate.

I shook my head. '*You're* the mad one here.' I glanced towards James who was standing and looked like he were wondering if he ought to come over and help. Which one of us needed it the most, I don't know. I turned back to my mother. 'I will only do this to prove to you that I'm fine. But you let me speak and you don't interrupt?'

'Yes of course,' Mum said looking ever so relieved. 'But when he finds you're not, you'll get the proper help, won't you?'

'*When?*' Angling towards the exit again.

'If,' Mum said, tugging at my sleeve and looking chastened. 'I meant "if".'

I gave her a 'sure you did' wither, turned and, under the heavy glower from the maître d', we crossed the café towards the confused psychiatrist, pulled out our chairs simultaneously and sat down.

James tentatively took his seat. He looked really quite mortified. As was I. But seeing as I was there, I was damn well going to prove my sanity to my insane mother.

I looked at James. 'Even if I'm unwillingly present here, *as are you*,' I frowned briefly at my mother, who frowned harder back, 'and we're in a restaurant, do patient privacy rules apply?'

'Yes, of course,' James said, looking more comfortable with a topic that made sense to him rather than Mum and I and the weirdness of our being there. 'The Hippocratic Oath of patient confidentiality and respect stands whether you are speaking willingly,' he glanced to my mother who raised her chin, 'or not.'

'Okay, good,' I said.

'Would you prefer to have this conversation alone?' James glanced in my mother's direction.

I gave my mother a look, one she returned with an expression that screamed 'turncoat'.

'She can stay.'

A waiter arrived, Mum and I ordered a coffee each, and when he was gone I turned to bewildered Doctor James and in a lowered voice told him everything. From the moment Chris died on the operating table, to my daughter's torment at the hands of a double-barrelled bitch.

Mum got out her hanky and did some dramatic eye wiping while I pushed on through, the strain in my throat the only indication that it was a painful process. James nodded, his expression empathetic at the difficult moments. I glossed over the details of the wrongful death payout but mentioned that I'd come into some money and that I was choosing to be charitable and have some fun with it.

'With *all* of it,' Mum interjected, leaning over the table, causing James's coffee to slop around in his cup and some of his couscous to rain down from his plate.

I shot her a glower and she shrank back.

'Not *all*,' I said then explained how spending the money doing entertaining things for my daughter and getting her involved in helping others had changed the physical shape of her; her posture, the drawn-down edges of her mouth and eyes, they were gone. And how now, with something else to focus on, it had reminded her that there was still fun to be had in life; that one bully's opinion of her did not need to dictate her self-worth. And I knew that money couldn't fix that fact that my husband and Hannah's father had died. And that money wouldn't stop a girl bullying my daughter. And that, no matter how much I wished there was, there was no online shop where I could buy back my child's self-esteem. And I was aware that I could be buying a bigger home, or a posh car, or investing in cryptocurrency. But by being charitable and fun with the money my daughter's eyes were alive and alert. Like a child's eyes should be. She was smiling again. And that was all I ever wanted.

I sat back and waited.

'Well,' the man said, giving me a smile and a lengthy look of profound compassion before turning to Mum. 'She has grief, of course, it's understandable and perfectly normal, and studies show that parents themselves can suffer anxiety from their child being bullied but . . .' he turned and smiled at me again. 'She doesn't need to see a psychiatrist.'

'What?' Mum spat.

I tried not to look smug. Not very hard though.

Doctor James looked at Mum, seemingly no longer marginally frightened of her. 'Brooke knows exactly what she's doing and, in regards to her windfall, is aware of all her options. It's . . .' he turned to me again, '. . . remarkably admirable, if I'm permitted an opinion.'

I smiled.

'Well,' Mum said, zipping closed her handbag with force. 'I'm rather sorry to say that you are *not* permitted one.' She scraped her chair back and stood. 'Thank you for your time,' she said leaving the unsaid words 'and for wasting ours' hanging heavily in the air, and she spun on her practical heels and stalked a zig-zag through the tables, past the maître d', and out on to the street.

'I'm sorry about all this,' I said to James. 'She thinks *I'm* mad; I think *she's* mad . . .' I smiled, pushed back my chair and stood.

James stood also and reached a hand across the table. 'It was an absolute pleasure to meet you,' he said, his intelligent eyes looking directly into mine.

'And you,' I shook his hand. 'Thank you. And sorry. Again.'

He nodded and I left. When I reached Mum outside I looked back through the giant window. James was still standing, watching Mum and me on the footpath. He gave a wave then took his seat.

'*Absolute* waste of time!' Mum clipped as she strode away from the cafe.

I trotted to catch up and linked my arm through my well-meaning mother's. 'And we still haven't eaten.'

'I wouldn't like anything in that preposterously pompous place anyway,' Mum said. 'Very pleased with itself, it was. Shall we pop by Marks and Sparks and get an egg sandwich?'

Chapter 20

Over the next few weeks a pattern emerged.

Hannah or I would come up with an idea. Trish and her students would execute it. It would be in a newspaper or on social media. Mum would ring to panic/reprimand/question her parenting because Martin was a drifter (she still didn't understand the concept of remote working), I was 'unstable', and everyone was mildly frightened of Sasha.

'How much did *that* cost?!' she'd screeched down the phone when ponies with coloured saddlebags were walked around the South Bank by handlers who'd give out more envelopes with notes and gift cards.

'What is the *matter* with you?' she'd exclaimed when she read about people in #NoReason T-shirts setting up tables in parks around London and playing Scrabble, Connect Four, Backgammon, and Rummikub with the public 'for no reason' other than to take a moment to connect with someone you didn't know during your lunchbreak rather than eating your Pret sandwich alone on a patch of grass.

'What are you scheming?!' she'd yell up to Hannah and me giggling in the tree hut.

'What are you scribbling?' she'd say if she saw me making notes.

'What did I say?!' she'd fret if I became animated while she babbled about the Pétanque club's struggles with the plumbing, or someone in the village who'd had their child's bike stolen.

'You've got a mania!' she shrieked when the news reported that every child at that day's performances of *The Cursed Child* had been given a free wand.

'I don't want any part of it,' she announced after she'd received a call saying the Pétanque clubrooms had been anonymously upgraded and there was to be a cocktail party to celebrate.

'I saw Joan in the village,' I said to her a week later. 'And she said you enjoyed a very *large* part of the cocktails.'

The *Daily Dispatch* was doing a regular column on the #NoReason activity and Julian P Tickle was tenaciously fixated on finding out who was behind it.

Is It A Long-Winded Campaign For Coca Cola? one column was headlined. *Is Banksy Branching Out?* read another. Hannah and I loved the speculations and would fall apart laughing at each wild guess.

When one called the person behind it an activist I thought it was hilarious but Mum had huffed that I wasn't 'active' in an area of life that actually mattered and that comment had stung. But the sting didn't last long because for the first time in nearly two years I had that little bud in my chest; the bud of anticipation. The desire to get up in the morning, that the day might just be okay. Enjoyable, even.

When London woke one Saturday morning to multi-coloured baubles in trees, each eco-friendly carboard one containing a note and gift card, Mum stormed in to my bedroom in Sussex.

'You're incorrigible! Insufferable! You're . . .' She stood at the end of my bed with her hands on her hips. 'You're . . . you're all of the "in" words!'

'Incredible? Insightful? Inventive?' I'd said, propped up on my elbows.

'In . . . fucking believable!' she said and stormed out only to storm right back in. '"UN"! I KNOW IT'S "UN"!' And she stormed out again.

On weekends the family would gather in the den and watch the evening news; Dad with a gleam in his eye, Mum with a sherry, a basket of corn that needed shucking and trepidation, Sasha with her phone and a dearth of interest (and awareness), and Hannah and I fidgety with excitement.

'I don't want to know who's behind #NoReason,' said an older man interviewed on the street. 'It takes the fun out of it.'

'Hell yeah, I wanna know!' said a guy on a bike in a courier uniform.

'There's an excitement about going to work, like, is there going to be a #NoReason on my Tube?' said a young woman in a suit standing next to a young man in a suit, both holding greasy Greggs bags. 'Or like, is our street going to be one that gets free tacos or that chalk art thing. It makes me look forward to going to work each day.'

'Yeah, right,' said the guy with an eyeroll and they both laughed.

It cut back to a reporter on a street busy with colourful #NoReason people. Next to him stood a young woman in a sherbet yellow #NoReason T-shirt and stripy rainbow shorts. 'It's not just the recipients who are loving this new phenomenon,' the reporter said. 'Lola here volunteered to the #NoReason team via Instagram.' He turned and held out his microphone. 'Lola, you didn't meet the people or person actually behind #NoReason, how did you know where to go and what to do?'

Lola bounced on the spot. 'I just sent a DM on Insta asking if I could be part of it and got a reply telling me to wear clothes that made me happy and to turn up here! The other #NoReasoners gave me this shirt and we've been handing out flowers and envelopes all day!' Lola said, still bouncing like an 80s jazzercize video. 'I love it! I'm going to do as many as I can fit in around my job.'

The screen cut to a dour-looking teen, his floppy fringe covering an eye. 'My sister made me come,' he said in a mumbled voice while glaring at Lola. 'I don't like big crowds. Or small ones. Or people.' He glanced at a multicoloured posy in his hands. 'Or flowers.'

A lanky man in a suit strode past at the edge of frame and the teen held out the flowers with a limp wrist. The lanky man looked at the flowers, cracked into a grin, then surprised the teen by wrapping him in a bear hug. The teen looked appalled for a moment then his lips curled into a minuscule smile.

I craned past Sasha, on the sofa scrolling, and gave Mum a triumphant grin. Which she returned with an indignant purse of the lips.

After it had been all over the media that carriages in some Tubes had been filled with jokes and pictures of baby wildlife (Hannah's idea) instead of adverts for nasal spray and car insurance, Mum had tried a calmer approach.

'Lovely idea,' she'd said, forcing a smile as I walked alongside her 4×4 back from the yurt field. 'I like it. Very nice. You've made your point now. Yes you have a lot of money and its very entertaining to go off and have fun with it, and the twitters and grammers all love it, and I can't tell you what to do, but . . . ' then the whole way back to the house she proceeded to tell me what to do.

'Don't you have any opinions on what I should be doing?' I asked Dad another sunny afternoon, having endured a hijacked trip to the village at a serious of open homes Mum just happened to drive past after 'getting lost' in a village she'd lived in for forty seven years. 'Mum certainly does.'

Dad smiled and the bristles of his white moustache lifted.

'My opinions are based on my experiences in life. I can never presume that what I would do is what you should do. I could give you my opinion but it will not be relevant to your specific situation; I have not walked in your shoes.'

I waited for more but Dad merely smiled and rested his hands on the book lying face down in his lap.

My parents. No guidance from one. All the guidance from the other. They balanced each other out, I guess.

'My client has offered me tickets to a concert next week,' Dennis said from behind his mask at Hannah's first brace check-up. '21 Pilots. It sounds like a big production. Would you like to go?'

I surprised myself, and Hannah, by saying yes immediately.

At the concert when the two band members took to the stage, Dennis's smile wavered. Confused as to why the band were missing nineteen of their pilots, he sincerely apologized to Hannah for it not being the big production he'd led her to believe. Hannah giggled hysterically and explained that two 'Pilots' was just the right amount because the name of the band was a morality lesson and had come from a play about the Second World War. Dennis stared at Hannah for a few seconds and, if at all possible, his opinion of her inched higher.

'She seems much more like herself,' Dennis said as she skipped ahead of us at the end of the concert, all of us in oversized 21 Pilots T-shirts.

'Yes,' I said, feeling proud. 'She's doing really well.'

'The young lass at school is leaving her alone now, is she?'

'No,' I said, thinking of the page ripped from an exercise book Hannah had found on the floor near her desk at the beginning of the week. The page had two columns; 'Who Hates Hannah Paige' and 'Who Likes Hannah Paige'. The 'like' side was empty and the 'hate' side had the word '*me*' written in different inks and handwriting. I thought about how Hannah had had a little cry, allowed me to cuddle her, refused to go to the head teacher, then thrown the page in the bin and spent the rest of the evening stuffing notes and gift cards into colourful envelopes while watching *CSI* reruns. 'But she's getting her joy elsewhere.'

A week later he called saying he had tickets to Queen with Adam Lambert. When we took our seats I noticed they weren't in VIP and said so to Dennis.

'No,' he said turning a deep red. 'I bought these ones myself.'

I looked at him, stunned.

'I thought Hannah would like to go,' he said, looking worried. 'I hope that's okay?'

I swallowed. 'It's more than okay.'

He gave a reassured smile, turned to the stage and clapped along, thoroughly out of time.

After that Dennis and I would exchange the odd text, mainly music trivia from his clients he thought Hannah might like to hear, or me sending him photos of Hannah's different rubber band colour combinations. It felt nice and weird to hear a *ding* on my phone and know that it could be someone other than Penny, Trish or my family.

★

'Will you tell Trish about sneaking gift cards into library books for people studying to be nurses?' Hannah said one night after we'd had a particularly busy evening of #NoReason planning.

'Yes, boss,' I said, following her from the bathroom to her bedroom.

'And can you tell Trish that when her students give out the envelopes they should say "I like your top" coz it makes people feel good,' she said climbing onto her bed and turning to face me. 'And they have to say it and mean it even if it's a top they wouldn't ever wear. Even if it's ugly. Because it might be that person's favourite top and someone else might have told them it's ugly and maybe they were thinking about not wearing it anymore. And that's sad that someone might not wear their favourite top just because someone else might not like it.'

'It is,' I said, realising how much Livie's comments had affected Hannah. 'Lie down now.'

'You'll tell Trish all that?' she said shuffling under her covers. 'Exactly all that?'

'Yes, boss,' I said.

I'd tucked her in in a squirm of giggles then settled back at the kitchen table opposite Trish and we'd clicked away at our laptops. After a while I'd felt her gaze on me and looked up.

'You're loving this,' she'd said, smiling.

I'd grinned. 'I really am.' I felt my grin fade.

Trish's expression became empathetic. 'Chris?'

I nodded.

'It's okay,' she said with an reassuring smile. 'You're allowed to feel happy.'

I nodded, not sure I fully agreed with her.

'It's nice to see you interacting with the world again.'

'It's good for Hannah.'

'It's good for *you*,' she said with one of her meaningful looks, and as she went back to loading tasks in to her calendar I had a sudden thought.

'I'm asking a lot of your time.'

'You are,' she said looking up again. 'But it's proving to be very beneficial for my students.'

'It is?'

Trish explained that there were some students who were harder than others to reintegrate into jobs or education. They'd had tougher childhoods and had been let down by people who should have been looking out for them. They were the ones who'd taken to the #NoReason acts more than others. 'Many of these kids have had to overcome extremely negative domestic situations. The emphasis on initiating joy in others is constructive in changing their view of the world.'

'Wow,' I said, marvelling at another positive aspect to the acts I hadn't considered. My grin came back, and we chinked glasses and got back to looking up Westminster Borough's policy on alpacas in Covent Garden.

After Trish left I opened my bank account, transferred her the required amount, as usual, then sat back and sighed. It felt good to see the balance lowering.

★

'This is getting crazy,' Penny said, shoving Julian P Tickle's card at my chest after slamming her front door in his chipper face again.

It was the Friday evening before midterm break and we were having a final dinner together before Hannah and I headed off to Sussex for the week leaving Penny in London with her mother-in-law.

'It's fine,' I said leaving my hiding place behind her living room door.

'That's all you say: *it's fine, it's fine,*' Penny grumbled as she headed back towards her kitchen, her impression of my British accent sounding Australian. And cartoon mouse-ish.

I sniggered and she scowled.

'These journalists are at the school,' she implored. 'They're knocking on our doors. And that smiley weirdo is positive someone from the school is behind it!'

'Well, to be fair, he's right.'

Penny glared and I dropped my grin.

'Unless they can follow the money from Trish's account to mine they'll never be able to find out it's me,' I said, spouting my usual argument.

'They probably *can* follow the money,' Penny said as we resumed our seats at her parquet oak dining table and checked on the kids eating in the sunny garden.

'But that's illegal,' I said, picking up my pizza.

'Do you think they care if it will get them off their horror tabloids and onto a *Times* column?! They do whatever they need to get the story. Believe me, *cariño*, I know about this stuff – my cousin is a journalist in Madrid. Hideous leeches! Except he's lovely and works with disabled children in his spare time and we all know he's Abuelita's favourite grandchild. Do you at least wear gloves when you stuff these envelopes?'

'Gloves?' I laughed. 'Of course not.'

'But the fingerprints?'

'If my fingerprints aren't on any database, which they aren't because I'm not a criminal, how could they ever find me? You're obsessed with crime shows as well, you should know that.'

'Ay, crime shows move too fast these days,' Penny said waving her hand and picking up her pizza. 'I was watching that *How To Get Away With Murder* the other day and I looked down to assemble a bit of salmon and an edamame bean on my chopsticks and by the time I looked back up I had no idea what was happening.'

I laughed and shook my head.

'*Por favor, cariño*, you have to think of what could happen, though. I worry for you.'

'Well don't. Worry about something else.'

Penny shot me a glower of betrayal. 'I'm worried about you leaving me for a whole week with my mother-in-law. Are you sure you can't have Hannah's birthday party on Monday? And then have it last all week?'

Hannah's birthday was on the Friday of the midterm break. Penny and the family would be coming down to celebrate but until then her mother-in-law was coming to stay to help ferry Penny's kids to and from their myriad activities.

Before class broke up that afternoon Hannah's teacher had written the names of the kids having birthdays during the holidays on the board. The class had sung them happy birthday then Miss Shuker had asked the three children to stand up and tell the class what they were doing to celebrate. When Hannah said she wasn't sure, Livie had laughed loudly. I was furious with Miss Shuker for being so insensitive.

While Penny riled about the agony of how there was never a holiday where she didn't get to see her mother-in-law naked and how it wasn't fair that Rog got to be in Berlin for a conference and miss out on all the geriatric nudity, I thought back to Hannah's last birthday.

Chris had been gone ten months and I'm ashamed to say, I'd organized nothing and given Hannah only money; the day *after* her birthday because I'd not gone to the cash machine on the actual day. And even though she did have friends at the time, we'd not had a party. Making chitchat with parents; organising games and presents and plastering on a smile – I just hadn't had it in me. Mum had offered to come up and help but even thinking about celebrating was too much. So, I'd let Hannah have the day off school, picked up a shitty cake from Sainsbury's Local, and we'd ordered pizza and watched a couple of Harry Potter movies for the millionth time; barely speaking for most of the day. I'd been truly disappointed in myself when I put her to bed, glad the day was over. Ten was supposed to be a big birthday.

I'd lain in my own bed that night and made a silent promise that for her next birthday I'd invite all her friends and organize a big party.

But that birthday was here, and Hannah had no friends to invite. The best I could do was a barbeque at Mum and Dad's. I'd invited Gus, Trish, Penny, Rog and the kids, a selection of Mum and Dad's friends from Pétanque and any grandchildren they had staying to make the party feel busy. Hannah had even asked me to invite Dennis, which I'd found weird, but they seemed to have a connection. He'd accepted reverently then called in a mini-stress every second day to discuss potential gifts.

I clicked back into Penny's diatribe and smiled.

'And does Rog ever see my mother's genitals?' she was saying through a mouthful of pizza. 'No. Because *my* mother keeps them where they are supposed to be, locked up and only out for the waxer and the husband. Not flapping them around for everyone to see like she's airing sheets.'

Chapter 21

'What's that?' Mum said, poking her head out of her open car window with a sneer.

'A finch. His name is Stefan.'

I rested the birdcage on the ground and put my fuller than usual suitcase in the open boot.

'Come on you two!' I called to Hannah and Tom who were dawdling across the train station car park watching something on Tom's phone.

Tom pocketed his phone and they raced to the car, where Hannah threw her duffle bag in the boot unceremoniously. Tom's parents were still on their film in Morocco so he was staying with us for the week. As they were often away, it had become a regular set-up and Tom had always stayed on a camp bed in Hannah's room. With him being twelve now and Hannah almost eleven I feared we were nearing a time where it would become inappropriate for them to share a room.

'Why did you get a pet finch?' Mum said, looking at the innocuous bird as if I'd told her I'd got a pet dogshit.

'We didn't,' I said, manhandling the metal cage inside into the middle seat, Stefan chirruping furiously. 'It's Hannah's teacher's. She's going to Rome for midterm and when she goes away someone in the class looks after him. Hannah's name was drawn out of the hat.'

'Well, that's unfortunate.'

'I *put* my name in the hat, Nan,' Hannah said, jumping in the back with Cookie and slamming her door. Tom got in the other side and pulled his door closed with a gentle click. 'Everybody did. Except the kids who are going away or the ones whose parents won't let them look after a bird.'

Mum gave me a sideways look. 'Why couldn't *you* be one of those parents?'

'What bother is it going to be to you? He'll just sit in the kitchen on the side table and Hannah will give him some seed every few days.'

'Inside?' Mum said, roughhousing the gears into position.

'Yes, inside,' I said, buckling up.

Mum harrumphed and muttered something about Florence being perfectly happy with her outdoor coop while swerving us out of the car park.

'You let Leo live inside.'

'Leo has impeccable manners and is a charming companion. Finches have no personality,' she huffed.

'Leo said the F-word this morning,' Tom offered from the back seat and Hannah giggled.

Mum threw Tom a traitorous look and when she turned back to the front noticed my raised eyebrows. 'Well,' Mum blustered. 'I'd spilt the cereal so he was using it in context.'

★

Twenty minutes later Mum swung the car through the old gates and had to brake to allow a rather good-looking young man and Dad to cross the gravel courtyard, each on one end of a rickety wooden ladder.

'Who is *he*?' I said, watching the tanned, blue-eyed man/ boy with a white-blonde bun tied at the nape of his neck walk in front of the car.

'That's Lars,' Mum said, lurching the car into her favoured parking spot and wrenching on the handbrake. 'He's from

Norway. He arrived yesterday. His English is very good and he's very tidy.'

'He's very handsome.'

'I wouldn't know,' Mum said, blushing.

Hannah and I dropped our suitcases at the bottom of the stairs then helped Mum lug in her huge shop while Tom carried cheeping Stefan into the kitchen.

'Where shall I put him?'

'Just on that side cabinet, thanks, Tom,' I said, pointing to the cabinet that held a sorry-looking vase of brown flower stems with 98 per cent of their petals absent. It was from the time Mum had tried her hand at drying flowers. Her bowl of decorative dried lemons and limes had only encouraged maggots.

Mum tracked the bird cage with an accusatory gaze while pulling the groceries from their bags. Some items not usually seen in my mother's kitchen came out; various cold cuts and some kind of rye cracker bread.

'Oh yum!' I said, pulling out a dill and juniper berry flavoured packet of smoked salmon.

'Those are for Lars.' Mum snatched it away from me.

I leaned against the bench. 'Oh, really . . .'

'My goodness, I'm glad Inga has gone,' she said, avoiding my gaze and moving from the kitchen bench to the pantry with various posh foodstuffs. 'She kept making this sour cabbage stuff. Gave your father terrible gas.'

'Gave *who* terrible gas?' Dad said, coming through the back door with Lars in tow.

Mum coloured right down to her shins.

Dad did the introductions then Lars mentioned he'd seen the drums and asked if he could have a go and Hannah dragged him down to the cellar, Tom and Dad trailing behind.

Within minutes, it became clear that Lars was a drummer.

For perhaps some kind of Norwegian death metal band.

'Now, I met a lovely young lady in the village last week and I've invited her over for afternoon tea today,' Mum said, wincing from the hectic beat and persistently crashing cymbals. 'I thought you two might get along.'

'I'm forty-three,' I said, raising my voice over the din. 'I don't need you to make friends for me.'

'She's new to the area. I don't care if *you* need any friends. She does.'

'What if I'm busy this afternoon?'

Mum stopped in the middle of the kitchen holding a melon and a pack of prosciutto. 'Are you?'

I thought about the #NoReason 'To Do' list on my Excel spreadsheet, not one item I could tell my mother about, and gave a reluctant 'No.'

'Well, then. That's settled. She'll be here at three.'

★

At seven minutes to three, a vision of composure arrived at the front door with clear skin, tiny feet and a dimpled smile. She was probably in her late twenties. Or early thirties with zero stress and a juice diet.

'Oh, hello, Leesa love, come in, come in,' Mum said ushering her in to the formal front living room that was only ever used to spy on Sasha's dates.

I followed like an awkward 9-year-old being forced into a playdate with a stranger. Mum hurried through the introductions then left Leesa and me facing each other on two horsehair-filled, button-back slipper chairs while she bustled off to make tea. I asked Leesa the polite questions you ask strangers; when did she move here (three weeks ago), where from (Acton), why (finished her studies/felt like a new start/country air) then Mum bustled back in, dumped a tray of tea and biscuits on the coffee table, plonked herself on the stiff Queen Anne love-seat and said, 'So Leesa, what do you do?'

Leesa looked at Mum for a brief second before answering in a melodic voice. 'I'm a life coach.'

'Interesting! Tell us what that entails. What does a life coach do?' Mum said, talking fast as though she needed this meeting over and done with. Or was on cocaine.

Leesa considered Mum for another moment before speaking and I wondered whether the pauses were a personality tic. 'Well, primarily it is about analysing a client's current situation and making an action plan. Which could be to achieve a specific goal, or to recognize the propensity to make poor choices, and to move towards making positive ones.'

Mum nodded emphatically.

Leesa paused again and at Mum's insistent look that she continue, glanced my way and carried on. 'We guide people who are confused or apprehensive about what to do with their lives and help them with goal-setting, taking control of future plans and—'

'Future plans!' Mum blurted with manic glee, she grinned and nodded at me then, clocking my dark expression, turned swiftly back to Leesa. 'And?'

'And . . . we can help people navigate an obstacle that is preventing their success, or to find their way after a traumatic experience—'

'Oh, that sounds like *such* an interesting job. Doesn't that sound like an interesting job, Brooke, love?'

'Yes,' I said through gritted teeth.

'Oh, something has just occurred to me, Brooke! Maybe you should join up, or . . . link in or . . .' She spun towards Leesa. 'What do you do with the coaching?'

Leesa had clearly already told Mum all of this and was now repeating herself. I watched as it dawned on her that this casual little meeting was a sham orchestrated by someone with the subtlety level of an industrial meat grinder. 'Become a client.'

'Right. Of course. Maybe you should become a client, Brooke, love?'

It was like Mum had taken her acting cues from a primary school play. Or the muppets on Sesame Street. And Leesa was her unwitting co-star.

Ignoring Mum's expression of appeal, I turned to Leesa. 'It's been very nice to meet you, but it is obvious that my mother,' I threw a fierce look Mum's way, 'has organized this meeting under false pretences. It's becoming a regular habit of hers.'

Leesa shot Mum a concerned look which Mum tried to dismiss with a jolly smile.

'I'm sorry to have wasted your time but I don't need your help. I don't need *any* help. I hope you meet lots of new people and enjoy living here and finds lots of clients but I will not be one of them.' I stood, gave Leesa, a blush growing on her pore-less cheeks, a perfunctory smile then left the room.

'You will,' Mum said, flying out of the room, instantly at my heel as I crossed the tiled floor to the stairs.

'Can you just leave it?' I sighed.

'No I cannot. As a mother I can't just stand by and watch this recklessness any longer! You have a daughter; you have a future to think of!'

I reached the bottom of the stairs and placed a foot on the first step.

'I'll tell the papers it's you,' she said in a hushed, threatening tone.

I turned. 'No, you won't,' I said shaking my head at her absurd tactics. 'I'd be sued and you know it.'

'I'll . . . I'll cut you out of my will.'

I raised my eyebrows. 'Mother, I'm incredibly, unwillingly wealthy.' I turned back and started up the stairs.

'I'll tell Hannah you haven't confirmed her place at the school yet,' she said, her voice barely a whisper.

I stopped, three stairs up, and spun around. Mum's expression was unyielding. 'You wouldn't?' I whispered.

She raised her chin. 'Try me.'

We held each other's gaze. There was steel in Mum's eyes, but I could detect a hint of desperation she was working hard to mask.

I walked back down the stairs and faced my mother. 'Chris and I scrimped and saved. We were responsible with money. We got a mortgage, planned for Hannah's education, and put money aside for the future. And look where "being responsible with money" got me – a dead husband and a daughter being bullied. Money didn't stop Chris dying. Money can't stop Hannah being bullied. Money can't fix anything that matters.' Instantly in a bleak mood, I turned and started up the stairs again.

'That's a broad sweeping statement,' Mum said, stepping closer. 'It can fix hunger and insecurity and—'

I spun round on the second step. 'To me!' I said, tears threatening. 'Money can't fix anything that matters *to me*!'

Mum's eyes became moist. 'Oh love, please speak to her?'

I wiped under my eyes and shook my head. 'No.' I was about to turn towards upstairs but noticed Leesa standing in the living room doorway behind Mum. How did she get there so noiselessly? Were her tiny feet made of silk?

'I think I can help you, Brooke,' she said in a soothing I've-done-a-weekend-life-coaching-course-in-Devon-and-my-Insta-feed-is-all-in-sepia voice. 'Iris told me a bit about your circumstances when we met. I'm very sorry to hear of your husband's death.'

Mum's chin trembled but she battled it back.

'I really do think I could help you. I could see you every fortnight?' Leesa said, taking a silken step closer.

'How about every day this week starting tomorrow?' Mum said, not taking her eyes off me.

'I have Hannah,' I said. 'And Tom.'

'You could do it while Hannah has her drum lessons,' Mum countered. 'And anyway, your father and I are here to look after them.'

We glared at each other. *Please don't do this?* I begged with my eyes.

Mum averted her gaze. 'Ten o'clock tomorrow morning suit you, Leesa?'

After some practised consideration, Leesa nodded. 'I think I can fit that in.'

'You said you have no clients,' Mum said, her voice curt and intimidating. 'So I'm sure you can.'

The apples of Leesa's cheeks flushed endearingly, like a milkmaid in love. God, even her embarrassed face was charming!

Hannah and Tom walked through from the laundry with Pablo, wearing one of Mum's scarves and his mane spiked up like Jon Bon Jovi circa 'Livin' On A Prayer', trailing behind and Leesa took a startled step back.

'We're writing a part for Pablo in our movie,' said Hannah.

'We just need to see if he can open a fridge,' said Tom.

And they carried on through towards the kitchen.

Leesa looked to Mum and me for an explanation but we were locked in a battle of wills. 'I'll see you tomorrow?' she said, breaking the silence.

Mum squared her shoulders, determination emboldening her. I knew then that she was desperate enough that she would tell Hannah. Like a deflating balloon, my resolve seeped out of me.

'Yes,' I said, defeated. 'See you then.' I shot Mum a look of disloyalty then trudged up the stairs.

Chapter 22

'MU-UM!' Hannah's voice echoed up the stairs and along the hall.

I kept my eyes shut and snuggled further into my pillow.

'STEFAN IS DEAD!'

My eyes flew open.

We'd gone to bed late after a boisterous (Mum broke a pencil. And a glass) family games night. Tom and Hannah were a team, Mum and Lars were a team, and Dad and I were a team. Pictionary. Mum got exasperated because Lars was useless but Lars was also very beautiful so she was unwilling to tell him how his uselessness was causing her to lose, which she usually would have done to anyone else. We'd been drinking; Dad and Lars on the lager, me on the wine, and Mum on the sherry, and we'd headed upstairs a little wobbly (except Hannah and Tom of course) after midnight.

As I grabbed my dressing gown I looked at the time. 9:51. I groaned. Leesa was due at 10am for our first forced session.

I jogged down the stairs to the kitchen to find Hannah and Tom with Stefan's night-time cage cover (used to enforce sleep and inhibit cheeping) lying on the kitchen table and Stefan belly-up at the bottom of his cage. Mum rushed in, gathering her dressing gown at her waist and pushing her grey bob back in place. It seemed the entire house had slept in.

'Oh dear,' said Mum, arriving next to us.

'Oh dear,' said Dad, arriving through a different door, fully dressed and with the morning paper tucked under his arm.

Lars arrived next, in just a pair of light cotton pyjama bottoms, his chest bare, causing both Mum and me to do a double take.

'Maybe he is just sleeping,' said Lars.

'While rare,' Dad replied, 'owls have been known to sleep lying down.'

Mum and I turned back to the cage.

'With their feet in the air?' I said.

'No,' Dad admitted.

'Anyway, this is a finch, not an owl!' Hannah cried.

'*Was* a finch,' said Lars, seemingly pleased with his grasp of English tenses.

I frowned at him, but my frown disbanded as he yawned and stretched. Mum too was momentarily distracted.

'Maybe it has narcolepsy?' said Tom.

Mum and I turned back to the cage.

'Well,' said Dad, stroking his beard. 'Narcolepsy is a neuro-logical disorder and birds can develop neurological disorders, although I've never heard of a case of avian narcolepsy.'

'Poke it,' Lars said, in his Scandi accent, pulling a dried flower stalk from Mum's awful arrangement and holding it out to anyone in the mood for a dead finch on a stick.

'No!' Hannah cried.

I snatched the stick away from Lars. Gus walked into the kitchen with his guitar case.

'Oh dear,' he said, arriving next to me and seeing the upturned body of Stefan.

Hannah slumped on a chair at the breakfast table. 'Noooooooo,' she groaned, the anticipation of Livie's potential cruelty causing her to tug at the sides of her face with her fingers, dragging her eye sockets down to expose the yucky red stuff.

'Stop that,' I said nudging her.

Tom sat on the chair beside her and rested an arm across her shoulders. 'Maybe he fell.'

Hannah wrinkled her nose. 'Birds don't fall.'

'Did the cat get him?' said Gus.

'We don't have a cat,' said Mum, looking at him as if he were dim.

'Morning,' said Sasha, arriving in the kitchen with a cat in her arms.

'That's not ours,' Mum said, off Gus's expression.

'What happened?' said Sasha.

'Why have you got a cat?' said Mum.

'What am I going to do?' said Hannah.

'It's Michael. He's a rescue,' said Sasha. 'You met him last night. When you were drunk. Don't you remember? It was after you broke the pencil because Lars couldn't get your picture of "Wi-Fi".'

Mum scowled.

'Wi-Fi, yes,' Lars grinned.

'I can't abide cats. They're rude. He'll have to go.'

Sasha scoffed and left.

Leesa arrived.

'Oh dear,' she said.

'Is he definitely dead?'

'Maybe he's in a coma?'

After much conjecture, and a bit of poking, we determined that Stefan was in fact dead. And after some Clouseau-type inquests realized that Mum had moved his covered cage off the sideboard and placed him on top of an ancient gas heater that absolutely did not need to be on and because of the cage cover Stefan had effectively spent the night in a little birdy gas chamber.

'I'll buy you a new one, Hannah, love,' Mum said.

'I'll drive,' I said, heading toward the door, glad to have a task that would take me away from my Leesa session.

'No, *I'll* drive.'

'You're probably still drunk.'

'I was never drunk in the first place!'

'So you always moonwalk to bed?'

'On occasion.'

'I'm coming. I like looking at the fish.'

'Fish yes, we go out for breakfast?'

★

Lars, Mum, Dad, Hannah, Tom, Gus and I stood in a line at the counter of the pet store. A ruddy-cheeked man wearing an apron with a pin attached to one breast that said *I ♥ animals* and another on the other side that said *Pets are family* looked up from what appeared to be a messy pile of stock-take papers with a start.

'Oh hello!' He pushed his glasses up his nose. 'How can I help you?'

I elbowed Lars. He stepped forward and plonked a plastic Ziploc bag on the counter. Stefan wobbled back and forth like a lone lemon. The man peered at the bag then looked up.

I smiled to let him know that what we wanted was to conduct a perfectly standard exchange. 'We'd like to purchase a finch that looks exactly like this one,' I said.

'Just a tad more animated,' Dad added, his beard twitching.

Gus failed to contain a snort.

'Ye-es,' The pet store man bent down and put his nose closer than I ever would to a dead animal. 'Old, was he?'

'No,' I said.

'He spontaneously died,' Mum said.

'He was gassed.'

Mum bristled, and gave me her best tut-tut face. The man gave another glance at plastic-wrapped Stefan, then back up to our gathering, who gave a simultaneous smile, then after a moment of deliberation, took us to the back of a shop where a mesh-fronted cage the height and width of a small wardrobe was alive with finches. The man unhooked a net from the wall and carefully stepped inside the cage. Lars, Mum, Dad, Hannah, Tom, Gus and I gathered around and the calls for which bird we needed began:

'That one looks like him!'

'There it goes!'

'What about that one?'

'Not *that* one! He's got too much white!'

'Too much black!'

'Stefan was fatter!'

'Ooooh *no*, not that one!'

'Stefan was browner!'

'Do finches recognize their owners?'

'That one!'

'He's above you!'

'He's behind you!'

'That one!'

'He's over there!'

'There he goes!'

Inside, the little man looked like he was doing a triple-speed version of the Macarena. Eventually, with his grey curls plastered to his sweaty temples, the man emerged with a shagged-out finch in his net. We followed him back to the counter and lined up again on the other side to watch him extract New Stefan from the net and put him in a little cardboard box with tiny breathing holes.

'I'm going to take this,' Dad said, picking up the bag with Old Stefan in it.

Our party stared at him.

'For research purposes,' he said.

The little old man blinked at Dad, then took our money, handed Lars the little box with New Stefan in it, made a deliberate show of handing Mum a print-out on caring for your finch, and sent us on our merry way.

At the house we couldn't agree on the best way to get

New Stefan out of the box and into the cage.

'Put the box in the cage.'

'There might still be gas remnants in there.'

'It's a structure of holes. It can't contain anything. Especially vapour.'

'Does a hole exist? Or is it merely the absence of something that *does* exist?'

'*Dad*. Not that donut thing again.'

'What donut thing?'

'Does a donut hole exist? If you ate the donut where does the hole go?'

'Does it?'

'What?'

'Exist?'

'Now *that*, young man, is the whole point. *Whole* point. Donut *hole*.'

'*Grandaaad*.'

'I'm just going to open the box and tip him in the cage.'

'We should do it outside.'

'We should do it *inside*.'

'I'll do it.'

'No, *I'll* do it.'

'I think I should do it.'

Eventually, I couldn't stand it any longer so put the box next to the cage on the breakfast table, opened it a slither, slid in my hand and New Stefan slipped out of the gap, out of the kitchen door, and out of our lives.

Lars, Mum, Dad, Hannah, Tom, Gus and I stood in a line at the counter of the pet store.

The little old man looked up from his papers, the hair around his temples still damp, and gave another little start. I elbowed Lars. He stepped forward.

'We would like anozer finches,' he said, placing the empty box with the little holes on top of the counter.

Chapter 23

Back at the house, Leesa was waiting in the dining room with her fairy-like feet crossed at her ballet dancer-like ankles.

'Gosh, sorry that took such a long time. You must have somewhere you need to be?' I said, quickly replying to a text from Trish.

She smiled. 'No.'

'Oh good,' I said faintly and slid into a dining chair opposite her. My phone lit up with Trish's immediate reply and I read it, replied then watched from across the expanse of mahogany table as Leesa dug out pristine coloured folders and unused notebooks with over-used inspirational quotes in swirly gold letters across the front of their tropical foliage covers. She placed an open folder on the chair to her left, out of my sight, and her tidy tote on the chair to her right. Poking out the top of the tote was a well-thumbed book. *Life Coaching For Beginners*.

After she'd settled her folders and pens (exactly perpendicular to her box-fresh notepad) she smiled and said 'Okay, shall we get started?'

'I guess,' I said, distracted by my phone lighting up.

Leesa looked at it, then me. Feeling chastised, I turned it so the screen was face down. She gave a nod as if that were the correct thing to do and I felt an instant desire to be rebellious.

'So,' she cracked a 'trust-me-I'm-a-therapist-and-now-we're-in-session' smile. 'What are you looking to achieve through coaching, Brooke?'

I frowned my 'I'm-a-captive-here-and-I'd-very-much-like-to-leave' frown. 'You're aware I'm being blackmailed to do this?'

Mum bustled into the room with a rattling tray of patterned cups and jugs. 'Thought you might like some tea,' she said in a faux sprightly voice. She placed the tray on the table, angled her head towards me, hissed *'behave'* then turned to Leesa and trilled 'milk and sugar?' ever so sweetly. I eyed my mother while she assembled Leesa's tea and left me to sort my own. Then with a thin-lipped, not-at-all furtive incantation of potential consequences if I didn't comply in my direction, she bustled out again.

Leesa smiled. 'How about we break it down to a smaller, less daunting notion. What would you like to achieve in *this* session?'

'I'd like to know what came first; the verb "duck" or the noun "duck".'

Leesa frowned.

'Do we duck because a duck ducks, or is a duck a duck because a duck ducks?'

Mum appeared in the doorway again, her face like thunder. If thunder had a big tax bill and a misbehaving cloud-ette. 'Scones?' she pretty much screamed.

Leesa tore her gaze from me and turned to Mum. 'I don't eat gluten, but thank—'

'Just something to keep your energy up!' Mum said, plonking a mountain of home baking that looked as dense as clay and could probably be used to facet diamonds in the centre of the table. While hacking curls out of a pound of butter she twisted my way. 'You *will* behave or so help me God I'll tell Hannah!' she whisper-shrieked. 'Butter?' she sang at Leesa and, without waiting for a response, smashed a cold curl of butter onto a scone, flung it on a plate, and bunged the plate in front of Leesa, showering crumbs all over the place.

Leesa thanked Mum, watched her leave the room, relocated the plate off her folder, swept crumbs from her forms, then settled her pale blue eyes on me and smiled. Again. She opened her mouth and Mum came in to view through the closed glass French doors into the adjoining conservatory with Leo on her shoulder.

'You think we don't know what you're doing?' I called out.

Mum set up a wicker chair at a dubious angle, lowered Leo on the side table, and sat down placing a basket full of garden peas on her aproned lap. She looked up at Leesa and me, affected an 'oh look it's you again, isn't this a nice surprise' expression, reddened at my slow shake of the head, motioned that she couldn't hear a thing, and got busy shelling peas.

I turned back to Leesa. 'She will keep doing this. Best to just press on.'

'Okay.' She glanced at Mum. 'Is that a—'

'Parrot. Yes.'

'Right,' she said, then after receiving no further explanation she pulled a phone from her tote, tapped at it with clean clear-polished nails and placed it on the dining table between us, a voice recording app on the screen. Her smile dropped at my expression. 'Did your mother explain I need to record our sessions?'

I turned towards the conservatory. 'No, she did not.'

Mum angled away from us, studying her current pea with more intensity than any pea deserved.

'Oh, I'm sorry.' Leesa flushed. 'I have to log a certain number of hours with clients for my certificate. Is it okay?'

With a significant dearth of enthusiasm, I nodded and Leesa pressed record.

'I'm here under duress,' I said into the phone and received

a sharp look from Mum. 'Only kidding,' I said, then in the direction of the conservatory mouthed *'no I'm not'*.

Mum silently fumed. Leesa considered me with an evaluating gaze I found uncomfortable. I stopped smiling and shifted in my seat. Leesa broke her gaze, unsheathed a bullet-pointed list from a clear file folder, placed in in front of her and after a brief glance at the list, clasped her hands over it, but not before I could read the title: *First Session Questions – Establishing Your Client's Current State*.

'I gather you don't want to work on your grief,' she said. 'Your mother said you've had counselling in the past but haven't found it useful?'

I picked up the teapot and poured myself some tea. 'I've been to many, many counsellors. They just make us sadder.'

'Us?'

'Hannah and me.'

'Well, life coaching isn't strictly counselling, it's more guidance.' She glanced down at her list then spoke like she were reciting a school speech. 'Life coaching can help you navigate through a new stage of life and assist you in recognising and achieving goals.' Leesa paused. 'Can you think of any goals you'd like to achieve?'

I never allowed myself to think of the future without Chris. I picked up my teacup and shook my head.

'That's fine,' Leesa said with a practised smile. 'We have techniques to help you figure out what it is you do want if you don't know.' She glanced at her bullet pointed sheet again then opened a folder with *Keep Going, Keep Growing* written on the front and flicked through plastic-coated pages. 'I'll get you to fill out a few forms, they help us see where you're at currently, then we can work from there. Does that sound okay?'

'I guess so.'

'Great.' She slipped stapled forms from a document protector and handed them to me. I scanned the headings; *Social and*

Recreation, Family and Home, Career and Financial, Physical and Health. Under the headings were a list of statements with tickboxes next to them and at the end of the list a box to record how many ticks. One statement under *Family and Home* immediately caught my eye: *I have a partner or spouse with whom I have a stable healthy relationship*. I swallowed.

'That one is about how you spend your day,' Leesa said when she caught me looking at a pie chart titled *The Wheel of Life*. 'You fill in the circle choosing how much of the pie you spend doing each of the activities listed down the side.'

I looked at the list. I looked up at her. She slid a pristine box of sharp, unused coloured pencils across the table towards me.

'You can use a different colour for each activity.' Leesa looked very pleased with herself.

I was not pleased with her. Or Mum.

'How long do you think this will take?' I said, taking note of the time on a hideous mantelpiece clock.

'Life coaching sessions are generally an hour, but your mother has asked if we can do longer sessions seeing as you're my only client and,' she cleared her throat, 'you have some free time.'

I thought about the 'To Do' list on my Excel spreadsheet, the emails that needed sending, the bookings waiting to be confirmed, the texts from Trish lighting up my phone, then looked at Mum sitting like a sentry in the conservatory, every fibre of her being alert to the goings on in the dining room. The sooner I got on with it, the sooner I was free. I grabbed a blue coloured pencil and both Mum and Leesa exhaled.

When I finished one form Leesa would take it and make notes while I worked on the next one. It went on and on and on for over an hour, while Gus and Hannah worked on Nirvana's 'Lounge Act' in stops and starts in the background, until I finally slid the last form across the table. Leesa spent a quiet couple of minutes reading it, made some notes, filed it neatly, then smiled across the table.

'I can see from your forms that Hannah is the most important part of your life.'

I nodded.

'Which is how many parents fill out the forms.'

I nodded.

'But,' she said, looking at the pie chart of how I spent my week, 'what I can also see is that there isn't much else.'

Ouch.

'You work from home at approximately fifteen hours a week? Can you tell me doing what?'

I explained my work.

'So, you don't have any contact with colleagues?'

'Just emails and the odd phone call.'

Leesa waited for more.

'It's a temporary position. My boss says my job is there for me when I feel ready to go back.'

Leesa nodded. 'And how long have you been doing the temporary job?'

I said nothing.

Leesa held my gaze, then looked back down at the pie chart and pointed to the tiny wedge allocated to *social*. 'This is quite small. Where do you socialize? Outside of your own home.'

'I don't. Not really.'

'Because you don't get invited, or you do but say no?'

Ouch again. 'I get invited,' I said with a bristle I tried to contain. I'd coloured in that wedge with the three concerts we'd been to with Dennis and the coffees I had in my kitchen with Penny in mind. They weren't much. I knew that. 'I just say no most of the time.'

'Why do you think that is?'

'I don't feel like going out.'

Leesa gave an ominous 'hmmm' and I bristled again. 'Your

world seems small,' she said, tact failing her. 'Studies have shown that isolation can cause not only depression but other physical health issues. Maybe it's worth saying yes to some invites?'

My body clenched at the idea of saying yes to a school function or brunch or dinner party.

Leesa broke her intense stare-down and looked at the hideous clock on the mantlepiece. 'Our session is up, I'm afraid.'

I wasn't. That obvious fact hung heavily in the air. I stayed in my seat as she packed up.

'Do you have any questions?' she said as she slid the box of coloured pencils neatly in the side of her tote.

'Yes.'

Leesa brightened.

'What exactly is a free radical?'

Leesa unbrightened. Mum stiffened.

'I always imagined them to be tiny people like Che Guevara running around inside our bodies saying *I'm free! I'm free!*'

Five minutes later, I was released and Mum walked Leesa out, confirming the time she'd be back the next day and apologising for my uncharacteristic obstructiveness while I ran up to my room and grabbed my bag and shoes.

'How do you think it went?' Mum asked as I clattered down the stairs and across the entrance hall.

'How do *you* think it went, Mum? You were there listening to everything.'

'I was not!' she said, falling into step behind me as I exited the front door and crossed the courtyard.

'She said I was doing really well, actually. And that I didn't need coaching and I should just keep doing what I'm doing because I'm fine.'

'She did *not*. She told you, you need to socialize more and I've been saying that to you for—'

I stopped in the middle of the courtyard and spun around, raising my eyebrows.

Mum's hands worried her necklace. 'Well, that's what I *gathered* from your expressions . . .'

'Your attempt at covert reconnaissance is atrocious.' I turned and carried on towards the cart shed, smiling despite myself. 'Also, Leesa doesn't even seem to know what she's doing. She keeps checking a folder hidden beside her and asks questions from a list. I don't even really know what we did today except colour in.'

'Well, she's not yet finished her training. You're her test subject.'

'I don't want to be her test subject.'

'You'll do it.'

'Why? What am I really going to get out of these sessions?'

'You'll do it because I say so and—' She stopped and watched me tug Martin's rickety bicycle from between the old Triumph and a barrel of rusting shovels and hoes. 'Where are you going?'

'Into the village?'

'What for?' she said, her eyes narrowing in suspicion.

'Crisps.'

'We have crisps.' Her eyes narrowed further.

'Not the ones I want,' I said and swung my leg over the brittle seat. 'Hannah and Tom are on the trampoline with Lars. I'll be back in an hour.'

★

When I got home Mum was fossicking around in the cart-shed.

'Where are the crisps?' she said, emerging in a puff of dust as I parked the bike.

'What?'

'The crisps?' She said following me inside while I fired off a text. 'That you went to the village for. Where are they?'

'Oh. I ate them.'

We paused in unison as we clocked a cage on the hall table containing a nervous-looking guinea pig.

My phone dinged with a reply and I smiled as I read it then ran up the stairs under Mum's mistrustful, narrow-eyed stare.

At dinner that evening Dad said that in Switzerland it was illegal to own one guinea pig. It was also law that Swiss fish experience day and night cycles, and cats, while not legally required to have a companion, must have access to a window in order to view other cats. Mum moaned about a bake sale fundraising afternoon she was attending and how Jeanette-from-Pétanque was making a pineapple upside-down cake 'even though *I* always make a pineapple upside-down cake' and Jeanette was only doing it because nobody had bought her wonky Battenberg for two years in a row.

'What is the bake sale fundraising for?' I'd asked and Mum had clamped her mouth shut, frowned at her grey slab of roast beef, then stated that it really was better that the big organisations give to the needy and the average struggling person should just focus on looking after their own, while Dad had fished around in his cardigan pocket and placed Old Stefan in his plastic bag on the table next to his glass of lager. Mum had knocked back some port and said she'd prefer not to have dead things at the table, Hannah and Tom pointed out that the beef she'd served was essentially a 'dead thing at the table', and Sasha had gagged. Then we'd received an extended oration on Aristotle, Socrates and Plato's various views on death, which led to Lars talking about Norse mythology, which led to Tom talking about Marvel's *Thor*, which led to Mum talking about Chris Hemsworth with a flush down her neck.

Chapter 24

The next morning Leesa's arrival was imminent and Mum, worried I was going to fly the coop, stalked in to my bedroom and I quickly got off the phone.

'Who were you talking to?'

'Trish.'

'About?'

'Nothing much.'

'I heard you say *three will be plenty*,' she said, her eyes slits of suspicion.

'Yes,' I said reaching for my laptop. 'We were discussing her sexual partners.'

Mum's face puckered as she watched me settle on the bed and begin typing. She frowned. 'Leesa is due any minute.'

'I have to send this email,' I said, angling the screen away from her and tapping out to Trish what I hadn't been able to finish saying on the phone. 'I don't know what use you think Leesa is going to be. It's a waste of time.'

'A waste of time?' she said, leaning to see the screen. 'What else have you got to do?'

Unable to say 'A shit ton, actually', I leaned away from her, tapped out the final line, pressed send, shut the laptop and slid off the bed. 'I resent being blackmailed by my own mother.'

'Well, needs must sometimes, love,' Mum said following me out of the room.

'I also resent being life coached by someone my own age.'

Mum frowned. 'She's not your age. She's younger. By quite a bit.'

'Even better,' I rolled my eyes and took off down the hall.

'It's like you've got body dysmorphia of the age,' she said still frowning. 'It's not attractive to want to be younger, you know.'

'Thanks, Mum,' I said, descending the stairs.

'Gus is here!' Hannah said, racing past us with Tom in tow. 'Tell him we're down there already!' They spun around the banister and clomped down the cellar stairs.

'Hello,' I said stopping at the bottom of the stairs as Gus arrived in the open doorway holding his ever-present guitar case. Mum stumbled into the back of me, propelling me across the entrance way into Gus's arms.

'Hi,' he said, propping me up with those tanned arms that Trish liked so much and sometimes still texted me about. He smelt of horse, which isn't as gross as it sounds.

'Thanks, sorry about that,' I said, glaring at Mum who was smoothing down her hair.

Leesa's hybrid crunched across the gravel.

'The kids are down there already,' I said, ushering him in. 'Do you need any help with today's lesson?'

Mum narrowed her eyes. 'Leesa is here.'

'Ah . . .' Gus looked from Mum to me as he crossed the threshold. 'I think we'll be okay,' he said, *I've seen you clap and I believe you have a distinct rhythmic impediment* written all over his face.

'I could alphabetize the sheet music?' I looked at him pointedly.

He looked back, I'd like to say with comprehension but it appeared to be more alarm.

Mum glared at me. I glared at her. The hallway was thick with nonverbal undertones that weren't clear to anyone.

'Good morning,' Leesa said, arriving in the doorway with her clear complexion, her folders of forms, and her (needs-a-bit-more-attention) life coaching instruction manual.

Gus flicked his Paul Newman eyes between Mum, Leesa and me. 'I'll leave you to it,' he said, after Mum gave him a none too subtle glance towards the cellar and me an obvious shove towards the dining room.

★

'What if I pay you double to *not* do the sessions?' I said from my position across the expanse of dining table.

'This is a mutually beneficial arrangement. I'm still learning so I'm not being paid.'

'What if I found you some local clients who did pay? Would that be a good exchange? For my freedom?'

Leesa looked up from her folders of colouring in pages. 'Who do you know?' She held my gaze, a mild challenge in her eyes. She was wearing a white cotton top with pretty lace flowers on the lapels. She was the devil, I tell you.

She smiled. 'Okay then,' she glanced at her forms. 'Seeing as you don't have a goal I'd like to try some visualisation. Would you like to lie down for this?'

'Sure,' I said, following Leesa to the musty chaise longue that had not one particle of comfort to its tightly packed upholstery. 'I detected a note of exasperation when you said "don't have a goal",' I said, lying down, 'but I'm willing to overlook it seeing as you're learning your craft.'

'Thanks ever so much,' Leesa said and I was immensely proud of her dripping sarcasm.

I squirmed and adjusted, coughed at the dust that puffed out of the upholstery, and eventually settled.

'We're going to create your Miracle Day,' Leesa said, putting on her 'I'm a very relaxing person' voice. 'Close your eyes and breath in and slowly out.'

I did as she said.

'First we get your mind into a calm state where it releases chemicals that create a positive mood,' Leesa said and it sounded like she were reading from a piece of paper. 'We do this by visualising a time or place that is positive and specific to you, and will trigger the release of those particular chemicals.'

'That's a complicated explanation. Do you mean you want me to go to my happy place?'

'Yes,' said Leesa with a wry tone to her voice. 'Go to your happy place.'

'Alright. I'm in a room. I'm alone.' I opened an eye. '*Completely* alone.'

Leesa gave me a 'ha-ha very funny' look down her cute button nose.

I smiled and closed my eyes again.

'Think about an instance when time stood still for you. Where you felt like your truest self? Take yourself to that place.'

Gladly.

★

Chris and I spent our first few nights in India at a fifteenth-century palace in Rajasthan. It was all stone corridors, arched windows, romantic four-poster beds, courtyard gardens with tinkly fountains, and tiny stone staircases circling up to turrets that overlooked fields and jungle. During a hot, fragrant night filled with unfamiliar sounds that kept us awake, charmed and delighted by the exoticness, Chris had shat the romantic four-poster bed. Then vomited. Luckily the bathroom was tiny and he spent the rest of the night on the toilet with his chin on the edge of the hand basin filling both receptacles. In the wee hours when his temperature rocketed higher and his moans became weaker, I'd called Mum from an ancient phone at the antique desk that counted as a reception, fretting that Chris was going to die of some disease never before documented in humans.

'Chris is going to die!!!' I'd wailed down the line.

'WHAT?!' she'd cried.

And when I'd explained the symptoms I got an earful for frightening fifteen years off her extremely busy life for a bout of food poisoning. Mum suggested I get Chris to a doctor to deal with the likely dehydration.

'I'll try,' I'd said, looking, unconvinced, out the glassless window in the palace wall and across the dark and noisy jungle.

The night manager was a man of about fifty who ceaselessly smiled. Even as I told him about the bed shitting. He summoned help and minutes later two men in white kurtas carried Chris to a waiting jeep. The manager hopped in the driver's seat and we bumped off into the velvety, aromatic night, Chris moaning weakly with each jolt of the tyres in the rutted mud road. After twenty minutes we arrived in a dirt road village and pulled up outside a squat concrete building lit by fluorescent bar lights and parked next to a cow. The manager rushed ahead as Chris, the two men and I made our way through the mud, around the cow, and past a child who should have been in bed and most definitely should not have been smoking.

'I'm going to die here, aren't I,' said Chris dramatically, as we arrived in a sparse concrete room to see four men playing checkers at a plastic table.

The manager spoke while indicating towards Chris and the men playing checkers hopped up and cleared the table. One of the men picked up a battered doctor's bag and placed it on the table.

'Now it's a doctor's surgery?' Chris had croaked in my ear and I'd managed a nervous giggle.

The men stood in a line with no inclination to give us privacy while the doctor tapped Chris's knee with a rubber hammer, listened all over Chris's chest with a stethoscope that looked like it had been thrown out during the Boer War, pulled at his eye sockets, and prodded his belly. Then handed over some generic-looking pills in a foil pouch, and sent us on our way. By the time we got back to the palace we'd decided against taking the nameless drugs and Chris was very much in need of the loo/sink. But a day later he was weaker, paler, half the size he usually was and I thought he was going to die so he knocked back the unidentifiable pills and twelve hours later he was bright as a button and we were knee-deep in a river surrounded by orphaned rescue elephants. We spent the morning scrubbing a 40-year-old elephant's leathery wrinkled skin with coconut husks, being introduced to a 3-year-old orphaned elephant who seemed terribly shy, and watching a 1-year-old elephant be confounded by the need to hold up his trunk while he lay in the water. Three hours with rescue elephants had felt like mere minutes.

*

'I'd gone from frightened Chris was going to die in the middle of the night in the middle of nowhere, to the happiest I'd ever been,' I said, my eyes still closed and the image of Chris grinning as he met the baby elephant in my mind. 'I felt like anything in the world could happen. Chris and I could do anything we wanted. Together.'

Leesa waited a moment before speaking. 'That sounds like true happiness.'

'It was,' I said quietly.

Leesa didn't speak for a moment and I greatly appreciated her letting me sit in that memory a little longer. I felt like I could fall into a deep restorative sleep. *Wow.* My heart rate really had lowered. I felt awake and asleep. And content. Was this what it was like to be a cat? Or my father?

'Do you feel ready to create your Miracle Day?' Leesa asked.

I nodded while keeping my eyes closed. I heard the rustling of a sheet of paper.

'Imagine you go to sleep tonight and when you wake tomorrow a miracle has happened during the night; your dreams, every single one of them, have come true.' Leesa paused,

I guessed to allow me to consider what those dreams may be. 'I'll walk you through questions one by one to help you build a step by step account of what happens in your ideal day.' Leesa paused and I heard the piece of paper being put down. 'Do you feel ready?'

I nodded.

'So you wake up. What's the first thing you notice?'

'Chris is there.'

Even with my eyes closed I could sense Leesa nodding. 'How would that feel?'

I let out a shaky breath. 'Wonderful,' I said through a strained throat. 'It'd feel wonderful.'

Leesa walked me through the rest of my 'Miracle Day' and it turned out all I wanted was Chris, Hannah and I together again. Things that, no matter how much 'goal work' I did, I couldn't ever achieve. These sessions seemed were even more of a waste of time than I'd first thought. My happy place chemicals began to expire.

'How would Chris being alive make a difference to your current reality?'

I opened my eyes. 'Are you fucking kidding me?' I said, but not viciously. I was more incredulous she'd even asked that question.

Leesa looked away from her sheet of paper, a little sheepish. Yet she raised a single eyebrow and waited.

'Hannah would have her dad and I would have my husband,' I said in a tone that suggested she were simple. 'Where did you say you were doing your diploma again?'

'I didn't. And how would Hannah having her dad and you having your husband make you feel?'

I frowned at this heartless pretty milkmaid but, when I realized she wasn't going to change her probing, pretty milkmaid expression, scowled and returned to my closed eye position.

'Tell me one word that sums up the feeling you have after experiencing your Miracle Day, your husband and Hannah's father present.'

I squirmed on the chaise longue. I wasn't sure what this exercise was going to achieve. Eventually a word came to me. 'Companionship.'

'Good. Do you get that feeling anywhere in your current life? And if not, do you feel that the way you're currently living will help you attain it?'

Penny had Rog, Mum and Dad had each other, Trish had . . . anyone she wanted. Who did I have? Did Cookie count? A sense of discomfort settled across me. A long time seemed to pass.

'If you don't socialize you don't let anyone in and won't achieve "companionship". We have to take steps to achieve our goals. Wanting them isn't enough.'

Leesa's Apple watch beeped and I opened my eyes.

'I'm sorry, our time is up,' Leesa said. 'Do you have any questions?' she asked.

'Yes,' I said pushing myself up from my prone position and watching her pack up.

Leesa smiled and raised her eyebrows.

'*Mork and Mindy* was the 70s; *ALF* was the 80s. *Third Rock From The Sun* was the 90s. Where is our modern day "alien in suburbia"? I feel like my daughter is missing out on an important cultural experience.'

Leesa pressed stop on her phone recording app, furnished me with a sardonic expression and followed me out of the room.

'Oh good,' Gus said, coming up from the cellar behind Hannah and Tom as I walked Leesa to the front door. 'Have you got time for a quick chat?'

'Why don't you go to the pub?' Mum said, materialising out of absolutely nowhere.

'Great idea,' Gus grinned.

'I have the kids . . .'

'Your father said he'd take them to see the new litter of piglets at the neighbours'.'

'There are seventeen!' Hannah squealed. 'Let's go find stuff to feed them!' she added, dragging Tom in the direction of the kitchen. 'Bye, Gus!' she called when she was already in the next room.

Leesa raised her stupid perfect eyebrows. Mum folded her arms.

I narrowed my eyes at both of them then forcing a smile, turned to Gus and said, 'I'll just get changed.'

Chapter 25

'Sounds like a date,' Trish said down the phone while I held a nice sleeveless blouse up and assessed my reflection in my bedroom mirror. 'It'll be all your vagina talk.'

'Nope,' I said, tossing the nice sleeveless blouse on the bed and snatching up a plain cotton vest. 'I'm not ready for a date. And especially not with a man obsessed with my vagina.' (The opposite of how I felt in my twenties.)

'It's a drink at the pub. What's the worst that could happen?'

'A tornado,' I said and hung up.

★

Gus and I made our way through the busy beer garden towards an outdoor table in the sun, both clutching glinting pints of golden lager. I'd changed out of my 'inside only' leggings to denim shorts and a plain cotton vest. The midday sun was already heating my bare shoulders. I scanned the garden and noticed groups of females watching Gus as he took his unhurried strides across the grass. As we threaded legs into our seats at an outdoor table I waved at an elderly couple sitting nearby who lived down the lane from Mum and Dad.

Once settled in our seats there was self-conscious silence where we both sipped our beer. I scanned the garden. I'd spent many an afternoon here with Chris. And Martin when he was in the country. I knew the landlady and her husband well. Their adult kids had worked at the pub during Uni holidays but were now off chasing their individual fortunes. I caught the eye of the girl who worked in the deli in the village and waved. I'd used to babysit her and now she was sitting in the sun drinking cider and vaping with her friends.

'So what did you want to talk about?' I said, returning my gaze to Gus sitting opposite me.

He smiled. Having kept him at arm's length over the past couple of months of Hannah's lessons I hadn't quite got used to his handsomeness. He was mid-forties and had the kind of golden tan that had sunk in to his DNA. He shaved once a week, on any random day, and if it happened to be the day I saw him, his smooth appearance shocked me.

'Hannah told me she's enrolled at the college,' he said and I looked into my beer glass, glad to be wearing sunglasses. 'We have one of the best school bands in the county, if I do say so myself,' he grinned. 'The drummer is graduating this year so there's an opening. They don't usually take first years because it's a big commitment; a lot of extracurricular rehearsal time and travel for gigs et cetera but Tom showed them a video of her playing, and the band are pretty keen on meeting her. They're auditioning over the next few weeks and I was wondering if you'd be up for bringing her in for a try-out?'

I took a sip of my beer and considered his question. When it became apparent that my beer sipping and considering was on loop Gus spoke again.

'I've not had a student as talented as Hannah,' he said, which made me stop sipping.

'Really?'

He nodded, the sun glinting off his metal-framed sunglasses. 'She's got natural talent for sure, but many people have. What sets her apart, *miles* apart, is that she also has passion and extremely high standards for herself. Did you know she's set herself a goal of mastering Alex Van Halen's "Hot For Teacher"?'

'Yes,' I said, thinking of how often I'd hear her roar in frustration while trying to move her sticks around her kit at the breakneck tempo.

'It's a really tough riff. Lots of top drummers struggle with it.' He picked up his beer, a thick silver ring he wore on his pinkie clinking the glass. 'But she'll achieve it. And probably quite soon.' He smiled. 'Although not soon enough for her.'

'She's determined,' I said, thinking fond thoughts about my daughter.

'I got her doing Simon and Garfunkel's "The Boxer" today, to teach her restraint. She has a tendency to race ahead, and she did the strike on the snare with this unimpressed heavy glare,' he said chuckling. 'It was so hard not to laugh.'

I smiled at Gus's obvious enjoyment at teaching my head-strong (when it came to music, at least) daughter.

'She calls them Simon and *Gargoyle* and it's too sweet to correct,' he said picking up his beer.

'Oh she knows,' I said, grinning. 'That's her way of telling you she hates it.'

Gus shook his head and laughed.

I picked up my own beer. 'So, tell me about these try-outs then.'

After he'd given me the details and explained the level of commitment being a member of the band entailed, and I'd said I'd think about it, the pints had their relaxing effect and we moved on to more personal topics. I asked where he lived – in a rented cottage on the outskirts of the next village; was he married: not anymore. He asked me why Dad walked around with chickens under his arm and if it was okay to teach Hannah Eric Clapton's 'Cocaine'. And I then found out he'd turned down a surf trip to South Africa with his friends to give extra lessons to his students over the break.

'I need the money,' he said with an unbothered shrug. 'The only place I could afford after my wife and I split up is quite far out. I'm saving for a place back in the village area.' He smiled. 'There's always next year.'

'It's a regular trip?'

'Sort of. We're all split from our partners and have been going away on the odd surf weekend. We call ourselves the Separated Surfers.' He grinned and took a gulp of his beer.

'When your divorce comes through, you'll need to change your sport.'

'Like the Divorced Divers?'

'Annulled Arm Wrestlers?'

'Estranged Egg and Spoon Racers?' he said and we both laughed.

'Here you go, my loves,' said Kay, the landlady, placing a mountain of wedges covered in sour cream and chilli sauce on the table.

'Oh, we didn't order these,' I said.

Kay smiled. 'On the house. It's lovely to see you back here.'

I felt my cheeks heat up at Kay's simple kindness. 'Thanks.'

She gave me shoulder a squeeze, collected our empty glasses and left.

Gus watched her go. 'People know you here,' he said with gentle curiosity. 'I've been a regular for nearly two years, but they all say hello to you.'

I nodded. 'I've been coming here since I was a kid,' I glanced over at the open grassy area where little girls in floral dresses were chasing each other, three boys were playing giant Jenga, and a couple in their early twenties sat cross-legged sipping vodka tonics. They all dissolved and Chris, tanned and youthful in a crisp white shirt, first two buttons undone and sleeves rolled up, took their place. I turned back to Gus. 'Chris and I got married here.'

'Oh,' Gus said, shifting in his seat.

'We were supposed to have the wedding at Mum and Dad's but we woke that morning to a broken sewerage pipe and a very stinky lawn. And some stinky chickens. And one stinky sheep.'

Gus wrinkled his nose. 'Gross.'

'Dad rang the plumbers; Mum rang Kay; Chris, Trish and my brother rang all the guests; and I cried. By late morning it was all sorted and the wedding went on exactly as planned, just here instead of at home.'

'It's a beautiful place for a wedding.'

'It was.'

Gus watched me for a few moments. 'Another pint?'

I smiled and nodded. 'Sure.'

Gus headed to the bar and I turned back to the grassy patch, scooped a wedge through the sour cream and popped it in my mouth, thinking back to that perfect, shit-lawn day.

★

Chris and I had traipsed downstairs that morning to find Mum in the kitchen in her dressing gown peering out the open back door with an indecent smell of farts in the air.

'Love, I think we might have a problem,' Mum said to me, her expression grave as she held her nose.

Dad and Martin arrived in the doorway, liquid 'mud' halfway up their wellingtons, faces greenish and solemn.

'Well?' Mum said, her hands at her dressing gown collar.

'It's shit,' Martin said.

'Literally,' said Dad.

I'd burst into tears, and Mum had followed. Sasha had walked in and accused us all of waking her up. Trish had made Mum a coffee with a generous slosh of whisky, and one for herself (minus the coffee). And Chris had pulled me to him and said, 'If I have to marry you surrounded by shit, I will.'

'You probably think that's romantic, but it really isn't,' I'd sniffed.

And by the time I'd dried my tears Trish and Mum had a plan.

★

Gus placed a pint in front of me, snapping me out of my daydream. As he took his seat he glanced at the empty bowl where there used to be wedges, then at me.

'I'm sorry,' I said.

Gus lowered his sunglasses, his aqua eyes flashing. 'You're not, are you?'

I grinned. 'Not even a little bit.'

Gus laughed and pushed his sunglasses back over his eyes.

'But I am sorry about not being sorry,' I said. 'And I shall get us some more.'

I ordered more wedges, and Gus and I chatted and ate as the sun made its way across the hot and buzzy beer garden.

'I married young,' Gus said after I'd asked him why he'd split up with his wife. 'I was in a band and she was wanting to get into fashion. Then I did my teacher training and as we got older we realized that, well . . .' He appeared to be searching for the right term. 'She wasn't a very nice person.'

I laughed. 'Did she realize that, too?'

'No. She realized I was only going to be a "music teacher".'

'What does she do?'

'She co-owns a fashion boutique in the next village.'

'Mantel's?'

'Yep.'

'I know it,' I said. 'Bit too glittery for my taste.'

Gus smiled. 'We still share custody of our dog, though. Month on/month off.'

'You have a dog?'

He picked his phone up, where he'd laid it face down after turning it to silent, a courtesy I hadn't given him in case Hannah needed me, tapped in his code then handed it over. 'That's Andrew.'

'Andrew?' I said, looking at the picture of a black and brown farm dog more suited to the name Rex or Jed. 'After . . . ?'

'No one.'

'Ok . . .' I said then after a beat we cracked up.

'Month on/month off is hard, though,' Gus said taking back his phone. 'Each time I hand him back I end up moping around for about a week. It's like a death.' His cheeks lost their colour. 'I'm so sorry,' he said, dropping his gaze to the table, the image of a man severely disappointed in himself. 'That's . . . That was . . .' he shook his head then looked back up. 'Sorry.'

I smiled and reached a hand across the table to squeeze his forearm. It was warm from the sun. 'It's okay,' I said.

I was used to the strange role reversal that happens when you've lost a loved one; comforting people who feel they may have accidently upset you and soothing away their mortification.

'Well, obviously you've met Cookie,' I said, moving us past the moment.

'Yes, we know each other. Intimately,' he said, and I detected a hint of violation-related shame.

'She humped your leg, didn't she?'

'Leg. Thigh. Foot pedal. Backpack.' He lowered his sunglasses and looked over the top. 'Paper bag with my sandwiches in it.'

My mouthful of beer went down the wrong way. 'Oh my God!' I said through choking coughs. 'I'm so sorry!'

'It's fine. Iris made me a steak and kidney pie to make up for it.' He winced. 'Mostly kidney.'

'Well, I'm sorry about that too.'

As we chatted it turned out that I was not the only one who ferreted bits of gluggy lunch offerings off my plate.

He reminded me that a few weeks before I'd brought Hannah's old plastic pencil case to the table and sequestered hunks of gloopy partially cooked scotch-egg and asparagus pie.

'You saw that?'

'I *copied* that! Except I used my fabric drumstick case and had to throw it out.'

'Fabric?' I laughed. 'Amateur.'

'She has a unique culinary view,' Gus said diplomatically.

'There isn't anything Mum doesn't think can be put in a pie,' I said. 'Leftover chicken laksa, pea and ham soup, oysters.'

Gus shuddered. 'I was there for that one.'

While we were laughing Kay arrived at our table.

'How much set-up time will you need, Gus, love? I want to get the lawn mowed beforehand.'

I listened as Gus talked stage logistics, amps and power cords, then Kay nodded and headed over to another table.

'What's that about?' I asked when Gus turned back to me.

'We have a gig here on Thursday. Our first one. I'm actually kind of nervous.'

'You've performed before, though?'

'Not with these guys. My mates have reached that stage of life where their teenage kids are never at home and they can get on with doing their own thing a bit more so we started a band. We're a little rusty.' Gus appeared to have a sudden idea. 'Would you come? You could bring Hannah and Tom. We could do with the numbers. I don't know who will come to a gig at 2pm on a Wednesday but that's all Kay could give us at short notice. Nothing like a band of four playing to a crowd of three.' He gave me a hopeful grin.

Before I could answer Kay walked past carrying a tower of empty glasses against her chest. 'You know Brooke here is a whizz at pub quizzes? Get her on your team and you may get your hands back on that ridiculous cup you named after yourself.'

'Believe me, I'm trying,' Gus said, grinning at me.

★

'Mum, Stefan is a girl,' Hannah said as soon as I walked through the open front door, feeling warm and fuzzy from the three pints in the sun and the surprisingly easy conversation with Gus. Tom stood at her side eating a radish (ew) with its greenery still attached. He reminded me of Crumpet, but without the tendency towards unprovoked violence.

'Don't worry, I'm sure Miss Shuker won't notice,' I said, sliding my sunglasses on top of my head and rummaging in my handbag for my phone to call Trish. I hadn't planned to be so long with Gus and I'd seen a bunch of missed calls and texts. 'How can you be sure, anyway?'

'She laid five eggs,' Tom said.

I stopped rummaging and looked up. 'Well, she'll notice *that*.'

The kids nodded sagely.

Mum, Dad, Hannah, Tom, Lars, Leo and I were gathered round Stefan/Stefanie's cage in the kitchen looking at the eggs when Sasha walked in with a hamster in a cage.

'It's for the other one,' she said in the face of our confusion.

'What other one?' Mum asked.

'Franco,' she said, referring to the guinea pig.

'Why?'

'Because Dad said!' Sasha said, indignant. 'About it being illegal in Switzerland to have only one guinea pig because they die of loncliness!'

Mum frowned at the cage then up at Sasha. 'But this is a hamster.'

Sasha affected a violent *'AND?'* expression.

'Well . . . they're different animals, love.'

'And we're not in Switzerland,' I added.

'And unfortunately, the two animals,' Dad said in a regretful tone, 'while both from the rodent family, do not get along. Alas, if we put them together the guinea pig will become irritated by the hamster and will attack it.'

Sasha glared at everyone. 'NOBODY EVER APPRECIATES WHAT I DO AROUND HERE!' She dumped the cage on the counter, stomped out of the kitchen, up the stairs, along the landing, into her bedroom, and slammed the door.

Mum, Dad, Hannah, Tom, Lars and I looked at the jittery occupant of the cage.

'So I guess we have a hamster now, aye, Nan?' said Hannah, poking her finger into that cage. 'What shall we call him?'

'We should take him back to Jeffrey,' Mum said, regarding the hamster with distaste.

'Paul,' said Lars, 'When a child I did have one called Paul, and I did love him.'

'Paul is a lovely name,' Mum said, breaking into a beatific smile and picking up the cage with sudden veneration. 'Let's introduce him to everyone else, shall we, Lars?'

★

Later that evening, Tom and Hannah sat in their beds with bowls of apples and copies of the latest Phillip Pullman. 'Lights off in ten minutes, okay?' I said, popping my head around the doorway. Cookie was curled on the bed next to Hannah.

They both nodded, absorbed. They were reading the same edition and racing to get to the end. It was something they'd been doing for years. I felt a deep tug of guilt that I still didn't know if moving to Sussex was best for Hannah and me, and that if I decided against it then this happy little set-up had a time limit.

'I didn't realize Gus was funny,' I said after a while.

'Yeah. He's really funny,' Hannah said without looking up from her book.

'He's hilarious,' Tom said, crunching his apple.

'Oh,' I said, crossing the room and sitting on Hannah's bed and running my finger through Cookie's fur.

She looked up from her book. 'It's okay, Mum, you've been busy.'

Chapter 26

'I don't get these,' I said, picking up Leesa's notebooks with motivational statements on the covers. *"You are enough." "You do enough", "You're fine as you are"*. They're so one-eyed.'

'Studies have shown that, when feeling unworthy, people respond to positive statements,' Leesa said as she scanned her instruction manual. 'Even when it comes in the form of anonymous declarations.'

'Maybe for some, yes, they shit on themselves unnecessarily and need reminding that they're worthy and "enough", but what about the people who are *not* enough? Who are *not* "fine as they" are but actual total assholes?'

Leesa regarded me from across the table.

'Like people who don't pay their child maintenance or repeatedly cheat on their partners? No, shithead, you could have done more. You could have done *a lot* more. These swirly statements need to come with a veeeery long disclaimer that says *If you are one of the following type of bastards then you do not get to read my swirly gold statement and feel good about yourself. Avert your eyes, snakey muthafucka.*'

I waited for a response from Leesa but she was entrenched in her Life Coaching manual.

After a few seconds she looked up with a patient expression. 'Finished?'

'Yes.'

Leesa then had me do a vision board with 'companionship' in mind. After a quiet half hour of cutting and pinning pictures from magazines on a corkboard she'd brought in, while Leesa read her manual and made notes, I said 'This is so "self-help" circa 1996' and Leesa snorted despite herself. When I finished I held it up.

'There's an awful lot of beaches and bottoms,' Leesa said, her eyes heavy with disappointment.

'You're not looking properly.' I moved the board closer. 'There are also nice cushions and margaritas.'

Leesa shook her head and we moved on to her favoured activity: form filling.

At the end of the session she said by the end of the week I had to accept an invite and extend an invite, and that I needed to get a gloop of sleep out of my eye because it had been driving her crazy all morning and I allowed myself a giggle at her sassiness.

'I feel like we're making progress,' she said, packing her things.

'Really? I feel like that's a line every therapist is trained to say so clients don't ask for their money back.'

Leesa smiled. 'Perhaps.' She picked up her tote and turned to me with a resigned expression. 'Do you have any questions?'

I grinned.

Leesa waited.

'Do you think amphibians have evolved *not* to have emotions?' I asked and Leesa rolled her baby blues. 'That they're looking at us like *Dude, check out those humans. They're still dealing with anxiety and depression and the angst of unrequited love. I'd have pity for them but I got rid of that useless shit, like, millennia ago, man?*'

Leesa left.

The next day she got me to fill out more forms and handed over eight books she wanted me to read that would help me find direction.

At the end of the session, as she collected her folders and manuals, she looked up. 'Do you have any—' she paused, 'thing that you'd like to add?'

I grinned. Clever girl.

'Did you know,' I said, and while Leesa packed her bag and left the room I told her that researchers set out to establish what makes a word funny and found that there are six basic categories; sex, bodily functions, insults, swear words, partying and animals. 'And the top ten funniest words were: upchuck, bubbly, boff, wiggly, yaps, giggle, cooch, guffaw, puffball and jiggly. As described in the *Journal of Experimental Psychology*,' I said, and waved Leesa, shaking her head and hiding a smile, out the front door.

★

'Look how you've grown!' Kay clutched Hannah to her substantial bosom as soon as we walked through the door of the Gentle Goose. Hannah grinned up at her. 'Oh, and those braces really do suit you! Did you know my Matthew had braces? Why don't you and Tom come and choose some crisps and I'll show a photo out back.' She looked at me with a 'that okay?' expression and, with a warmth in my heart, I nodded.

After Leesa's 'extend/accept an invite' comment Mother, who I can only assume had a full debrief with Leesa after each session, or had the dining room bugged, hounded me relentlessly, and to stop her setting me up on any more 'play-dates', I texted Gus and said I'd love to see his gig. I was also keen to get out of the house. It was hard to do any #NoReason work with Mum's hypervigilance anytime I got on the computer or phone so I thought I could sit in a corner of the beer garden and make a few plans. But Hannah and I hadn't had much of a chance to talk about #NoReason so there weren't many plans to be made. I'd noticed that even though #NoReason acts were continuing while we were away, she didn't check the social media responses as often as she usually did in London. She was too occupied with Tom and her movie script and Gus's lessons and neighbour's piglets and seeing if Pablo could swim or liked burritos.

Tom, Hannah and Kay disappeared behind the bar and I headed out to the beer garden feeling weirdly nervous about seeing Gus.

Outside, the band was setting up on a makeshift stage at the back of the sunny garden and seemed mildly stressed about what went where. While I was deliberating on whether to go over, a woman in a navy sleeveless playsuit, with tanned freckled limbs, salmon-coloured sandals, a straw hat, and bright red lips appeared in front of me.

'Brooke?'

'Yes.'

The woman cracked into a grin, her teeth perfect and naturally shiny white. 'I'm Michelle. Mich. Gus told me to keep an eye out for you! Come, we're sitting over here.'

I followed her across the lawn to a table where another woman and man, both in their forties, were sitting with glistening pints, glossy sunglasses, and smelling of cologne and tropical suntan lotion.

'Guys, this is Brooke!' Mich said and my arrival seemed expected. 'This is Amanda, she's married to Danny up there on bass.' Mich pointed from the woman in a white broderie top and her blonde hair in a casual ponytail, to the beefy armed guy untangling cables on the stage. 'This is Blake, he's Dan's partner,' she said pointing from the tanned and toned man at the table wearing a fitted black T-shirt and lots of leather bracelets to the slim guy in a trucker cap adjusting a pedal behind the keyboard. 'Yes, we have two Daniels in the band. And my husband is the drummer, Robbie,' Mich said, nodding her head at the man who was on the stage in shorts and a pale blue T-shirt with a surf label on the front and had just dropped all the song sheets.

She laughed and Gus and Robbie looked up.

Gus grinned, said something to Robbie, then jogged across the quiet garden.

'Hey,' he said. 'You came!'

'Of course. I wasn't going to miss – what's your band's name?'

Gus's smile faltered. 'The Van Dans?'

'Because we have two Dans,' Blake explained. 'And they arrive in a van.'

'I thought it was The Van *Dammes*?' said Amanda. 'Like Jean Claude Van Damme.'

'Why would it be that?' Blake said.

'Because Dan and Robbie do martial arts.'

'When did they change it from Four Pete's Ache?'

'When they realized they didn't know a "Pete",' said Mich. 'Let alone four of them.' And they commenced arguing.

'We're still working it out,' Gus said laughing. 'You look really nice.'

'Thanks,' I said, blushing under his smiling gaze. I'd left my hair out and, after a rummage through Sasha's cornucopia of beautifying products, had found a subtle bronzer that I'd rubbed with an amateur fingertip along my cheekbones. I wore a black cami, black linen shorts, and leopard print slides. Nothing special but it was nicer than the leggings/T-shirt/maybe-not-yet-washed-my-hair-topknot combo Gus was used to seeing me in.

He smiled at me for a moment longer then scanned the garden. 'Not much of a turnout,' he said, noting the smattering of people, some reading newspapers at tables and looking at the band set-up with concern.

'I'm sure more are on their way,' I said, unconvinced.

There was a sudden screech of feedback and everybody covered their ears.

'I'd better get back, we'll lose our audience before we start,' he said with a grimace then turned and jogged back to the stage.

Mich beckoned me to sit next to her and handed me one of the waiting pints. Once I was seated I answered everyone's questions about where Hannah and Tom were, how the midterm break was going, if my sister had really dated everyone in Sussex and how my parents came to have so very many animals; the fact they seemed to know all about me giving me an unexpected sense of belonging.

Hannah and Tom raced to the table asking for lemonades and I got them to introduce themselves while I went inside and ordered another round.

'Tom is writing a movie,' I heard Hannah say as she sat next to Mich who turned out to be an English teacher at a school a few villages away.

'And Hannah's doing the music,' Tom said, shuffling in next to Blake.

'And we're going to move to Hollywood and get a flat.'

'And a dog.'

When I got back balancing a tray of drinks Tom and Hannah were re-enacting a scene from their movie that involved Pablo the donkey making quesadillas for Leo the parrot. When they were done they moved to sit on the grass at the foot of the stage.

'They're adorable,' Mich said. 'A real double act.'

'They are,' I said, the familiar guilt rearing its head whenever anyone mentioned how sweet Tom and Hannah were together.

The twang of Gus's guitar sounded and we faced the band as they kicked into a shaky version of Bruce Springsteen's 'Glory Days', Gus on lead guitar and vocals. After a song or two the band found their groove and the garden slowly filled up. As the afternoon wore on and the beer flowed, Mich, Amanda and Blake shimmied in their seats, eventually making their way to standing when the band played REO Speedwagon's

'Keep On Loving You' while I stayed sitting and tapped my foot. With the band gravitating towards our table in each break I felt like a groupie.

'She took everything,' Mich said in a divulging manner in the final break.

The band were doing rounds of people they knew in the garden and Mich, Blake, Amanda and I were sun-warmed and beer-merry at our table.

'Everything?' I said.

'Yep,' Blake said. 'She said her business had paid for the house whereas his teacher's salary barely covered bills and in the end he didn't want to fight anymore so he walked away from it all.' He made a face and I got the sense none of them missed Gus's ex all that much.

'He got shared custody of their dog, his music gear, surfboard and that crusty horse of his but that's it,' Amanda added. 'We even had to lend him a sofa.'

I looked over at Gus, holding his pint at his chest and laughing. 'He doesn't seem bitter at all.'

'Oh he had some dark weeks,' Blake said.

'He looked at voodoo dolls online,' said Amanda.

'And drank,' added Mich.

'And came on to *everything*,' said Blake.

Mich, Amanda and Blake shuddered in recollection and we cracked up.

A few minutes later the band, minus Robbie who was heading our way, moved towards the stage.

'Robbie needs a break,' Gus said into the microphone. 'He's getting on a bit so we'd like to call our resident rock drummer to the stage.' He gestured to Hannah at the front who squealed and threw her hands over her face. But a second later she'd clambered behind the drums, adjusted the seat, pedal and snares, and was looking expectantly at Gus – excited and nervous.

Gus said something in her ear, she nodded with serious

authority that made our table make 'awww' noises, then she hit the sticks together in a one, two, three motion and they launched in to Metallica's 'Enter Sandman', Hannah beating the drums with her giant brace-filled grin just visible over the cymbals, and aimed fully at Gus.

'She's amazing!' Amanda said, flipping her glasses on her head, her eyes wide.

'Wow!' Mich said.

'I think I'm out of the band,' Robbie said and there was a tiny note of realism in his statement.

As I watched my daughter become the star of the gig I was overcome with pride. Gus moved from singing at the front of the stage to her side, I assumed to give her confidence, but by the look of her she didn't need it. She was in her element. Tom had moved closer to the stage and was dancing energetically as close to Hannah on the drums as he could get, probably just of proud as her as I was.

Hannah played three songs with the band; all rock and drum heavy. After they'd smashed out the last note of a Van Halen song and the swollen crowd had cheered, Gus leaned forward, and said something in Hannah's ear that caused her ecstatic grin to drop. She glanced at me then said something to Gus, a pained look on her face.

'What are they up to?' Mich said.

'We're going to play a song now,' Gus said, looking at me with a gleam in his eye while Hannah slunk down behind the drums looking mortified, 'that apparently always gets someone special in this audience dancing.'

Blake leaned towards me. 'I think *you're* that special someone,' he said, having trouble with his 's's.

Hannah turned and said something to Dan behind the keyboard. He cracked up, removed his trucker cap and handed to her, and she jammed it on her head and pulled it low in an incognito way, making the crowd laugh.

'One, two, three!' Gus chanted, and they launched into 'MMMBop' by the Hanson Brothers.

'Oh no!' I said, giggling.

Mich, Amanda, Robbie and Blake leapt up.

'Come on!' Blake said, dragging me to join them. 'You *have* to dance to this one!'

Soon all the kids in the garden were bopping, then a few more, until eventually the whole garden was dancing. Even me. A little bit. I noticed Gus's eyes on me. Mich noticed me noticing and smiled. I watched Tom leap about, delighting in watching his best friend excel at what she loved most. Hannah grinned at him, despite hating the cheesy song, and a mantle of happiness settled across me. I moved closer to Amanda, Blake, Mich and Robbie dancing in the middle of the lawn and allowed them to pull me in to their knot of MMMbopp-ing, sun-kissed limbs.

*

Around 5 o'clock the band wrapped up. Mich and Robbie had to drop their teen sons at a party, Amanda and Danny had a BBQ to get to, and Blake and Dan were off to a wine bar. They invited Gus but it was somewhere his ex frequented so he declined.

'I think I'll just head home,' he said.

'We're having a games night if you want to join us?' I said, shocked at where that had come from. I blamed the beer. And MMMbop.

Mich, Robbie, Amanda, Danny, Blake and Dan were *dreadful* at hiding their interest in Gus's answer as they gathered their bags, hats, vapes and jackets.

'It's just Monopoly,' I said, my heart quickening at Gus's apparent interest. 'We lost the dog and the battleship so you can either be my father's old prefect badge or half a walnut shell.'

Gus shook his head at his friends, now openly observing

our exchange, and turned to me with a grin. 'I think I'll go for the walnut shell.'

Everyone left with kisses on the cheek and declarations of meeting up at the next gig. Gus said he'd meet us at Mum and Dad's once he'd dropped the gear home, and Hannah, Tom and I headed home in an Uber; Hannah absolutely fizzing at performing in her first gig and listing all the songs she wanted to play at the next one.

Gus turned up around 6:30pm, his hair wet and smelling like pine and sea salt, even more tanned from his afternoon in the sun, and handed over a bottle of rosé with a dragonfly on the label. While I poured us a glass each he surveyed, with amused interest, the noisy family occupying various areas of the kitchen. Hannah was at the table showing whoever was listening a beat on some upturned Tupperware. Leo was pacing the table picking up bits and pieces and saying the odd swear word. Mum was burning every item she was intending on serving. Lars was cheeping bird calls he'd learnt off YouTube to Stefanie. Clint was watching from the back door. Dad had picked up Gus's wine bottle and was telling us that in order to avoid the males bothering them for copulation, the female dragonfly fakes her own death. And Tom was Googling copulation.

Dinner was served (toad in the hole that looked more like burnt penis in custard) then we replenished our drinks, moved to the den and the family games night began. Mother was upset that no one landed on her Old Kent Road collection despite her declaring irrefutably at the beginning of the game that that was the only way to win; Gus, with his half walnut shell, quietly collected up the railways stations and amassed a tidy pile of ratty paper money; Tom pointed out that while Dad (missing opportunities, losing desperately and not at all concerned) was informing us of the mating ritual of the dung beetle he'd missed out on collecting rent yet again, and Dad retorted that he didn't need money and quoted Socrates: *He who is not contented with what he has, would not be contented with what he would like to have.*

'Why on earth do you play then, Spike?' Mum had blustered. 'If you're not even going to *try* to win.'

Meanwhile Lars had assembled a strip of hotels down one side and made paupers of the lot of us.

Once Hannah and Tom were in bed I walked Gus out to his bike, giggling about the rifts caused during a typical family games night.

'Your mother cheats,' Gus said, pulling his bike out from the cart shed.

'I know. Everyone knows. And she *knows* everyone knows.'

'And not even subtly,' he said with disbelief. 'She just took money whenever she needed some.'

I laughed.

Gus smiled. 'See you tomorrow. 4 o'clock, was it?' Gus said, meaning Hannah's birthday barbeque.

'Yep.'

He smiled. 'Thanks for coming to the gig today. I've always dreamed of playing to a crowd of twelve.'

I laughed. 'Anytime. It was fun,' I said surprising myself by actually meaning it. I'd enjoyed being with his friends. And I'd enjoyed how often his gaze would find me from the stage. 'And thank *you* for letting everyone know I dance to "MMMbop" and humiliating me in front of twelve people.'

Gus grinned. 'Anytime. It was fun.'

He leaned forward and kissed me on the cheek, just the same way that Mich and Robbie and Blake and Amanda and all the Dannys had done, but his caused an unexpected flutter under my ribs and a hyper awareness of the exact spot of skin his lips had touched.

Blushing in the dark, I waved goodbye as he pedalled out the gate.

Chapter 27

Early the next morning Mum, Dad, Sasha, Lars and I woke Hannah (and Tom) by bounding in to her room blaring Stevie Wonder's 'Happy Birthday' from a Bluetooth speaker; all of us singing in our varying levels of talent, with Martin part of it all via Facetime from Cuba.

Hannah shuffled up in bed amid giggles and grins, her hair an adorable bird's nest. After a mass cuddle we piled her bed with presents. She squealed with delight at new cymbals and drumsticks (a routine gift for the past few years), tie-dye T-shirts, band T-shirts, rugby balls, and multi-coloured socks. Lars made her a tin of a delectable buttery biscuit, and Tom gave her a vintage Sheila E. T-shirt his parents had found in a market in Marrakech, which she put on over her pyjamas the second it was out of the wrapping, and a clear file folder of printed-out sheet music of songs he wanted her to learn.

After pancakes everyone showered then leapt in to party prep. People were arriving at 4 pm and the day was expected to be hot. Mum was in charge of making sure the animals were secured, filling the vol-au-vents she insisted were *not* out of fashion, and making the downstairs loo presentable, while the rest of us scoured the barn and cart-shed for extra outdoor tables and chairs, cleaned the rusty barbeque, and stacked up picnic plates and cups.

At 10 on the dot Leesa turned up, despite me trying to cancel her, and asked when I'd last felt joy.

'When I realized that the word "double-barrelled" was double-barrelled,' I'd said.

Leesa had deadpanned me.

'Is there any area in your life where you feel unfulfilled,' she'd asked next.

'Yes. I learned the word "ombudsman" this year and I'm upset I've never had the opportunity to use it in a sentence.'

'You just did.'

'You're clever,' I'd said, beaming. 'Problem solved. Shall we wrap up for the day?'

And Leesa had smiled and handed over more forms.

★

'There you are, birthday girl!' I said, arriving in Hannah's bedroom doorway after hustling Leesa out bang on time. 'It's time to pick up your cake, Tom's waiting in the car.' My good mood dropped as I noticed her on her phone, a furrow between her brows. 'Hannah?'

She turned her phone face down on her lap. 'Yeah?'

'Time to pick up your cake. Go brush your teeth, okay?' I smiled, waiting to see if she was going to tell me that something was up.

'Okay.' She put her phone under her pillow and headed out.

I waited until I heard her electric toothbrush before slipping the phone out from under her pillow. I tapped in her passcode and the screen lit up to what she was looking at. An Instagram post of Livie, Zara, Mackenzie, and three other girls who used to be friends with Hannah standing on a jetty next to a shiny boat, their arms linked as they stood grinning in their fruit-coloured bikinis. Melody was with them in a floaty open kaftan displaying her whiter than white bikini and her tanner than an Irish Setter tan.

The caption said #*girlsquad boat day* – *love being with all my* #*bestfriends!* I scrolled down her feed; the other girls had also posted variations of the same photo with similar '#*bestfriends all together*' captions. I knew Livie would have organized her #girlsquad boat day on Hannah's birthday on purpose. Pushing down a swell of anger I slipped the phone under Hannah's pillow and headed downstairs even more determined to make Hannah's day special.

'Why don't you leave the kids here?' Mum said, appearing at the bottom of the stairs carrying a box of bunting.

'It's Hannah's cake. She wants to pick it up.'

Mum watched me fire off a quick text, read its instant reply, grin, and fire off another. She narrowed her eyes. 'You've got something planned, haven't you?'

'No.'

'You're up to another mischief, I can feel it,' she accused. 'You're all twitchy and—' Hannah clattered down the stairs and out the front door at the same time as Lars walked past in the opposite direction wearing just a pair of denim shorts and carrying a folded trestle table, his chest bare and his pecs bulging. With Mum momentarily sidetracked I took the opportunity to escape, and fifteen minutes later I'd parked the car on the outskirts of the village. Hannah and Tom trotted ahead on the sunny footpath discussing a TikTok life-hack they wanted to try but when we reached the square they stopped in their tracks.

'A #NoReason?!' Tom said, gaping at people in colourful #NoReason T-shirts approaching locals. 'What are they doing here?'

'We must be lucky!' I said, grinning at Hannah who grinned right back.

A girl in pink shorts, heart-shaped sunglasses, and a baby blue #NoReason T-shirt approached us. 'Hello!' she said with a megawatt smile. 'We're doing a treasure hunt in the village today. Would you like to play?'

'Yes!' squealed Hannah and Tom at the same time.

'It's my birthday!' Hannah blurted as the girl handed over a clue.

'Well, happy birthday to you!' the lady said, grinning wider. 'I love your T-shirt!'

Half an hour later Hannah and Tom chose a free book each from the bookstore and the man behind the counter handed them their next clue. They'd had free milkshakes at the cafe, a scrounge in a lucky-dip from the toy shop, multicoloured candies from the old-fashioned sweet shop, and cake-pops from the bakery. Each store owner handed them a clue and each time Hannah had squealed 'It's my birthday!' at them. As we criss-crossed the village Hannah and Tom compared clues and loot with other children who couldn't believe their luck. I snapped photos and sent them to Trish who was in a meeting in London before heading down for the party but she replied to each one all the same.

'This one's for you,' Tom said, handing me the note as we stepped out of the bookshop onto the sunny footpath now teeming with families who'd heard about the treasure hunt.

Hannah read over my shoulder.

Are you with an adult? I bet they're thirsty. Take them to the bottle store to visit Kirsty.

I laughed at Hannah's eye roll then followed her and Tom as they clattered along the cobblestones. At the bottle shop Kirsty was on the footpath next to a wine barrel used as a table, wearing a straw hat adorned with multicoloured flowers and pouring paper cups of cool sangria for grateful parents and grandparents. Knots of children stood alongside showing each other their haul and giggling with the adventure of it all.

'It's my birthday!' Hannah said, bouncing in front of Kirsty.

'I know, my love!' she said. 'Run inside and see Henry, he has your present behind the counter.'

Hannah ran inside followed by Tom.

'You didn't need to do that,' I said.

'Oh pish posh,' Kirsty said, handing me a sangria with an overjoyed beam. 'Isn't this exciting?!' Her ruddy cheeks were even more flushed than usual. 'I got the call from the #NoReason person last week and I couldn't believe it!'

As she handed out drinks she recounted how a #NoReason 'representative' had called and talked her through the plan and how all the shop owners were thrilled they'd chosen our village while I grinned along and pretended I hadn't co-ordinated the whole thing in the preceding weeks and wasn't actually sitting next to Trish when she'd made that phone call to Kirsty.

'To think all the fun that's been on the news is here in our village!' Kirsty said.

Hannah bounded out of the shop, thanked Kirsty for the new drumsticks by way of a giant hug, accepted a clue, then Kirsty turned to the next group of adults and children and started her story again.

Tom and Hannah cracked the final code Trish and I had written then ran all the way to the village green where bouncy castles and inflatable slides were set up, music played, and kids could get ice lollies and pony rides while adults could order cocktails from brightly decorated hipster drinks tucks.

A lively, laughter, music, play-filled hour later we were home and Mother was at the front door.

'I'm speechless,' she said as the kids hustled inside while I followed behind holding the cake we'd picked up before leaving the buzzing village.

I smiled. 'I wish that were true.'

But her inquiries/reprimands could go no further because Clint and Pablo got loose and found the tray of vol-au-vents and Leo was refusing to go into his cage in the dining room because he couldn't be trusted to not cuss at the children, and Hannah and Tom accidently exploded the vol-au-vent piping bag all over the kitchen.

'There are so many comments already!' Hannah said, scrolling through Instagram on my phone while I wiped vol-au-vent filling off her Sheila E. T-shirt with a flannel in the bathroom. 'I can't believe all the kids in the village got presents for my birthday!' She giggled and looked up from her phone. 'I love you so much, Mum,' she said, leaning into me and I thought my heart might burst.

Trish arrived direct from her meeting and immediately got among the worker bees and moments after we'd cracked open the last deck chair, Mum had folded the toilet paper into a peak, and Crumpet had been walked back to his field, people began to arrive.

Dennis handed over an exquisitely-wrapped gift and Hannah opened it to find a book of Def Leppard sheet music, not just signed but with a personal message to Hannah from Rick Allen, and a new set of coloured rubber bands for her braces.

'Thank you!' Hannah said and threw her arms around his waist.

He smiled at me over the top of her head and I had the urge to fling my arms around his neck myself and thank him for the constant kindness he showed my daughter.

'*That's* Hannah's orthodontist?' Trish said as he was herded away by Mum to help hand out vol-au-vents. 'Think I might have to chip myself a tooth.'

'Sorry we're late, dance recital,' Penny said as all four doors of their 4×4 flung open, liberating the hot and bothered family.

'That teacher,' Penny said, stepping away from the car and leaving Rog and the kids to unload. 'Ay, she needs a fuck or a taco or *something*, she's miserable. The looks we got for leaving as soon as they were off stage! What a horrible life, I hope Rosa gives it up soon before that three-ounce stickwoman starts telling her her thighs are too chunky. God, it's hot! I need a drink. You said there were mojitos, no?'

Gus, the yurt guests, Mum and Dad's friends and their grandchildren arrived next then all of a sudden we had a party. Kids ran through sprinklers, climbed trees and jumped on the trampoline in the baking sunshine. Dad, Lars and Leo supervised them in the pool and Mum screeched when Hannah traipsed them all through the house looking for towels. They wrapped sausages straight off the BBQ in buttered white bread while still in their dripping swimming costumes and ran back into the water with tomato sauce down their chins.

The adults introduced themselves to each other and the sun (we all blame the sun) made us down mojitos and Pimm's at a considerable pace. We stopped to sing happy birthday round the drum-themed cake and Hannah grinned while looking out at the ragtag bunch of friends we'd cobbled together.

As the hot afternoon turned into a balmy early evening the adults, except for Sasha who left to get ready for a date, settled in to fold-out chairs, loungers, and camping chairs, and sipped on frequently refreshed drinks, while the kids ventured in a big gang, all clutching rapidly melting ice lollies, out to the orchard looking for Clint and Pablo.

I handed Penny and Trish their renewed mojitos and apologized for taking longer than expected. 'I was talking to Dennis.'

'Yes, we noticed. And we think so did someone else,' Penny said, tipping her head towards Gus.

'Hardly,' I said, but felt myself blushing as I settled in my deck chair. I'd been conscious of Gus's attention as I'd been floating around and quite liked the warm, fluttery feeling in my stomach of him noticing where I was during the party.

'You're much more chatty than usual, *cariño*,' Penny said after testing her mojito. 'It's good.'

'Am I?'

Penny and Trish nodded emphatically.

'How's the life coaching going?' Penny asked as we watched Rog, Gus, and Dennis try to string up a piñata.

'She gave me all these books to read about finding my purpose because she thinks I'm directionless.'

I noticed Penny and Trish resolutely avoid making eye contact.

'They've got names like *Finding True North*, *Finding Your True North*, *Finding Your North Star*, Following *Your North Star*. What's so good about north? Many good things are south. We all want south-facing properties.'

'Birds head south for the winter,' Penny offered.

'South Korea is the better Korea,' said Trish.

'*South* Park.'

'*South* of France.'

'Going "south" is always good,' Trish said, sexual connotations all over her eyebrows.

★

'That's Rocky, and Wilma, and Keyser Soze, and Brad, and Linda Carter,' I said, introducing Gus to the chickens and ducks a few more mojitos later.

The setting sun was casting long shadows across the lawn and the combination of alcohol and relief at Hannah having a good time on her birthday was making me feel euphoric. I'd found myself wanting to chat to Gus so had suggested a tour of the outdoor animals.

'I actually helped your father dig the pond,' he said.

'Oh. So you've already met them,' I said, feeling silly.

'Well, not formally,' he said with a grin that gave me goosebumps.

We walked back to the party area and stood under an old oak, watching the kids attack a piñata that Penny was hoisting higher and Rog was trying to lower.

Gus was warm and funny and I found myself wanting to crack up. Then wanting to hold it in. Then wanting to forget about my moniker of 'sad widow' and just laugh. Without it being followed by a wave of guilt. Gus chuckled at Penny and Rog having a skirmish over the piñata and as he did our arms touched. The feel of his sun-hot arm against mine sent a ripple of desire across my abdomen. And other areas. A feeling I hadn't had in so long it shocked me. My head swam. I looked at Gus. He was smiling at me. He was saying something. I made an excuse about needing to check the vol-au-vents, raced across the garden, and Trish and Penny found me a few minutes later sitting in the dining room in the exact seat I sat in when I had my Leesa sessions.

'What happened?' Penny said, pulling out Leesa's usual chair. 'You were laughing and having a good time and then you took off while Gus was mid story.'

I told them about the laughing, the arm brush, the mojitos, and the 'feeling'.

Penny frowned. 'You . . . you were flirting?'

'Yes,' I said, the admission causing all manner of confusing emotions.

'And?' Trish said.

'And I think he was flirting with me.'

'*And?*' Penny said.

'And . . . and I liked it!' I burst into tears.

While I ran my arm under my running nose Trish and Penny exchanged a look.

'*Cariño,*' Penny said, her eyes sympathetic. 'Don't be so hard on yourself. We know it is tough for you, but it's okay to have feelings. Chris has been gone a long time.'

'Not even two years,' I spluttered.

'It'll be two years in a couple of weeks,' she said gently. 'And it's okay to flirt. It's okay to *want* to flirt. It's even okay to think about dating.'

I looked at her, horrified. She nodded. I looked to Trish. She nodded too.

'Since Chris has been gone, have you ever felt a stir?' Penny said. 'You know, in the place where stirs occur?'

I spent a good minute wiping my running nose with a tissue Trish handed me. 'I've had a stir occurrence,' I admitted.

Penny gave a nod of encouragement. 'That's good, that's good. When?'

'There's a scene in *The Lion King*,' I sniffed. 'You know when Simba and Scar are fighting and it's in slow-mo and Simba's back is all muscly?'

Penny sneered and said, 'No. There's something very wrong with you,' at the same time Trish nodded and said 'Yes. Excellent.'

'And just then. With Gus.' I burst into tears again.

Penny and Trish talked me through it being okay to start to have these feelings and after I'd calmed down and pretended to agree with them, Trish went to refresh our drinks but came back empty-handed.

'Your sister just arrived back from her date, and she's dressed as Cher,' she said, grinning from the doorway. 'It is definitely worth coming back to the party.'

We headed outside to find Sasha standing around the outdoor table (in a full-noise Cher outfit – the one that's a high-cut, mesh and sequin leotard with feathery headdress) regaling Mum and Dad, their stunned Pétanque friends, and the rest of the party with her most recent humiliation. One poor old man, sitting on a rickety chair at Sasha's crotch height, didn't know where to look.

Apparently, a date had invited her to a 'share' club and she'd thought it was a 'Cher' club (why she didn't investigate this further I don't know), so had hired the feather/sequin/mesh leotard and turned up at the private room of a distinguished wine bar to see ladies and gentlemen with French twists, tailored jackets, and buffed nails sipping Chablis and discussing their stock market investing club.

'Ugh,' she said, flumping on a chair, her feather head-dress knocking the old man's glasses skew-whiff. 'This shit is exhausting.'

Dennis walked over, his eyes alight. 'Cher!'

'Yeah?' Sasha said, unimpressed.

'She's my favourite singer,' he beamed.

Finally, one he knew.

Twenty minutes later Hannah had convinced partygoers to schlep the equipment up from the cellar and well into the evening – with Gus on guitar, Hannah on drums, a yurt guest from Bulgaria on synthesizer, and Dad on his ukulele (rather pointlessly but he enjoyed it all the same) – Dennis sang Cher songs. *All* of the songs and *all* of the words. And harmonies. Not well, not well at all. Enthusiastically, sure. But not well.

Around 11pm the party wound up. I'd managed to avoid being alone with Gus for the rest of the evening, rushing off to refresh drinks or clear up discarded vol-au-vents from the lawn if he happened to venture near me. Dennis left in an Uber, saying he'd come over early in the morning to help tidy up, the tired and contented kids were sent up to bed, followed by Mum and Dad, then Penny and Rog, until only Gus, Trish and I were left. When Trish made a not-so-subtle quick exit to bed I walked Gus across the peaceful, party-littered lawn to his Uber.

'I'm sorry about earlier,' I said as we did that slow foot-swinging kind of walk. I knew he'd know what I meant. 'I was just . . . I was . . .' I couldn't find the words so made crazy hands around my head. 'You know.'

We reached the side of the house and Gus stopped to look at me. His sunglasses were on top of his head and the yellow glow spilling from the windows touched on the tanned angles of his face. He was extremely attractive.

'I think I do,' he said. 'And,' he smiled. 'Well, I think I'll leave that ball in your court.'

I nodded and wrapped my arms around myself. We stood silently for a few minutes then he leaned forward, kissed my cheek goodbye, and jumped in his Uber.

Chapter 28

I was woken by my phone at some sinful hour in the depths of the night.

''Lo?' I croaked.

'Brooke, I'm ever so sorry to call you so late but I've been stabbed.'

I bolted upright in bed. '*Dennis!?* Is that you?!'

'Oh yes, I should have led with that perhaps, it's—'

'Oh my God, are you OKAY?! Where are you?! Who stabbed you?!'

'Er, myself, actually. Ah . . . it's not a *great* story. But I'll have to fill you in a little later. See the thing is, I'm being discharged but because of the medication and the location of the stab wound, near my lung, I can't be alone. I know it really is a most inconvenient time, but I was wondering if you had a spare sofa I could kip on? Just for the night, so I can be around other people in case of any complications. I could get an Uber to you? I'm so sorry to ask, but my Airbnb cottage is rather remote, and the stairs to the bedroom are really more of a ladder and I already fell down it once and the doctor says I can't risk splitting the stitches.'

It was a lot of information to receive at, I looked at the screen of my phone. Almost 2am.

'Of course, I can definitely find you somewhere,' I said, thinking of our full house and full yurt field and where to locate more bedding. 'Why don't I come and get you? What hospital are you at?'

'Oh no no no, I wouldn't dream of it! And also, wouldn't you be, I'm so sorry to assume, a tad over the limit still?'

'I'm fine.' I tossed the duvet back, swung my feet out of bed, and put them on the ground. The room moved substantially. 'Nope. It's an accurate assumption.' I rested my spare arm upright on my knee and cradled my head in my hand.

Dennis doubled, triple, quadruple checked if it was okay (Dennis, just order the Uber), asked if we needed him to pick up any milk on his 2am journey across sleepy West Sussex (er, no thanks), and said he'd leave as soon as the nurse came back with a stab-wound care instructions (righto).

I gave my bedroom a few moments to sober itself up then tiptoed out of the door in my shorty pyjamas and down the hall past all the closed doors; Martin's where we'd put Penny and Rog; my old room, which was now the foreign student's room and where Lars was snoring; Hannah's room, her door open (a rule if Tom were staying) to reveal Tom, Hannah and Penny's kids blissfully asleep with limbs akimbo; and finally Sasha's where we'd put Trish (Sasha kindly staying at a friend's for the evening – after she'd changed out of her Cher eyesore of course).

I jumped as Sasha's door creaked open a crack. I stopped and waited for my friend to emerge with her long limbs but instead as the door slowly creaked open further I saw . . .

'MARTIN!' I shriek/whispered, feeling a rush of love at seeing my brother followed by confusion as to how he was there. Hadn't I spoken to him in Cuba that morning . . . ?

'Shhh!' he whispered back, beaming. He was tanned and skinny like people who spend a lot of time in tropical countries are.

'What are you doing here?' I whispered, grinning back at him. Then I noticed the towel wrapped around his waist, realized he was probably naked under it, remembered where he'd emerged from, and replaced my grin with a scowl. 'In *Trish*'s room!?'

He looked sheepish. 'I decided to go to the airport after speaking to Hannah this morning. I just really wanted to be at the party with all the family and mojitos. So as soon as I hung up from you, I turned around and booked the next flight home. But then my flight kept getting delayed and Customs were being weird about something in my luggage,' he said, looking shifty. 'Then I couldn't find a cab that would bring me out here for ages and when I finally got here it was after midnight and everyone was asleep.' He shrugged. ''Cept Trish.'

I gave him a 'she was awake because you called her, wasn't she?' look.

He grinned back. 'So how are you, sis?'

He put a tanned arm out for a hug, leaving the other to clutch together the corners of the very small towel.

I tried to maintain my scowl but couldn't. Martin was my favourite person in the whole world, aside from Hannah and Chris. I smiled and took a step towards his outstretched arm then froze. I looked away. 'Your towel is coming apart. Do you *wax?*'

'Language barrier at a Balinese massage place.'

'I like it,' Trish whispered, arriving in the doorway.

I screwed up my nose. A door down the hall creaked open and the three of us turned.

Lars emerged in his tiny Scandi boxer shorts and walked sleepy-limbed down the hall to join us.

'Hello,' he said as if it were perfectly normal to be whispering in a hall at 2am with a man he'd never met who waxed his boy places. 'I am Lars from Norway.' He stretched out a hand to Martin and they shook. Martin's towel split again. Lars grinned at everyone.

Another door creaked open and the four of us turned.

Penny emerged. 'What's going on?' She tiptoed towards us, a champagne slinky dressing gown cinched round her tiny waist. 'Martin? Is that you?'

'Hey,' he whispered and waved.

'Hold your goddamned towel!' I whisper-yelled.

Penny reached us. 'Why are we all up?'

'I needed the loo,' Martin said.

'I needed water,' Trish said.

'I needed to check ze egg finch babies,' Lars said.

'I needed some chocolate,' Penny said.

'Dennis stabbed himself,' I said.

★

Martin put on some underpants, went to the loo, and after some heavy glaring (and a knuckle-out punch to the bare upper arm), extracted his luggage from Trish's room and agreed to sleep in the living room with Dennis – a man he'd never met who'd stabbed himself. Trish and I hunted down some bedding; Penny and Lars sourced crisps and chocolate and checked on the egg finch babies. And Dennis arrived half an hour later, surprised to be greeted by a middle-of-the-night pyjama tea-party of semi-sober people.

'Well, I went to bed, but I couldn't settle because of the splinter,' Dennis said after Martin had made him a tea and we'd all inspected the bandage on his ribs. I'd been surprised to see a substantial set of abs that Trish, Penny and I all agreed, via silent glances, were bloody fantastic.

'What splinter?'

'I got a splinter when I was climbing trees looking for the chicken.'

'What chicken?'

'Chickens can't climb trees.'

'It flew up.'

'Chickens can't fly.'

'Why was a chicken in a tree anyway?'

'It was Florence. Mum put her up in a branch because Cookie was after her.'

'Was she drunk?'

'I'd say so. Because then she forgot which tree she put Florence in and by the time we found her she'd kind of hopped up branch by branch until she was out of reach and then Mum panicked that Florence would fall and damage a tail feather and Dad wouldn't be able to show Florence.'

'Show her to who?'

'Florence is a show chicken. They're judged on their tail feathers.'

'Dad is a very serious competitor in the show chicken world. Florence has won distinction the last two years.'

'Sorry, I think I missed a part. Was your mother drunk or the chicken?'

'Mum. Although Florence actually did get stuck into Dad's lager once. She slept for a *really* long time.'

Dennis's attention darted from speaker to speaker. When we turned to face him he looked back at us blankly.

'The splinter?' Penny encouraged after a silent few seconds.

Dennis blinked. 'Oh, yes! Well . . . yes. I couldn't find a needle or pin anywhere in the cottage I'd rented so I got out my pocketknife and tried to dig around.' He looked down at the heel of his hand as he said this. Penny, sitting next to him, narrowed her eyes at his palm that, from my spot on the other side of the coffee table, appeared normal. 'I managed to get it out and then went to the bathroom to clean off the little bit of blood. When I came back, I tripped while unlacing my slippers and fell backwards on the bed. My elbow hit the bottom of the pocketknife that I'd regrettably left on the bed and, rather more regrettably, with the blade still out, which upended the knife making it stick straight up and when I fell on it, it went between my ribs. It missed my lung by a couple of millimetres. Rather fortunate, I think.' Dennis finished with a smile.

Penny leaned forward, frowning at Dennis's open hand. 'The splinter is still in there,' she said, looking up at Dennis as if he were very, *very* strange.

'Ah, yes,' he said, glancing down at his palm with cheerful interest. 'After I'd fallen on the knife I'd pushed myself up by putting my hand on the nightstand. Which is where I'd placed the splinter. So . . . ah . . . yes, the splinter is, unfortunately, back where it started.'

The room was silent for a few moments, processing the story.

Martin frowned. 'Why do your slippers have laces?'

Chapter 29

'Rise and shine,' Mum said, coming into my bedroom and opening the curtains to another sunny day. 'Leesa will be here in less than an hour and you need a shower.'

'I cancelled her,' I croaked from under the covers.

'I uncancelled her.'

I groaned. 'It's Saturday. Why does she want to tell people how to live their lives on a *Saturday?* Doesn't she have a wholefoods market she needs to be at or a microgreen-scented yoga class?'

'I have no clue what you're talking about – get up.'

I pushed myself up. Oh, I felt awful. I blinked my eyes into focus to see Mum sitting at my dressing table in her dressing gown rubbing her forehead, uncharacteristically quiet. 'Mum, are you hung-over?'

'Nothing of the sort!' she said, then burped.

'You are.'

Mum pursed her lips but didn't move. 'The children are watching a movie, your father has gone for his morning walk, the rest of the house is still asleep, and Lars is downstairs making some kind of Norwegian breakfast. It's quite fish-orientated.'

I gagged. 'I think I speak for everyone when I say "firm pass".'

Mum stood, gave a grimace and another burp slipped out,

took a second to steady herself then grabbed my dressing gown off the back of the door. 'Into the shower,' she said, tossing it in my direction but failing and tripping on it as she left.

★

Half an hour later, Mother found out Dennis had been stabbed and had had a sleepover, and that her favourite child was back in the country and was annoyed with all of us for not informing her. Hannah raced into the living room and pounced on her uncle and Mum forced the entire house up for the fishy breakfast in celebration of his return.

'Happy birthday!' Martin said, arriving in the kitchen freshly showered, followed by Trish, also freshly showered (for which I scowled at the both of them) and placed two figurines on the table in front of Hannah who'd been watching Tom devour the fishy breakfast with disgusted fascination.

The figurines were a llama and a donkey, about six inches tall, decked out in South American-style tassels and headdresses. It looked like they were made out of old crisp packets and plastic bags.

'They're made out of old crisp packets and plastic bags,' he declared proudly, and Penny sneered over her coffee.

'I love them!' Hannah said, her face alight. 'Thank you!'

'The saddle bags open and you can store stuff in there,' he said, demonstrating. 'I got them from a women's initiative in Peru. They're able to earn enough money to send their children to school with the proceeds. *And* it cleans up rubbish from the local area.'

'Really?' I picked up the donkey and inspected it. 'Do they have a website?'

Dennis, Trish, Lars and I searched up the initiative, Mum watched with suspicion, Sasha scrolled on her phone, Hannah and Tom tested the fishy breakfast again, and Martin clocked Leo perched on the back of Tom's chair, the guinea pig in a cage next to Stefanie in a cage, and Clint watching from the open kitchen door. 'Things haven't changed much around here,' he said, grinning.

After a second round of coffees everyone helped clean up the garden; Mum trailing Martin in case he did some of his 'weeding'. Sasha left for work, Gus arrived and he, Hannah and Tom schlepped to the cellar, Trish and Dennis shared a ride to the station, and Penny and Rog packed up their exhausted children and left. Then returned three minutes later because they'd forgotten Lorenzo.

And just like that Hannah's birthday was over. And I was a single mother of an 11-year-old.

★

'Did you read the books I gave you?' Leesa asked once we'd settled in the dining room.

I frowned. 'You gave them to me two days ago.'

Leesa looked up blankly.

'You gave me eight books forty-eight hours ago and you want to know if I've read them?'

She blushed and put her manual to the side. 'Did you at least start any of them?'

'I read the titles. Lots of north-based activity.'

'They're well-respected books that can help you find direction.'

'If I wanted to only go north.'

Leesa waited a moment. 'The sessions we've had so far, specifically the miracle day and the vision board, are tools that help guide you towards discovering your own personal values and goals. Are you starting to get an idea of what you want to aim for in your near future?'

'*Near* future?' I said. 'A burger and coke.'

Leesa gave me an insistent look.

I yawned. 'I don't know . . .'

'Give it a go,' Leesa said. 'What do you, Brooke Paige, want out of life?'

As another yawn overtook me, I tuned in to Gus and Hannah working on Phil Collins' 'In The Air'. It was an easy track for Hannah, she'd been playing it for years, but I expected that was an intentional choice, seeing as we were all weary from the party. I pushed the shy 'hello' Gus and I had exchanged in the front entrance out of my mind, and forced myself to think about what I, Brooke Paige, wanted out of life.

'Still a burger.'

Leesa's gaze drilled into me.

'Alright, all right!' I said, flumping back in my chair and thinking about life in a general sense. 'You know what I actually want?'

Leesa's expression brightened with interest.

'I want to be able to go to the supermarket and buy food and know that it hasn't come from a farm covered in pesticides that kill bees and that isn't worked by people being paid less than minimum wage,' I said, making Leesa frown. 'I want to be able to be able to buy a cucumber that isn't covered in plastic wrapping. I don't want my choice of plant-based packaging to actually have been made from a crop being grown in an area that's been cleared of natural rainforest in order to grow it! I want to know that when I buy an avocado it hasn't come from a farm controlled by a cartel who terrorize the local community. I don't want my socks to be made by an 8-year-old in Bangladesh. I want to know the daily choices I have to make to keep my family fed and clothed and heathy don't have horrible repercussions for another family. I want to live my life without having to research every damn thing first so that I'm not making choices that hurt the environment or cause monkeys to be chained up and have shit put in their eyes. I want that to be the norm! Why is the world so fucked up that in order to live an undamaging life you have to put in so much goddamned research? It's upside down! All the people who do want to cause damage should be the ones to put in hours of research in how to achieve that. And living an undamaging life should be the status quo. Everything is the wrong way round and I'm tired of trying to navigate my way through it.'

Leesa blinked. 'Okay,' she said. 'But what do you want to do with your career?'

I raised my eyebrows. 'I don't know,' I sighed. 'Maybe I'll be an Instagrammer and take pictures of doors in Notting Hill. People do that these days, you know. I know because I follow them. And I like the door pictures.'

Leesa watched me. 'Do you think you have a problem with self-expression?'

'Probably. I don't think I'll ever be able to convey how desperately I wanted to be in *Jem and the Holograms*.'

Leesa clasped her hands together on top of her folder and looked directly at me. 'Are being pig-headed and obstructive the type of personality traits you'd like your daughter to inherit from you?'

Shocked at Leesa's directness (and on-the-money-ness) I blinked a few times. Then swallowed and looked down at the table. 'No,' I said, my tone repentant.

Leesa watched me for a few moments longer than was comfortable then moved her hands and glanced at her folder. 'Did you feel fulfilled in Events? When you worked in it properly, I mean?'

I shifted in my seat. 'Yes. I guess. It paid the bills and I didn't get bored. I liked my colleagues.'

'What do you think your purpose in life is?'

'I don't believe in a purpose,' I said, fiddling with the pack of coloured pencils. 'I think people who are lost in life need to have this "purpose" that gets talked about. We're just here. Living life. Like the tiger and the flea, and chrysanthemums, and bacteria.'

'That seems like a defeatist attitude.'

'I think it seems freeing. It's exhausting trying to figure ourselves out all the time. Shouldn't we just live? Like the cat or the snake or the prawn? I bet they don't worry about their purpose in life. Shouldn't we just *be*?'

'Exactly.'

'Huh?'

Leesa smiled. 'That's what I believe anyway. We are supposed to just "be" without the social construct of what we "should" be and the angst of figuring ourselves out.'

I narrowed my eyes. Was this a trick? 'Well . . . Then why am I doing all of this . . . figuring shit out and filling out forms and stuff if I'm supposed to just "be"? Why do we need life coaches? You have a belief that means your job is a waste of time. You're weirder than I thought.'

'Because you've got your social conditioning that you're acting on subconsciously. We as a species need to get to the point of just "being" without social constructs. But I'm afraid that will be many generations away. This,' she waved across the table at the scattered forms and life coaching paraphernalia, 'is only here to try and help us move closer to that state of just "being". You yourself will probably never get there.'

'Thanks.'

'And neither will I. But as a species we are making steps towards it. And in generations perhaps we won't have anxiety or depression.' She paused. 'And we will be like the prawn.'

I regarded Leesa with suspicion/a hangover. She smiled serenely back.

'I think we should do some more visualisation,' she said after a moment.

'Great,' I said, making to move to the chaise longue for some shut-eye.

'No, you're going to write it down this time.' She pushed a blank notepad across the table.

'Oh,' I said, settling back in my chair.

'Keeping in mind the work we've done so far, I want you to imagine your future. Really *see* it; the house you're in, the clothes you're wearing, who you're with, where you go during the day. If we can get a clear picture of what you're aiming for then we can start putting down some building blocks in the here and now. Let's start by projecting yourself forward twenty years.'

I looked at her and twirled the pen in my fingers.

'You'll be . . .' Leesa flicked her eyes upwards and did some mental math. 'Sixty-three, right?'

'God, that sounds old.'

Leesa smiled. 'Where do you see yourself when you're sixty-three? Write down what you're doing, using the present tense. Are you overseas? Are you in a country home, a city apartment? Do you work?'

I sat still. Nothing came to mind. Nothing at all. When I was sixty-three Hannah would be thirty-one. She might have a baby of her own. Chris wouldn't be there. I couldn't picture it. Cookie would be dead. She'd still look exactly the same, though. She looked half run-over already. I twitched my pen.

'Okay,' Leesa said. 'How about just ten years? When you're fifty-three. How do you spend your days? Do you have a different job? Or are you still doing event admin from home for fifteen hours a week?'

I gave Leesa 'I-know-what-you're-doing-and-I'm-not-impressed' glare.

She waited for a few minutes of silence before adding, 'Are you still living in your place in Earlsfield? Hannah might have moved out by then?'

The idea of Hannah moving out struck horror through me. I'd be alone. Fifty-three and alone in that house with my memories.

I looked down at my pen. I tried willing myself to even

be able to have a glimpse of what my future might look like. Ten years from now. Fifty-three. Hannah would be twenty-one. She might be at Uni. Or overseas. Chris wouldn't be there. Eventually I looked up at Leesa, helplessness, I'm sure, written all over my face. My hands felt sweaty and panic fluttered in the base of my throat. Alone. I could be truly alone.

'Perhaps that's still too big a time frame. How about five years?' Leesa watched my expression. 'Two?' She waited. 'Next year?'

The room felt stuffy. I used to be able to see myself and Chris travelling. We'd make all sorts of plans and goals. Move to Sussex, Hannah's sixteenth, her eighteenth, her twenty-first (Chris had already started planning his outfit). Retire in Greece next to an eccentric older couple, take in stray dogs and putter about in a tiny fishing boat, casting out a line for a seafood dinner. But now . . . I couldn't see anything. It was like I *had* no future. I could hear a rushing sound in my ears. A clammy dizziness smothered me and my hands trembled.

'Okay, we can stop,' Leesa said. She slipped the pen out of my shaking hand and pushed a glass of water towards me.

★

For the second half of the session I, surprising even myself, was semi-co-operative. I realized that being unable to even conjure up a mental image of what I wanted in the future had scared me. We filled in a few charts; ones with titles like *The Benefits and Drawbacks of Change* and *Assessing Your Next Move* then, with a blush, Leesa asked me to fill out my evaluation form on her. I said all good things.

'So,' Leesa said as we reached the end of our session. 'What do you think, if anything, you've achieved in this week we've had together?'

'Are you sure it's been only a week? I definitely think you've had at least two birthdays since we started.'

Leesa stared me down so I gave her a few examples, which

included realising I needed new cushions, then Leesa declared us all done and began packing up.

'So,' I said, watching Leesa pile up her folders and manuals, 'in your not-yet-professional opinion,' I paused to give Leesa a cheeky grin and allow her to return it with a mildly amused simper. 'Where do you think I'm at? Life-wise?'

I'd asked with a light tone but found that I really did want her opinion.

Leesa smiled, seeing through my artificial light-heartedness. 'I think you are a loving, loyal, independent, fiercely determined, and profoundly broken-hearted woman.'

My façade dissolved and my throat constricted.

'I think you use humour as a way of deflecting the reality of how you feel. Which is lost. I think you feel guilty at the idea of moving forward,' she said, sliding more folders and forms into her tote. 'I think you're waiting for someone to give you permission to do so but it can only come from yourself.'

I swallowed and looked at the dull surface of the dining table where Leesa's phone sat, recording us. She reached across the table and pressed 'stop' with her fingertip. Her nail polish was clear and her nails neat with a perfect cream-coloured half-moon.

'You've got grit and determination,' Leesa said, her voice gentle and encouraging. 'You've just been applying it, fiercely, to not moving on. Shift that focus and you'll find that that grit that has kept you stationary will get you moving towards creating a fulfilling and loving future for you and Hannah.'

I nodded.

'Brooke?'

'Yeah?' I said, looking up.

'Thank you for letting me practise with you,' Leesa said. 'You've been a real help.'

'Have I?' I said, scratching at the edge of my eyelid where

a dab of moisture was collecting. 'I thought I was a real pain in the ass.'

'You were.'

I looked up to see Leesa grinning. I smiled and shook my head and followed her out.

'Do you have any clients yet?' I asked when we reached the open front door where sunlight was streaming in.

She coloured. 'No.'

'Well,' I said. 'I'm here every weekend so . . . if you're okay to come Saturdays while Hannah does her lessons we could keep going?'

Leesa looked surprised. And actually, so was I. But I realized that when I was with Leesa I didn't feel like a widow. She didn't handle me with kid gloves or tiptoe around me. She was honest with me. Rude on occasion. And I'd come to rather enjoy the sassy banter.

'Really?' Leesa said.

'If it's helpful for you, sure,' I said. 'I won't be co-operative, though. Obviously.'

Leesa broke into a wry smile. 'No, no of course not. Where's the challenge in that?'

Chapter 30

'Good morning,' Sasha sang the next morning as she arrived in the kitchen and glided towards the fridge.

Martin, still jet-lagged, looked up from his coffee. Hannah and Tom shared a confused glance over their Rice Krispies. Dad smiled over his newspaper, and Mum and I checked each other's responses, unsure as to how to proceed in the face of this uncharacteristic pleasant address.

In the resulting silence Sasha peered around the open fridge door and replaced her smile with a scowl. '*God,* everyone is always so *serious* in this house. It's *so boring!*' She slammed the fridge door shut and the rest of us exhaled.

'You're in a good mood,' I said, joining Sasha at the kitchen bench where she was pouring herself a juice.

'I met someone last night.'

'Someone nice, it seems.'

'*Finally!*' she said, a smile escaping. 'I'm meeting him again today. Just for coffee but it might lead to lunch,' she shrugged as if it were a casual arrangement and she hadn't been thinking about it every second since the night before.

'That's great! Where did you meet him? Tinder?'

Sasha opened her mouth to answer but became aware of a hovering presence and spun around coming face to face with Mum who immediately affected innocent disorientation in her own kitchen. Sasha scowled and left the room. Mum shrugged and followed.

★

A short while later I was under the outdoor table retrieving one of Hannah's multicoloured socks so we could head back to London that afternoon with the majority of what we'd come with, when Mum motored up on her 4×4 and slammed on the brakes.

'I just got a text from Kirsty saying a journalist from the *Daily Dispatch* popped into the store and was asking a lot of questions about your little treasure hunt!' she hissed.

I crawled backwards out from under the table and stood, the stinky sock in my hand. 'Really?'

'Yes,' Mum snapped. 'He wanted to know if she knew of anyone local who might have a connection to the school in Earlsfield! Luckily, she has no idea what school Hannah goes to.' She shot me a reprimanding look. 'And, of course, everybody wants to know why they chose our village.' I thought I caught the faintest flicker of pride, then Mum was back to being severe. 'At some point, someone might figure out that *you* have a connection to both areas. Have you thought about that?'

'Actually, no . . .'

Mum gave an appeased sigh, like she'd finally found something I would listen to.

'Okay,' I said, moving across the lawn towards one of Hannah's shoes, Mum motoring behind me. 'I won't do anything else in an area attached to me or Hannah.'

'No!' Mum exclaimed. 'It's the last term of school, journalists are sniffing around! It's time to be serious now; confirm Hannah's place at the school, and stop all the extravagant nonsense! You know, I don't believe you have full control of your faculties anymore.'

'Thank you, Mother,' I said, bending to pick up the shoe before turning to face her. 'I appreciate your input.'

'No you don't,' Mum stated then became quizzical. 'Do you . . . ?'

I looked back at her, deadpan. 'No.'

She scowled. 'Oh you're a wicked child, you are.'

'Have you noticed the difference in Hannah?' I said, bending to pick up a neon hair tie. 'She's happy. Even though she has no friends. Except Tom of course.'

'All the more reason to confirm her spot at the school *with* Tom.'

The idea of leaving Chris behind in the memories in our home in Earlsfield still filled me with nausea. I spied another sock by the veggie patch and took off in that direction. 'I don't know if that's what I want.'

Mum made a pooh-poohing noise as she juddered the 4×4 alongside.

'Look, I'm not asking you to live the same way I do,' I said, picking up the sock and recoiling at the smell. 'I'm not even asking you to agree with what I do. I don't need your approval. But I'd like your support.'

Mum blinked and appeared to consider my statement, then sighed and turned the 4×4 towards the house. 'I'm afraid I can't give you that.'

'What's the big deal with me spending it anyway?' I said, walking alongside the bike towards the house. 'Having money doesn't make you happy. This notion has been around for years.' I stopped at the kitchen door, Clint blocking my entrance, as Mum motored past towards the laundry.

I scuttled round Clint and into the kitchen where Lars was teaching Dad to roll what looked like little biscuit cones over the handle of a wooden spoon. The room smelt like vanilla and Hannah demonstrating her drum prowess to Martin reverberated up from the cellar.

'We're making krumkake,' Dad said.

'He is a natural,' Lars said, and I nodded and took a moment to appreciate his shirtless back.

'If I thought money made you happy,' Mum, said coming through to the kitchen from the laundry with the vacuum cleaner and placing by the back door. She gave Lars a triple take then reluctantly turning her attention back to me, 'I wouldn't have married your father; a philosophy student with no real career prospects outside of lecturing.'

Dad looked up from a patterned waffle-iron type thing. 'Thank you, my love,' he said, and weirdly, he genuinely meant it.

'I'd have gone on that road trip with Leo Sayer.'

I filled a water glass. 'You dated Leo Sayer?'

'We . . . dabbled.' She gave a flirty look.

I grimaced while gulping my water then followed her to the laundry where I helped load the dirty linen into the huge washing machines.

'The point is,' Mum continued, carrying a mountain of laundry that obscured her face, 'of *course,* money alone can't make you happy. But it can make you secure. And security breeds contentment and being content is a perfectly acceptable state in which to live. No need for the highs and lows of joy and despair. I don't know why you're so against doing anything conventional.'

'Conventional?!' I scoffed. 'There's a parrot pacing the kitchen table calling everyone a shithead, an alpaca at the back door *who you're about to vacuum*, and a miniature donkey is rambling around the house wearing your coral bead necklace.'

Mum pursed her lips then turned back to the washing machine. 'I *should* tell Hannah about the school,' she said, twisting a dial. 'That would get you to stop.'

I gave her a levelling look. 'If you do, I'll tell Karen from Pétanque you think she cheated in the tournament.'

Mum gasped. 'You wouldn't!'

'And that you think her teacakes taste like dryer fluff.'

Mum looked scandalized. 'Oh, you are a wicked, wicked child! I don't know where you get it from!'

A little later, Martin and I took the kids and Cookie for a walk in Hesworth common. At the top of a hill we sat on a bench seat looking out over the lush green landscape and while Tom and Hannah collected sticks in the bush behind us Martin read the latest articles on #NoReason.

'Shit, Brooke,' Martin said, looking up from Julian P Tickle's *Daily Dispatch* column. 'They're calling you an activist.'

'I know,' I giggled. 'Mum is outraged.'

Martin stared at me.

'You think I'm mad?'

'Yes. But I did before.'

I nudged him with my shoulder and he chuckled.

'At the risk of sounding Mum-like,' he said. 'Is this something you're doing to distract yourself from making plans for your future?'

I turned away and looked out over the fields. I felt his gaze assessing me.

'I wouldn't be a good little brother, who is younger than you, and more good-looking, intelligent, personable . . .'

I turned to face him, a smile twisting at the edges of my mouth.

'. . . a better cook,' he continued as I shook my head and grinned. 'Lighter on my feet, a much better tennis player, and Mum's favourite if I didn't ask,' he paused and looked at me, the edges of his eyes crinkled in a smile which then un-crinkled as he became serious. 'Do you know what you're doing?'

I swallowed. 'Does anyone?'

Martin gave a nod of concurrence then draped an arm across my shoulder and pulled me close so we were shoulder to shoulder looking out over the fields.

'So this life coach,' he said after a quiet moment. 'Is she single?'

I rested my head on his shoulder. 'Would you stay in the country if she were?'

Martin's silence said everything.

★

Back at the house I checked Hannah and Tom's packing then left them helping Lars cleaning out Stefanie's cage, and after wandering aimlessly outside for a few minutes, I found myself searching for Dad. My session with Leesa had been playing on my mind. I'd been hungover and had let my guard down. I'd tried to glimpse my future and it wasn't there. I located Dad on a lichen-covered bench with a book face down on his lap and his eyes closed. If he never actually read the books how *did* he get all his info?

'Dad?'

'Hmmm,' Dad murmured as if my arrival was expected. He didn't even open his eyes.

'Can I ask you something?'

'Always,' he said and gestured, with eyes closed, to the space next to him.

I sat down and quietly contemplated the gaping nothing I felt when forced to look at the future. Eventually Dad opened his eyes and looked at me patiently, like we had all the time in the world.

'Did you ever have a time in your life where you didn't know what was next?' I said. 'Like there were too many options but also no options? Like you've lost what direction you're supposed to go in and lost all future plans and there is just this . . . blank nothingness?'

Dad's astute eyes searched mine. 'Is that how you feel?'

I looked out across the garden and thought about the money, the #NoReason acts, Hannah's smile that had returned, and the fact that with less than two months of school left I still hadn't confirmed her place at the high school or where we would live or what I should do with the money. Should I do what normal people would do and invest in stocks and bonds and make myself and Hannah even richer instead of making strangers smile with prepaid coffee cards and glitter and ice cream? I turned to my father, waiting good-naturedly.

'Sometimes I think, why did this happen to me? What is the reason for it? And am I actually fulfilling the reason it happened or am I just fucking it up?'

'Ahhh,' Dad smiled. 'My dear, you are doing just fine.' He patted my hand with his roughened, aged one. 'Just fine indeed. For there is no reason for anything. *We are here on Earth to fart around.*'

I frowned.

'Kurt Vonnegut,' he added, closing his eyes again. I studied my father. So serene, so at peace with his place in life, so—

'Dad, you have a cricket in your beard.'

Dad's moustache twitched. 'Two, I believe,' he said, indicating to the other side of his beard with a thickened finger.

I leaned around and there, settled in his beard chirruping his legs, sat a second cricket. I watched my dad for a moment. His closed-eye, face-tipped-a-fraction-towards-the-sun expression was that of a man content. Content with two crickets on your face.

In the distance Mum drove past on the quad bike, wearing a giant pair of BluBlockers; Leo perched on the handlebars like he were in charge of navigating and Clint clomping behind eating vegetables out of a basket on the back. From the other direction Martin shot across the lawn carrying a suspicious-looking plant to the back of the barn. He clocked me and held up his finger in a 'shh' motion. Then Lars, Hannah and Tom walked out of the kitchen back door and headed towards the orchard followed by Pablo the miniature donkey looking smashing in Mum's 80s necklace and his mane in plaits tied with scrunchies. I leant back against the garden bench and tipped my own face towards the sun. How did I ever expect to be able to make normal-person decisions with these loons as my nearest and dearest? And who wanted to be normal anyway?

★

On the way to the train station later that afternoon I asked Dad to swing by the bottle store.

'Oh hello, Brooke love,' Kirsty said. 'Are you and Hannah back to the city today?'

'Yes,' I said, placing a bottle of Chardonnay I didn't need on the counter.

'Wasn't that treasure hunt the other day a treat? You know, we had a journalist in here asking all sort of questions.'

I smiled, I knew I wouldn't have to bring it up. 'Really?'

'Yes, it was so exciting! Like being in one of those murder mystery movies – except without the murder.'

'I bet. Did he leave a card?'

'Oh yes,' she said, immediately plucking one from a little pile in prime position on top of the register and handing it to me. 'You going to call him? You might get in the paper – wouldn't that be a treat?'

I looked at the little rectangle in my hand then back up to Kirsty, forcing a smile. 'Wouldn't it?' I said, pocketing Julian P. Tickle's card.

Chapter 31

'What if she notices?' Hannah said, crossing the playground holding Stefan/Stefanie's cage with the bird cheeping away. She was nervous that Miss Shuker would realize we were handing over a different bird and Livie would have ammo for a whole new round of torment.

'Hopefully she won't,' I said, walking alongside. 'Grandad checked, remember?'

And he had. By holding up dead, frozen Stefan (why he still had him, I didn't want to know) alongside Stefan/Stefanie's cage while Mum, Tom, Hannah, Sasha, Lars, Martin and I had compared the two. But new Stefanie had fluttered crazily.

'Perhaps she thinks you're a family of bird murderers and you're showing her her fate,' Martin had said with a grin.

Amid the fluttering, and the fact that frozen Stefan's colours had faded somewhat over his few days in the freezer, we'd only been able to determine that they looked mostly alike. Before we left Lars had taken the 'egg finch babies', with the intention of raising them as his own.

Miss Shuker beamed (at the cage – not us) as we walked into the classroom. Despite her week in Rome she was still as pale as the whiteboard she was writing on.

Hannah placed the cage on a desk and Miss Shuker shuffled over.

'Hello, my little friend,' she said with a warmth she didn't use towards the children. She peered into the cage. 'Did you miss me?'

Hannah and I stood alongside, fixed grins on our faces.

Miss Shuker frowned and moved her miniscule potato-shaped nose closer to the cage. Hannah and I shot each other a worried look, then when she straightened and faced us we stretched our grimaces into grins.

'He looks like he's had a great midterm break. Thank you for taking good care of him, Hannah.'

I said goodbye to Hannah at the classroom door, a silent 'phew' passing between us, then joined Penny at the school gates where she'd been with a conglomerate of mothers who liked to chat for ages.

'Why's he doing the drop-off?' I said, referring to Livie's dad who, as I spoke, checked out the lycra-clad rear of one of the more toned 'heading-to-Pilates' mums. 'Melody never misses an opportunity to one-up everyone else's holiday.'

'Jendi said she's in the hospital. Having her boobs taken out again, apparently.'

'Christ. In out, in out. Shake 'em all about at the school fundraiser. She's doing the hokey-cokey with her bosoms.'

Penny snorted. We were silent for a while as we watched Justin flirt with another couple of mums.

'It's gross how he openly flirts,' I said.

'And cheats.'

'Really?'

'Jendi said Melody found out over the break that he'd been sleeping with a colleague.'

I wrinkled my nose. 'What a bastard.'

Penny nodded.

'I feel sorry for Melody.'

'Me too.'

'I still don't like her though.'

Penny sighed. 'Nobody does.'

We stopped for a coffee at a new place on the high street on the way home. Being out at a café rather than at Penny's or mine was new and Penny had been delighted, and surprised, when I'd suggested it. The man behind the counter greeted Penny by name and made her coffee without her having to ask. I ordered mine then joined her at a table near the window.

'How do they know you here?' I said. 'Didn't this place just open?'

Penny looked up from stirring her coffee. 'A year ago.'

'Oh.' It seemed I really had been locking myself away.

'So, did you see Gus again after the party?'

'Briefly – when he arrived for Hannah's lesson the next morning.'

'And?'

'And nothing. I said hi.'

'Raunchy.'

'But he texted me yesterday. And again last night.'

Penny grinned. 'Oh yes?'

'Just sending me a link to a Spotify playlist he'd made for Hannah.'

Penny's grin fell. 'Thrilling.'

I fiddled with the mug of paper sugar sticks. 'When I saw his name pop up on my phone I . . . I got those "feelings" again.'

'Oh yes,' Penny said, back to grinning.

'And when I got into bed I thought, *This is mine and Chris's bed and I'm thinking about feelings that I might be feeling for another man.* And it felt so wrong. And all of Chris's stuff is still in his bedside table and—'

'It is?'

I nodded. 'And the slats are still broken from that time we . . .' I gave a coy look and Penny smiled and shook her head. But my coy look faded as I remembered 'the feelings' and my throat tightened. 'And the dent is still on Chris's side of the mattress where he slept and when I was sitting there thinking about Gus I felt like . . . I felt like I was cheating.'

Penny was quiet for a moment, observing my distress in the way I picked my nails, then a wide smile spread across her face. 'This is good.'

'Huh?'

'Yes,' she said, gazing out the café window, nodding to herself. 'Very good.' She snapped her attention to me, eyes shining. 'We will go bed shopping! You will get a new bed. And it will be a fresh start. Man-wise. You need this. It's like a clean slate. On which to have sex.'

My mouth gaped.

She jabbed at her phone. 'Okay, let's see. I can go bed shopping with you on Wednesday after drop-off if we make sure I'm back to pick up Rosa early for her dance exam with that crazy bitch. Or next Tuesday, if it's after Lorenzo's morning interview and candle ceremony at that Steiner school. Jesus, I don't know why Rog listens to his mother about that crap! But we will do the candle ceremony and Lorenzo will hate every second and then I can tell her we tried.' She tapped at her phone some more. 'Or . . .' She looked up. 'Or today actually. Like, right now?'

I stared at my friend, outraged. 'No!'

Penny fixed me with a hard glare. 'Why not?'

'I – I can't . . .' Getting rid of the mattress Chris and I had slept on our entire married life was too abhorrent an idea to process.

Penny's hard stare softened. 'You have broken slats and dents on a side that hasn't been slept in for nearly two years.'

'So?'

'How old is your mattress?'

'Fourteen years.'

The hard stare came back. 'You need a new bed. We will

go today.' She picked up her coffee. 'It will open up the opportunity for new life and new love.'

I looked at Penny, dismayed. I didn't want those things.

She shrugged. 'Or you can tell yourself you're getting it to avoid backache. But whatever the reason, *you are getting a new bed.*'

★

'I don't like high ones,' I said two hours later, after a salesman in a dark suit had shown us yet another bed. 'They make me think of old ladies called Sylvia under eiderdowns listening to Radio 4 in the middle of the night with a nightstand full of pills and a glass of water that's got bits of fluff and dust floating on the surface.'

'Sylvias,' sighed the long-suffering salesman.

Penny huffed. 'This bed makes you think of Sylvias and the last bed made you think of guys called Liam wanking to an Arsenal game. At John Lewis you had Tracey and Phil, both in accounts, who break up after they both get off with somebody at their Christmas work do. Then Drew and Jason who work in TV and are off to walk the Appalachian Trail to fundraise for their buddy having chemo and who you'd rather be friends with than have the same bed as.'

'Drew and Jason sounded cool, admit it.'

Penny scowled. 'We had intense-yogi/grows-her-own-wheatgrass-but-secretly-hates-the-taste Bethany on the futon, working-in-IT/mummy-issues/wears-socks-to-bed Nathaniel on the inner sprung, and Francine and Leanora the organic-macadamia-farmers on the organic latex.'

'And Adrian the cricketer/muscly-arms-but-skinny-legs/cheats-on-his-partner on the breathable bamboo inner with memory foam topper,' the salesman reminded us. 'A personal favourite of mine,' he said, and I didn't know if he meant the bamboo bed or Adrian the Cricketer.

I shrugged. 'These are very real feelings for me.'

Penny shook her head and shunted me past two impecca-bly-dressed men standing at the foot of a pine-framed bed that looked like it belonged to Heidi and Fred who were saving their pennies because they were about to start a family, and on to the next contender – a low, sleek bed with a dark leather base and seemingly endless flat mattress.

'No,' I said immediately.

'What's wrong with this one?' Penny demanded while the salesman twinkled at one of the impeccably dressed men.

'It reminds me of a man in a macho apartment with floor-to-ceiling windows that he doesn't drop the electric blinds over when he has sex, and there's a leather chair with chrome legs in the corner that's draped in a crumpled pencil skirt from a lazy day in bed with a woman he picked up the night before. There'd be a crystal tumbler of whisky glinting on the oak floating nightstand, and a drawer full of extra-large ribbed condoms and Rolexes. It would smell like coffee and sex and expensive aftershave, and the sheets would be imported and washed daily by a maid. It reminds me of Jon Hamm. This is Jon Hamm's bed.' I paused. 'I'll take it.'

The impeccably dressed men had joined us. 'We will too.'

★

Hannah got home from school and told me Livie had talked non-stop about her #girlsquad boat trip and that nobody had asked how her birthday was. Or remembered that it had been her birthday over the holiday. Not even Zara. But before I could offer any platitudes Hannah shrugged and said she didn't really care because she'd had the 'best birthday ever' and appar-ently Mackenzie had gotten seasick and had vomited in Melody's Louis Vuitton. I felt immature for loving that particular detail.

After dinner I joined Hannah on the sofa, where she was curled up with Cookie and grinning at her phone.

'Let me see?' I said, expecting it to be a social media post of any of the number of events still going on around London; the stalwarts of #NoReason like the food trucks, the games in the parks, and people in the street giving out compliments and gift cards. But when Hannah angled the screen to me I saw a photo of Tom sneaking fake flies into the boarding house spaghetti.

The next day, while Hannah was at school, a truck containing the new bed arrived and in a matter of seconds two muscled men, one short one tall, had flipped the old mattress up against the wall and were dismantling the old frame while I watched from the doorway. As the bed base came apart an old flat cap was revealed.

'Ma'am,' the taller of the two said as he handed it to me then, after briefly clocking my sudden drained expression, got back to the bed frame.

I turned the cap over in my hand, brushing off the dust and remembered Chris coming home with the horrible new hat on his head.

'Great, huh?' he'd said, grinning.

'Not at all,' I'd said.

And I'd hidden it. And he'd found it and halfway through a friend's barbeque appeared wearing it.

And I'd hidden it.

And he'd found it and come back from the bathroom at a restaurant wearing it.

And I'd hidden it, and he'd found it.

And I'd hidden it again and he'd found it again.

It went on that way for a year and then I'd hidden it and he'd never found it.

'Excuse me, ma'am,' the tall man said, and I moved to the hall as they trekked the bedframe pieces out to the truck.

When they came back for the mattress and began hefting it down the narrow hall towards the front door I followed, my eyes on the two dents.

'Stop,' I said as they neared the office door. 'You can just put it in there.'

The taller of the two looked at the tiny office, making the obvious assessment that it was too big to be living there permanently and turned back to me. 'The fee only covers pick-up and disposal on the day of delivery. You'll have to organize for it to be collected and pay the dump fee yourself if you do it later.'

I nodded. 'That's fine.'

The men looked at me and I looked back, willing the moisture in my eyes to not spill over.

'It's really expensive,' the shorter guy said. 'You'd be better to let us—'

'She wants it in here, mate,' the taller guy said, and with a nod in my direction, he tugged the mattress into the office, shifted a chair, and laid the mattress down on the remaining floor space, the edges of it curling up the wall.

Back in my bedroom the new bed was put together swiftly and was much bigger than the old one.

'Does this need to be kept here?' the shorter guy said, pointing to Chris's guitar that rested between his bedside table and the wall.

A memory flashed in my head of Chris perched on his side of the bed ironically strumming Eric Clapton's 'You Look Wonderful Tonight', to me while I stood in the doorway in unflattering onesie pyjamas that had a saggy bottom, my hair in a 'sleep bun' on the top of my head, and brushing my teeth; my giggles making toothpaste dribble down my chin. The memory faded and the delivery man was still there, waiting.

'I don't suppose it does, no.'

The man handed me the guitar then moved Chris's bedside table against the wall, his things that I refused to get rid of rolled and clinked inside. Twenty minutes later, the new bed was up, and the delivery men took the plastic wrapping and the signed delivery form and left. I stood in the doorway of the office holding the Egyptian cotton John Hamm sheet set Penny had insisted I buy and looked at my old mattress filling the floor of the office, the two hollows on each side. I remembered the day Chris and I had bought the bed and how we'd felt so grown up signing the delivery form at Ikea then, after a pit stop at the hotdog counter, going back to our newly purchased home to wait for it. It had been well and truly christened that whole weekend.

I turned away from the marital mattress and walked down the hall to my bedroom. Forcing myself to think about other things, I briskly made up the new bed then immediately left the house to pick up Hannah way earlier than I needed to.

'Why have you got a new bed?' she said, coming into the living room after her shower that evening.

'The old one was broken.'

'Why did you keep the mattress?'

I looked at her and shrugged.

She came to sit on the sofa next to me and wriggled herself under my arm. After an hour of quiet TV watching I tucked Hannah in to bed and not too much later brushed my teeth in the quiet house, then stood at the foot of the new bed in my pyjamas.

It was wide, flat and, without the hollows, impersonal. The whole purpose of the new bed was for moving on; shedding my old life.

Shedding my husband.

I tugged the duvet off, grabbed a pillow, and made my way down the hall to the tiny office. As soon as I laid my eyes on the old mattress, not quite fitting in the space so that the foot of it curled up the wall, the warmth of familiarity moved down my spine. I tossed the pillow on the bed, curled up in Chris's hollow and pulled the duvet over me. Ten minutes later, footsteps padded down the hall.

'Mum?' Hannah said, her silhouette dark in the doorway. 'What are you doing?'

'I just wanted to sleep here,' I said. A tear, not seen in the shadows, trickled from the corner of my eye and ran across my cheek as I lay on my side.

Hannah stood silently for a beat, then left. Seconds later, she was back with her own pillow. She tucked under the duvet I held open, curled against me, and I wrapped my arm around her.

Chapter 32

'Hello, love,' Mum said. 'I just wanted to check in on you and Hannah. Make sure you're all right.'

'Thanks, Mum,' I said, rolling over on my mattress on the floor. It had been two weeks and I was yet to sleep in the new bed.

'Are you sure you don't want us to come up? I could make a nice meal?'

That was debatable. 'We're okay.'

'But—'

'I don't want to acknowledge today. I want to recognize his birthday and our wedding anniversary and . . . and *any* other day. Not this day.'

'But Hannah might want—'

'Hannah and I have discussed it. It's what she wants too.'

'Well, okay, love. If you're sure?'

'I am. Thank you though.'

'Did you know about the Open Day at the school on Friday for next year's prospective students? Are you and Hannah coming down for that?'

The email had been in my inbox for a month. Mum's question reminded me of the text I'd received from Gus the night before, asking if we were attending the Open Day and if we were, would I like to go out for dinner after. I hadn't replied yet.

'I'm not sure.'

'Okay, love. I'm sure they can accommodate you if you decide you can make it last minute,' Mum said and I appreciated her atypical unbossiness.

I hung up and rolled back over. I did not like today. And I did not want to get up. Was there anyone in the world who wanted to get up less than I did? People on death row, soldiers leaving their young family to go into a warzone, a lonely person getting their faithful old dog put down, somebody who had to tell their staunchly homophobic parents they were gay. Thousands. Truly, truly fuckloads of people wanted to get out of bed less than I did. I got over myself, shuffled out of the covers and headed to the bathroom. On my way there Trish called.

'Yes, we're okay,' I said.

I peed, flushed, washed my hands, and stared in the mirror. Penny called.

'We're going to have a quiet night in,' I said to the offer of dinner at her place. 'But thanks.'

I went back to looking in the mirror. Chris had died two years ago today. Two whole years without my best friend. I knew that throughout the day I'd get heart emojis from friends I no longer saw, and texts from Martin who knew I didn't want to speak to anyone. (He'd left a couple of days previously. The invites had started and he was positive he'd seen the back of his ex's head in the village and it was too much to handle.) I'd call Chris's parents in the evening, their morning in New Zealand, and we'd have a stilted conversation where none of us wanted to speak but felt obliged to connect with each other. It was the kind of day where I'd do absolutely nothing but fall into bed exhausted. I looked at myself in the mirror. Two years since I'd felt my husband's eyes on me. I had grey hairs now. Just a few in the front. Chris never got to see me with grey hair. Lucky bastard. I wiped under my eyes, and headed to the kitchen to make coffee. Hannah had already been in and had her breakfast. Her cereal bowl was in the sink. I filled Cookie's dish with biscuits then stared into nowhere while listening to the kettle to boil and rumble in the quiet house. As it flicked off Hannah came in in her uniform; her school bag over one shoulder and her eyes haunted. We looked at each other; words failing both of us. She dropped her bag to the ground, stepped forward and we hugged.

'You sure you're going to be okay?'

Hannah nodded against my chest. She hadn't wanted to alter that morning's routine of walking over to Penny's then going in to school with them.

I gave her tiny body another squeeze, then released her. She gave Cookie an extended cuddle then gathered her bag from the floor and headed down the hall. From my spot at the kitchen bench I watched. Her head didn't turn to look at the family photo on the wall and her pace didn't falter. She reached the front door, put her hand on the doorknob then stopped. Was she coming back? I watched as she rested her head on the door for a brief second, her shoulders rose and fell then she lifted her head and turned the doorknob.

'Hannah,' I said, stepping into the hall, my throat aching.

She turned. Her was chin puckered with the effort of holding back a sob and her school bag dwarfed her tiny frame.

'Stay with me?' I said, my voice cracking.

Her face crumpled. She dumped her bag and ran into my arms.

★

I emailed the school saying Hannah wouldn't be in then went to the living room and found her curled on the sofa with Cookie.

'Are you hungry?' I said, sitting next to her.

She shook her head and snaked her fingers through Cookie's fur. 'Mum,' she said eventually, 'I think . . .' Her bottom lip wobbled. 'I think I'm starting to forget him.' A tear escaped and trickled down her cheek.

'Oh, sweetheart.' I gathered her to me and she buried her face against my chest. I smoothed her hair and let her cry, blinking back tears of my own. 'We talk about your dad all the time,' I said once her breathing had settled and she lay with her cheek against my chest. 'We talk about the things he liked to do and the funny stories he used to tell. Every night I tell you how much he loved you.'

'I know,' Hannah sniffed. 'But we only remember the good things. And . . . and it makes me feel like he wasn't real.' Her voice wobbled again. 'Like he was a perfect person from a storybook that only babies read. I want to remember my real dad.'

Fresh tears soaked my cotton T-shirt. I held her close and after a few minutes, when her breathing steadied again, she sat up.

I smiled as I wiped at her cheek with my thumb. 'How about we talk about all the things he did that annoyed us?'

'Um . . . okay,' she said, running a hand under her nose.

I thought back. 'He picked his toes while he watched TV.' Hannah frowned, confused at my aim.

'He left wine bottle tops on the bench even though the bin was right there,' I continued, looking through to the kitchen at the bin next to the kitchen bench. 'He stole every plug and charger in the house. He . . . He sang the lyrics to songs wrong on purpose. He wore those horrible ripped tartan slippers.' I paused as I thought about the slippers at the back of the wardrobe that I'd nagged Chris for years about throwing out and now that he was gone I couldn't bear to part with. A lump formed in my throat and my eyes watered. How could he be so real in my head yet not exist?

'His farts smelt like rotten carrots and Marmite,' Hannah ventured, the edges of her mouth curling up.

I turned to her and gave a watery smile, then made an 'ew' face. 'They really did.'

Hannah giggled. 'What else?'

'He never put the bathmat back up.'

'He never remembered my teacher's names.'

'His sneezes were too loud.'

'He put used matches back in the box.'

'He called quinoa "quinollia" just to annoy us.'

'He laughed at his own jokes before he'd even finished them.'

'He didn't like *SpongeBob*.'

'He didn't like tomato sauce.'

'He didn't like bananas.'

'But he liked banana cake!' we both chorused then erupted into giggles.

For the next hour we ate Maltesers and listed Chris's shortcomings, and at the end, for some strange reason I felt closer to him. As though he was in the corner of the room in the armchair, rolling his eyes at the two ladies in his life giving him shit.

I looked at my daughter. 'You're a clever girl,' I said, squeezing her tight.

★

'Do you want to do any #NoReason stuff today?' I said a little while later when Hannah came back from the bathroom.

'No,' she said, sitting next to me and tucking her legs up. 'I've been thinking what Dad would want to do if he could come back for a day.'

'Oh yes?' I said, swallowing. The thought of Chris being allowed back to us for a day, the thought of my daughter contemplating that possibility, was overwhelming.

'I think he'd want to go out for ice cream. A giant one with chocolate sauce and chocolate sprinkles and a chocolate flake.'

I smiled and nodded. Chris had been a massive chocoholic.

'And then go watch the boats near Tower Bridge then come home and order pizza and watch a movie from the 80s that has, like, really bad special effects,' Hannah said with a roll of her eyes.

I was quiet for a moment and she stopped grinning, worried she'd upset me.

'Oh sweetheart, you haven't forgotten him,' I said. 'If Dad could come back for one day I think he'd want to do exactly that.'

'So . . . can we?'

★

Hannah and I Tubed to London Bridge. We ordered colossal ice creams with all the chocolate toppings we could pile on at Borough Markets then walked the sunbaked streets, cutting down towards the river near HMS *Belfast*. We found an empty bench facing the water near the bridge and sat in the sunshine pointing out different boats to each other and reminiscing about the person we both missed so desperately. While Hannah was lost in a happy memory I watched the people around us and remembered that before all the #NoReason stuff this was how I'd spent my days. Cookie and I watching the people who passed us. But now it was different. These people didn't all look dreary or lonely or grim. There were people laughing with their friends, making a phone call and smiling at something the person on the other end said. I watched people taking photos of the bridge and the boats and each other. People hugging each other hello, kissing each other goodbye. A mother giggling at a baby. Had I only seen the sad and the lonely because I was sad and lonely? But being happy, was that a betrayal of my husband?

I looked at Hannah, swinging her legs on the bench next to me while she watched the boats her father had loved to watch; trying so hard to be happy with so much on her little shoulders. I looked out at the boats. Yes, Chris was in our home in Earlsfield but he was also on a bench watching boats. And at the barn in Sussex. Or anywhere there was a chocolate ice cream or a food truck. I looked back at my daughter.

'There's an Open Day at Tom's school next week,' I said.

Hannah looked up, chocolate ice cream round her mouth. 'Really?'

I nodded. 'Do you want to go?'

'Ah, *yes*,' Hannah said with an emphatic look.

'It's on Friday so you'd have to take a day off school.'

'Duh. Even better!' Hannah said and when a boat sounded its deep horn she turned back to the water, her feet swinging with renewed enthusiasm.

'You're sure you want to go to that school?' I said, feeling like I was holding on to the last strand that tied me to my husband. 'It would mean leaving our home? The place where we were a family.'

Hannah looked up at me. 'You and I are a family,' she said. 'A little one.'

'We are,' I said, leaning in to her.

'And Cookie.'

'And Cookie.'

Hannah and I watched the boats for a short while longer then headed home. We ordered pizza, vegetarian with double pepperoni (Chris's favourite) then watched *Back To The Future*, Hannah giggling at the clothes and the special effects that she'd giggled at before, just with her father alongside defending the technology of the time. I tucked her into bed then sat at the kitchen table and cast my eyes around the room. The cracked glass in the French doors, the dented floorboard, the paint stripes. They weren't Chris. Chris came with us wherever we went.

I opened my laptop, RSVP'd 'yes' to the Open Day then

curled up on the old mattress quickly before I changed my mind.

★

'Mum,' Hannah said, slapping a reminder notice on the kitchen bench where I was standing as soon as she got in from school the next afternoon, her bag still on her back.

'Oh. I forgot about this.' I put the notice on the kitchen bench and pulled out the junk drawer looking for a pen to sign the permission form that allowed Hannah to go on the 'Father Daughter Bushcraft Day' and allowed me to attend as an honorary father or lesbian or appointed guardian seeing as we had 'unique circumstances' and didn't fit the 'normal' mould. It showed how truly out of touch Ms Galloway was that anything other than Mom/Pop and 2.5 kids was considered out of the norm.

'Mu-um,' Hannah pressed. She slid the notice across the bench. 'Look at the date.'

I shut the pen-less drawer and scanned the sheet of A4. It was being held on the second to last Friday of the school year. It was also Chris's birthday. 'Oh.'

Hannah, Trish and I had planned a colourful, musical #NoReason in town as a secret celebration on what would have been his forty-fifth. I was going to let Hannah have the day off school and go into town to be among all the fun.

'You don't have to go,' I said. 'I can just email Ms Galloway and—'

'I want to go.'

I frowned. 'To the bushcraft day or Dad's #NoReason day . . . ?'

Hannah went red and looked at her feet. 'To the bushcraft day.'

'Oh.'

'I'm sorry, Mum,' she said. 'I do want to come to Dad's birthday thing, but I really *really* want to do the bushcraft day.

It's the Bear Grylls one and . . . and Dad loved all that stuff too.' She looked at me with pleading eyes.

'Honey, you don't need to apologize,' I said. 'You can go.' I looked at the sheet on the bench. 'What about the #NoReason stuff? I guess I can see if we can do it another day but so much has already been put in place—'

'No, we should still do it. It's for Dad's birthday,' she paused as she gathered the right words. 'Can't you do it without me? And I can look at the photos when I get home?'

I flattened the notice for no particular reason. 'Well, I guess so. If that's what you want.' I looked at Hannah and her cheeks flushed. 'Who will go with you to the Father/permitted lesbian/permitted female guardian/permitted widow Bushcraft Day?' I said, forcing a smile. 'We could call Grandad and see if he can go with you?'

'Okay.'

'Oh bother,' Dad said down the phone when I called to ask. 'We're away on a Pétanque tournament. I might be able to get out of it . . .'

'No,' I said. 'Mum has been muscling her way up the Pétanque social ladder for months. I can't let you.'

'Ye-es. Your mother might have something to say about it – but then again, she has been wanting to partner with Neville lately because he's a much better thrower than I am. I can suggest it to her?' he said, not sounding very sure on the idea. 'Do you think they'll skin a rabbit? I'm not certain I could stomach it, but I will rally, my dear, I will rally.'

But Mum rang five minutes later and said he most certainly could *not* miss the Pétanque tournament. She'd had matching uniforms made.

'Can I ask Dennis?' Hannah said when I told her.

'Really?'

She nodded. 'I know Ms Galloway said you could come but you'd be the only mum. Except for Liam's two mums and

Sanjeet whose aunty is coming because he lives with his grandparents and they're too old. You aren't mad, are you?'

'Of course not, honey,' I said, ignoring the sting.

'Do you think Dennis would want to come?'

'He might have patients. But I can ask.'

Hannah's face broke into a broad smile and she handed me my phone.

Dennis answered immediately and I explained the situation. He said he'd need to check his calendar with Bev and I waited on the line while he did just that.

'You have Miss Bunton at 10:30 and that fellow who has that football team at 1pm,' Bev's voice said. I could hear taps at the keyboard. 'Then at 3:30pm you have Baron Fletcher. He's not really a baron, is he? He wears awfully cheap shoes.'

'We can move them,' I heard Dennis say.

'All of them?' said Bev.

'Yes. A very important engagement has just been brought to my attention.'

There was some muffled phone movement sounds and then Dennis came back on the line.

'I'm completely free that day and it would be an absolute honour to accept.'

'Are you sure you've not got anything on?' I said, thinking about Baron Fletcher's cheap shoes.

'Not at all. Free as a bird.'

I gave Hannah, who was anxiously listening to my end of the conversation, a thumbs up and she dropped her nervous expression and clapped her hands. 'I'll email you all the information. Thank you so much for doing this.'

'Oh, it's . . .' I heard a sniff. 'Really is an absolute honour to be considered.' He sniffed again and made his excuses.

Chapter 33

'Welcome,' said a senior boy as Hannah, Trish and I walked through the college's grand entrance with a mass of other neatly dressed children and parents, all keen to make a good impression.

Children looked shyly at each other, wondering if they were each other's future classmates, future BFFs. Hannah kept picking at her braces. She'd had them tightened the day before and when she'd told Dennis about the Open Day he'd asked what the school colours were then dug out the corresponding rubber bands. Hannah had a green and gold smile.

'I wonder if we'll meet Mr Taylor,' Trish said in my ear.

She'd insisted on accompanying me under the guise of seeing Mr Taylor but I knew it was for moral support.

Another senior student, a girl, directed us with an open arm down a corridor lined with trophies, and gold-lettered honours boards, to a wood-panelled hall. Standing beneath oil paintings of founding members of the board I felt out of place. Martin, Sasha and I had gone to state school and here among the seniors in their £200 blazers and parents who'd arrived in Range Rovers and Porsche Cayennes, I felt like an imposter. Even though it had been months now with a bank account that meant I could easily afford the school I still felt like the money wasn't mine.

After a brief welcome speech by the suited head teacher,

we were given sticky name tags, split into groups of about twenty and guided to departments around the campus by two graduating students each. Both ours, a boy and a girl, spoke like they were leaving school and flying straight to placements in the UN.

In each department students were demonstrating the best that subject had to offer. It was like doing an interactive museum tour. In Science students made a beaker of blue liquid froth over, a lemon-powered electrical circuit light up, and another couple were dissecting something far too red and floppy for my liking. In the Design department Hannah got to design her name into a logo and 3D print it as a keyring. In Languages, students spoke in Chinese, French, Japanese and Korean as they offered us snacks in the corresponding language.

When we arrived in the Drama department and saw Tom on stage Hannah did a little squeal. We watched a mini Greek comedy then as we were guided out Tom beamed and waved vigorously from the stage.

'I can't wait to go here!' Hannah said, and Trish gave me a lengthy look.

We carried on through Mathematics, English, the fitness centre, and all the sports fields (where Trish mysteriously disappeared), and Hannah was wide-eyed throughout. Occasionally she saw a friend of Tom's or a boy she knew from rugby and they'd greet her excitedly, making the other children in our group develop a sort of fascination with her.

When we arrived in the Music department a full band, including saxophones and violins, started up and Hannah's eyes grew wider. Gus grinned in our direction then turned back to the band, keeping time. Hannah's eyes were fixated on the drummer; the senior boy who was graduating. She followed his stick work with the concentration of a Heathrow air traffic controller. Or Trish and a good-looking suitor aged 18–87.

When they finished our group applauded, then each

musician approached a family, and showed them round with impeccable manners and confidence.

'Hi,' Gus said, walking over to us with a smile.

'Hello,' I said aware of other parents noticing us receive his attention.

It was strange to see him not in shorts and a T-shirt but suit trousers and a button-down shirt. Only the peak of his forearm tattoo was visible beneath his partially rolled sleeves and for some reason it was sexier than seeing the whole thing.

He looked around. 'I thought you said Trish was coming?'

'We lost her around the sports department.'

'Mr Taylor?'

I grinned and nodded.

'We lose a lot of the ladies round that department,' Gus said with mock jealousy. 'So,' he said, turning to Hannah who was ogling the drum set up, 'do you want to see the recording studio?'

'You have a recording studio!?' she said, nearly leaping out of her skin.

Gus grinned. 'This way.'

While the other kids in our group had a go on some of the instruments Hannah got to record herself playing the drums in a padded room, then fiddle with buttons and dials which distorted or sped up her drumming. When Gus walked us out Hannah was fizzing.

'Can you do real whole songs in there?'

'Uh huh,' Gus said.

'Oh my God, oh my God,' Hannah chanted and Gus and I laughed.

As we were about to leave I turned to Gus and he smiled, the unanswered invite to dinner on my mind and, I assumed, his.

'I'm sorry I never replied about dinner tonight,' I said in a low voice so the other parents couldn't hear.

'That's okay,' he said, still smiling, but perhaps slightly forced.

'I'd love to come,' I found myself saying.

Gus looked surprised. And really, *really* happy, which was a tiny bit intoxicating. 'Great. I'll pick you up?' he said, the crack in his voice and subsequent cheek flush causing more attraction on my part.

We settled on a time then Hannah and I moved on to the next part of the tour with our group.

When it was over tea and biscuits were put on in the canteen for the adults. It opened out to a grassy area called The Quad where prefects were directing the new kids and some current students in team-building type games. Hannah was immediately in the thick of it and I stood on the edges of other couples sipping my tea.

'There you are,' Trish said, sidling up to me.

'Where have . . . Never mind, I don't want to know.'

Trish grinned.

'She's having a ball,' I said as we watched Hannah tumble over another boy, fall apart laughing, then leap up and dust herself off.

'She is.'

I watched my daughter for a moment longer then nodded to myself. 'Hold this?' I said, handing my tea to Trish.

It took me a short while to find reception and after another minute the receptionist had located Ms Potts, the school registrar.

'I'd like to confirm Hannah Paige's place in September, please,' I said, my heart beating fast.

'Oh yes, Hannah Paige,' Ms Potts said, leading me into her office and closing the door. She located the correct forms and instructed me where to sign. 'I hear we're getting a star on the drums,' Ms Potts said as I filled in Hannah's details. 'And on the rugby field.'

Five minutes later Ms Potts shook my hand and said she

was delighted to be welcoming Hannah to the school and reminded me to sign Hannah up for the band try-outs.

I arrived back next to Trish feeling jittery.

'Where'd you go?' Trish said, handing me my tea.

'I just confirmed Hannah's place.'

Trish said nothing but squeezed my forearm and smiled. Then we both turned back to watch Hannah.

'You know I'm your number one supporter . . .' she said after a few minutes.

'Yes,' I said, my voice immediately wary.

She processed my reaction for a beat. 'Do you feel like perhaps you've done enough now?'

'Enough what?'

'You know what I mean,' she said. 'Maybe it's time to start thinking about what you *really* want to do with the rest of the money.'

I stayed silent.

'I get it, I do. The things you've been doing have helped Hannah immeasurably. But maybe it's time to make some proper plans.'

'I've just been doing what you suggested. Creating her some joy and connection.'

Trish looked at Hannah, running around with kids she didn't know and laughing, each cheek a bright spot of colour. 'Then I think you've achieved it. That is one joyful girl.'

A lump formed in my throat.

'And look at the connections you've made for her,' Trish said, waving her arm across the busy quad. 'Not least the one you've strengthened between you and her.'

I chewed the inside of my lip and kept watching Hannah.

'Now that you've confirmed Hannah's place, maybe it's time to make this next #NoReason your last. And think about what *you* are going to do.'

*

Trish went to the train station direct from the Open Day and back at Mum and Dad's Hannah raced immediately upstairs to change out of her 'gross neat clothes' while Mum arrived in the front entrance with a question she was desperately trying to hold in.

'I confirmed her place,' I said. Then waited.

There was no 'finally you've seen sense' or 'I told you this was the right thing to do'. Her expression merely softened and all the tightness seemed to leave her body. She stepped forward, put both hands on my cheeks, looked into my eyes and nodded like she understood. Then stepped back again, said 'You'll stay here as long as it takes for you to find the perfect home for you and Hannah,' and with a brisk swipe at her cheeks she left the room and I stood alone in the front entrance for a while after.

The rest of the afternoon I enjoyed Hannah flitting round the house, unable to keep still as she asked when she'd get to choose her subjects or have her uniform fitting. I felt, not exactly happy, but at least not nauseous about the decision I'd just made.

'If I signed up for Drama would we get to do a play together?' Hannah said, buckling in next to Tom in the back of Dad's car in the late afternoon. He was taking them to a movie (Dad loved dissecting the philosophy hidden in Pixar) then out for burgers.

'Probably,' Tom said and while they giggled about how gross it would be if they had to *kiss* I luxuriated in the warmth blooming across my chest. Yes. It was the right decision.

As they drove off with the windows open I heard Tom filling Hannah in on which teachers were nice, which ones would let you hand an assignment in late, and which ones smelt of chicken gravy.

I turned towards the house and the warmth was instantly replaced by nerves. I had to get ready for dinner with Gus.

I found Sasha in my room wearing box-fresh exercise gear, her nose to the mirror, applying lashings of mascara. 'Another date?' I said, zipping open my overnight bag.

Mum arrived out of nowhere. 'Do you have a date, Sasha love? That's nice. The London lad again, is it?'

Sasha gave me a heavy-lidded stare in the mirror. 'Couldn't keep your trap shut, could you?'

'The woman is a sorcerer,' I said. 'She must have learnt to apparate whenever the word "date" is uttered.'

Mum pursed her lips at me then turned to Sasha and raised her eyebrows.

'Yes, I have a date. And yes, it's the guy from London. He's come down again.' She spun away from the mirror beaming and I felt a rush of affection at seeing her so happy. 'To *specifically* see me. We're going for a walk.'

'Lovely,' Mum said, clasping her hands together. 'Where?'

'I'M NOT TELLING YOU, WOMAN!' Sasha spun back to the mirror.

Mum didn't even bother to look taken aback. 'Why don't you ask the young fellow to stay for lunch? I'm making a pie with the leftover goat sausage?'

Sasha gave Mum an 'I don't think so' look in the mirror's reflection, slicked on a fourth layer of lip-gloss, brushed down her unblemished Lulu Lemons then stalked towards the door. 'Do not follow me!' She left in a cloud of organic perfume oil and menace.

Mum followed her.

Soon after Mum went out to a Pétanque committee meeting and Yegor, the latest student, went to the pub with his language school buddies. In the unnervingly quiet house I showered and tried on every item of clothing I had, fussed with hair up or hair down, got overwhelmed by a rifle through Sasha's make-up, then it was time.

A date.

Neither of us had 'officially' announced that fact but when we stood in Mum and Dad's front entrance freshly shaved (in different bodily areas), hair attended to, and doused in fragrance it said as much. I took a deep breath as I followed Gus to his car.

I could do this.

Dinner was delicious and the conversation was easy, but from the moment we sat down, from the arancini starter to the shared tiramisu, I felt like we were hurtling towards the end of the night and the potential 'kiss moment'. Like a butterfly in the rain attempting to revitalize its sodden wings, my heart would flutter when he smiled but the flutter was closely followed by a nauseous plunge of guilt at being out for dinner, and attracted to, a man who was not my husband. Then all of a sudden, the bill was paid, the Chianti was finished, and we were outside, the summer night air warm and alluring on my shoulders. We walked to his car, so close that my bare arm touched his, and I could hardly concentrate on the story he was telling me about the time he broke his collar bone and his mother said it was just a sprain and still made him go to his horse riding competition and how he'd . . . won? lost . . .? fallen off again? Then we were at his car in the velvety warm darkness. We faced each other; both having done this dance before and knowing it was a 'moment'. For a kiss, going to a bar, going to someone's place, or just going home and calling it a night.

Gus took a step towards me and held out his hand. 'I like you,' he said, looking down at me.

'I like you too,' I said, putting my hand in his and feeling the fizz across my chest at the sensation of our fingers intertwining.

He took another step, his eyes enquiring and I gave a faint nod. His lips were warm and soft, his aftershave was fresh and sea-breezy. The sodden-winged butterfly tried her wings again.

His hands moved to the small of my back sending prickles down my arms. We kissed deeper and I leant back against his car. After a moment we pulled apart, checking each other's reaction. His lips were pink from the crush of kissing, and his pupils dilated. He smiled.

'I didn't like it,' I blurted.

The butterfly fell flat.

Gus's smile faltered then dissolved into confusion. 'Wh—What . . . ?'

'I did not enjoy that.'

'Oh.'

'I have to go,' I said. And I ran away.

I. Ran. Away.

I RAN AWAY?!?!?

Chapter 34

'You ran away?!' Penny snorted into her takeaway coffee.

'It's not funny,' I said, feeling the mortification of that night rise up in me again.

'I completely disagree. It *is* funny. It is very funny.'

I gave her a look.

'For me, obviously, not for you. What did this Gus do?'

'I don't know. I was running away.'

Penny cackled again, her navy manicured hand not holding a coffee flapping in front of her chest.

'Stop laughing!' I said, humiliated.

'I'd love to, *cariño*, but I cannot, I cannot. How did you get home?'

'I called an Uber when I'd run far enough away.'

I allowed Penny another round of laughter and turned to watch Earls Court Road coming to life in the early morning light. A shipment of thirty llamas and donkey figurines made out of old crisp packets and plastic bags had arrived from Chile the week before and Trish's students had stuffed the saddlebags with a #NoReason note and pairs of tickets to movies, musicals, footballs games, and concerts. At 5:30 that morning they'd hidden them in locations around London, snapping photos which would be uploaded to the #NoReason Instagram page at precisely 6:30am, in time for the early morning commuters. Trish had texted me a few of the chosen locations so at 6am

I'd knocked on Penny and Rog's door, exchanged a sleepy Hannah for a sleepy Penny, and we'd jumped in an Uber, leaving Rog to get all five kids fed and to school and nursery. In the car I'd told Penny I'd confirmed Hannah's place at the new school. I'd received a sad face, a fierce hug then a plea for her own room at my new home. Penny and I were now outside a Costa looking across the street at a llama figurine sitting on an electrical box next to a gyros shop, its crisp-packet body glinting in the morning sun.

★

'Have you called him to explain?' Penny said, wiping under her eyes with an index finger.

'I sent a text.'

When I'd been in the back of an Uber on my way home, my cheeks aflame and my stomach in knots, I'd sent Gus a message:

> I'm sorry. I guess I'm not ready for what was happening between us.

He'd replied immediately saying he understood. Then followed it with:

> I thought it was because I'd had the anchovies.

He'd added a winky emoji and I'd replied with a laugh emoji and that was it. The next day when he'd come for Hannah's lesson I'd avoided him by being in the dining room ready for Leesa before she got there and ensuring our session overran, making Leesa chuffed, Mum delighted, and myself annoyed.

'A text?' Penny's mirth evaporated and was replaced with a stern look. 'Your only contact with him since then is *a text?!* But you must call him! The poor man will be feeling terrible!'

'I know! I know!' I said, pulling at my face.

'Stop that, you'll get wrinkles. Ay, have I taught you nothing? Here, let me find my cream.' She shoved her takeaway coffee at me and dug around in her giant tote.

While she fossicked and nattered about Rog's mum and what she'd done last weekend with a group of other free-love orientated people she'd been on a barge trip with, I thought about the kiss with Gus and how the real problem was that I *had* enjoyed it. And that that enjoyment had been immediately followed by such a fierce surge of guilt I'd felt physically sick. Those lips I'd kissed? And had wanted to kiss again? They hadn't been my husband's lips. What I'd done had felt like cheating. The rest of the weekend I'd walked around with that horrible nauseous feeling you get when you've done something very, very wrong and someone you care deeply about might find out and be irrevocably hurt. But that person couldn't be hurt. Ever again.

I sighed.

Penny looked up from her tote, sans cream, and cocked her head to the side. 'Ay ay ay,' she said, an empathetic corners-down smile on her red lips. '*Cariño*, it is tough for you, I know. Come,' she said, and wrenched me into one of her tiny, vice-like hugs that verged on torture and I shoved my arms out to the side like a mid-flight seagull in order to avoid crushing the coffees between our chests.

She stopped when I fake gasped and took back her coffee with a smile.

'So,' she said, turning back to look across the road. 'How long do we have to stand here?'

Penny had increased her noises of concern at the #NoReason acts. She'd shut the door on a handful of journalists now and was getting exponentially worried about her lying face.

'Till someone finds it and you can see how much joy it brings them and see why Hannah and I like doing this.'

Penny sneered. 'They're made out of rubbish.'

I laughed and checked my phone. Only one minute till Jamal, Trish's student who was the social media whizz, uploaded the photos to the #NoReason feed. The streets had a smattering of people walking purposefully, grabbing coffees, texting as they headed to the station. Penny was yawning incessantly. At 6:30 I refreshed my screen. The posts popped up and I elbowed her mid giant yawn.

'Any moment now,' I said, showing her the feed then looking across the road.

Forty-five minutes later Penny had had another two coffees, two trips to the loo and nobody had noticed the llama figurine. After another ten minutes Penny was complaining of a sore back.

'Fine,' I said, deflated. 'We can go.' But as I took a step towards the station Penny's tiny hand clutched me with unfathomable strength. 'Ow!'

'Look, *cariño!*'

I looked. A young woman in a Ryman's uniform was slowing down her listless meander as she passed the figurine. She stopped a pace or two past it then stepped back and frowned at the twinkly rubbish llama. She scanned up and down the street, her eyes wary, and Penny and I immediately affected being deep in conversation.

'I think Brad Pitt is overrated.'

'I don't believe in tectonic plates.'

We giggled while glancing sideways at the young woman as she picked up the figurine and turned it over in her hands. She fiddled with the saddle bag flap then pulled out a folded envelope.

'She's opening it!' Penny whispered, clutching my arm.

'Shhh,' I said, grinning. 'And also ow again!'

The young woman read the contents of the envelope then her head shot up and she looked up and down the street, her eyes alight. Penny tightened her grip.

'Jesus!' I said, prying her talons off me.

When the young woman could find no source of her good fortune she placed the figurine back on the electrical box, snapped a few photos with her phone, then shoved it in her bag and strode down the street, a smile on her lips.

'Oh my God!' Penny exclaimed. 'That was . . . Where are we going now?' she said as I dragged her towards the station instead of ordering an Uber.

'To show you more.'

For the next couple of hours we Tubed across London, looking at the stalwarts of #NoReason. Penny joined the queue for a free ice cream in Hoxton and was upset her non-alcoholic cocktail had no alcohol in Soho. We watched people playing Connect Four and Rummikub in St James Park, Scrabble and chess in the Embankment Gardens. After chowing down a free taco we headed over to South Bank to see if we came across any of Trish's students handing out coloured envelopes and flowers.

'Doesn't matter!' I said when we couldn't find any. And I pulled out two caps and a tiny stack of coloured envelopes.

'What's in them?' Penny asked as I dumped a cap on her head and the other on mine.

'A #NoReason note. And money.'

'How much?' she said adjusting her cap so her hair still looked good.

'£50.'

'What?!'

She watched with her mouth gaping as I wove through a crowd, covertly slipped an envelope in a lady's Primark shopping bag, then circled back to her standing at the railing overlooking the river.

'What if someone catches you?'

'I just screw the envelope up and pretend I was getting rid of some rubbish.'

Penny frowned at my system. 'I know this makes you feel good and everything. But the part of me that is married to a finance guy is so worried about what you're doing.'

'What does the other part of you think?'

'That I'd love to slip a stranger some cash.'

I placed an envelope in her hand. 'Do it. It feels great!'

Penny held the envelope against her chest. 'I can't! It goes against everything Rog believes in! The frivolity – the waste! Ay, I couldn't! I couldn't!' she said then trotted into the crowds, slipped the envelope in to the bag hanging off the shoulder of a mother pushing a double carriage pushchair then scuttled back to the railing. 'Ay *Dios mio!*'

We grinned at each other.

'Give me another one!' she said and she took off into the crowd, beaming.

Ten minutes later we reached the end of the small stack and collapsed against railings further along the bank, laughing. I opened my bag towards Penny to reveal it stuffed with envelopes.

'More?'

'Yep,' I beamed.

Penny's brow dropped. 'You should stop. It's too much.'

'You were doing it five seconds ago!'

'I don't know what came over me. I blame the dopamine. It's like a high. But I'm back down now and that is a very large pile of envelopes and I think maybe you need someone telling you to rein it in.'

'I have my mother for that.'

She was distracted from her reprimand by a sudden shriek from two girls sitting on the grass.

'She got a #NoReason!' one girl shrieked and a handful of people drew towards the excited pair while I giggled and trotted away, Penny eventually following, smiling despite her earlier caution.

I dug out another envelope, high on gaining my friend's approval but as I rounded a corner, Penny still a few feet behind me, I bumped into someone, making me drop the envelope. Before I could snatch it up, manicured male hands had picked it up and when I stood I was face to face with Will. My lawyer.

'Hello,' I said, my cheeks reddening.

'Hi, Brooke,' he said, smiling as he held the envelope out towards me.

At that moment the two girls from the grass skipped past, one on them holding up the exact same envelope yelling 'I got a #NoReason! I got a #NoReason!' and I cursed their extrovert nature I'd usually applaud. Beyond them was Penny, gawking at me. I made the tiniest motion with my head that she was to leave. *Now.* Then turned back to Will.

His expression shot a chill down my spine.

Chapter 35

'I can't stress enough the severity of what can happen to you if you break the terms of the agreement,' Will said from across the boardroom table.

Being back in that room was sobering. I'd sat in that exact spot repeating the details of Chris's death over and over and over until I was emotionally numb; signing bits of paper I was too immobilized with grief to comprehend.

'I'm not breaking the rules,' I said, pushing aside the memories. 'I'm not telling anyone what happened to Chris.'

'You were out there, in public, dropping envelopes into people's bags.'

'Yes,' I admitted.

'Alone?'

'Yes,' I lied.

Will looked down at some papers that looked like internet printouts. 'So, the sky banner over the school in Earlsfield was you? And the street party that same day?'

'Yes.'

'And the treasure hunt in West Sussex?'

'Yes.'

'The donkeys on South Bank?'

'Yes.'

Will looked up at me for a moment, his expression unreadable, then continued to flick through the printouts. 'The ice cream trucks, the sing-along on the Tube, the dancers in Cavendish Square, the people playing board games in parks, the gift cards and the cupcakes at volunteer organisations. The people handing out envelopes in the street, and the ones in bookstores. These were all you?'

'Yes,' I said.

Will let the corners of the papers fall and watched me with mounting concern. 'There is a significant level of public interest in this #NoReason campaign. People want to know who is behind it and why they're doing it. If they find out it's you then—'

'How will they find out it is me? My friend Trish does the bookings over the phone and the payments are cash deposits. Everything is online or over the phone. Always. And nobody has contact with me at all. I just turn up and pretend to be a spectator.'

'Your friend Trish,' Will said. 'I take it she knows of the money and its origin?'

'Yes,' I said. 'From the beginning. You met her at one of the mediations. She's the most trustworthy person I know. She would never *ever* tell anyone.'

Will gave me an extremely sombre look and a sick feeling bubbled in my stomach. 'Do you transfer money to her from your account?'

'Yes.'

He raised his hands from the desk a few inches, his palm splayed, as if to say 'there you go'.

'They can't look into our accounts. That's illegal!'

'Maybe. But easily, and frequently, done. Illegality is not a disincentive for a journalist hoping to break a story.'

My mind raced. 'Well . . . Well, so what?' I said, scrambling. 'Even if they find out it's me, that doesn't mean I'm going to tell anyone about the payout.'

'You won't need to. When they see where and how you

live, find out your job and your income, they'll know the money has not been earned by you. They will want to know where you got it and why you're doing these public acts. They will look into it until they find it. They just need to know who is behind it. These newspapers have vast resources and yes, many of them unscrupulous.'

I chewed my fingernail.

'Brooke,' he said, his expression patient yet severe. 'The stipulations of the contract you signed were very clear. These conglomerates can and do go after people who threaten their businesses. They go after them brutally. I'm not saying it's right. I'm informing you of the harsh reality of dealings within the pharmaceutical world.'

I swallowed down my mounting fear.

'You could end up being sued for more than you received. It could ruin your and Hannah's future.' He paused to allow that information to register. 'I will do my very best to protect you but if it comes out I can't promise you it will be okay. I really can't.'

I suddenly saw in harsh reality what I had been doing. How risky it had all been and how I'd ignored all the warnings from my mother. I'd been so clouded by the guilt of even having the money I'd just wanted it gone. Was my mother right? Was I manic? Did I have a mania?

Will typed some notes on his sleek silver laptop. 'Do you have any more planned?'

'Just one. But I can cancel it,' I said, wanting to do anything Will told me to.

'Yes, do that,' he said, looking away from his screen. 'Immediately.'

'There are probably still envelopes in books and bags that haven't been found. And those figurines that went out today. What should I do about those?'

'Leave them. If you try to collect them it is another chance of being caught. Do nothing else, dismantle the campaign, and hope like hell for a big story that distracts the press.'

With a final warning to lie very, very low, I left Will's shiny offices and called Trish.

'We need to cancel the birthday party for Chris.'

'What happened?'

In a breathless panic I regaled her with the details of my meeting with Will.

'On it,' Trish said, authoritative and in control.

Calmed a fraction by Trish's assurances that all would be cancelled by the end of the day I said goodbye.

When Hannah got home from school I had a whole speech prepared and was ready for her devastation at having to say goodbye to #NoReason but when I explained the situation (glossing over how very scary Will's warnings were) she surprised me with her response.

'That's okay, Mum. If we kept doing it all the time then it wouldn't be special and people might get bored with it.'

I smiled. 'You know, I sometimes forget how truly clever you are.'

'Duh.' Hannah grinned. 'Now can I tell you what happened at school today?'

'Sure,' I said surprised at the tiny sting I felt at her readiness to say goodbye to our #NoReason acts.

Hannah jiggled excitedly. 'We were learning about palindromes. Words that are the same back to front, you know like kayak and noon and level,' she said and I nodded. 'And Mr Moody asked if anyone knew any others. Liam yelled out "poop" and everyone laughed. And then Mr Moody said that someone's name in the class was a palindrome.'

'Yours,' I said, smiling.

'Yep,' she grinned. 'And when Mr Moody wrote my name up on the board he said, "Hannah — exactly the same back to front" and Livie said, "how *boring*".'

'Oh, that little—'

'But Mum, guess what I said to her?'

'What?'

'Yours backwards is "Evil"!'

I gasped. 'You *didn't?!*'

'I did!' Hannah giggled into her fists, cute as a cheeky button.

My heart swelled at her finally being able to laugh at a Livie altercation.

'Mr Moody said it wasn't a palindrome but he wrote it up on the board anyway and Livie was *so* angry!'

'Well, God bless Mr Moody,' I said and Hannah fell apart laughing.

★

That night Hannah and I dismantled the #NoReason nerve centre at our dining table and I put everything in a box for when she was older. The rest of the week Hannah went to school and I lay low and watched the #NoReason activity on social media. Envelopes were still being found, as were the better-hidden rubbish figurines, but there were no longer any ice-cream trucks, or games being played in parks or people in crazy outfits handing out envelopes. Trish had undone everything. She'd sat her students down and explained that #NoReason had run its course. They were disappointed, it had brought as much joy to them executing the events as the people on the receiving end, but they'd accepted that it had to end at some point. When I told Mum she'd rung every single day, sometimes twice, to check what I was doing and when I said 'nothing' with a note of melancholy, she'd say 'excellent' in a chipper tone and hang up.

The fear that Will had put in me dissipated as the week went by. I did the usual invoices for Abdul; work I had told myself and everyone else was ten to fifteen hours a week and now realized was probably only two to three, and without

#NoReason occupying my time my days were long and lonely again. When I looked at my bank account I no longer felt the thrill of watching it go down.

It took till the end of the week for the public to notice. I'd been watching the news, with Hannah and Cookie curled on the sofa, when a shot of the familiar #NoReason lettering came on screen.

'Almost as suddenly and without explanation as it arrived, it has disappeared, leaving the public a little sad,' the news anchor said.

They cut to a shot of a man in a suit with his sunglasses on. 'I miss it, you know? I work near James Park and me and my colleagues would go down in our break and play a game. I think the council should make it permanent.'

'I never got a #NoReason envelope but friends did,' said a woman in a London Aquarium polo shirt. 'So yeah, I guess I'm sad I won't get the chance now.'

It cut to a reporter standing with the man from the original ice cream van from the Sports Day. 'It's been really cool,' the guy said, smiling. 'And amazing exposure for us. We'll miss it for sure, but I get it, it couldn't go on forever. I'm just really grateful we got to be a part of it, you know. We were there on the first day!'

'And you never knew who was behind it?' asked the reporter.

'Nope. All online and anonymous.'

'What would you ask the person, or people, behind this if you ever met them?'

The guy looked thoughtful. 'I'd probably ask why? I mean, I know it was to make people smile and spread a bit of joy but there must be more. Maybe. Yeah, I guess I'd just ask why.'

The reporter came back on the screen and spoke directly to camera. 'I think a lot of people would like to ask that very question.'

They finished with a vaguely cheesy montage of #NoReason photos and I switched off the TV and looked at Hannah.

'It's kind of sad it's over,' she said.

I nodded.

'But good too.'

'Why's that?'

'I don't like keeping secrets from Tom.'

Chapter 36

In Sussex on Saturday morning Gus arrived for Hannah's lesson and we ran into each other in the front entrance.

'What's going on?' he said as Mum, Tom and Hannah scooted past into the formal living room, followed by Dad with Leo on his shoulder, who was followed by Cookie, followed by Antoni from Poland.

'Mum turned up on Sasha's brunch date and Sasha is on her way home,' I said, hustling him in the door.

'Oh dear,' he said stepping inside. When we faced each other he gave a tentative smile and the 'kiss and run' came flooding back.

I gave him a hasty half smile then, babbling to cover my discomfort, hustled him into the living room where Mum, Dad, Hannah, Tom and Antoni were already at the window. 'Sasha is talking about him being "the one",' I said, 'and has been refusing to give Mum any details about his name or job or *bank balance*—' I gave the back of Mum's head a hard stare as I crossed behind her, she merely flapped a dismissive hand my way '—or anything at all and it's driven Mum past her usual levels of insanity, which of course are higher than any normal person's, and she's entered a whole other state of feverish stalkerism.'

Mum turned away from the window with pursed lips.

'Feverish Stalkerism is what you have,' I said, taking up a

position at the window next to Antoni. 'It's a new condition and they're going to name it after you: Iris McVale Feverish Stalkerism Syndrome.'

Mum opened her mouth to contest my medical findings but was distracted by a car turning in to the property. Gus stepped up to the window next to me, close enough for his arm to brush mine, causing a flutter in my stomach. We locked eyes and he opened his mouth as if to say something.

'Here she is!' said Dad, breaking the moment.

'Oh dear God,' said Mum as Gus and I turned to look out the window.

'It's just Leesa,' said Hannah.

'Oh dear God,' said I.

'Brooke,' chastised Mum.

'In here!' said Antoni.

We frowned at him leaning out of a sideways opening window that we didn't know opened and beckoning Leesa in with a cheerful, ruddy-cheeked beam. Leesa gave a brief, confused wave and a few seconds later arrived in the living room and took up a position at the window with the rest of us.

'What are we doing?' she said.

'Front row seats. Fight Night,' said I.

Mum turned away from the window, hair a-fluff, lips a-purse. 'Now Brooke—' she began but the acceleration of a vehicle coming down the lane broke her off and our gathering leaned closer to the windows.

Two seconds later, Sasha roared her crapped-out old white and red mini into the courtyard, sending a cascade of gravel over Dad's sweet peas.

'Aw,' he said dejectedly.

Sasha flew from the car, slammed the door shut and strode towards the house, her expression thunderous.

'Oh goodness,' Mum said as she put her hand to her chest

and stood back from the window to address us. 'Well, it was nice knowing you all.' And chin-first, she left to meet her fate.

'WOMAN, YOU'VE GONE TOO FAR!' Sasha boomed and Mum shut the door behind her.

The living room vigil moved closer to the closed door in a huddle.

'I don't know how Mum is going to get out of this one,' I said.

'I don't know what you're talking about Sasha, love,' we heard Mum say.

'By bluffing, it seems,' said Dad, rocking on his plimsoles.

'I SAW YOU! WE BOTH SAW YOU! IT WAS SO *EMBARRASING!*'

'Where?' said Mum, still maintaining that affected innocence was the way forward.

Tom and Hannah, in the middle of a huddle of adults, looked at each other with delight.

'YOU WERE BEHIND THE WAITER!'

'I was not.'

'THAT LADY AT ANOTHER TABLE CALLED YOUR NAME!'

'Must be another Iris.'

'THERE ISN'T ANY! IT WAS YOU!'

'It wasn't.'

'IT WAS!'

'It *wasn't!*'

'WHO *ELSE* WALKS AROUND WITH A PARROT ON THEIR SHOULDER?'

'Plenty of people!' said Mum, getting desperate and not at all believable. 'Why, I've seen at least three people with parrots on their shoulders in the village this week alone.'

Dad shook his head. Hannah and Tom stifled giggles; Leesa gave Antoni, grinning at her with eager intensity, a double-take then stepped closer to me. Gus and I chuckled. The shared amusement made me shy and I looked away.

While Sasha and Mum spoke over each other in an ever increasing volume nobody except me noticed the man exit the passenger side of Sasha's mini and head towards the house.

My stomach dropped.

Was that . . . ? It couldn't be?

A clammy feeling crept up my neck as he got closer. Light-headed, I scanned the living room while the rest of the room continued to snigger at Mum and Sasha. There was nowhere I could hide. And if I left the room I'd be walking right into him at the front entrance. In any case it didn't matter.

He was here.

'Hello, it's *so* lovely to meet you,' came Mum's sickly sweet greeting.

'Jules, this is my mother, Iris. She has boundary issues.'

We heard Mum scoff then she was telling the man to come into the living room and meet the rest of the family and 'assorted riff-raff.' And while the 'assorted riff-raff' (Leesa, Gus and Antoni) glanced at each other, checking if it were worth being offended, and I hid behind Gus, he entered the room.

Sasha's boyfriend was Julian P Tickle.

'Hello,' he said cheerfully.

'Hello, shithead,' said Leo the Parrot and Julian's affable grin faltered for a moment then he appeared to be delighted by the greeting.

I agreed with Leo. Had Julian conned his way into my sister's affections to get to me?

Mum apologized, and Sasha began the introductions while I shuffled to the back hoping for a sudden earthquake or ceiling fire or stampede of bison.

'And this is my sister, Brooke,' Sasha said, getting to me before the bison did.

Julian turned away from Leesa and held out his hand to me. 'Very nice to meet you.'

'You too,' I said, lowering my head.

Julian shook my hand, his brow creasing. His hair still had that sticky-up tuft. 'Have we . . . met before somewhere?'

'I don't think so,' I said, pulling my hand from his. 'I just have one of those faces. Plain. Like a blank canvas. People think they know me all the time.'

He kept his gaze on me for a moment longer than was comfortable and I noticed Mum frown and both Sasha and Gus shift uncomfortably. Gus's discomfort caused my stomach to flip.

'Right,' Mum said, clapping her hands together. 'Who'd like some scones?'

The correct answer was 'nobody' but Julian was new so he answered in the affirmative.

★

My session with Leesa was an excellent escape from Julian but a waste of time. I couldn't concentrate. I was too busy fretting that over scones as palatable as scoria, Julian would remember where he met me and put two and two together. Hannah switching cheekily from Simon and 'Gargoyle's' 'The Boxer' to AC/DC's 'Shoot To Thrill' and being made to switch back again amid giggles that could be heard from the cellar did nothing to soothe my jitters. After an hour of distracted visualisations, Leesa left. Gus and I had another self-conscious exchange at the front door, and then he left. Hannah and Tom raced off to see if Pablo could fit a tutu, and I found Mum and Sasha at the kitchen table discussing how extraordinary it was that Crumpet, who'd wandered in to the property as Julian were leaving, hadn't kicked him and had even nuzzled his stomach.

'Why'd he leave?' I asked, heading to the kitchen counter and fiddling with a pile of cherry tomatoes sitting on a chopping board.

'He said he had some urgent work,' Sasha said, sounding annoyed. 'He'd come down here to be with me so I'm not really sure what *work* he needed to do all of a sudden.'

My stomach flipped. Was his work figuring out where he recognized me from? Or did he already know and was only dating Sasha to get proof that I was behind no reason? He didn't seem to be that calculating. He didn't have calculating hair.

'I'm meeting him later,' Sasha added.

'Oh lovely. Where?' Mum asked. You had to admire her shameless persistence.

Sasha merely shook her head.

'What does he do for a job?' Mum endeavoured.

'He's a journalist. For the *Daily Dispatch*,' Sasha said. She scraped her chair back and strode out of the room, leaving Mum utterly delighted Sasha had deigned to impart a nugget of information about the boyfriend.

In the quiet left behind, I watched my mother's delight falter. She turned to me. 'The *Daily Dispatch*?'

Chapter 37

'Do we try and break them up?' I said, pacing the chook enclosure while Mum paced in the opposite direction, giving me a stern look each time we crossed.

'We can't!' she flustered. 'Sasha's finally happy! She *smiled* the other day.'

'You're right.' I chewed my fingernail.

'Do you think he knows it's you?'

'I don't know. I think he recognized me but I'm pretty sure he's only seen me at my house. And anyway, if he does suspect anything he won't be able to get any proof. It's all finished now.'

We paced for a few seconds.

'How did she even meet him?' I asked.

'Well,' Mum said, throwing me a severe look of reproach. 'He came down here to investigate that treasure hunt thingy you did! And when he popped to the pub at the end of the day Sasha was there and their Tinderfaces linked in.'

'Right,' I said, and we paced some more.

'Oh Brooke, you could lose everything!' Mum said suddenly.

We stopped pacing and looked at each other. The fraught silence was broken by my phone ringing. I slipped it out of my pocket to see it was Tom's mum, Vanessa.

'Hey?' I said down the phone. We did a brief catch-up on how the movie was going, how great the souks were in

Marrakech, and I asked (for Mum) if George Clooney were still married, then Vanessa's voice took on a more solemn tone.

'I have something to tell you,' she said. 'We've been offered a four-year contract at the studios in LA. It's extremely last minute but . . . well, we're moving over in the summer break.'

'All of you?' I said, my stomach plummeting.

'What?' Mum mouthed, clocking my expression.

Vanessa paused. 'Yes. This contract means no travelling around so we can be together. We haven't had time to look at schools yet but the studios say they'll help Tom get into a good one.'

My mind went back to Hannah at the open day; playing rugby, her grin wider than it had been in months, her and Tom stuck to each other like glue. 'Hannah's going to be devastated.'

Mum stepped closer to me, her face stricken.

'Tom too,' Vanessa said. 'We're telling him this weekend. He doesn't know yet.'

'Can you please ask him to not tell Hannah yet? I want to find the right time to break the news.'

'Of course,' Vanessa said. 'We'll get the kids to Facetime all the time. And I hope you'll visit once we're all set up?'

'I'll make sure we do,' I said miserably. 'Oh my God, I'm so sorry. Congratulations!' I said, forcing cheer into my voice.

We brushed over the nightmare logistics of getting back from Morocco, packing their cottage, flying to LA, and setting up over the summer break then she had to get back to set. I hung up and looked at Mum, bereft.

'What? What is it?' Mum said.

'They're moving to LA. With Tom.'

Mum's face fell. 'Shit.'

'Shit.'

★

Back in London the week slipped by in a tangle of worries. School was still a lonely place that Hannah endured and I was afraid her new happiness was too fragile to take on the news about Tom, her one friend, moving away. I wanted to have a solution before I presented her with it but I couldn't come up with one. And if I wasn't worrying about Hannah I was worrying about Julian. Each day I scoured the news, but when nothing about me or #NoReason was in the *Daily Dispatch,* and our gentle probing of Sasha about her boyfriend brought forth no concerns, Mum and I allowed ourselves to relax. About that, at least. Then all of a sudden it was the Father/Daughter Bushcraft Day. And Chris's birthday.

I placed his favourite breakfast on the table in front of Hannah.

'Happy birthday, Dad,' she said, and blew out the candle on top of her pancake stack.

I smiled. 'Happy birthday, Chris.'

After breakfast we looked at photos of Chris, had a cuddle, then not too much later Dennis arrived, fifteen minutes earlier than I'd suggested and in beige shorts, a vest with multiple pockets, a beige bucket hat, and enough sunblock on his face to pass as a mime. It was nice to see him. Hannah walked into the kitchen with her daypack. She'd gone over the equipment list four times the night before and we'd both decided it was a good idea to pack extra plasters for Dennis.

He took a solemn step towards her. 'I would like to thank you for the supreme privilege of accompanying you today.'

Hannah gave him a shy smile. 'You're welcome.'

'We'd better head off,' I said, checking the time. 'The bus leaves in twenty minutes.'

Dennis pulled tightly on his backpack straps so that his pack sat high up on his back and joined Hannah in the hall. 'Your braces are looking good,' he said as they made their way to the front door, Cookie and me following behind. 'Are the kids at school giving you any trouble about them? Any name-calling? Any new ones I might not have heard? I feel I've heard them all but am always keen to see what the young folk are coming up with.'

'I get called Brace Face and Metal Mouth sometimes,' Hannah said, opening the front door.

'Classics.' Dennis nodded following her outside where they waited on the footpath for me to lock up.

'And Cheese Grater and Tinsel Teeth.'

'Lesser used, but still standing the test of time, I see.'

I joined them on the footpath and they turned and walked, side-by-side, in the direction of the school with me following.

'One time someone called me Staple Smile.'

'Now *that's* new,' Dennis said, as if he were an extremely keen botanist and had just been shown a new species of fungus.

'Tom says they're all brace-ist,' Hannah said and they both chuckled.

They exchanged stories from their recent lives all the way to school and, feeling a swell of affection for the unlikely pair, I waved as they took their seats on the bus. They barely even noticed me as they gabbed like old friends.

'See you at Nan and Grandad's!' I said through the open bus window.

Dennis and Hannah were getting a lift there after the bush-craft day which was in the South Downs, a mere twenty minutes away, rather than get the school bus back to Earlsfield.

Penny waved off Elise and Rog, who couldn't have looked more out of his element, then joined me as we watched the bus depart.

'Hannah looks happy.'

'Hmmm,' I said, clocking Livie and her father occupying seats at the front of the bus with a knot of giggling girls and teachers surrounding them.

Penny considered me. 'What?'

I shrugged and we began walking. 'I thought she'd want to be with me today, that's all.'

'But it's good that she *wants* to be at school, right? That's been your aim this whole time, no? To get her confidence back and for her to be happily off to school?'

I nodded. We reached the corner of the street where we needed to go in opposite directions.

'I'm sorry I can't spend the day with you,' Penny said, her red lips in a downward smile.

Now that Lorenzo was about to start school Penny had thought she might go back to work. She'd emailed round her resumé and immediately had requests for interviews. She stood before me in her smart clothes, off to go talk luxury interiors.

'That's okay.'

She stepped towards me and pulled me into a hug. 'Happy Birthday, Chris.'

'Happy birthday, Chris,' I said, breathing in her expensive jasmine and fig shampoo.

★

I shut the door behind me at home and Cookie's claws on the floorboards echoed in the otherwise silent house. I felt aimless. I had no #NoReason tasks to attend to, my Excel spreadsheet now defunct. As I boiled the jug and looked at the spot where the whiteboard had been I realized I'd enjoyed being so busy. What was I going to do now? Go back to walking Cookie? I sat with a cup of tea and my laptop and opened my emails. One from Abdul asking to chase an unpaid invoice for a small engagement party. It would take no more than fifteen minutes. I sighed and opened the invoice as my phone buzzed, Trish's name on the screen.

'Hey,' I answered. 'Aren't you—'

'It's going ahead,' Trish's voice came down the line fast and uncharacteristically breathless.

'What?'

'Chris's #NoReason birthday party. I just got a call from Jamal and apparently the singers are planning on doing it because they'd already been paid. And the volunteers are still heading in and the musicians and everything.'

My heart was immediately in my throat. 'What? But you told them to stop!?'

'I know, but Jamal says the volunteers love doing it so much they don't want to. They called it a movement and said it was in the public's hands now.'

'Oh my God.'

'I know. Look, I have to go, I'm due on camera in one minute. I don't know what you can do about it but I thought you should know.'

I hung up, grabbed my keys, kicked my feet into some sneakers and flew out the door. An hour later I was on Carnaby Street in the thick of Chris's 'birthday party'. Saxophonists in ballgowns, chalk artists, caricaturists, and people in #NoReason T-shirts handing out envelopes. But what were they stuffed with? They must be doing their own donations. Tables were set up and people in bright outfits were playing board games with strangers. It was joyful and colourful and kind; all the things #NoReason had become. But this time it wasn't me. It had taken on a life of its own.

I checked my phone. Social media was loving it.

It was a multicoloured fucking nightmare.

Appalled, I walked through the throng in a daze which was broken as the twenty-strong a cappella group we'd booked, *and* cancelled, launched into a beatbox version of Club Nouveau's 'Lean On Me', one of Chris's favourite songs. A whoop came from the swelling spectators as a girl in bright green overalls and two puffs of hair sticking out the top of her head like Mickey ears bounced forward and performed a solo beatbox, then was joined by a guy with a chest like a tank who sang and strutted in front of the a cappella group.

I was rooted to the spot, watching in horror, as a crowd grew around them. The a cappella group fell into a synchronized three-step routine eliciting more whoops and applause from the crowd. They were moves I'd seen on a filmed rehearsal weeks previously. Then it had made me clap with joy, now it filled me with dread. As they reached the end of the song there was an explosion of cheers. Dismayed at the happy, colourful, vibrant spectacle I no longer had any govern over I realized I had to get out of there. I turned to leave but was blocked by a familiar face.

'I *knew* it was you.'

Fuck.

'What?' I turned away. 'Sorry, I have somewhere I need to be.'

Julian P Tickle sidestepped, blocking my path. 'You're the one behind #NoReason.'

A man who'd been filming the singers jerked his head in our direction.

Why had I come? Why hadn't I just stayed at home? What the hell was the matter with me?

I sidestepped Julian's sidestep and took off down Carnaby Street, Julian keeping pace as I wove through the multi-coloured crowd, my pulse racing.

'Your daughter goes to the school where the first #NoReason act was. Your family lives in the village where the treasure hunt was. You're *here*.'

'So are lots of people.'

'And I have this,' he said, thrusting a sheet of paper in front of me.

I glanced at a grainy image of Hannah and me outside a bookstore, our faces hidden by our disguise caps. I looked away and stepped around a group of tourists watching a #NoReason person handing out envelopes. 'That could be anyone, you can't even make out the faces.'

'You're carrying the exact same handbag,' he said, almost apologetically, as if he hated to be the one to break it to me.

Still weaving around the crowd, I cursed Martin for sending me the distinctive woven handbag from Nepal.

'What I don't get is how you pay for it all,' Julian said, skipping to keep up. 'I've seen where you live. I know you work part-time from home. So, are you acting on behalf of someone funding it? Is it a social statement campaign?'

Panic tightening my chest, I tried to turn down a side street but it was blocked by a crowd circling a violinist in a sequined jumpsuit playing Europe's 'The Final Countdown'. She was unbelievable and at any other time I would have been captivated. I reversed and skipped round a knot of people, Julian relentlessly at my heel.

'You must have a reason why you're doing all this,' he said, matching my pace as I wove in and around the crowds, the increasing pace of the violin music increasing my anxiety. 'Nobody would put this much effort and expense into something without a purpose. I mean, let me be very clear, I think it's wonderful and that's why I want to write about it.'

I ducked to the left but was hemmed in by a swarm gathered around a #NoReason girl in a leopard-print leotard, stripy tights and shredded tulle bat-wings playing chess on a neon light-up chess set with an elderly man in a turban.

'Imagine if the public knew who was behind it?' Julian said as I wiggled my shoulders through the crowd. 'You might get donations. In fact, I'm sure of it.'

I saw a gap and took off. Julian, again, at my side.

'If they could just put a name and a face to it all there is no limit to where you could go with this.'

I quickened my pace, but was blocked by a throng of people watching a chalk artist draw a kangaroo on a trampoline.

'Do you have an end goal?'

I tried to go down a lane but was blocked by a girl in a #NoReason T-shirt handing out flowers.

'Are you working on behalf of someone high-profile?'

I took off down another lane but hit a cluster of tourists taking photos of the festival-like atmosphere.

'Don't you want the accolades from being behind something so nationally loved?'

I spun around and Julian was right in my face. I tried to squeeze past another swelling crowd, my shoulder scraping on the brick wall as I got hemmed in.

'I don't know what you're trying to achieve but the publicity can help you get what you want.'

'No, it can't!' I cried, falling back against the wall as a crowd pushed past us following the violinist as she danced down the lane like the Pied Piper.

Julian's mouth fell open. 'It *is* you!'

Fuck it. Fuck it all over the place.

I scanned the dancing crowd filling the whole lane. Finding no avenue for escape I turned back to him waiting, stunned. 'Look,' I said, my voice low. 'You can't write the article.'

Julian expression became genuinely mystified. 'Why not?'

'Because you just can't.'

'I can,' he said sympathetically, as if I were very naïve. 'You can either be part of it, or—'

'You can't use my name if I don't give permission.'

'I can,' he said, and again he seemed sorry to be informing me of that fact. 'You've been doing public acts. But I can assure you, the article will be written from a positive standpoint.'

'Is this why you're with my sister? To get to me?'

Julian looked confused. 'What? No,' he said, shaking his head. 'What you've been doing is amazing! People will want to interview you—'

'That can't happen!'

'Why?'

'Please, *please* don't write anything about me,' I said feeling frantic. 'I can pay you to not write anything.'

Julian's resolve wavered and then returned. 'It's not about the money.'

'I'll do whatever it takes for you to walk away from this. I want to be left alone.'

Julian frowned. 'Why? You've been doing *very* public events. If you wanted to be left alone, why do them?'

I shook my head.

'If I don't write about it somebody else will eventually find out who you are and *they* will write it. And who knows what angle they'll take. I can assure you that my take on it all is extremely positive.' His face lit up. 'What you have been doing . . .' he cast his arm out at the bustling, happy crowd, 'it's inspiring!'

'No,' I said. 'Please.' Hannah and I could lose everything. I started to feel sick.

'This . . . This could be the story of my career,' Julian said, squaring his shoulders. 'And . . . and I will write that article.'

'NO, YOU WILL NOT!' said a voice that had said *no you will not* many times to me.

Julian and I spun around.

'What are you doing here?!'

My mother arrived at my side. 'I have Feverish Stalkerism Syndrome, remember.'

I smiled despite the fraught situation.

Mum gave me a brief smile then rounded on Julian. 'If you write this article you have no idea of the ramifications for Brooke.'

Julian's eyes flicked to me, assessing and inquisitive, then back to Mum. 'I—'

'Now, you seem like you're not a bad fellow,' Mum railed over him. 'You like animals, which makes me willing to give you the benefit of the doubt. And Crumpet seems to like you and he's a faultless barometer for character. But I cannot abide this kind of work for a potential suitor for my daughter.'

Huh? I looked at my mother. *Was this about me or Sasha?*

'Sniffing around people's private lives and writing about them in the media with no thought except your name in the tagline. It is not an honourable way to make a living. You should be ashamed of yourself! And if you want to see my daughter again, you'd best think what the right thing to do is. And so help me God, if you have used my youngest to get to my eldest you'll wish you'd never gone to journalism school. If you even need to these days!'

I was surprised and proud of my mother's fierceness, despite her concerns leaning a little more towards Sasha than I thought appropriate for the situation.

'Sasha and I met at a pub . . .' Julian said. 'I had no idea . . .'

Mum narrowed her eyes, evaluating his expression.

'It's the truth,' Julian said firmly and I believed him.

'Well then,' Mum spat. 'What are you looking for here, exactly?' She flicked her head in my direction.

Julian glanced at me and I thought I could detect a hint of guilt, 'Breaking a major story like this, it's . . . it's every journalist's dream. It could change my entire career trajectory.'

'So, it's your name on the front page you want? Fame?' Mum stared him down.

'Well, yes. But it's more than that.'

We all paused as a guy with a lot of facial hair and a baby-pink #NoReason T-shirt flounced in front of us, proffering three single yellow gerberas, and complimented our attire. We dropped our variety of fraught expressions, smiled and thanked the man, then as he flitted to another group, spun back to each other and resumed our serious demeanours, only now each holding a cheerful bloom at our chests.

'Tell us what it is that you want,' Mum demanded. 'Money?'

Julian explained that a shift worker at any news publication had it tough but that it was especially ruthless at the *Daily Dispatch*. If you didn't deliver on the editor's outlandish and unrealistic demands, getting a senior footballer to comment on another footballer's indiscretions by lunchtime for example when you were only asked at 10:30am, then you could be out of a job before the afternoon trip to the vending machine. Every day you turn up to work could be your last. 'And that kind of insecurity is no way to make a life.'

Mum's expression remained hard. Julian's grey eyes flicked my way then went back to Mum. He knew who was in charge.

'Delivering a story like this,' he said. 'It could get me off shift work and become a staffer. A staff position brings not just better stories but job security. A contract and a salary.'

Julian shrugged and all of a sudden he looked like every other guy in his late twenties struggling to find a job that would pay rent on a shared flat in an area only marginally acceptable to call home. 'I want to be able to save for my own place, so I don't have to live with a flatmate who maintains a very loose relationship with soap, and an unhealthy obsession with the cat from *Hello Kitty*. And has a pet snake. Which we can't currently find. Or a wardrobe so damp it grows mushrooms. I want to do normal things like plan a holiday. Or actually be able to turn up to my friend's birthday dinners when I say I will. And, you know, pay insurance on my car when it's due. Being a shifter,' he shrugged again, 'it's too precarious.'

Everyone had their own struggle and I felt a pang of sympathy for him and his mushroomy wardrobe and his weird flatmate. And really concerned about that missing snake.

For a moment, Mum was silent and Julian turned to me.

'What you've been doing,' he said, smiling again. 'It's brought a sense of fun to people. You've reminded the public to notice each other – and that when they do, life can be a little bit more joyful. It's *amazing!*' He cracked into a wide smile. 'And if you just let me quote you—'

My stomach dropped. Julian just wasn't getting it. I turned to my mother, my eyes, I'm sure, desperate.

Mum looked back at me, her brain whirring. She didn't flap and fluster or call anyone wicked. She gave me a single nod, then turned to Julian, cool and calm. 'I have a deal for you.'

Chapter 38

Mum and I sat rocking to and fro on the Tube towards Victoria. Mum's mouth was in a thin line and I'd made a shredded mess of the skin around my nails.

As the Tube approached Victoria Mum threaded her arm through her handbag and turned to me.

'I'm sorry, Mum.'

'Let's just see what he says. Then we can do apologies.' She gave me a nod then when the train doors opened at the station she strode out towards the connection that would take her back to Sussex and her Pétanque tournament, and I was left with a nasty feeling in the pit of my stomach.

As soon as I walked in the front door at home I emailed Will.

Are you able to stop an article being written? Or get a gag order or something?

Then with shaking hands I grabbed mine and Hannah's overnight bags, Cookie and her lead, and headed back to the station to get the train to down Mum and Dad's.

When I was on the train Will phoned back.

'What happened?'

I slunk down in my seat, relieved no one was within earshot, and in a hushed voice, told him what had happened.

Silence.

'It's bad, isn't it?' I said.

Will waited a second before answering. 'Is your mother going to be able to pull this off?'

'I don't know.'

'Let's hope she does. It will be your best shot. In the meantime I'll start putting together a defence.'

I ended the call and felt sick. This was real. Will, my sharp-suit-wearing lawyer from a law firm with glass walls and its own gym, was relying on my mother striking a deal with her retired news editor neighbour; the bargaining chip being a virile alpaca called Clint.

When the Uber dropped me at Mum and Dad's they'd already left for their Pétanque championship in Bournemouth. Sasha was at a hen weekend in the Peak District and the latest student had gone back to Latvia, homesick. The house was uncharacteristically silent.

Mum had left a note on the kitchen bench with a giant 'To Do' list.

I got to the end of the note that covered yurt changeovers, checking guests in and out, hamsters/parrot/donkey/alpaca/sheep/chicken and duck care, egg deliveries, instructions on how to get the washing machine working when it stuck on 'spin cycle', and ways to get Crumpet to do what you want, and had a sudden pang of extreme love for my mother. She did so much. And still expended a vast amount of energy worrying about her adult children.

I tended to the most pressing of chores, let an indignant Leo out of his cage, then paced the kitchen waiting for a call (Leo pacing the kitchen bench in mimicry). It came an hour later.

'Noel is on board and Julian is going to take the deal,' Mum said, the sound of the car engine in the background.

'Oh, thank God,' I said, my legs giving way as I sunk to the floor. I leant back against the fridge.

'I have to drop Clint off when we get back after the weekend,' Mum said, her voice cracking. 'Do you think Noel might still let me vacuum him?'

Oh Jesus. I flicked open Mum's drinks cupboard with my foot and looked at the bottles. 'I . . . I don't know, Mum,' I said, wondering if the sentence 'Would it be okay if I came over and vacuumed your alpaca occasionally?' was one that had ever been uttered by anyone else in history. 'Maybe.' Pimm's. What did that taste like straight? 'I'm so *so* sorry, Mum. I don't know how to make it up to you.'

I grabbed the Pimm's. Yuck. It tasted yuck straight.

'You can stop all this nonsense.'

'I have.'

'You can make a solid, responsible plan for your and Hannah's future.'

'I will.'

'And you can weed the vegetable garden.'

I called Will and let him know that Mum's neighbour had agreed to swap Clint for arranging an introduction for Julian to his former underling, the editor at Reuters News Agency. The editor had agreed to it on the proviso that Julian had an exclusive with the anonymous (and *remaining* anonymous) person behind #NoReason.

'Mum says Julian has agreed to the terms.'

We just had to hope that Julian was going to do what he said he would – interview me, keep my name out of it, and take the job offer, if there even was one. And then never let on who I was. *Ever.* There were a lot of 'ifs' and a reliance on trust. But that was all we had. And my mother would have to give up Clint.

I felt awful.

'Do you trust him to keep his word?'

I thought about Julian. And his uncalculating hair tuft. 'I do.'

An hour later, I'd weeded the vegetable garden and was

sitting at the sunny outdoor table with a margarita wondering how I could make the loss of her beloved Clint up to my mother, when Dennis and Hannah walked around the side of the house; muddy (Hannah), limping (Dennis), and grinning (both). I pushed my worries to the side, an act aided by the fact I was two margaritas in (okay, three), and asked Hannah and Dennis how their day was.

'We learnt how to build and light a fire, make a shelter, and cross a river!' Hannah said once I'd got them both a cold drink and we were sat around the outdoor table in the late afternoon sun. 'And we did knife safety, and abseiled down a waterfall! Well, Dennis fell down it.'

'Did you?'

'Only half way,' he said cheerily, as if falling only half the way down a waterfall were a jolly good fortune.

'And we learned to set snares and traps, and to navigate by the sun, and find water in moss. And we made spears! Dennis got a splinter.'

'Another one?'

'It's small . . .'

'And we learned how to purify the water and then got split into adult and child teams and had to make our own way back to the base camp. And we had to eat *grubs*!'

'Did you?'

'Dennis did. He got its butt stuck in his teeth!' Hannah squealed with disgusted delight.

'Ew!' I said to Dennis who appeared to be delighted by Hannah's delight.

'Well, it was either the ah . . . rear . . . or . . . or the head . . . that got lodged in my upper centrals.'

I shuddered. 'What did it taste like?'

'Not *too* bad . . .'

'He vomited!' Hannah said, then collapsed into giggles.

I looked to Dennis for confirmation.

'I did,' he admitted with a sheepish grimace then we both laughed as Hannah crumpled with increased giggles.

★

A little while later, Hannah went inside to call Tom and tell him about her day, and I suggested we order pizza for dinner before Dennis headed back to London.

'How about I make dinner?' he said. 'I am, if I am permitted to say myself, a fairly decent cook.'

After a fossick in the fridge, we perused the herb and veg garden, a journey that was peppered with stories about the time he mistook one berry for another in Australia and ended up having his stomach pumped, or the time he was desperate to reach a particularly delicious-looking plum and landed in a virulent patch of poison ivy, while wearing a friend's too-small-for-him swimmers, or the time he nearly choked on a Vietnamese mint leaf from a fresh spring roll at Camden Markets and coughed so vigorously he fell in the canal. He had such an unhurried calmness about him. And he was funny. Although most of the time not intentionally. I introduced him to all the animals then we went back inside and Dennis made himself at home in the kitchen while I mixed more margaritas. He whipped up a Mexican chicken dish that had Hannah rudely scraping the plate with her finger, and a strawberry and coconut rice dessert that had us all licking the bowl.

'Oh, I shouldn't,' Dennis said when I went to top up his drink as he was putting the last dish in the dish rack. He dried his hands with a tea towel draped over his shoulder. 'I ought to be heading off.'

'Can you stay?' Hannah said, bouncing across the kitchen to him. 'Then you can watch my drum lesson in the morning?'

Dennis looked across the kitchen at me. 'Ah . . .'

'That's okay, Mum?' Hannah spinning to face to me.

'Oh . . . um,' I said, caught off guard by the notion. Hannah's eyes pleaded with me. 'Sure. Martin's old room is set up.'

Hannah grinned and spun back to Dennis. 'Can you?'

Dennis glanced at his watch. It was just after 9pm and the kitchen door was open to the pale violet twilight, the scent of a summer garden wafting through on the warm breeze. 'I could, I guess . . .'

'*Please?*' Hannah said, stepping closer and clutching her hands under her chin in a begging motion. 'We can make pancakes in the morning! Mum makes *the best* pancakes ever.'

I smiled at my oblivious daughter. I made godawful pancakes. But had learned to disguise that fact with lashings of cream and syrup.

'Okay,' Dennis said with a gracious nod. 'Pancakes sound delicious.'

Hannah squealed as she jumped up and down then after I'd topped up our glasses she dragged us both to the cellar to hear her latest Sheila E. beat. Half an hour later Hannah vehemently denied exhaustion at the same time as allowing me to tuck her in to bed. I didn't tell her about the volunteers going rogue and the #NoReason day going ahead. That could wait until Dennis left the next day. Her eyes were shut before I'd even left the room. When I went back downstairs, I found Dennis waiting patiently at the garden table, Cookie on his lap. Cookie didn't usually like anyone's lap. She was a dog that liked to sit on the floor and lick her areas.

'She's cute,' he said.

'She isn't.'

'No. Not really.' He smiled.

I took my seat at the table and for a moment we sat looking at each other. There had never been any time that we'd hung out, just the two of us, and it suddenly seemed weird. The only sounds were the faint braying from a donkey a few fields down the lane, the last of the crickets, and the odd cheep and flutter of a bird nesting up for the evening.

'How is your girlfriend?' I asked, topping up his glass then mine.

'Oh,' Dennis said, straightening in his seat. 'I think she broke up with me.'

'I'm sorry,' I said pointlessly because I wasn't, and it seemed neither was he.

'Yes, it was all rather unusual. One day she was making plans for lunch at a members-only restaurant that didn't serve milkshakes and talking about booking a weekend break to a members-only farmhouse in Oxfordshire . . .'

'Is she a member?'

'No, but I got the impression she rather hoped I would be.'

'Are you?'

'No.'

'So, you didn't go on a weekend break?'

'Well, yes, actually. To an Orthodontic Symposium in Hounslow. But I don't think she enjoyed herself.'

'Can't imagine why.'

It took a moment for Dennis to get my meaning and then we both chuckled.

'Then one day I saw her with a plastic surgeon who has a practice a few doors down.'

'He has memberships?'

'I believe so, yes.'

'Sounds like you had a lucky escape, if you don't mind me saying.'

Dennis chortled softly. 'I don't mind at all.'

Well into the night we talked. I found out that his grand-mother had taught him to cook and she was now eighty-seven and he still saw her every week. And she still made a better soufflé than him. I found out that he'd only had one serious girlfriend when he was in his mid-twenties and since then had been open-heartedly looking but perfectly content on his own. I found out that his favourite TV show was *Night Court,* a show I had to google to remember, his favourite movie was *Finding Nemo*, and that he found peaches too fuzzy. As I regaled him with my idiosyncrasies he watched me with a charmed expression and I felt funny and clever and interesting under his smiling gaze.

'Thank you for accompanying Hannah today,' I said. 'She had a brilliant day.'

'As did I,' Dennis said. 'Hannah is delightful company.'

Pleasure bloomed within me at the praise of my daughter. 'She is pretty special.'

'I was impressed with her focus on the tasks. And she relates very well to adults.' Dennis's smile faded somewhat. 'She pointed out which young lady had been giving her some trouble. Livie, was it?'

I nodded.

'You can tell something is going on with the young lady. She was incredibly competitive and pointed out whenever another child did something incorrectly. It's worrying when children bully. It is never a happy child who picks on another.'

'No,' I said. 'But I find it hard to muster any sympathy for a child who chose to pick on a girl who'd recently lost her father.'

'Yes,' Dennis said, looking stricken.

And then because he was so easy to talk to, and I'd had several strong margaritas, I told him how worried I'd been about Hannah over the past year and that perhaps some of her confidence troubles had been my fault. Perhaps I'd isolated her too much because I didn't feel up to seeing people.

'I just have this fear that I haven't been the mother I should have been,' I said, noting the difficulty I had with any 's' words. 'And maybe that's why Hannah didn't feel strong enough to stand up to Livie?' I'd been pushing this thought to the back of my mind for months; finally, the margaritas had released it.

'What are you talking about?' Dennis said, with a look of

disbelief. 'Hannah is one of the most delightful creatures I have ever met. She seems confident despite the hurdles she's had. And that's down to you. *All* you.'

I thought about Hannah and through Dennis's eyes saw, not a child without a father but just a child. Taking the very first steps towards becoming a teenager. And doing it with the burdens of grief and victimisation. Doing it with grace.

Chapter 39

'MUM!' Hannah's voice tore me from the depths of sleep.

I barely had time to collate the fragments of thoughts. The sun was too bright. Why hadn't I shut the curtains? I was naked. Extremely hungover. Dennis was next to me . . .

Wait. Dennis was next to me!?

I was naked?!

Dennis was naked!

I WAS NAKED NEXT TO NAKED DENNIS!

The door flew open. Hannah gasped. Dennis woke. Dennis gasped. Hannah flew out the door and slammed it behind her.

★

'It's completely understandable,' Dennis said as I hustled him up and out of my bed, apologising.

In my mind, and in the harsh light of morning, we were back to being orthodontist and client's mother, yet we were naked in my bedroom at my mum and dad's house looking for his clothes. And we'd shagged (twice!) on my dead husband's birthday.

'It's an alarming way for her to find out about us,' he said as he pressed confirm on his Uber.

Us?! No no no no no NO!

I threw on an old hoodie of Chris's from the musty drawers and pulled on shorts from my open suitcase. At the front door, Dennis mentioned calling later and meeting up and, rather than address the colossal mistake we had both just made, I said 'yes, great, yes, goodbye, speak later, thanks', and accepted his kiss. He crossed the courtyard to his Uber, his shirt buttoned incorrectly and his hair tousled and strangely roguish for a geeky orthodontist, then waved cheerily as the Uber drove out the gate. I turned and raced through the house calling Hannah's name.

She wasn't in her drum room, the formal living room, the dining room, the lounge, the kitchen, the laundry, or any of the upstairs bedrooms or bathrooms. I flew back down the stairs and out of the kitchen door into the garden. No Hannah.

Trampoline – no Hannah.

Tree hut – no Hannah.

She wasn't in the barn, the cart-shed, or with the chickens. I raced through Clint's paddock and he and Pablo raised their heads and watched me streak across their field towards the yurt field. No Hannah. But I did see a man in boxers standing in the doorway of the toilet block, his hair a-squiff, prevented from exiting by Crumpet who was munching stolen produce menacingly two feet from his bare stomach.

'I'll be back in a second!' I said as I ran past the orchard. 'He's friendly!' I lied.

But when I got to the back paddock, extremely out of breath, she wasn't anywhere. And the school rugby field was full of teen boys and I had no bra on. I raced back to the house, took the stairs two at a time and dashed down the hall to my bedroom. I took a second to stand in the doorway looking at the tumbled duvet and wrestled-in sheets, shame and regret curdling in my stomach. I needed to call Hannah. Where was my phone? It began vibrating somewhere on the dressing table. I scrambled through yesterday's clothing, discarded in a frenzy of ill-advised lust, following the vibrations. When I finally found it, I saw not Hannah's name, as I was hoping, but Vanessa. Tom's mum. Maybe Hannah had gone there?

'Hi, Vanessa,' I said, pacing at the end of the bed.

'Oh hi, Brooke, I'm so sorry to call early on a Saturday. Did I wake you?'

'No, no I'm awake!' I said affecting a perkiness I didn't feel. 'What's up – is Hannah with you?'

'With us? No, is she not with you?'

'I just can't find her at the moment. I'm sure she's about somewhere,' I said trying to sound casual but feeling desperate. *Where was she?*

'Ri–ight. Well, I might know something about that,' Vanessa said. 'Tom just came to me very upset. They were messaging each other and he accidently mentioned us moving to LA. She called him and when he said we were leaving in August she hung up and now her phone is off.'

'Oh.' I slumped on the end of the bed. 'That explains a lot,' I said, no longer faking sprightliness. 'I think she's run away.'

'Oh no! Shall we . . .' The phone muffled for a moment and I heard her repeat the information to Tom. Tom's voice sounded panicky and Vanessa said something about it being okay and 'she'll be found soon enough' then she was back on the line. 'Tom says he thinks he knows where she'd go. He says he can bike over now and look for her. Is that okay?'

'That would be great. Thank you.'

I waited while Vanessa reminded Tom to take his helmet and keep an eye out for cars and then she was back.

'I'm so sorry about this,' she said. 'Tom feels terrible because he knows you wanted to be the one to break it to her, but they were apparently sharing their biggest worries or something and Tom said "moving away" before he'd properly thought about it. He's very distressed. I hope Hannah is okay?'

I rubbed my forehead. 'I've been waiting for the right time to tell her but there just hasn't seemed to be one.' It felt like a pathetic excuse. Why hadn't I just told her?

'It's sounds like she's had a bit of a tough year at school.'

'She has. But still, I should have told her. This is completely my fault.'

'You were just protecting your daughter.'

Vanessa's kindness made me want to cry. 'I thought I was.'

I promised to let her know when we'd found Hannah then we hung up. I stayed on the end of the bed wondering if I should go with Tom to look for her but decided I would let him find her alone. She ran to get away from me. I needed to respect her claim for space. I needed to let her process what she'd just found out. I needed to let her process what she'd just *seen*. I took a deep breath. I needed to vomit.

*

I wiped the flecks off the avocado toilet seat (a hue that definitely aids vomit in its upward journey) then sat on the floor of the bathroom with its chipped old tiles and took slow steadying breaths, assessing my current situation. My phone, discarded on the floor, lit up with a silent text from Trish. And one from Penny. Then another from Trish again. I snatched it up, swished toothpaste around my mouth, left the bathroom and while trudging down the stairs opened the texts from Trish.

> Ignore the fuckers.

Huh?

Her one before that said:

> Have you read the article?

What article? I closed down Trish's texts and opened Penny's.

> It's an asshole article! They're virtue signalling wankers!

What article? I pressed dial.

'What article?'

'Oh *cariño*, I'll send you the link. Read it and call me back.'

'Okay,' I said and hung up.

Two seconds later my phone lit up with the link to a broadsheet newspaper article. I sat on the third bottom step in the quiet entrance hall, the front door still open from where I'd shooed out Dennis, and clicked it.

I could barely take in the words, my vision was swimming and my mind was racing over what I'd done with Dennis, where Hannah was, how she must be feeling. Sentences jumped out at me as I scanned the text. *'Frivolous and arrogant waste of money in a time of austerity still for many' 'handing out coffee cards when they should be putting the money to good use', 'rehabilitating prisoners' 'the environment' 'pointless and wasteful' 'showy and thoughtless' 'a load of expensive wasteful nonsense', 'most likely a talentless trust fund brat looking for fame'.*

I scrolled to the comments that were popping up at the bottom of the article.

'So glad I'm not the only one who thinks this is a load of shite.'

'London-centric as usual. What's the bet it's a group of privileged tw*ts telling us all how to live and thinking they're doing something great for humanity. Feck off.'

'It went away. Why is it back?'

'I actually found it really annoying when I was trying to get to work and there are all these people in my way giving out crap I don't want.'

'Why don't they do something useful with all that money like solve climate change.'

Oh God. Would Hannah read this vitriol and it be her lasting memory of #NoReason? A sour feeling twisted in my gut.

I heard footsteps and looked up to see Leesa in the doorway. 'Hi!' she said with her customary fresh-faced smile of wholesome goodness but when she registered the look on my face, her brow creased. 'Brooke?'

I burst into tears. Leesa dropped her bags and rushed over.

'What happened?' she said, sitting next to me and placing her arm around my shoulders. She smelt like sun-warmed jasmine blossoms.

'Hannah has run away because I didn't tell her that Tom was moving to LA,' I said through sobs. 'And I slept with her orthodontist.'

I heard movement and looked up to see Gus in the doorway.

I had thought I was at rock bottom but the cold look in Gus's eyes proved me wrong.

'I . . .' I stood and took a step towards him.

Gus's expression remained impenetrable. Leesa watched from the stair.

'I . . . I can't.' I walked out.

I got to the kitchen and stopped. Clint was in the middle of the room eating a peach from the fruit bowl, gazing around the kitchen as though he was thinking about redecorating it but perhaps not until after summer because it was such a busy time for social callers. I couldn't even scold him. Not least because it was my fault for leaving his gate open but also, he looked so happy. And soon he'd just be another alpaca in a field being periodically vacuumed by a woman he used to live with. I manoeuvred around him and sat at the table.

'Hello, shithead.'

I looked at Leo in his cage, bobbing his head the way he did when he wanted to be let out. I opened his cage door and he hopped on to the kitchen table where he paced between Clint and the fruit bowl.

'Tom is here and he and Gus have gone to look for Hannah,' Leesa said arriving in the kitchen moments later and clocking Clint. 'Oh. I'll take him back to his paddock, shall I?'

'Thanks,' I said miserably.

She leaned over me, plucked a peach from the bowl then navigated the tight space around Clint's woolly rear. 'It's going to be okay,' she said, walking backwards out the door to the garden, Clint following, his large chestnut eyes on the fuzzy fruit she held out.

I picked up my phone and typed Tom a message.

Text me as soon as you find her please.

He replied with a thumbs up emoji and I sat staring at the screen. Leesa came back ten minutes later and I hadn't moved.

'Crumpet was holding a man hostage in the toilets.'

'Oh God, I forgot about him. Is he okay?'

Leesa made a 'not really' face. 'He'd been there for nearly an hour. He didn't speak a word of English.' She pulled out a chair at the table. 'Except "asshole". I took Crumpet back. He's a handful, isn't he?'

I nodded, only briefly registering somewhere in a tiny corner of my mind that Leesa being able to lead Crumpet away was a big deal. I then realized that Mum was probably going to get a terrible TripAdvisor review from the man stuck in the toilets. I was making a mess of everything. I shook my head and the tears tumbled again.

Leesa dragged her chair next to me, put her arm around my shoulders and made soothing noises. 'They'll find her,' she said. 'She won't have gone far. She's a sensible girl from what I've seen of her.'

'It's not just that.'

'Is it the orthodontist?'

'It's everything,' I sobbed.

And while Leo inspected every piece of fruit in the fruit bowl I told her about the bullying, and the devastation of witnessing the gradual loss of Hannah's confidence, the paling of her cheeks, her sunken eyes.

'I just wanted to see her smile again,' I said. 'To see the little nose wrinkle she did before losing it to laughter. It got less and less and then . . . it was never.' I looked up. 'The school wouldn't help and I didn't know what else to do. So I organized dancers outside her school.'

Leesa frowned. 'Dancers . . . ?'

'And a sky banner and free ice creams and a street party. With alpacas.'

'Street party?' Leesa's eyes searched the ether then widened. 'You're . . . ?'

I nodded. 'I'm #NoReason.'

Leesa's jaw dropped.

I told her that it was only meant to be that one-time distraction at the Sports Day. But that it got put on Instagram with a hashtag and Hannah wanted to do more and things took a kind of crazy turn. But Hannah was smiling again so I didn't care about the news articles and the journalists at the school.

'Then Mum found out and tried to get me to stop but I wouldn't so she called you in. But you didn't know the real reason you were here so how could you get me to stop? And also, I didn't want to be life coached.' I shot her a guilty look. 'Sorry.'

Leesa shrugged.

I told her about not wanting to leave London and move to Sussex even though that had been 'The Plan' and everyone kept reminding me of it. And how after I did finally confirm Hannah's spot Tom's parents said they were moving.

'And then today she found out about him moving and that I hadn't told her. And she saw me in bed with her orthodontist,' I said, my voice rising. 'And there was this sort of not-really-a-thing but maybe-a-thing with another man—'

'Gus,' Leesa said. 'I know.'

'You do?'

Leesa smiled as if it had been plainly obvious.

I shook my head and handed Leo a lemon that had rolled out of his grip. 'And now Mum has to give away Clint, and there was this horrible article about #NoReason and Hannah will read it and her final memory of it will be all this mean stuff people wrote. And . . .' I swallowed. 'And it's my fault Chris is dead.'

Chapter 40

Leesa frowned. 'He died in surgery, didn't he?'

I nodded. 'Yes. But it was my fault.'

'What do you mean?'

I told her that Chris had had a clicky jaw that had made my skin crawl. And he'd always wanted Eggs Benedict at this particular café because he said they did the best hollandaise but I never wanted to go because they served it on ridiculously chewy ciabatta and I couldn't handle the clicky-clunk of his jaw as he ate. And he'd roll his eyes and we'd go to a different café which served bread that required much less jaw labour.

And sometimes I'd put surgeon brochures in his bag or send him links about different kinds of clicky-clunky jaw surgery. And it sort of became a long-standing joke. But there were times when I would actually get up from the table and eat my dinner in a different room. I just couldn't stomach the dull click-clunk of cartilage on cartilage. So, a little over two years ago he booked his surgery. And when he was recovered, we were going to have Eggs Benedict at the chewy ciabatta café. But then he died.

'And Mum steamrolled me into a big legal claim and one day I had all this money.' My eyes watered. 'So much money.' I blew my nose. 'And I hated every single penny. Because I'm the reason we have it.' I looked at Leesa. 'He had the surgery because of me. I'm the reason Hannah doesn't have a father.'

Leesa was silent. A rarity. The silence was pierced by a text notification and I snatched up my phone.

'Oh thank God,' I said, the air releasing from my tight chest in a gasp. 'They found her.' I replied to the text, placed my phone on the table and looked back at Leesa.

'Chris's death is not your fault,' she said.

I nodded. I nodded because counsellors had told me that. I nodded because Mum had told me that. Trish had told me that and Penny had told me that. And the logical part of me knew it. But my heart didn't let me believe it. So I nodded because it was easier.

Leesa reached across and squeezed my hand. 'I'll make us some tea.'

A few minutes later the forceful beat of Metallica's 'Sad But True' reverberated up the stairs. I crumpled and hid my face in my hands. I desperately wanted to go down there and explain everything to her but decided to let her work her emotions out on the drums. I couldn't face seeing Gus anyway.

While Leesa pottered around the kitchen opening cupboards and drawers and not once asking where anything was, I listened to the cymbal-smashing beat that matched the anger I'd seen in Hannah's eyes. And Gus's. I really had fucked everything up. I wanted to wrestle free of my own skin and go embody someone else.

Leesa placed a steaming mug in front of me, then took her seat. We blew on our mugs and listened to Hannah and Gus finish the song then the house fell silent as they probably dissected Hannah's stick work. When the first bars to 'Dreams' by Fleetwood Mac drifted up from the cellar, a memory of Chris dancing around me, prancing suggestively with a tea towel, while I cooked dinner flashed in my mind. I wiped away moisture gathering at the corners of my eyes and Leesa gave an empathetic smile.

'I still look for him in a crowd,' I said. 'I think that maybe

I've had a blip in my time consciousness and that actually he's only just gone out of sight for a minute. I feel like I can't tell anyone that, because I'm supposed to be over it by now. I'm supposed to be over him. But I don't want to be over him. The idea of it makes me so sad.'

Leesa nodded. '*Sometimes we don't want to heal because the pain is the last link to what we have lost,*' she said. 'Jim Storm.'

I wiped away another tear. 'Did you just do a quote?'

'He's an Instagram poet who used to be a mechanic.'

'My father would be very proud.'

Leesa smiled. She watched me for a few moments before speaking gently. 'You don't have to say goodbye to your husband in order to move on to the next stage of your life. He will always be a part of you, you'll carry him forever. A part of your heart belongs to him. And that's okay. But that's the wonderful thing about a heart. It doesn't have a finite capacity for love. There's room to be happy again. There's room to love again.' She paused. 'You *haven't* moved on, Brooke. And that's okay. Moving on is very, very hard. But moving forward doesn't mean you're leaving him behind.'

'But that's exactly what it feels like,' I said, tears tumbling. 'I can't leave him behind. He'd *never* leave me behind.'

Leesa handed me another tissue. 'What do you want?'

I shook my head. What I wanted didn't come into it. It was what was best for Hannah.

'No,' Leesa chided, reading my thoughts. 'It's important you know what you want. If you aren't happy, your daughter won't truly be either. You know the metaphor about safety masks? About putting on your own mask on before helping others less able?'

I nodded.

'You've done really well making Hannah happy again.'

I gave her a look.

'Not necessarily *today*,' she said, and we exchanged wry

smiles. 'But now it's time to do well by you.' She paused. 'Put on your own mask.'

'But . . .' I searched my scrambled thoughts. 'But what if I don't know which mask to put on? Or I can't even find a mask?'

Leesa smiled. 'You will. You have to give yourself permission to think about what it is *you* want.'

I nodded. I'd pushed any concept of what I wanted to the back of my mind for so long I had no idea where to start. Everything I wanted seemed to be tied to Hannah. But like the visualisation exercise that had thrown me, I realized that had been a dangerous thing to do. Who would I be when Hannah grew up and left home? What did *I* want? I forced myself to consider the question. Again, and again, and again. All the while Leesa watched me with her baby blues. I don't know how long we sat there. It felt like a year and also thirty seconds. She'd nod encouragingly when I looked up at her, feeling helpless and adrift. And I'd go back into my thoughts. I ran over my life with Chris. I ran over the two years without him. I asked myself again. The answer made me weep.

I looked up. 'I don't want to feel guilty anymore,' I said, tears falling.

Leesa nodded.

'I'm so tired of feeling this way but then I feel like a horrible person for being over being sad. I want . . .' I sniffed. 'I want to have moments of happiness that aren't followed by guilt that I get to be happy and Chris doesn't even get to be alive. That I get to love our daughter and Chris doesn't. That I get to hug her . . .' my voice caught in the back of my throat. 'He will never see her get married. Or have her first job. Or first boyfriend. And I will. I'll see *all* of that.'

Leesa waited for my sobs to subside. 'Chris would want you to be happy, don't you think?'

She was right, of course. That is all Chris would want for me.

My phone beeped with a text from Tom saying the lesson was over and asking if Hannah could go to his place for lunch. I replied that it was fine. 'I have to check out some of the yurt guests,' I said noticing the time on my phone.

'Do you need any help?'

'That'd be great. Thank you.'

Leesa and I strolled across the grounds that was alive with bees, cabbage butterflies and birds, the sounds of happily clucking chickens, and the faint low of a faraway cow.

We passed Clint, Pablo and Audrey the sheep, and I looked away from the woolly alpaca feeling like the worst daughter possible. 'Everything is such a mess,' I said. 'What do I do?'

Leesa glanced at me. 'Are you really asking me?'

I thought about that. 'Yes,' I said. 'I'm really asking. I have no idea.'

'About the money or the orthodontist or Gus or the press or your future?'

I snorted at her list. 'All of it.'

Leesa nodded as if she'd already come up with a nine-point plan that would address and solve everything. 'Go on a trip.'

I stopped walking. 'What?'

'Take Hannah and get yourself some space.'

'Run away from my problems? That's your recommendation?' I frowned. 'That's the exact opposite of all those "face your fear" self-help books. You should look for a different career, I think.'

Leesa chuckled. 'Sometimes it's the only way to view a problem from a different angle. It's not running away, it's changing your viewpoint.'

Leesa gave me a few moments to absorb that concept.

'So just forget about the money, and that horrible article, and the fact I don't know where to live or what school to send Hannah to. Or that I've been having feelings for a man I kissed then ran away from, and that I slept with a different man I *don't* have feelings for, who is actually Hannah's orthodontist, and just . . . go on a trip?'

Leesa smiled. 'Well, no. I think you need to deal with all those things first, *then* go away.'

'Hmm,' I said. 'I was a bit more with you on the running away . . .'

Leesa laughed. Then, after a beat, so did I.

'But also,' Leesa said, becoming serious. 'Decide to be happy.'

'Decide to be happy?' I looked at her, doubtful. 'It's that easy, is it?'

'It's that easy and that hard,' Leesa said. 'You are as happy as you decide to be. So, just decide.'

I nodded. Decide to be happy. What a simple notion. Could it work?

'You know,' Leesa mused as we reached the orchard gates, 'I think we've probably achieved more in the last two hours than our entire time together.'

'Yes,' I said contemplating that fact myself. 'I wanted help today.'

*

Leesa helped me check out a couple from the yurts, remake beds, direct a young family to a good park nearby, and make sure the Italian family had everything they needed including my number in case of more asshole pony visits. I was shocked to learn Leesa spoke French, German and Italian, and could understand Bulgarian. When we walked back to the house and I asked how she came to be a such linguistic magician she told me she used to be a UN translator based out of Geneva.

'What?' I said, as stunned as if she'd told me she used to be Kirk Douglas. 'Why are you doing this life coaching? It must be so unchallenging for you.'

Leesa smiled but it was a sad smile. 'Have you heard of the wounded healer?'

I shook my head.

'It's a term created by Carl Jung, a psychologist. It's the idea that someone who treats patients treats them because they themselves are, or have been, wounded.'

I stopped next to the chicken enclosure and waited for more.

Leesa stopped also and after a moment where she gazed across the grounds, she turned to face me. 'My fiancé died in a boat accident six years ago.'

'Oh. I'm so sorry.' I swallowed. 'So . . . you know.'

'I do,' she said, her eyes glistening.

I held out my hand. She grabbed hold of it and we squeezed. For the first time in forever I didn't feel so alone.

Chapter 41

'Hannah found out about Tom moving,' I said down the phone to Penny.

'Oh no! Is she okay?'

'She ran away.'

'Oh *no!*'

'But she's back now.'

'Oh good.'

'There's more.'

'Oh . . . ?'

'I slept with Dennis.'

'Not Gus? Who is Dennis? The dentist?'

'Orthodontist, yes.'

'That's the first time since . . . ?'

'Yes.'

'How was it? Emotionally.'

'It was . . .' I said trying to assess how I felt among the angst and the hangover and the guilt. 'Strange.'

'And physically? How big? Circumcised? Did it bend to the left? I only met him that one time but he seems like the kind of guy who would have a substantial bend.'

I clapped my hand to my forehead as flashes of skin on skin came back to me. Two years without sex, and multiple margaritas, had made me a bit of an animal in the bedroom.

I felt my cheeks burn at the memory but also, it had felt good to be held by someone. 'It was kind of nice, actually.'

'Oh good!'

'But that's bad!'

'It is?'

'Yes, he's *Hannah's* friend. That's how she sees him. And she found us in bed. Naked.'

'Oh no.'

'And I had to get Dennis out quickly and his underpants, he wears *actual* underpants, are still in my room and then Hannah ran away, and that article, and I realized my first sexual encounter after my husband died was *on his birthday*, then Gus heard me tell Leesa about sleeping with Dennis, and an Italian got imprisoned in the toilets by a pony and . . .well, it's been a very average morning on the whole.'

'Yes, yes I see that. So, do you like the dentist like that?'

'Orthodontist. And no. Not *at all*. He's a friend, I guess,' I said, surprised by the fact I did actually think of him that way. 'And he was being so kind and I haven't had sex in ages and I was *so* drunk and I just wanted that feeling of being close to someone, you know?'

Penny uhuh-ed.

'But now Hannah hates me. Dennis will hate me when I tell him I regret it. I'm pretty sure Gus hates me.' I sighed. 'Even *I* hate me. It's just a big fucking mess all for a drunken shag. And Mum has to give away Clint.'

'Who is Clint? Did you sleep with him too?'

'No, Clint is Mum's alpaca. It's a long story.'

'Ri–ight.'

'I feel so guilty.'

Penny waited a beat. 'Because of Hannah or Dennis or Chris or Gus?'

'All four. And Clint.'

I could tell Penny was nodding.

'What should I do?'

For the first time in her life Penny said, 'I don't know.'

★

A couple of hours later, Vanessa texted to say Tom was bringing Hannah back and I waited on the front steps for them. They arrived through the gates and I crossed the gravel courtyard to greet them halfway. Hannah trudged right past me, her eyes on the ground. I watched her disappear inside then turned back to Tom.

'I'm sorry,' he said, looking distraught. 'I didn't mean to tell her.'

'Tom, you do not need to apologize. This is my fault. I should have told her before. I shouldn't have asked you to keep such a big secret. Can you forgive me?'

He nodded and his cheeks coloured.

'Come here,' I said, holding my arms out and wondering if the 12-year-old boy who'd been part of our lives since he was seven would accept my hug. He did and it warmed my fragile heart. 'You are Hannah's most favourite person. Thank you for looking after her so well today. We're all going to miss you so much.'

'I'll miss you too,' he said, his cracking voice betraying his emotion, and I realized how hard it must have been for him to not share his own worries with his best friend.

I really had been a poor decision maker.

After Tom left, I searched the house for Hannah then headed into the garden. I found her sitting under the willow tree, Leo perched on her outstretched legs eating the grapes she was offering him one by one.

'Hi,' I said through the droopy branches I'd parted like a stage curtain.

Hannah looked up then turned her attention back to Leo.

I stepped through and let the branches swing together behind me; the outside world evaporated, leaving Hannah and me in a shadowy cocoon. 'May I?' I said pointing to a spot beside her.

Hannah shrugged, which I took as a good sign so I sat beside her, leant up against the trunk and exhaled.

'I've a lot to apologize for,' I said after a moment. 'Where would you like me to start?'

Again, Hannah shrugged.

'I'm sorry about not telling you that Tom was moving away. That was wrong of me.'

I watched Hannah feed Leo another grape.

'I didn't know if you'd still want to go to school here, if Tom wasn't going to be there. I thought maybe you'd rather stay in Earlsfield. At our home. But then that would mean you'd go to the local school with Livie and . . .' I looked at my daughter being burdened with my excuses for not doing the right thing and sighed. 'I should have told you. I'm sorry that I didn't. The truth is,' I sucked in a breath. 'I haven't known what's right. I . . .' I shook my head and sighed. 'I've been lost.'

Hannah looked up at me, her eyes blank.

'And I'm very sorry because I'm the parent.' I felt a tear spill over. 'I'm the parent and I *should* know what to do. But I just don't.'

Hannah watched me, her expression strained. She hated to see me upset but she was still angry with me. I wiped under my eye. She went back to feeding Leo. We sat in silence.

'What do you want?' I asked eventually.

Hannah looked away from Leo, her expression quizzical.

'Do you still want to go to the school if Tom isn't there?'

Hannah's face became miserable and she shrugged.

'It doesn't matter what you decide, as long as we're together. Sussex or home, or somewhere totally new if you want? We can make anything work.'

Hannah turned her attention back to Leo who was rotating

a grape in his claws. The question was too big for an 11-year-old. I was about to reframe it when she spoke.

'I don't want to be sad anymore,' she said. She glanced up at me, her expression guilty, then she looked back down at Leo. 'I don't want *you* to be sad anymore. I don't want to be the sad girl whose dad died. I just want to be Hannah. And you to be Mum.' She looked up. 'Does that make me a bad daughter?'

'Oh honey,' I said my heart breaking. 'You're the best daughter I could have ever asked for.'

'I don't mean to you,' she said, her chin trembling and her eyes welling. 'I mean to Dad. Does wanting to stop being sad make me a bad daughter to Dad?'

A fat tear ran down her gorgeous youthful cheek. It took me a moment to push back the wave of tears threatening to run down my much less youthful cheeks.

'Not at all, sweetheart,' I held out my arms and after a second she leaned into them. Leo hopped off her lap indignantly. 'We'll miss him, we'll miss him forever and ever. And we'll continue to have sad moments. But there is nothing wrong with wanting to be happy.' I held my daughter tight. 'Dad would want that, wouldn't he?'

Hannah didn't answer and for a while we sat in our willow tree cocoon listening to the sounds of the world carrying on outside the droopy branches.

'Dad would want you to be happy too,' she said eventually.

I eased out a long breath as I realized that Hannah and I had today both expressed the same desire. Permission to be happy. Leesa was right. The only people who could give us that permission was ourselves. 'I know.'

Hannah stayed in my arms and we watched Leo hop about on the ground picking up bits and pieces and examining them. After a minute or two she sat up and Leo climbed back on her lap.

'Mum?' she said, wiping her cheeks.

'Hmmm?'

She went red. 'What about Dennis?'

It was my turn to go red. 'That was a mistake.'

Hannah nodded.

'And I'm sorry. Very sorry.'

She stroked Leo's feathers with the back of her index finger. 'I think he likes you, though.'

Again, we lapsed into silence.

'We've got a lot to sort out, don't we?' I said, leaning over and stroking Leo's feathers just like Hannah was. It seemed so soothing.

Hannah nodded. 'Mum?'

'Yes.'

'Livie told the kids on the Bushcraft Day that I was going to a boys and girls school because you were trying to stop me becoming a lesbian.'

'Right.' I let out a tight sigh. 'Well, there's nothing wrong with being a lesbian of course, but when we get back to London Livie will be the first thing we sort out.'

Hannah gave a resigned nod.

I touched my finger to the tip of her nose and when she offered the tiniest smile I was overcome with relief. 'Shall we go back inside?'

As we left the protection of the willow tree and stepped into the bright sunlight I turned to Hannah. 'You know, if you don't want to go to the school here without Tom we don't have to choose another school just yet.'

'But it's the end of the year?' Hannah said.

I smiled. 'Well, Leesa came up with an interesting idea . . .'

Chapter 42

'She took a turn for the worse, I'm afraid,' said the woman with multiple rings crammed along her wrinkled yet well-maintained fingers who'd answered Livie's parents' front door on Sunday evening. She'd introduced herself as Justin's mother; Livie's grandmother.

She spoke as if we knew what had been going on in the Smith-Warrington household. 'It doesn't look like she'll be coming home any time soon. The one in the breast hadn't been the primary and they found it everywhere, I'm sorry to say. The doctors here say they've done all they can but they're looking at a clinic in Mexico who have different approaches and some quite fantastic results.'

'That's good,' I said.

'Yes. They didn't want to tell wee Livie and spoil her Bushcraft Day. She'd been so looking forward to it. Livie is quite the outdoorswoman, I'm sure you noticed on the trip.' She directed that comment to Hannah who God bless her, smiled and nodded.

'She doesn't get it from me, mind. Oh no, I prefer my own bed and eiderdown. Always have. I don't do any of the gallivanting about Europe like this lot do.' Her face fell. '*Did*, I suppose now . . .' She looked past us wistfully and toyed with a heavy and expensive-looking gold pendant that hung down her cream top to her mid chest.

'We are so sorry,' I said. 'Is there anything we can do?'

'Would you like the name of the hospital she's at? Livie would love to see a friendly face, I'm sure. They kept the serious nature of the illness from her so it's come as a bit of a blow to the wee lass.'

'Sure,' I said and Hannah and I waited silently at the front door while the lady popped back inside. She came back with the name of the hospital written in fancy loopy writing on fancy flowery notepaper. 'There you go, loves. I'm so sorry to give you the sad news like this. It must be quite shocking to hear because she'd been such a trouper through it all, always keeping positive and hoping for the best.'

'Will Livie be coming back for the last week of school?' Hannah asked.

'I don't think so, my love.'

Hannah nodded.

'Alright then, bye now.' And she shut the door.

Hannah and I walked away from the house in silence. Hannah turned to look at the big bay windows of their impeccably painted house, then turned back to me.

'Is Livie's mum going to die?'

I put my arm over Hannah's shoulder. 'I don't know.'

We carried on down the footpath for a while, my arm resting on Hannah's bony shoulder, our footsteps slow and occupied, the early evening sun warm on our backs.

'Poor Livie,' Hannah said. 'We should send her something.'

How my heart swelled for my empathetic, forgiving daughter. She had forgiven me and, in a flash of a second, seemed to have forgiven Livie. I bent down and kissed the top of her head.

★

On Monday morning Hannah headed off for her last week of school with her shoulders back, her multicoloured basketball under her arm, hoping to challenge the boys to a game at recess. She was brilliant in the end of year concert and received an award at the Leavers Ceremony for 'Originality and Authenticity in Creative Writing'. Ms Galloway approached me at the canapé table that night.

'I think Hannah ended up having a good year,' she said, with an 'I'm-a-professional-and-knew-how-this-would-turn-out' smile.

I put down my mini sausage roll. 'I don't give a rat's rectum what you think,' I said and walked away.

On the last day of school I dropped Hannah at the gates with a giant water soaker and an even gianter grin.

'Ava and I are going to gang up on Mr Moody,' Hannah giggled, walking a pace or two ahead of me.

'Aw that's mean. Mr Moody is lovely,' I said, skipping to catch up.

The final day of school was a teachers versus students water fight and Hannah had wanted the biggest, soak-iest water gun there was.

'That's why we're going to gang up on him!' she shrieked.

When she saw Ava at the gates with the exact same super-soaker she squealed with excitement, said 'BYE!', and without a backward glance, raced over to the first girl who had apologized off her own back for standing by and saying nothing during Livie's reign of terror. I watched my daughter run happily through the school gates then walked toward Penny, who'd been watching me.

'You got her through it,' Penny said, smiling. 'You did do it in a rather dramatic, crazy-person way, but you got her through it.'

I linked arms with my friend as we turned in the direction of the café where they knew her order and now mine. 'Everybody got her through it.'

★

'All you need to do is tell Dennis it was a one-time drunken encounter, a huge fucking mistake, and is never happening again ever,' Penny said, taking her seat opposite me.

'In a better way.'

'Naturally,' she said, emptying a sugar packet into her coffee. Then another one. 'Talk to Gus re the kissing, then the telling him you hated the kissing, then the running away, the avoiding him, and then the sleeping with Hannah's dentist.'

'Orthodontist.'

Penny rolled her eyes. 'Then figure out where you want to live, what school Hannah will go to, what to do about the article, the rest of the money, and your future in general.' Penny picked up her flat white and shrugged like the 'To Do' list she'd just outlined was no more taxing than going to the corner store to get tampons, a trashy magazine and four Galaxy bars.

★

I knew it was going to be hard by the look of outright joy in Dennis's eyes as he crossed Cavendish Square Gardens to greet me later that day.

I'd been practising all the way into town. I would tell him that while I very much enjoyed our one night together I'd come to think of him as a good friend and just wasn't ready for anything right now. That I needed to focus on Hannah and our future and that I was very sorry but that I hoped we could still be friends because Hannah very much enjoyed his company. As did I. *As a friend.* I was nervous and jittery. I really didn't want to hurt Dennis. I'd grown very fond of him.

'It was just a one-time drunken encounter, was a mistake, and is never happening again,' Dennis said as soon as I'd opened my mouth.

I blinked. *Had Penny called him?* 'I . . .'

He smiled. 'I paraphrased for you.'

'Oh . . .'

'I'm right, though, aren't I?'

'Well, I wouldn't have put it quite like that but, essentially . . . yes.' I looked up at his kind and handsome and unguarded face. 'I'm sorry.'

Dennis looked back at me for a moment then smiled. 'It's okay. Really it is. I value our friendship. And if that's all we will be . . . well, then. I just couldn't be happier.' He stretched his hand out on the bench between us, the open palm an invitation.

I smiled and placed my hand in his. We sat for a little while watching the city workers kick their uncomfortable shoes to the side, peel off socks, and eat their sandwiches and bento boxes in the sun. I liked Dennis. I wanted to be his friend. He closed his eyes and raised his face towards the sun. I smiled and did the same, my hand comfortably in his.

*

'Don't jazz it up or anything. I want it to be my words.'

Julian looked at the handwritten statement I'd handed him, wary. 'Not even the bad grammar?'

I affected a gasp. Julian smiled. He seemed to be a nice guy, after all. I'd gone straight from Dennis to Canary Wharf to meet him. We'd found a shady spot in Jubilee Park and I'd given him my statement which he was intending to take straight to the editor at Reuters. I watched Julian scan the statement again, his eyes flickering, I assumed, at the parts his journalistic brain wanted to correct.

'Can I ask you a personal question?' I said.

Julian looked up from my statement and frowned.

'You asked *me* a whole bunch.'

He conceded his frown and smiled. It looked far more natural on him 'Okay. What?'

I tried to form a sentence diplomatically. 'What . . . What is it about Sasha . . . ?'

Like butter in the sun his features softened. 'Sasha is . . .' he said through a soppy smile I never thought would be brought about by the thought of my brusque, tempestuous sister. 'She's sweet and thoughtful and . . .' Julian said, his eyes like a cartoon in love. 'She's always looking at ways to improve herself. Even though she's already perfect.' Julian looked at me like that were an obvious fact and she were just so adoringly *silly*. 'And she's so funny!'

'Funny?'

'Yeah,' he chuckled. 'She's always making jokes.'

Was he talking about *my* sister? 'She is?'

He nodded and his smile waned. 'She says she tries not to joke around you too much ever since . . . since your husband passed away.'

'Oh.'

'Yeah, she's really thoughtful like that. She had enough saved for a deposit for a flat a year ago but decided she wanted to stay around to support your parents, your mum mainly, while they supported you.'

I was floored.

He watched me for a moment. 'It sounds like it's taken quite a toll on your mother. Sasha was worried about you both. She talks about it often. She's been in tears on occasion.'

'I . . . I had no idea,' I said, shocked yet again at how far-reaching the effects of a death can be. It wasn't just Hannah and me.

'I guess I'd better get this off.' He waved the handwritten note I'd given him. He seemed eager to get up to those Reuters offices.

I smiled. 'And no names,' I reminded him.

'No names.'

'Thank you for taking this deal,' I said. 'I know you don't know why but it's very important nobody ever finds out it was me. And I know you could have decided not to.'

Julian gave a humble kind of shrug. 'It's okay.'

'You think you'll get a job here?' I said, nodding in the direction of the buildings where Reuter's head offices were.

Julian's face broke into a grin. 'The editor is really keen on this story so . . . I really think I will.'

I smiled. 'I do too,' I said, feeling his optimism leach into my system.

Julian grinned wider.

'I guess I'll be seeing more of you, then?' I said as we walked out of the park and stood on the street.

'I guess we will,' he said. 'Brooke. Potential sister-in-law.' He winked as my mouth dropped open. 'See you!'

I smiled to myself as I headed down the escalator towards the Tube and home. Julian seemed to be a thoroughly decent man. And ridiculously in love with my sister.

★

Hannah had been invited to an end of year sleepover at Ava's and Penny was busy with last day of school celebrations with her various offspring. On the way home from town I picked up some antipasti and a bottle of bubbles then sat in my garden in the late afternoon sun with a notepad and series of scrawled words under a title that said 'New Fucking Plan #2'. After some time I called Trish.

'Do you think Julian will keep up his end of the bargain?' she asked.

'I do.'

After we reminisced over what our favourite #NoReason moments were we said our goodbyes and I moved inside, put the half bottle of bubbles in the fridge and made a peppermint tea. I sat on the sofa with my laptop and scrolled through to a favourite photo of Chris. He was in Mum and Dad's pool with Hannah. Her arms were around his neck and both of them were grinning at the camera. I zoomed in to his face and stared at him for a long while.

'She's okay,' I said to him.

After I'd locked up, turned all the lights off, let Cookie out for a final wee and brushed my teeth I stood in the doorway of the office looking at the old mattress. It was being picked up in the morning. I walked down the hall towards my new bed.

★

The next day I picked up a tired but very happy Hannah from Ava's. I made plans with Ava's mother for Ava to come and stay in Sussex for a few nights over the summer holidays, then we went home, packed up Cookie and our bags, and piled on to the train to Mum and Dad's.

After an early dinner of incinerated chops Mum (Leo on her lap), Dad (book on his lap), Sasha (on her phone), Vanko (the Ukrainian who spoke better English than the rest of us), Hannah, and I gathered around the evening news in the TV room, the windows flung open to the hot summer's evening.

'Shhhh!' Mum said as she turned the news up.

Sasha looked up from her phone with a scowl. 'Nobody was talking!'

'I said shhhhh!' Mum flapped, slopping sherry over Leo as it made its way towards her mouth.

'And now, a statement has been released from the elusive person behind the anonymous acts of joy that happened in London all of a sudden and came to be known as #NoReason.'

Everyone, with the exception of Sasha who was absorbed by her phone, leaned forward in their seats. Dad's eyes landed on me briefly.

'I didn't go into the whole thing with a plan,' the news anchor read out. 'I didn't really know what I was doing. This statement hasn't been written by a spin doctor. Or even someone who can spell very well.'

My mouth dropped open − Julian had added that part! Cheeky bugger.

'I'm not a public figure and, most importantly, have no

desire to be. I do not have limitless wealth, I am not making a long-winded political statement. And neither am I Banksy, but thank you very much for the flattery.

'This has not been a convoluted advertising campaign for a telecommunication company. I'm not trying to sell you a smartwatch or get you to vote one way or another.

'I'm sorry that I don't have enough money to solve the climate catastrophe. It's going to take a lot more than the money I've spent to change anything in the environment. We all need to make changes for that. I'm just someone who needed to make a little fun and bring a sense of worthiness to someone close to me. And to bring some joy to the strangers I walk this world with.

'I hope I achieved that.

'As you go about your day, look at the people you pass. Everyone is dealing with something. People's children are sick, their marriages are failing, their finances keep them up at night, their mothers have died, their hearts are broken. They might be walking their path feeling alone and unseen. Give them a smile. Tell them the shade of blue they're wearing really suits them. That easy smile, that little compliment might have the power to turn their crap day into a good one. It could even last a lifetime. That's a phenomenal gift. And it's free.

'Life is precarious and it can be hard. It's the little connections that make it better.

'Talk to the stranger, take the time to play Connect Four with a loved one, try to laugh more, try to make others laugh more.

'#NoReason is taking a rest. Maybe we'll be back in some shape or form when a little joy is needed again. Goodbye for now.'

The news anchor smiled at her co-host as the changing pictures of #NoReason behind her stopped on the original ice-cream truck man beaming at the camera and pointing to his #NoReason T-shirt. 'It all began here, and while we don't know if it will ever be back reports came in today of some hefty anonymous donations at the following charities.'

Mum shot me an outraged glare across the living room and I smiled sweetly back as the charities Hannah and I had chosen were read out. Hannah and I had realised that we didn't need to be rich. It had never sat well with me anyway. We'd put aside some money so that we were comfortable and secure, and would be for life, then gave the rest away.

The news anchors said their final piece then moved on to the weather and Mum turned the TV down. 'You're really done now?'

I smiled at Hannah, who grinned back, then turned to my anxious mother. 'Yes, Mum. We're done.'

Sasha jerked her head up from her phone, her eyebrows in her hairline. 'That was you!?' She scanned the room. Everyone nodded. Including Leo, which made Sasha do a disgusted double take. 'NOBODY TELLS ME ANYTHING!'

Chapter 43

'I haven't been myself. For a while,' I said to Gus as we walked side by side down the little path that followed a stream through the neighbour's fields. The sun warmed my bare shoulders as we moved in and out of shade cast across the path from a line of ancient oak trees. The scent of hot summer grass mixed with Gus's soap and suntan lotion created an alluring holiday feel. 'I don't think I even know who I am now. You've only met me like this but . . .' I shrugged. 'I used to be normal – hey! Hello!' I waved across a field to Clint. 'I used to live with that alpaca!' In the face of Gus's alarm I dropped my arm. 'Not in comparison to the general public, but in comparison to the current me.'

A hint of a smile twitched at the corners of Gus's mouth. After Hannah's lesson he had agreed to come on a walk with me so I could 'explain myself.' I wasn't doing the most fault-less of jobs.

'I guess what I'm trying to say is that how I've been behaving . . . Well, it's not how I'd act if I was who I was a few years ago – when my husband was alive and everything felt normal. I wouldn't have kissed you then freaked out and told you I didn't like the kiss and then run away.' I frowned. 'Actually, if my husband was alive, I wouldn't have kissed you at all.'

'I was going to say that.' Gus tried to bite back a smile and I was shocked at how attracted to him I was.

The attraction still caused a wave of guilt. But Leesa had said that the wave would become a splash, and then a trickle until maybe it'd just be a mist. And mist didn't knock you down.

'So . . .' I said. Our arms brushed and a shiver of desire ran down my spine, making me lose my train of thought. Maybe that mist wasn't as far away as I thought. 'Um . . . Where was I?'

'The kissing.'

'Right, yes.'

'And the running away.'

'That too.' I stopped walking and turned to face him. I felt like I was at the bottom step of a new path. A difficult upwards one that resembled an ancient temple that disappeared into the clouds. And was covered in snakes and scorpions. But at least I'd chosen one. I took a breath. 'I guess what I'm actually trying to say is that I like you.' I felt my cheeks heat as Gus settled his gaze on me. 'And I wanted to kiss you. In that moment. But when I did, it freaked me out and made me say that stuff about not liking it. Which wasn't strictly true. It wasn't the kiss I didn't like – it was all the feelings that came after the kiss. *Because* I liked it. And then I told you I didn't like the kiss and you looked mortified so, as any mature woman in her forties would have done in my situation, I ran away.'

Gus was quiet as we began to walk again.

'I'm sorry,' I said. 'I wasn't ready to kiss anyone.'

'But sleeping with someone was okay?' he said. He appeared to be trying to mask his hurt and I had to urge to pull him to me and kiss him all over his gorgeous face.

'Ye-es,' I said. 'That was the next point I was going to address.'

'I'm listening.'

'It's actually a very reasonable explanation.'

Gus stopped walked and looked at me, waiting.

'I was very, very drunk.'

Gus was silent for a few seconds then seemed to drop his hostile resolve. 'We've all been there.'

'So, to sum up – I like you. I like kissing you. I don't like the feelings that come after it. But I'm working on those. I did sleep with Hannah's orthodontist. I won't again. And . . . I hope that we can go back to how things were before the kiss?' I finished and looked up at him hopefully.

'Friends?' Gus said, and I noted a hint of disappointment.

'Yes,' I said, hoping by saying so I hadn't lost him. 'With . . . an open mind.'

The corners of Gus's lips turned up and a tiny spring of hope developed in my chest.

'So. What next?' he asked.

'I want to start afresh,' I said. 'Not just with you and me, with my whole life. I don't want to be the sad widow wherever I go. I want to be Brooke. Brooke and Hannah and . . . and whatever their future is. So . . . Hannah and I have come up with a plan.'

Gus tilted his head.

I stepped towards the fence, leaned my elbows on the sun-cracked wooden railing facing a field dotted with fluffy sheep, and told him our new plan. He moved to the fence, matched my stance and listened. When I reached the end, he smiled.

'Can I?' he said putting his arms out in invitation.

After a moment's hesitation, I stepped into his arms. He wrapped them around me and rested his cheek on the top of my head. We fitted together nicely.

The butterfly fluttered.

'Have you told Iris yet?' he said, pulling back.

'No,' I said, making an 'eek' face. 'Can you tell her?'

Gus threw his head back as he cackled then settled into a serious countenance. 'Absolutely not.'

I wrinkled my nose as I giggled. 'Didn't think so. If I do it now will you be there to morally support me and/or resuscitate her?'

Gus laughed and threw an arm over my shoulder.

We walked back through Mum and Dad's gates and stopped next to his waiting bike. He gave me the briefest kiss on the forehead. For some reason, it seemed more intimate than the cheek. When I turned towards the house I saw Hannah's face watching from the living room.

★

Two weeks later Mum, Dad, Vanko from Ukraine, Lars, Gus and I sat on loungers by the pool and sipped on glasses of rosé watching Hannah and Tom splash and dive and wrestle. To be fair, Mum was watching Lars, not the children. He had popped back one day to introduce us to his 'egg finch babies' and ended up being offered a job renovating the barn with the new builders in exchange for accommodation in Martin's old room. He worked with his shirt off and now resembled an oiled blonde Spartan. Tom and his parents would be leaving for LA at 7:15 the next morning. They'd flown in on Tom's last day of school and greatly appreciated Tom spending every day with us while they packed up their cottage. Tom and Hannah whiled away their summer break on the trampoline, in the tree hut, on e-bike trips with Gus, at the movies with Dad, dressing the animals in Mum's outdated scarves and necklaces and acting out scenes from their movie, on picnics with Gus and me, and hours and hours in the pool perfecting bombs. When Vanessa and Alex finished their packing they came around for a barbeque. It was bittersweet as we sat at the outdoor table reminiscing.

Around 10:30pm we all walked them to the gate; the night air warm and fragrant. Hannah and Tom hung behind, walking at a snail's pace as if their slowness could halt the inevitable. We exchanged hugs and well-wishes then stood back and let Hannah and Tom say their final farewells.

They faced each other on the driveway, after all these years, suddenly awkward.

'I'm going to miss you,' Hannah said, always the one with her heart on her sleeve.

Tom wiped away a tear then shot an embarrassed glance our way. 'Me too.'

'I made you a playlist,' Hannah said, getting out her phone.

Tom grinned through welling eyes. 'I made you one.'

They giggled as they clicked the various buttons that allowed you to share a playlist then slipped their phones back in their pockets.

'Come on, then,' Vanessa said putting her hand on Tom's shoulder. 'We've got a very early start.'

'Bye then,' Tom said and threw his arms around Hannah.

She buried her face in his shoulder. Vanessa and I locked watery eyes over the children's heads. I covered my mouth to stop a whimper and Gus put his arm around me.

When they let go of each other both of them were crying.

Mum gave a titter of a sob then stepped forward and pulled Tom to her. 'Oh my love, I am going to miss your friendly face around here!'

Hannah giggled through her tears as Tom's face half disappeared in her grandmother's bosom.

When he was released, flushed of cheek and gasping for oxygen, we said goodbye again then watched as they walked down the lane, Tom walking backwards waving until they were fully out of sight. Hannah fell into my arms and burst into heavy sobs.

*

The rest of the summer holidays saw the heatwave truly kick in and we spent most of our time by the pool. Hannah had weekly lessons with Gus but I saw him almost daily and as each week went by, the wave of guilt got smaller. We went on walks with the dogs, he came to family games nights, and

Hannah and I attended his daytime gigs. There was no more kissing but we did some hand-holding. Saucy, I know.

I even finally went along to his quiz night. The questions had flown. Robbie was too busy telling stories and we'd missed the second one. The fourth was missed when Blake did a coaster trick, and a whole lot more when someone did a trick with the only pencil and it went flying across the room. When Gus went to get drinks Mich had turned to me.

'Is this a date?' she'd said, her eyebrows raised, and I'd blushed deeply. She'd squeezed my shoulder. 'That's okay. One day at a time.'

Gus didn't get his trophy back that night but he assured me they'd gotten more questions correct with me on the team.

Hannah had been to London and stayed with Ava, and Ava had been to Sussex twice; both times begging her mother to let her stay an extra night.

We'd rented out our home in Earlsfield, putting all of our belongings in storage, and Hannah had been involved in helping choose the tenants. A single dad who had his two children every second week.

Leesa still came once a week for our sessions and I found her to be wise and bossy and I enjoyed her company more and more. We'd even attended a gallery opening together (for which I was only there for the canapés) and it felt like the seed of a new friendship.

Hannah had had a brace-tightening appointment. Dennis had shown us his bruised chin from paddle-boarding and Bev, after sneaking four extra boxes of rubber bands into Hannah's backpack, had shown us photos of her new twin grandsons.

*

Noel, the retiree next door, was aggrieved because not only did Crumpet still break out of his field to visit us, but now he brought Clint with him. And Mum was less than hasty with their return.

Livie's mother had gone to Mexico and Livie was at home with her grandmother. Word from Jendi was that the prognosis wasn't good. Hannah had thought long and hard about what to send Livie, in the end choosing to make her a Spotify playlist of songs that had cheered her up. And because Livie liked fashion we'd put together a hamper of nail polishes and jewellery making kits, and Trish had managed to wangle her two tickets to a recording of a Gok Wan TV special. Hannah hadn't gone so far as to want to drop it off herself but when she received a polite thank you text from Livie she'd smiled and tucked the phone away, and I sensed she had drawn a line under that part of her life.

I'd made an official complaint about Ms Galloway's handling of Hannah's bullying but had yet to hear back from the council. But, really, I didn't care anymore. She was out of our lives.

And as quickly as the public had been infatuated with #NoReason the media moved on and I had the briefest notion that it had all been a dream. I missed the secret thrill of being involved with something so big and outrageous and public. But Hannah and I still had the odd secret huddle over the summer holidays which caused Mum's suspicions to rise again.

*

Towards the end of the summer Hannah and I stood in Mum and Dad's courtyard with a farewell party of the human and animal variety. Sasha stood next to Julian, whom Crumpet had become inordinately fond of, and was nuzzling his neck. Mum stood next to Clint, who she'd insisted needed to come over to say his goodbyes (and who had received a quick morning vacuum). Dad had Leo on his shoulder, Leesa stood alongside Dennis, the two of them meeting and immediately forming a bond over the power of positive thinking and ocean swims. Penny stood next to Pablo with a look of discomfort. Lars held Cookie to his bare chest, and Trish and Gus were finishing up their chat about new educational policies. When he and

Dennis had seen each other that morning it had the potential to be very awkward. But Dennis had cracked into a genuine smile, stepped towards Gus with his hand outstretched, tripped on Cookie and landed in Gus's arms like a 1930s actress with consumption. Ice officially broken.

Mum eyed me checking the contents of our backpacks, then rounded on Leesa. 'I thought you were supposed to help her see reason?'

'I help people to discover what they want out of life.'

'That was *not* what I paid you for!'

'You didn't pay me,' Leesa said.

Mum turned back to me. 'What if you get lonely?'

I smiled at my daughter. 'We've been lonely before, and we survived.'

Hannah smiled back.

'What if you need a doctor?'

'They have doctors in other countries,' Julian said.

'Yes, I can confirm we have some in Spain,' Penny said, giggling.

'And Norway,' Lars said proudly.

'Dentists too, I hear,' Leesa said smiling at Dennis.

'And orthodontists,' I added. 'They're cooler.'

Dennis smiled broadly.

Mum rattled off more potential issues which Trish, Penny, Gus, Sasha, Julian, Leesa, Dennis, Hannah and I batted back. She'd spent the last month trying to talk me out of my plan and had already run through every hazard the world had to offer.

'And what is this cyber schooling anyway? How is she going to get a decent education?'

'Mum, I've told you. It's online and it's all official. They have Zoom classes with real teachers and assignments and grades and everything.'

'We're even doing online drum lessons, aren't we?' Gus said, nudging Hannah affectionately with an elbow.

'Yeah Nan, don't worry. It's going to be so fun!' Hannah said. 'I can do my lessons in my pyjamas!'

Mum shot me an appalled look.

'And,' I added, 'Ms Potts said that when she comes back it'll be a seamless transition.'

'*When* she comes back,' Mum scoffed. 'You can't just run away from your problems, you know!'

'I'm not running away,' I said, looking at Leesa. 'I'm changing my viewpoint.'

Leesa smiled and Mum scowled at her.

'Well?' Mum said, rounding on Dad. 'Don't you have anything to say?'

We all looked at Dad.

He rested his pale grey eyes on each one of us before settling on me. '*Once a year go someplace you've never been before.*' He smiled. 'The Dalai Lama.'

Mum glared at him. 'The ruddy Dalai ruddy Lama?!' She shook her head. 'Anyway, he said "once". *Once* a year. Not *for* a year!'

'*If we were meant to stay in one place we'd have roots instead of feet,*' Dad said.

Our gathering looked at him, waiting.

'Anon,' he added, then rocked on his plimsoles.

Mum shook her head but was stopped from berating him by a sudden outburst from Hannah.

'*OH THE PLACES YOU'LL GO!*' she said as she flung her arms out.

We all looked at her.

'Dr Seuss,' she added with a shy smile and Dad's eyes glistened with pride.

Mum opened her mouth to continue her fussing but I stepped forward and stopped her with a hug. 'Thank you,' I said in her ear. Her hair smelled like Elnett hairspray and transported me to the comfort of childhood cuddles.

'What for?' Mum said, stiff with anxiety beneath my arms.

'For caring so much. For loving Hannah and me so much.' I felt her soften in my hug. After a moment I stepped back. 'I wouldn't have survived the past two years without you. But I'm okay now.' I looked at Hannah laughing at Dennis. 'We're going to be okay.'

Mum dropped her desperate expression, wiped her eyes and nodded as an airport taxi nosed in through the gates and stopped by the cart shed.

'I guess it's really goodbye time now,' I said, feeling instantly both nervous and exhilarated. Hannah and I were starting afresh. Without Chris.

Mum grasped Hannah to her while Lars and Dad loaded our backpacks in the boot of the taxi.

I approached my sister who was expressionless and beautiful with her trendy sunglasses up on her head. 'I'm so happy you're happy,' I said, glancing at Julian who was giving Crumpet a chin rub. 'But I'm okay, Hannah is okay, Mum is okay.' Sasha's stern expression softened into hope. 'Go and live your life now,' I said and hugged her tiny frame. 'I transferred some money into your account this morning,' I whispered in her ear. 'And there's a super cute barn conversion down the road . . .'

Sasha said nothing but clutched me tight then stepped back, flipped her sunglasses down over her reddening eyes and fell in to Julian's outstretched arms, hiding her face in his shoulder.

I moved to stand in front of Trish. My best friend. My rock.

'It's been a fun ride, babe,' she said, one perfect eyebrow arched.

I grinned. 'I can't think of anyone I'd rather have done it with.'

I hugged and said goodbye again to each and every one of the people I loved and had grown close to until only Gus was left.

'I'll miss you,' I said to him in a quiet, private voice.

Gus swallowed and bobbed his head in agreement. 'I'll miss you, too.'

'I'm still in love with my husband. But when I'm ready . . . I feel like I'll be ready with you.'

Gus smiled. 'I'll wait.'

'I don't know how long that will be.'

'I'll wait.' He squeezed my hand.

I looked over at Hannah, suffocating in Mum's embrace. Leesa was putting Dennis' number in her phone, Penny and Trish were admiring Lars' shirtless form, Sasha was taking photos of Julian being nuzzled by Crumpet, and Dad was . . . watching the clouds.

'Come here,' I said, dragging Gus around the side of the house and out of view. I smiled then leaned forward and placed my lips on his. He was hesitant at first but as the kiss deepened his hand at my waist pulled me close.

When we drew apart, Gus smiled down at me. 'How was that?'

I thought about the butterfly in my stomach desperate to be allowed to fly but not quite making it. 'Okay, I guess.'

Gus was stunned but when I broke into a grin he shook his head and laughed. I stepped forward and we kissed again, deeper this time and more sure of each other.

'This is going to look like I'm running away again,' I said, moving out of his embrace and pulling him back to the group. 'But the one-way ticket is in no way linked to that kiss.'

'Right,' he said, returning my wide grin.

'Ready?' I said to Hannah who managed to extract herself from her grandmother's clutches.

'One more hug,' Hannah said, taking Cookie from Lars and squeezing her so tight her bulging eyes bulged a little further.

'I will teach her hoop jumping and will send you a video every day,' Lars said, taking Cookie back from Hannah.

Mum turned to Leesa. 'Hiring you was an absolute disaster.'

'I can see how you feel that way,' Leesa replied. 'We can work on that feeling of betrayal next week.'

Mum harrumphed.

'Thank you for everything,' I said to Leesa. 'I'm sorry I was so difficult at the beginning.'

Leesa gave me a look.

'And the middle.'

Leesa maintained her look.

'Basically, the whole time up until now.'

Leesa dropped her stern look and smiled. 'Believe it or not, you aren't my most difficult client.'

'Who is?'

She hesitated for a moment. 'Your mother.'

We considered each other, then erupted into laughter.

After another round of hugs Hannah and I climbed in the back seat of the taxi and closed the door. It was just us.

Everyone has an opinion on what you should do with your life. And as the taxi headed towards the gate I looked out the window and could see it in the faces of the people who loved us.

Mum was horrified.

Sasha probably thought we should have gone earlier.

Leesa was approving.

Lars was excited.

Julian was wondering if there was a story in it.

Penny was apprehensive.

Trish was supportive.

Dennis was delighted.

Dad was . . . looking at clouds.

And Gus seemed sad.

But nobody else had walked in our shoes for the past two years. We had to live our own life.

I was in the 'now what' stage. Staying in bed, warm and

enveloped is sometimes still what my body wants to do. But you've got to get on with existing. Throw back the covers and let the chill of real life hit you. Then take a step. Take another. And another.

Before you know it, you're in your kitchen. And it's a place to start.

I know that one day every happy instance won't be followed by a debilitating lurch of pain. There are times when it begins and I tell myself – no, it's okay to be happy right now. But whether I ever truly achieve that I don't know.

Grief wasn't ever going to leave me. I'd carry it around like a pebble in the corner of my pocket for the rest of my life. But it was a pebble now not a boulder. And I can carry a pebble.

We all can.

As we turned into the country lane, we looked out the back window at everyone who'd stepped on to the road and were standing in a line waving.

It may take a village to raise a child, but it takes one to get you through grief too. I waved back at the people I loved most in the world – and I'd added three more. Gus and Dennis and Leesa. Four if you counted Lars – and Mother certainly did.

'I can't wait till they get their surprises,' Hannah said, still waving out the back window.

'I know,' I said and smiled thinking about everyone's potential reactions, Mum's especially.

Hannah noticed my eyes on Gus and his on mine.

We waved until we reached the end of the lane. We turned the corner and it was just my daughter and me in the back of the airconditioned taxi.

'I know you'll probably be with someone else one day,' she said, turning away from the back window. 'It might take me some time to get used to it, that's all.'

'Me too,' I said. 'Me too.'

I held out my hand on the seat between us and she grabbed it.

'Ready for an adventure?'

'Totally,' she said, and her nose wrinkled as she grinned.

Epilogue

Late August – Villa in Sardinia

'Who is it?' Penny said from underneath her giant hat.

'Brooke,' Rosa said. 'She's Facetiming you.'

Penny threw her hat to the ground and sat up on her ergonomic sunlounger. 'Pass it to me! Pass! *Pass!* Quickly Rosa, ay for a ballet dancer you move like a tortoise!' Penny snatched her phone from her daughter and swiped the screen. '*Cariño*, I am so excited to speak to you! *Cariño?* . . . I can't hear you?? What are you saying? . . . Ugh the service sucks! Can you hear me? . . . You're nodding? Shall I keep talking? . . . You're nodding? Okay, so this villa you booked us is *amazing!* I can't thank you enough, the chef is unbelievable and the housekeeper won't let me lift a finger! I thought I loved you before but now I want to marry you. Rog ended up having to get back for work unfortunately and, *cariño*, you won't believe it but he flew his mother out here to "help me" with the kids! And no joking with you, she has hooked up with the pool boy! He's twenty-two! And he's not even *our* pool boy, no, she went *hunting* for a pool boy! Oh we are *so embarrassed*. But what can you do?! We loved the photos of Hannah and Tom at Disneyland yesterday. And I can't *believe* you met Jeff Goldblum getting a poke bowl! You are so lucky to be in L.A. with all the stars and the shopping. Oh no, you've frozen. You look mental . . . Are you there? . . . Brooke? . . . Ay, *mierda*.' Penny tossed her phone on the side table next to her cocktail and suntan lotion, and looked over at her mother-in-law in the pool in a tiny bikini kissing her pool boy.

'Noooo,' Penny groaned. She fell back on her ergonomic sunlounger and jammed her hat over her face. 'No no no *no*.'

September – A Beach in Crete.

'I've got an email from Brooke!' Iris exclaimed from her lounger under the sun-umbrella they'd paid a handful of euros for. 'I can't believe she hasn't been in contact for three days! Leaving us worrying what they've been up to. Here, I'll read it out to you. Sasha, love! I've got an email from your sister! . . . Sasha?'

Iris looked over at her daughter lying four loungers to the left and pretending she wasn't on holiday in Greece with her parents.

'Suit yourself. Okay, now let's see what they've been up to . . . She says she is sorry they haven't been in touch for a while but it's because they've been out of range at a dude ranch in Colorado. What's a *dude* ranch? . . . Oh my goodness, Hannah has been bareback horse riding. You should see these photos, Spike, love, she's riding up such a steep hill and on *such* a huge horse! And they went white water rafting! . . . And she's learnt how to muster sheep and fix a fence! And they slept under the stars one night with no sleeping bag or pillow and could hear *coyotes* at night! Coyotes?! What kind of holiday has she taken her on!? Are there snakes in Colorado?'

'Rattlesnakes,' Spike said from behind his *Guide to Greek Philosophers* travel book and fourteen layers of 50+ sunblock.

'*Rattlesnakes?!*' Iris turned back to the iPad. 'Oh my gizzards. She says they went to an ancient Native American cave site. They sound very busy, I don't know how they find the time to do Hannah's online school class thingies. But she says here the science class went very well. The experiment made a huge mess of their B&B bathroom though! Ha! Oh well, I guess that's the way of it all these days. She says they're getting a flight tomorrow morning to Seattle to go to some music festival! A music festival? Do you think Hannah should be going to a music festival at her age? She's asking if we like the guesthouse she booked and if Lars is doing okay looking after the yurt guests and the animals. I still cannot believe she managed to organize all this without me knowing about it. I *always* know what's going on. Love, is there anything you want me to put in my reply? Oh love, you should see this photo of Hannah with a rescued baby mountain lion, she looks so grown up. I do miss her, I—' Iris looked up from her iPad as a group of Greek men in tiny tight swimmers began a game of football. 'I think I'll reply later . . . yes, I think I'll sunbathe for a bit,' she said, sliding the iPad in to her bag and settling down to her view while Spike twinkled at her over the top of his book.

October – Pottery Studio in Peckham

'I got a postcard from Hannah yesterday,' Dennis said, mirroring Leesa's stance at his own pottery wheel. 'They're in Hawaii.'

The teacher at the front of the clay-splattered room encouraged the Sunday morning class of twelve adults of varying ages and abilities to start their wheels and begin to form their cylinders in the manner she'd demonstrated when they first arrived. With absolute unfamiliarity yet no lack of enthusiasm, Dennis mimicked Leesa as she depressed her pedal and beamed as his wheel began to rotate, the lump of clay the teacher had centred for him spun wet and heavy in the middle.

'Apparently,' he said, settling his wet hands on the lump and watching as it wobbled upwards not at all like the smooth elevation of the teacher's cylinder. 'They went on a walking tour over cooled lava and as a lot of it is made of glass it crunches under your feet. And they – oh, you're very good at this,' he said, noticing Leesa's lump of clay transforming into an even cylinder. He turned back to his own lump and focused. 'And they went mountain tubing down an old irrigation system through tunnels, and ziplining over a rainforest, and snorkelling with sea turtles. I could just picture her smiling face as she did all those things. She really is a delightful creature. I do miss them.'

'I got a call from Brooke earlier in the week actually,' Leesa said, not moving her attention from her wheel. Her delicate hands rested on either side of her cylinder that appeared to rise from the wheel as if by its own devices. Dennis, his hands still around his wobbly and rapidly rising tower, looked over transfixed. 'She and Hannah had a surf lesson in Maui,' Leesa continued, her gaze on her clay and Dennis's progressively admiring gaze on her, 'Their instructor turned out to be an old friend of mine from Geneva and they called me after their lesson. Brooke sounds very happy.'

'I'm so pleased she booked us these classes,' Dennis said, his enraptured gaze still on Leesa expertly moving her delicate hands over her clay.

'Me too,' Leesa said. She looked up at him with a smile which she dropped immediately. 'Your clay!' she exclaimed, her eyes wide.

'Wha—' Dennis turned. 'Oh dear!' he said jerking at the sight of his towering pillar of wet clay. The startled motion caused the pillar to collapse in the middle and, like the arm of a hammer thrower it spiralled violently, swung around, whacked Dennis across the cheek with a splat, and floored him like a dropped marionette.

'Dennis!' Leesa exclaimed, unable to remove her hands from her whirling clay cylinder.

'I'm quite all right,' he said, leaping up as the arm made another flailing rotation and floored him again.

November – Converted Barn in West Sussex

'She's so tanned!' Sasha said, flopping on a box labelled 'books' that Julian set on the wonky floorboards.

He stood and counter-stretched his back. 'Where shall we put the table?'

'They fed kangaroos,' Sasha said, pointing at a spot by the cottage-paned windows without removing her eyes from her phone. 'And held baby koalas orphaned by those bush fires . . .'

Julian disappeared down the narrow stairs as Sasha continued to scroll.

'OMG they went to Byron Bay! I'd love to go to Byron Bay . . .'

Julian staggered up the narrow stairs carrying an antique walnut drinks cabinet. 'Does your mother know you took this?' Julian said, placing it on the floor with an oomph.

'No.' Sasha continued to scroll.

Julian jogged back down the stairs.

'I cannot *believe* the colour of the water. Have you been to Australia?' Sasha called out. 'Brooke and Hannah are on a sailing trip around Great Barrier and got to sleep on deck one night and they saw dolphins at sunrise. *Dolphins,*' she said with an envious pout. 'At *sunrise.*' Sasha stopped scrolling and looked around the white-walled kitchen/dining/living room of their newly purchased barn apartment and sighed. 'Do you think that instead of buying a place with the money Brooke gave me we should have gone on a trip?'

'No,' Julian strained as he struggled up the stairs and across the room with another heavy box. 'Best that we got on the ladder now while I have a contract and you're in full-time employment before we start planning things like trips.' He lowered/dropped the box to the ground and let out an involuntary groan as he straightened. 'Or kids . . .'

Sasha jerked her head his way.

Christmas Eve – Busy Pub in Hammersmith

'What are you smiling at?' Martin said, placing two pints on the battered wooden table by the fire.

'Brooke just sent a video.'

'Oh start it again!' Martin said, taking his seat and shuffling close to Trish.

Trish held the phone up and pressed play.

'Hi! Merry Christmas! Well, merry Christmas Eve for you. Hannah's not here right now because, get this, she's gone crayfishing. That's why we're up so early! They have crayfish and salads and prawns for Christmas lunch in New Zealand. Hannah is having a ball, it's so hot here she's in the sea every day! She loves her cousins and it's been so nice spending time with Chris's parents. We sat around last night looking at photo albums. All these pictures of Chris as a baby and teenager . . . There were tears from everyone. . . And . . . I'm happy, though. I am. God, sorry.'

Trish and Martin's eyes watered at the sight of Brooke's chin dimpling and her eyes welling. Martin grabbed Trish's hand and squeezed.

'I'm happy. I am. And so is Hannah. Anyway, ugh, I wasn't going to cry. Okay, I'm fine now. I'm sending this as a video because I'm guessing you're doing the Christmas Eve usual at a busy pub and tomorrow you'll head off and do burnt turkey and raw Brussel sprouts at my parents'? You know, if you don't sleep with my little brother on Christmas Day that'd be fine with me.'

Trish grinned at her friend grinning.

Martin shook his head. 'My penis, my decisions.'

'Anyway I sent your little Christmas present to Mum and Dad's

so call me when you open it! Okay I'd better go and start making salad—'

'Brooke, would you like some champagne? I thought we'd take it to the beach and check out the crays they got?'

'Great idea!

'Okay, I'd better go. That was Chris's sister offering me champagne on the beach before 8am. Ha! I'll send a photo of the crayfish. Love you! Bye!'

Trish put the phone down and wiped under her eye.

'I know what she got you,' Martin said, wiping under his own eye. 'It's not little.'

Trish grinned a watery grin and shook her head. 'Neither is yours.'

Martin laughed and moved his hand to Trish's thigh.

Trish glanced at his hand. 'You heard your sister. No sleeping with her brother.' She gave Martin the exact opposite of a discouraging smile.

'On Christmas Day,' Martin said. 'She said nothing about Christmas *Eve*.'

February – Borneo Orangutan Rehabilitation Facility

Brooke looked through to Hannah, sprawled on her bed under the mosquito nets. It was dawn and already muggy on the balcony of their treetop lodge. She ran a palm across the first blank page of a cream and gold journal Leesa had given her. A letter unread? What is that? Wasted energy? Wasted emotions? At the very least, wasted paper. She started writing anyway.

Dear Chris,
I miss you. I miss you every day with every inch of my soul. I love you so much and I always, always will.

I feel like I'm ready to start moving on. I know you'd want me to.
Until another time. If that even exists.
Your adoring, heartbroken wife.
Xxx

She closed the journal and as she did, noticed some writing at the back of the journal. She flicked to it and recognized Leesa's perfect handwriting.

Sometimes we put up a wall not to keep people out,
but to see who cares enough to break it down.

Socrates

She swallowed and gazed out across the jungle. Then grabbed her phone.

February – School Hall in West Sussex

Sleety rain peltered the windows echoing across the silent, freezing hall as Gus adjusted the projector screen on the stage. His phone vibrated with a text and as he pulled it from his jeans pocket his heart leapt. It was from Brooke.

I'm ready. Any chance you could meet us in Cape Town for the Easter holidays?

'FUCK YES!' Gus cried, pumping his fist.
The hall of students looked up from their exam papers.

April – Airbnb Above Clifton 4th Beach In Cape Town

Vanessa, Alex and Tom flew out for the Easter break. They took Hannah for an overnight whale-watching trip and when

Gus flew in, nervous, excited and gorgeous, Brooke picked him up and they went straight to their Airbnb.

Reader, she moved on.

And she was okay.

Acknowledgements

My first thanks goes to my agent, Alice Lutyens, for her patience and support while life threw a few challenges at me and writing took a back seat. At no time did I feel any pressure from her. That lack of pressure allowed me to get back on track and finish Brooke and Hannah's story when I was ready. A big thanks to Molly Crawford at Simon & Schuster who inherited this book in its later stages and has been a positive guide to the finish line. And for her chatty notes in the margins! Also, I'd like to thank cover designer, Sarah Whittaker, for the cute rainbow raindrops. And thank you to Paul Simpson for his thorough copyediting and lovely note about this book and its characters.

Special thanks to Dr Ross Anning for answering all my questions about orthodontics and to Dan The Ambo Man (real name Dan Bentley) for his assistance with the paramedic scene. Any mistakes are my own.

Thank you to Sonia Voldseth for explaining the ins and outs of Life Coaching and for being an amazing neighbour! Apart from the fact you currently have builders on scaffolding who can see into my bedroom and which I totally forgot about and undressed in front of last week. Then forgot and did it again yesterday. And this morning. I do believe they think I'm doing it on purpose.

Another thank you has to go to my mother, Tricia Brown (she likes it when I put her actual name in). Try as she might, she can't seem to avoid situations that get her in a book. I've already got three scenarios for my next book. Four! I just thought of a fourth! I await with excitement (and my pen) for her next ridiculous instalment. So thanks Mum for being a terrible a Facebook stalker and for the petanque gossip. Everything is made up. Perhaps . . .

Thank you to my sister, Stephanie Brown, for sharing her tinder date disasters with me before she found her own 'Julian P Tickle', forcing Mum to give up her stalking career and move on to pottery.

Now to my other sister, Andrea Cammell. It was pointed out (by her) that for the last book she looked after my boys for two weeks and did a lot more than bake us a slice that no-one liked. So for the previous book, thank you to Andrea Cammell for all the stuff you did. And for this book, thank you for putting your builders on scaffolding at my neighbour's place and turning my bedroom into a low-budget Amsterdam window. Grrr.

Thanks to Kathleen Whyman for being the best beta reader and sender of funny Facebook messages that I laugh at first thing in the morning then forget to reply to for months. And thank you to Leesa Kahn for letting me borrow her weirdly spelled 'Lisa' and for always being a hugely supportive champion of my writing.

Thank you to my son's friends who bravely shared their experiences with bullies with me. And to the others I spoke to, adults and children, who did the same. Sadly, no one seems immune to it.

Thank you to the stranger who secretly paid for my breakfast after I'd shared my worries about achieving my deadline following a long lockdown with two boys and a husband overseas. I went home that day and wrote a whole chapter and was in a good mood for the rest of the week. Little kindnesses have far-reaching effects.

And lastly thanks to my husband for his ongoing love and support. And to my two sons who I adore. Without you I'd be, well, more productive. Fitter. Richer. I'd probably even have better hair. But I'll let all that go for an extra squishy smooshie snuggle. Yeah I know, *so embarrassing!*

While not exactly a thanks I think this deserves a mention. Stefan The Dead Finch is named after my brother-in-law who was annoying me the day I was writing that scene by sending photos of "books he found that were about me", including *Awful Auntie.*

So I made him into a rotund finch then killed him.

Andaz London Liverpool Street is a 5 star lifestyle luxury hotel in the heart of vibrant East London.

Opened as the Great Eastern Hotel in 1884, the hotel is housed in Liverpool Streets station's beautiful redbrick Victorian building, designed by the architects of the Houses of Parliament, with interiors seamlessly blending modern and heritage designs by Conran + Partners.

Capturing the hotel's location and history, our 267 rooms and suites aim to be creative spaces where the traditionally conservative City meets the vibrant artistic vibe of East London with illustration tattoo art by local artist Sophie Mo and photography of the local area by Hoxton Mini Press' Martin Usborne.

For the foodies, there is something to suit all dining tastes at any of Andaz London Liverpool Street's 5 restaurants and bars, from specialty morning coffee and healthy breakfasts to fresh Japanese, brunches galore, traditional pub fare and perfectly grilled dishes.

To find out more visit andazlondonliverpoolstreet.com and follow @andazlondon